GREAT JEWISH SHORT STORIES

Edited and with an Introduction by
SAUL BELLOW

"Most of the stories in this collection are modern; a
few are ancient. They were written in Hebrew, German, Yiddish, Russian, and English, yet all are, to a
discerning eye, very clearly Jewish.... In some cases
I have chosen the best translation rather than the
best story of a given author, and I am afraid there is
no way to disguise my own irreverence or my Jewish
obstinacy.... A story should be interesting, highly
interesting, as interesting as possible—inexplicably
absorbing. There can be no other justification for
any piece of fiction."

—Saul Bellow
From the Introduction

GREAT JEWISH
SHORT STORIES

SAUL BELLOW

A LAUREL BOOK
Published by
Dell Publishing
a division of
The Bantam Doubleday Dell Publishing Group, Inc.
1 Dag Hammarskjold Plaza
New York, New York 10017

Laurel ® TM 674623, Dell Publishing,
a division of the Bantam Doubleday Dell Publishing Group, Inc.

ISBN: 0-440-33122-6

Printed in the United States of America

Published simultaneously in Canada

Two Previous Dell Editions

June 1988

10 9 8 7 6 5 4 3 2 1

KRI

CONTENTS

GREAT JEWISH
SHORT STORIES

Introduction

Most of the stories in this collection are modern; a few are ancient. They were written in Hebrew, German, Yiddish, Russian and English, yet all are, to a discerning eye, very clearly Jewish. The oldest of them, *Tobit,* is pious and moral but its comedy and pathos have a familiar and contemporary flavor. Carried into exile, Tobit will not eat the bread of the gentile, he remembers God with all his heart, he defies the law of the land in observing the divine law, and gives burial to the dead of his nation. But when his son Tobias sets forth on his errand with the disguised angel his dog follows them. The presence of that dog on such an errand is a characteristic touch of Jewish wit. And the poor bride persecuted by the demon Ashmodai—seven times married she remains a virgin—is saved only because Tobias is instructed to make a dreadful stink by burning fish in the bridal chamber to rout the demon. The story is both touching and funny. Obstinate, righteous, sententious Tobit is a charming old man. His prayers are heard; an angel is sent, but the dog, trotting after the angel, is also slyly introduced—and the burning of the fish. Some two thousand years later, in the stories of Isaac Babel and Bashevis Singer, the world and the works of mankind are seen in an oddly tilted perspective very similar to that of Tobit. In a recent story by Singer, "The Spinoza of Market Street," there is another wedding. This time a dusty old scholar, devoted to Spinoza, is rejuvenated. His bride, a homely charwoman, is rescued from barrenness and from ugliness. She is transformed, becomes lovely. Happy but dazed, the old groom in the night mumbles his apologies to Spinoza for this absurd lapse from seriousness.

The religion of the Jews has appeared to the world as divinely inspired history. The message of the Old Testament, however, cannot easily be separated from its stories and

metaphors. Various commentators, unrestrained by orthodoxy and looking at the Bible with the clear or cold eye of
the twentieth century, have spoken of the books of both
testaments as novels. The late Ernest Sutherland Bates
edited a bible "to be read as living literature" and D. H.
Lawrence spoke of the patriarchs and King David as though
they were fictional characters. Thomas Mann in one of his
Joseph novels suggests that in having a story to tell, the
nearly tragic account of the envy of his brethren (how he
was given a coat of many colors; how his brothers were
angry; how he was sold into Egypt by them; how his father
mourned him; how he was molested by Potiphar's wife and
imprisoned; how he interpreted dreams and rose to greatness; how there was a famine in the land and his brothers
came to buy grain; how he revealed himself at last to them)
—that in having such a story to tell Joseph may have been a
greater man than the Pharaoh, his master. For there is
power in a story. It testifies to the worth, the significance of
an individual. For a short while all the strength and all the
radiance of the world are brought to bear upon a few human figures.

Hamlet, dying, says to his friend:

> O God, Horatio, what a wounded name,
> Things standing thus unknown, shall live behind me.
> If thou didst ever hold me in thy heart,
> Absent thee from felicity awhile,
> And in this harsh world draw thy breath in pain,
> To tell my story.

In defeat, a story contains the hope of vindication, of justice. The storyteller is able to make others accept his ver-
sion of things. And in the stories of the Jewish tradition the
world, and even the universe, have a human meaning. Indeed, the Jewish imagination has sometimes been found
guilty of overhumanizing everything, of making too much
of a case for us, for mankind, and of investing externals
with too many meanings. To certain writers, Christianity
itself has appeared to be an invention of Jewish storytellers

whose purpose has been to obtain victory for the weak and the few over the strong and numerous. To such accusations Jews would apply the term *bilbul*. A bilbul is a false charge; literally, a confusion.

For the last generation of East European Jews, daily life without stories would have been inconceivable. My father would say, whenever I asked him to explain any matter, "The thing is like this. There was a man who lived . . ." "There was once a scholar . . ." "There was a widow with one son . . ." "A teamster was driving on a lonely road . . ."

> An old man lived all alone in the forest. He was the last of his family and he was so sick and feeble that he could hardly cook his gruel. Well, one cold day he had no more firewood and he went out to gather some. He was stooped and old and he carried a rope. In the woods he spread the rope on the snow and he laid his fuel on it and tied a knot but he was too weak to lift the bundle. This was too much for him. He lifted his eyes and called to Heaven. "Gott meiner. Send me Death." At once he saw the Angel of Death coming toward him. And the Angel said to him, "You sent for me, what do you want?" And the old man thought quickly and said, "Yes, as a matter of fact I did. I can't get these sticks up on my back and wonder if you'd mind giving me a hand."

"So, you see, when it comes to dying . . . ," my father said, "nobody is really ready."

> Three Jews were boasting of their rabbis, and one said, "My rabbi's faith is so great and he fears the Lord so much that he trembles day and night, and he has to be belted into his bed at night with straps so that he doesn't fall out." The second said, "Yes, you have a marvelous rabbi, but he really can't be compared to my rabbi. Mine is so holy and so just that he makes God tremble. God is afraid of displeasing him. And if the world has not been going so well lately, you can figure

it out for yourselves. God is trembling." The third
Jew said, "Your rabbis are both great men. No doubt
about it. But my rabbi passed through both stages. For
a long time he trembled, too, and in the second stage,
he made God tremble. But then he thought it over
very carefully and finally he said to God, "Look—why
should we both tremble?"

I would call the attitudes of these stories characteristically
Jewish. In them, laughter and trembling are so curiously
mingled that it is not easy to determine the relations of the
two. At times the laughter seems simply to restore the equilibrium of sanity; at times the figures of the story, or par-
able, appear to invite or encourage trembling with the secret
aim of overcoming it by means of laughter. Aristophanes
and Lucian do not hesitate to involve the Olympian gods in
their fun, and Rabelais's humor does not spare the heavens
either. But these are different kinds of comic genius. Jewish humor is mysterious and eludes our efforts—even, in my
opinion, the efforts of Sigmund Freud—to analyze it. Recently one Jewish writer (Hymen Slate in *The Noble
Savage*) has argued that laughter, the comic sense of life,
may be offered as proof of the existence of God. Existence,
he says, is too *funny* to be uncaused. The real secret, the
ultimate mystery, may never reveal itself to the earnest
thought of a Spinoza, but when we laugh (the idea is re-
motely Hassidic) our minds refer us to God's existence.
Chaos is *exposed*.

Not all the stories in this collection approach the summits
of laughter or of feeling. In some cases I have chosen the
best translation rather than the best story of a given author,
and I am afraid there is no way to disguise my own irreverence or my Jewish obstinacy. For instance, I do not
wholly admire the stories of I. L. Peretz. This is heresy, I
know, but I find them slow going; they depend too much
on a kind of Talmudic sophistication which the modern
reader, and I along with him, knows very little of. As for
Sholom Aleichem, his language gives the Yiddish reader

indescribable pleasure, but his stories themselves are by a more general standard often weak. He was a great humorist, but a raconteur rather than a literary artist.

There are of course certain writers who can never be well translated. I remember a long afternoon during which I tried, and failed, to convince the Spanish novelist Pío Baroja that Walt Whitman was an admirable poet. "Not in Castilian," Baroja kept saying, and I suppose the most considerate non-Jewish reader in Minneapolis might take a similar view of some of our Yiddish classics in their English versions. The effort to describe their uniqueness may lead us into exaggeration and inflation, from inflation to mere piety. And from piety to boredom the path is very short. I do not see the point of boring anyone for the sake of the record. Opening a book in order to pay our respects to a vanished culture, a world destroyed to the eternal reproach of all mankind, we may be tempted to set literary standards aside. Still, a story should be interesting, highly interesting, as interesting as possible—inexplicably absorbing. There can be no other justification for any piece of fiction.

Quite understandably, to the writer in the Russian Pale it seemed most important to present Jewish life as sympathetically as possible. Because the Jews were remorselessly oppressed, all the good qualities of Jewish life were heaped up in the foreground of their stories. Raw things—jealousies, ambitions, hatreds, deceptions—were frequently withheld. The Jewish slums of Montreal during my childhood, just after the First World War, were not too far removed from the ghettos of Poland and Russia. Life in such places of exile and suffering was anything but ordinary. But whatever it was, ordinary or extraordinary, harsh or sweet, it was difficult to recognize it in the work of most modern Jewish writers. These writers generally tended to idealize it, to cover it up in prayer shawls and phylacteries and Sabbath sentiment, the Seder, the matchmaking, the marriage canopy; for sadness the Kaddish, for amusement the schnorrer, for admiration the bearded scholar. Jewish literature and art have sentimentalized and sweetened the ghetto; their "pleasing" pictures are far less interesting of course than the real thing.

In this century, so agonizing to the Jews, some people may think it wrong to object to such lack of realism, to insist on maintaining the distinction between public relations and art. It may appear that the survivors of Hitler's terror in Europe and Israel will benefit more from good publicity than from realistic representation, or that posters are needed more urgently than masterpieces. Admittedly, say some people, *Exodus* was not much of a novel, but it was extraordinarily effective as a document and we need such documents now. We do not need stories like those of Philip Roth which expose unpleasant Jewish traits. The Jews are much slandered, much threatened, greatly sinned against—should they for these reasons be unfairly represented in literature, to their alleged advantage? The question is a very ticklish one. It could be shown, I think, that the argument based on need is also the one used by Khrushchev. The Russian oligarchy approves only of what it quaintly calls "socialist realism." It would prefer to have us read Simonov rather than Pasternak. Paradoxically, therefore, the American Jewish public buys Uris and Pasternak for entirely different reasons—*Exodus* because it is good for *us*, and *Doctor Zhivago* because it is bad for *them*. In literature we cannot accept a political standard. We can only have a literary one. But in all the free countries of the world Jewish writers are able to write exactly as they please, in French (André Schwarz-Bart), Italian (Italo Svevo), in English, or in Yiddish or Hebrew.

In Jerusalem several years ago I had an amusing and enlightening conversation with the dean of Hebrew writers, S. J. Agnon. This spare old man, whose face has a remarkably youthful color, received me in his house, not far from the barbed wire entanglements that divide the city, and while we were drinking tea, he asked me if any of my books had been translated into Hebrew. If they had not been, I had better see to it immediately, because, he said, they would survive only in the Holy Tongue. His advice I assume was only half serious. This was his witty way of calling my attention to a curious situation. I cited Heinrich Heine as an example of a poet who had done rather well in German. "Ah," said Mr. Agnon, "we have him beautifully translated into Hebrew. He is safe." Mr. Agnon feels secure in his ancient tradition. But Jews have been writing in languages other than Hebrew for more than two thousand years. The New Testament scholar Hugh J. Schonfield asserts that parts of the Gospels were composed in a sort of Yiddish Greek, "as colorful in imagery and metaphor as it is often careless in grammatical construction."

With less wit and subtlety than Mr. Agnon, other Jewish writers worry about using the languages of the Diaspora. They sometimes feel like borrowers, compelled by strange circumstances to use a tongue of which their ancestors were ignorant. I cannot recall that Joseph Conrad, a Pole, ever felt this to be an intolerable difficulty. He loved England and the English language. I do remember that James Joyce, an Irishman, did feel such a difficulty. Stephen Dedalus in *A Portrait of the Artist* somewhat envies an old English Jesuit, perfectly at home in his own language. But then, young Dedalus was at this period of his life still rather parochial. In a story by Meyer Levin, one character exclaims, "I was a foreigner, writing in a foreign language ... What am I? Native, certainly. My parents came to this country ... they were the true immigrants, the actual foreigners. ... But I, American-born, raised on hot dogs, I am out of place in America. Remember this: art to be universal must be narrowly confined. An artist must be a perfect unit of time and place, at home with himself, unextraneous. ... Who am I? Where do I come from? I am an accident. What right have I to scribble in this American language that comes no more naturally to me than it does to the laundry Chinaman?"

Theories like those expressed by Mr. Levin's character, as Mr. Levin is at pains to show, about the "perfect unit of time and place" seldom bring any art into the world. Art appears, and then theory contemplates it; that is the usual order in the relations between art and theory. It cannot be

argued that the stories of Isaac Babel are not characteristically Jewish. And they were written in Russian by a
man who knew Yiddish well enough to have written them
in that language. Before he disappeared from view during
one of Stalin's purges, Babel had been put in charge of
publishing the works of Sholom Aleichem in Yiddish. Why
should he have chosen therefore to write his own stories in
Russian, the language of the oppressors, of Pobedonostev
and the Black Hundreds? If, before writing, he had taken
his bearings he could not have found himself to be "a
perfect unit of time and place." He wrote in Russian from
motives we can never expect to understand fully. These
stories have about them something that justifies them to the
most grudging inquiry—they have spirit, originality, beauty.
Who was Babel? Where did he come from? He was an
accident. We are all such accidents. We do not make up
history and culture. We simply appear, not by our own
choice. We make what we can of our condition with the
means available. We must accept the mixture as we find it
—the impurity of it, the tragedy of it, the hope of it.

SAUL BELLOW

Tobit is a book of the Apocrypha. The word "apocrypha" generally designates a body of near-scriptures, works of doubtful inspiration, not accepted in the canon. Tobit is thought to have been written during the Graeco-Roman period. A secular story, it is pervaded however by intense religious feeling. Tobit, in exile, cannot forget that he is a Jew. It is possible to compare him with Joyce's Leopold Bloom.

Tobit

Chapter 1

The book of the words of Tobit, son of Tobiel, the son of Ananiel, the son of Aduel, the son of Gabael, of the seed of Asael, of the tribe of Nephthali;

2 Who in the time of Enemessar king of the Assyrians was led captive out of Thisbe, which is at the right hand of that city, which is called properly Nephthali in Galilee above Aser.

3 I Tobit have walked all the days of my life in the way of truth and justice, and I did many almsdeeds to my brethren, and my nation, who came with me to Nineve, into the land of the Assyrians.

4 And when I was in mine own country, in the land of Israel, being but young, all the tribe of Nephthali my father fell from the house of Jerusalem, which was chosen out of all the tribes of Israel, that all the tribes should sacrifice *there,* where the temple of the habitation of the most High was consecrated and built for all ages.

5 Now all the tribes which together revolted, and the house of my father Nephthali, sacrified unto the heifer Baal.

6 But I alone went often to Jerusalem at the feasts, as it was ordained unto all the people of Israel by an everlasting

decree, having the firstfruits and tenths of increase, with that which was first shorn; and them gave I at the altar to the priests the children of Aaron.

7 The first tenth part of all increase I gave to the sons of Aaron, who ministered at Jerusalem: another tenth part I sold away, and went, and spent it every year at Jerusalem:

8 And the third I gave unto them to whom it was meet, as Debora my father's mother had commanded me, because I was left an orphan by my father.

9 Furthermore, when I was come to the age of a man, I married Anna of mine own kindred, and of her I begat Tobias.

10 And when we were carried away captives to Nineve, all my brethren and those that were of my kindred did eat of the bread of the Gentiles.

11 But I kept myself from eating;

12 Because I remembered God with all my heart.

13 And the most High gave me grace and favour before Enemessar, so that I was his purveyor.

14 And I went into Media, and left in trust with Gabael, the brother of Gabrias, at Rages a city of Media ten talents of silver.

15 Now when Enemessar was dead, Sennacherib his son reigned in his stead; whose estate was troubled, that I could not go into Media.

16 And in the time of Enemessar I gave many alms to my brethren, and gave my bread to the hungry,

17 And my clothes to the naked: and if I saw any of my nation dead, or cast about the walls of Nineve, I buried him.

18 And if the king Sennacherib had slain any, when he was come, and fled from Judea, I buried them privily; for in his wrath he killed many; but the bodies were not found, when they were sought for of the king.

19 And when one of the Ninevites went and complained of me to the king, that I buried them, and hid myself; understanding that I was sought for to be put to death, I withdrew myself for fear.

20 Then all my goods were forcibly taken away, neither

was there any thing left me, beside my wife Anna and my son Tobias.

21 And there passed not five and fifty days, before two of his sons killed him, and they fled into the mountains of Ararath; and Sarchedonus his son reigned in his stead; who appointed over his father's accounts, and over all his affairs, Achiacharus my brother Anael's son.

22 And Achiacharus intreating for me, I returned to Nineve. Now Achiacharus was cupbearer, and keeper of the signet, and steward, and overseer of the accounts: and Sarchedonus appointed him next unto him: and he was my brother's son.

Chapter 2

Now when I was come home again, and my wife Anna was restored unto me, with my son Tobias, in the feast of Pentecost, which is the holy feast of the seven weeks, there was a good dinner prepared me, in the which I sat down to eat.

2 And when I saw abundance of meat, I said to my son, Go and bring what poor man soever thou shalt find out of our brethren, who is mindful of the Lord; and, lo, I tarry for thee.

3 But he came again, and said, Father, one of our nation is strangled, and is cast out in the marketplace.

4 Then before I had tasted of any meat, I started up, and took him up into a room until the going down of the sun.

5 Then I returned, and washed myself, and ate my meat in heaviness,

6 Remembering that prophecy of Amos, as he said, Your feasts shall be turned into mourning, and all your mirth into lamentation.

7 Therefore I wept: and after the going down of the sun I went and made a grave, and buried him.

8 But my neighbours mocked me, and said, This man is not yet afraid to be put to death for this matter: who fled away; and yet, lo, he burieth the dead again.

9 The same night also I returned from the burial, and slept by the wall of my courtyard, being polluted, and my face was uncovered:

10 And I knew not that there were sparrows in the wall, and mine eyes being open, the sparrows muted warm dung into mine eyes; and a whiteness came in mine eyes; and I went to the physicians, but they helped me not: moreover Achiacharus did nourish me, until I went into Elymais.

11 And my wife Anna did take women's works to do.

12 And when she had sent them home to the owners, they paid her wages, and gave her also besides a kid.

13 And when it was in my house, and began to cry, I said unto her, From whence is this kid? is it not stolen? render it to the owners; for it is not lawful to eat any thing that is stolen.

14 But she replied upon me, It was given for a gift more than the wages. Howbeit I did not believe her, but bade her render it to the owners: and I was abashed at her. But she replied upon me, Where are thine alms and thy righteous deeds? behold, thou and all thy works are known.

Chapter 3

Then I being grieved did weep, and in my sorrow prayed, saying,

2 O Lord, thou art just, and all thy works and all thy ways are mercy and truth, and thou judgest truly and justly for ever.

3 Remember me, and look on me, punish me not for my sins and ignorances, and *the sins of* my fathers, who have sinned before thee:

4 For they obeyed not thy commandments: wherefore thou hast delivered us for a spoil, and unto captivity, and unto death, and for a proverb of reproach to all the nations among whom we are dispersed.

5 And now thy judgments are many and true: deal with me according to my sins and my fathers': because we have

not kept thy commandments, neither have walked in truth before thee.

6 Now therefore deal with me as seemeth best unto thee, and command my spirit to be taken from me, that I may be dissolved, and become earth: for it is profitable for me to die rather than to live, because I have heard false reproaches, and have much sorrow: command therefore that I may now be delivered out of this distress, and go into the everlasting place: turn not thy face away from me.

7 It came to pass the same day, that in Ecbatane a city of Media Sara the daughter of Raguel was also reproached by her father's maids;

8 Because that she had been married to seven husbands, whom Asmodeus the evil spirit had killed, before they had lain with her. Dost thou not know, said they, that thou hast strangled thine husbands? thou hast had already seven husbands, neither wast thou named after any of them.

9 Wherefore dost thou beat us for them? if they be dead, go thy ways after them, let us never see of thee either son or daughter.

10 When she heard these things, she was very sorrowful, so that she thought to have strangled herself; and she said, I am the only daughter of my father, and if I do this, it shall be a reproach unto him, and I shall bring his old age with sorrow unto the grave.

11 Then she prayed toward the window, and said, Blessed art thou, O Lord my God, and thine holy and glorious name is blessed and honourable for ever: let all thy works praise thee for ever.

12 And now, O Lord, I set mine eyes and my face toward thee,

13 And say, Take me out of the earth, that I may hear no more the reproach.

14 Thou knowest, Lord, that I am pure from all sin with man,

15 And that I never polluted my name, nor the name of my father, in the land of my captivity: I am the only daughter of my father, neither hath he any child to be his heir, neither any near kinsman, nor any son of his alive, to whom

I may keep myself for a wife: my seven husbands are already dead; and why should I live? but if it please not thee that I should die, command some regard to be had of me, and pity taken of me, that I hear no more reproach.

16 So the prayers of them both were heard before the majesty of the great God.

17 And Raphael was sent to heal them both, that is, to scale away the whiteness of Tobit's eyes, and to give Sara the daughter of Raguel for a wife to Tobias the son of Tobit; and to bind Asmodeus the evil spirit; because she belonged to Tobias by right of inheritance. The selfsame time came Tobit home, and entered into his house, and Sara the daughter of Raguel came down from her upper chamber.

Chapter 4

In that day Tobit remembered the money which he had committed to Gabael in Rages of Media,

2 And said with himself, I have wished for death; wherefore do I not call for my son Tobias, that I may signify to him *of the money* before I die?

3 And when he had called him, he said, My son, when I am dead, bury me; and despise not thy mother, but honour her all the days of thy life, and do that which shall please her, and grieve her not.

4 Remember, my son, that she saw many dangers for thee, *when thou wast* in her womb; and when she is dead, bury her by me in one grave.

5 My son, be mindful of the Lord our God all thy days, and let not thy will be set to sin, or to transgress his commandments: do uprightly all thy life long, and follow not the ways of unrighteousness.

6 For if thou deal truly, thy doings shall prosperously succeed to thee, and to all them that live justly.

7 Give alms of thy substance; and when thou givest alms, let not thine eye be envious, neither turn thy face from any poor, and the face of God shall not be turned away from thee.

8 If thou hast abundance, give alms accordingly: if thou have but a little, be not afraid to give according to that little:

9 For thou layest up a good treasure for thyself against the day of necessity.

10 Because that alms do deliver from death, and suffereth not to come into darkness.

11 For alms is a good gift unto all that give it in the sight of the most High.

12 Beware of all whoredom, my son, and chiefly take a wife of the seed of thy fathers, and take not a strange woman to wife, which is not of thy father's tribe: for we are the children of the prophets, Noe, Abraham, Isaac, and Jacob: remember, my son, that our fathers from the beginning, even that they all married wives of their own kindred, and were blessed in their children, and their seed shall inherit the land.

13 Now therefore, my son, love thy brethren, and despise not in thy heart thy brethren, the sons and daughters of thy people, in *not* taking a wife of them: for in pride is destruction and much trouble, and in lewdness is decay and great want: for lewdness is the mother of famine.

14 Let not the wages of any man, which hath wrought for thee, tarry with thee, but give him it out of hand: for if thou serve God, he will also repay thee: be circumspect, my son, in all things thou doest, and be wise in all thy conversation.

15 Do that to no man which thou hatest: drink not wine to make thee drunken: neither let drunkenness go with thee in thy journey.

16 Give of thy bread to the hungry, and of thy garments to them that are naked; and according to thine abundance give alms; and let not thine eye be envious, when thou givest alms.

17 Pour out thy bread on the burial of the just, but give nothing to the wicked.

18 Ask counsel of all that are wise, and despise not any counsel that is profitable.

19 Bless the Lord thy God alway, and desire of him that

thy ways may be directed, and that all thy paths and counsels may prosper: for every nation hath not counsel; but the Lord himself giveth all good things, and he humbleth whom he will, as he will; now therefore, my son, remember my commandments, neither let them be put out of thy mind.

20 And now I signify this to thee, that I committed ten talents to Gabael the *son* of Gabrias at Rages in Media.

21 And fear not, my son, that we are made poor: for thou hast much wealth, if thou fear God, and depart from all sin, and do that which is pleasing in his sight.

Chapter 5

Tobias then answered and said, Father, I will do all things which thou hast commanded me:

2 But how can I receive the money, seeing I know him not?

3 Then he gave him the handwriting, and said unto him, Seek thee a man which may go with thee, whiles I yet live, and I will give him wages: and go and receive the money.

4 Therefore when he went to seek a man, he found Raphael that was an angel.

5 But he knew not; and he said unto him, Canst thou go with me to Rages? and knowest thou those places well?

6 To whom the angel said, I will go with thee, and I know the way well: for I have lodged with our brother Gabael.

7 Then Tobias said unto him, Tarry for me, till I tell my father.

8 Then he said unto him, Go, and tarry not. So he went in and said to his father, Behold, I have found one which will go with me. Then he said, Call him unto me, that I may know of what tribe he is, and whether he be a trusty man to go with thee.

9 So he called him, and he came in, and they saluted one another.

10 Then Tobit said unto him, Brother, shew me of what tribe and family thou art.

11 To whom he said, Dost thou seek for a tribe or family, or an hired man to go with thy son? Then Tobit said unto him, I would know, brother, thy kindred and name.

12 Then he said, I am Azarias, the son of Ananias the great, and of thy brethren.

13 Then Tobit said, Thou art welcome, brother; be not now angry with me, because I have enquired to know thy tribe and thy family; for thou art my brother, of an honest and good stock: for I know Ananias and Jonathas, sons of that great Samaias, as we went together to Jerusalem to worship, and offered the firstborn, and the tenths of the fruits; and they were not seduced with the error of our brethren: my brother, thou art of a good stock.

14 But tell me, what wages shall I give thee? *wilt thou* a drachm a day, and things necessary, as to mine own son?

15 Yea, moreover, if ye return safe, I will add something to thy wages.

16 So they were well pleased. Then said he to Tobias, Prepare thyself for the journey, and God send you a good journey. And when his son had prepared all things for the journey, his father said, Go thou with this man, and God, which dwelleth in heaven, prosper your journey, and the angel of God keep you company. So they went forth both, and the young man's dog with them.

17 But Anna his mother wept, and said to Tobit, Why hast thou sent away our son? is he not the staff of our hand, in going in and out before us?

18 Be not greedy to add money to money: but let it be as refuse in respect of our child.

19 For that which the Lord hath given us to live with doth suffice us.

20 Then said Tobit to her, Take no care, my sister; he shall return in safety, and thine eyes shall see him.

21 For the good angel will keep him company, and his journey shall be prosperous, and he shall return safe.

22 Then she made an end of weeping.

Chapter 6

And as they went on their journey, they came in the evening to the river Tigris, and they lodged there.

2 And when the young man went down to wash himself, a fish leaped out of the river, and would have devoured him.

3 Then the angel said unto him, Take the fish. And the young man laid hold of the fish, and drew it to land.

4 To whom the angel said, Open the fish, and take the heart and the liver and the gall, and put them up safely.

5 So the young man did as the angel commanded him; and when they had roasted the fish, they did eat it: then they both went on their way, till they drew near to Ecbatane.

6 Then the young man said to the angel, Brother Azarias, to what use is the heart and the liver and the gall of the fish?

7 And he said unto him, Touching the heart and the liver, if a devil or an evil spirit trouble any, we must make a smoke thereof before the man or the woman, and the party shall be no more vexed.

8 As for the gall, *it is good* to anoint a man that hath whiteness in his eyes, and he shall be healed.

9 And when they were come near to Rages,

10 The angel said to the young man, Brother, to day we shall lodge with Raguel, who is thy cousin; he also hath one only daughter, named Sara; I will speak for her, that she may be given thee for a wife.

11 For to thee doth the right of her appertain, seeing thou only art of her kindred.

12 And the maid is fair and wise: now therefore hear me, and I will speak to her father; and when we return from Rages we will celebrate the marriage: for I know that Raguel cannot marry her to another according to the law of Moses, but he shall be guilty of death, because the right of inheritance doth rather appertain to thee than to any other.

13 Then the young man answered the angel, I have

heard, brother Azarias, that this maid hath been given to seven men, who all died in the marriage chamber.

14 And now I am the only son of my father, and I am afraid, lest, if I go in unto her, I die, as the other before: for a wicked spirit loveth her, which hurteth no body, but those which come unto her: wherefore I also fear lest I die, and bring my father's and my mother's life because of me to the grave with sorrow: for they have no other son to bury them.

15 Then the angel said unto him, Dost thou not remember the precepts which thy father gave thee, that thou shouldest marry a wife of thine own kindred? wherefore hear me, O my brother; for she shall be given thee to wife; and make thou no reckoning of the evil spirit; for this same night shall she be given thee in marriage.

16 And when thou shalt come into the marriage chamber, thou shalt take the ashes of perfume, and shalt lay upon them some of the heart and liver of the fish, and shalt make a smoke with it:

17 And the devil shall smell it, and flee away, and never come again any more: but when thou shalt come to her, rise up both of you, and pray to God which is merciful, who will have pity on you, and save you: fear not, for she is appointed unto thee from the beginning; and thou shalt preserve her, and she shall go with thee. Moreover I suppose that she shall bear thee children. Now when Tobias had heard these things, he loved her, and his heart was effectually joined to her.

Chapter 7

And when they were come to Ecbatane, they came to the house of Raguel, and Sara met them: and after they had saluted one another, she brought them into the house.

2 Then said Raguel to Edna his wife, How like is this young man to Tobit my cousin!

3 And Raguel asked them, From whence are ye, breth-

ren? To whom they said, We are of the sons of Nephthalim, which are captives in Nineve.

4 Then he said to them, Do ye know Tobit our kinsman? And they said, We know him. Then said he, Is he in good health?

5 And they said, He is both alive, and in good health: and Tobias said, He is my father.

6 Then Raguel leaped up, and kissed him, and wept,

7 And blessed him, and said unto him, Thou art the son of an honest and good man. But when he had heard that Tobit was blind, he was sorrowful, and wept.

8 And likewise Edna his wife and Sara his daughter wept. Moreover they entertained them cheerfully; and after that they had killed a ram of the flock, they set store of meat on the table. Then said Tobias to Raphael, Brother Azarias, speak of those things of which thou didst talk in the way, and let this business be dispatched.

9 So he communicated the matter with Raguel: and Raguel said to Tobias, Eat and drink, and make merry:

10 For it is meet that thou shouldest marry my daughter: nevertheless I will declare unto thee the truth.

11 I have given my daughter in marriage to seven men, who died that night they came in unto her: nevertheless for the present be merry. But Tobias said, I will eat nothing here, till we agree and swear one to another.

12 Raguel said, Then take her from henceforth according to the manner, for thou art her cousin, and she is thine, and the merciful God give you good success in all things.

13 Then he called his daughter Sara, and she came to her father, and he took her by the hand, and gave her to be wife to Tobias, saying, Behold, take her after the law of Moses, and lead her away to thy father. And he blessed them;

14 And called Edna his wife, and took paper, and did write an instrument *of covenants,* and sealed it.

15 Then they began to eat.

16 After Raguel called his wife Edna, and said unto her, Sister, prepare another chamber, and bring her in thither.

17 Which when she had done as he had bidden her, she brought her thither: and she wept, and she received the tears of her daughter, and said unto her,

18 Be of good comfort, my daughter; the Lord of heaven and earth give thee joy for this thy sorrow: be of good comfort, my daughter.

Chapter 8

And when they had supped, they brought Tobias in unto her.

2 And as he went, he remembered the words of Raphael, and took the ashes of the perfumes, and put the heart and the liver of the fish thereupon, and made a smoke *therewith*.

3 The which smell when the evil spirit had smelled, he fled into the utmost parts of Egypt, and the angel bound him.

4 And after that they were both shut in together, Tobias rose out of the bed, and said, Sister, arise, and let us pray that God would have pity on us.

5 Then began Tobias to say, Blessed art thou, O God of our fathers, and blessed *is* thy holy and glorious name for ever; let the heavens bless thee, and all thy creatures.

6 Thou madest Adam, and gavest him Eve his wife for an helper and stay: of them came mankind: thou hast said, It is not good that man should be alone; let us make unto him an aid like unto himself.

7 And now, O Lord, I take not this my sister for lust, but uprightly: *therefore* mercifully ordain that we may become aged together.

8 And she said with him, Amen.

9 So they slept both that night. And Raguel arose, and went and made a grave,

10 Saying, *I fear* lest he also be dead.

11 But when Raguel was come into his house,

12 He said unto his wife Edna, Send one of the maids, and let her see whether he be alive: if *he be* not, that we may bury him, and no man know it.

13 So the maid opened the door, and went in, and found them both asleep,

14 And came forth, and told them that he was alive.

15 Then Raguel praised God, and said, O God, thou art worthy to be praised with all pure and holy praise; therefore let thy saints praise thee with all thy creatures; and let all thine angels and thine elect praise thee for ever.

16 Thou art to be praised, for thou hast made me joyful; and that is not come to me which I suspected; but thou hast dealt with us according to thy great mercy.

17 Thou art to be praised, because thou hast had mercy of two that were the only begotten children of their fathers: grant them mercy, O Lord, and finish their life in health with joy and mercy.

18 Then Raguel bade his servants to fill the grave.

19 And he kept the wedding feast fourteen days.

20 For before the days of the marriage were finished, Raguel had said unto him by an oath, that he should not depart till the fourteen days of the marriage were expired;

21 And then he should take the half of his goods, and go in safety to his father; and should have the rest when I and my wife be dead.

Chapter 9

Then Tobias called Raphael, and said unto him,

2 Brother Azarias, take with thee a servant, and two camels, and go to Rages of Media to Gabael, and bring me the money, and bring him to the wedding.

3 For Raguel hath sworn that I shall not depart.

4 But my father counteth the days; and if I tarry long, he will be very sorry.

5 So Raphael went out, and lodged with Gabael, and gave him the handwriting: who brought forth bags which were sealed up, and gave them to him.

6 And early in the morning they went forth both together, and came to the wedding: and Tobias blessed his wife.

Chapter 10

Now Tobit his father counted every day: and when the days of the journey were expired, and they came not,

2 Then Tobit said, Are they detained? or is Gabael dead, and there is no man to give him the money?

3 Therefore he was very sorry.

4 Then his wife said unto him, My son is dead, seeing he stayeth long; and she began to bewail him, and said,

5 *Now I care for nothing*, my son, *since I have let thee go*, the light of mine eyes.

6 To whom Tobit said, Hold thy peace, take no care, for he is safe.

7 But she said, Hold thy peace, and deceive me not; my son is dead. And she went out every day into the way which they went, and did eat no meat on the daytime, and ceased not whole nights to bewail her son Tobias, until the fourteen days of the wedding were expired, which Raguel had sworn that he should spend there. Then Tobias said to Raguel, Let me go, for my father and my mother look no more to see me.

8 But his father in law said unto him, Tarry with me, and I will send to thy father, and they shall declare unto him how things go with thee.

9 But Tobias said, No; but let me go to my father.

10 Then Raguel arose, and gave him Sara his wife, and half his goods, servants, and cattle, and money:

11 And he blessed them, and sent them away, saying, The God of heaven give you a prosperous journey, my children.

12 And he said to his daughter, Honour thy father and thy mother in law, which are now thy parents, that I may hear good report of thee. And he kissed her. Edna also said to Tobias, The Lord of heaven restore thee, my dear brother, and grant that I may see thy children of my daughter Sara before I die, that I may rejoice before the Lord:

behold, I commit my daughter unto thee of special trust; wherefore do not entreat her evil.

Chapter 11

After these things Tobias went his way, praising God that he had given him a prosperous journey, and blessed Raguel and Edna his wife, and went on his way till they drew near unto Nineve.

2 Then Raphael said to Tobias, Thou knowest, brother, how thou didst leave thy father:

3 Let us haste before thy wife, and prepare the house.

4 And take in thine hand the gall of the fish. So they went their way, and the dog went after them.

5 Now Anna sat looking about toward the way for her son.

6 And when she espied him coming, she said to his father, Behold, thy son cometh, and the man that went with him.

7 Then said Raphael, I know, Tobias, that thy father will open his eyes.

8 Therefore anoint thou his eyes with the gall, and being pricked therewith, he shall rub, and the whiteness shall fall away, and he shall see thee.

9 Then Anna ran forth, and fell upon the neck of her son, and said unto him, Seeing I have seen thee, my son, from henceforth I am content to die. And they wept both.

10 Tobit also went forth toward the door, and stumbled: but his son ran unto him.

11 And took hold of his father: and he strake of the gall on his father's eyes, saying, Be of good hope, my father.

12 And when his eyes began to smart, he rubbed them;

13 And the whiteness pilled away from the corners of his eyes: and when he saw his son, he fell upon his neck.

14 And he wept, and said, Blessed art thou, O God, and blessed is thy name for ever; and blessed are all thine holy angels:

15 For thou has scourged, and hast taken pity *on me*:

for, behold, I see my son Tobias. And his son went in rejoicing, and told his father the great things that had happened to him in Media.

16 Then Tobit went out to meet his daughter in law at the gate of Nineve, rejoicing, and praising God: and they which saw him go marvelled, because he had received his sight.

17 But Tobit gave thanks before them, because God had mercy on him. And when he came near to Sara his daughter in law, he blessed her, saying, Thou art welcome, daughter: God be blessed, which hath brought thee unto us, and *blessed be* thy father and thy mother. And there was joy among all his brethren which were at Nineve.

18 And Achiacharus, and Nasbas his brother's son, came:

19 And Tobias' wedding was kept seven days with great joy.

Chapter 12

Then Tobit called his son Tobias, and said unto him, My son, see that the man have his wages, which went with thee, and thou must give him more.

2 And Tobias said unto him, O father, it is no harm to me to give him half of those things which I have brought:

3 For he hath brought me again to thee in safety, and made whole my wife, and brought me the money, and likewise healed thee.

4 Then the old man said, It is due unto him.

5 So he called the angel, and he said unto him, Take half of all that ye have brought, and go away in safety.

6 Then he took them both apart, and said unto them, Bless God, praise him, and magnify him, and praise him for the things which he hath done unto you in the sight of all that live. It is good to praise God, and exalt his name, and honourably to shew forth the works of God; therefore be not slack to praise him.

7 It is good to keep close the secret of a king, but it is

honourable to reveal the works of God. Do that which is good, and no evil shall touch you.

8 Prayer is good with fasting and alms and righteousness. A little with righteousness is better than much with unrighteousness. It is better to give alms than to lay up gold:

9 For alms doth deliver from death, and shall purge away all sin. Those that exercise alms and righteousness shall be filled with life:

10 But they that sin are enemies to their own life.

11 Surely I will keep close nothing from you. For I said, It was good to keep close the secret of a king, but that it was honourable to reveal the works of God.

12 Now therefore, when thou didst pray, and Sara thy daughter in law, I did bring the remembrance of your prayers before the Holy One: and when thou didst bury the dead, I was with thee likewise.

13 And when thou didst not delay to rise up, and leave thy dinner, to go and cover the dead, thy good deed was not hid from me: but I was with thee.

14 And now God hath sent me to heal thee and Sara thy daughter in law.

15 I am Raphael, one of the seven holy angels, which present the prayers of the saints, and which go in and out before the glory of the Holy One.

16 Then they were both troubled, and fell upon their faces: for they feared.

17 But he said unto them, Fear not, for it shall go well with you; praise God therefore.

18 For not of any favour of mine, but by the will of our God I came; wherefore praise him for ever.

19 All these days I did appear unto you; but I did neither eat nor drink, but ye did see a vision.

20 Now therefore give God thanks: for I go up to him that sent me; but write all things which are done in a book.

21 And when they arose, they saw him no more.

22 Then they confessed the great and wonderful works of God, and how the angel of the Lord had appeared unto them.

Chapter 13

Then Tobit wrote a prayer of rejoicing, and said, Blessed be God that liveth for ever, and blessed be his kingdom.

2 For he doth scourge, and hath mercy: he leadeth down to hell, and bringeth up again: neither is there any that can avoid his hand.

3 Confess him before the Gentiles, ye children of Israel: for he hath scattered us among them.

4 There declare his greatness, and extol him before all the living: for he is our Lord, and he is the God our Father for ever.

5 And he will scourge us for our iniquities, and will have mercy again, and will gather us out of all nations, among whom he hath scattered us.

6 If ye turn to him with your whole heart, and with your whole mind, and deal uprightly before him, then will he turn unto you, and will not hide his face from you. Therefore see what he will do with you, and confess him with your whole mouth, and praise the Lord of might, and extol the everlasting King. In the land of my captivity do I praise him, and declare his might and majesty to a sinful nation. O ye sinners, turn and do justice before him: who can tell if he will accept you, and have mercy on you?

7 I will extol my God, and my soul shall praise the King of heaven, and shall rejoice in his greatness.

8 Let all men speak, and let all praise him for *his* righteousness.

9 O Jerusalem, the holy city, he will scourge thee for thy children's works, and will have mercy again on the sons of the righteous.

10 Give praise to the Lord, *for he is* good: and praise the everlasting King, that his tabernacle may be builded in thee again with joy, and let him make joyful there in thee those that are captives, and love in thee for ever those that are miserable.

11 Many nations shall come from far to the name of the Lord God with gifts in their hands, even gifts to the King of heaven; all generations shall praise thee with great joy.

12 Cursed *are* all they which hate thee, and blessed shall all be which love thee for ever.

13 Rejoice and be glad for the children of the just: for they shall be gathered together, and shall bless the Lord of the just.

14 O blessed *are* they which love thee, *for* they shall rejoice in thy peace: blessed *are* they which have been sorrowful for all thy scourges; for they shall rejoice for thee, when they have seen all thy glory, and shall be glad for ever.

15 Let my soul bless God the great King.

16 For Jerusalem shall be built up with sapphires, and emeralds, and precious stone: thy walls and towers and battlements with pure gold.

17 And the streets of Jerusalem shall be paved with beryl and carbuncle and stones of Ophir.

18 And all her streets shall say, Alleluia; and they shall praise him, saying, Blessed be God, which hath extolled it for ever.

Chapter 14

So Tobit made an end of praising God.

2 And he was eight and fifty years old when he lost his sight, which was restored to him after eight years: and he gave alms, and he increased in the fear of the Lord God, and praised him.

3 And when he was very aged, he called his son, and the six sons of his son, and said to him, My son, take thy children; for, behold, I am aged, and am ready to depart out of this life.

4 Go into Media, my son, for I surely believe those things which Jonas the prophet spake of Nineve, that it shall be overthrown; and that for a time peace shall rather be in Media; and that our brethren shall lie scattered in the earth from that good land: and Jerusalem shall be desolate,

and the house of God in it shall be burned, and shall be desolate for a time;

5 And that again God will have mercy on them, and bring them again into the land, where they shall build a temple, but not like to the first, until the time of that age be fulfilled; and afterward they shall return from *all* places of their captivity, and build up Jerusalem gloriously, and the house of God shall be built in it for ever with a glorious building, as the prophets have spoken thereof.

6 And all nations shall turn, and fear the Lord God truly, and shall bury their idols.

7 So shall all nations praise the Lord, and his people shall confess God, and the Lord shall exalt his people; and all those which love the Lord God in truth and justice shall rejoice, shewing mercy to our brethren.

8 And now, my son, depart out of Nineve, because that those things which the prophet Jonas spake shall surely come to pass.

9 But keep thou the law and the commandments, and shew thyself merciful and just, that it may go well with thee.

10 And bury me decently, and thy mother with me; but tarry no longer at Nineve. Remember, my son, how Aman handled Achiacharus that brought him up, how out of light he brought him into darkness, and how he rewarded him again: yet Achiacharus was saved, but the other had his reward: for he went down into darkness. Manasses gave alms, and escaped the snares of death which they had set for him: but Aman fell into the snare, and perished.

11 Wherefore now, my son, consider what alms doeth, and how righteousness doth deliver. When he had said these things, he gave up the ghost in the bed, being an hundred and eight and fifty years old; and he buried him honourably.

12 And when Anna his mother was dead, he buried her with his father. But Tobias departed with his wife and children to Ecbatane to Raguel his father in law,

13 Where he became old with honour, and he buried his father and mother in law honourably, and he inherited their substance, and his father Tobit's.

14 And he died at Ecbatane in Media, being an hundred and seven and twenty years old.

15 But before he died he heard of the destruction of Nineve, which was taken by Nabuchodonosor and Assuerus: and before his death he rejoiced over Nineve.

The term *Haggadah* is derived from the Hebrew verb *higgid*, to tell or to relate. The Haggadah is a body of Rabbinical tales. It is defined by Webster as "collectively, the nonlegal portion of Rabbinical literature . . . that exegesis or exposition of the Scriptures consisting chiefly in imaginative developments of thoughts suggested by the text." This and the tale following are from the Haggadah.

The Lord Helpeth Man and Beast

During his march to conquer the world, Alexander, the Macedonian, came to a people in Africa who dwelt in a remote and secluded corner in peaceful huts, and knew neither war nor conqueror. They led him to the hut of their chief, who received him hospitably, and placed before him golden dates, golden figs, and bread of gold.

"Do you eat gold in this country?" said Alexander.

"I take it for granted," replied the chief, "that thou wert able to find eatable food in thine own country. For what reason, then, art thou come amongst us?"

"Your gold has not tempted me hither," said Alexander, "but I would become acquainted with your manners and customs."

"So be it," rejoined the other, "sojourn among us as long as it pleaseth thee."

At the close of this conversation, two citizens entered, as into their court of justice. The plaintiff said,

"I bought of this man a piece of land, and as I was making a deep drain through it, I found a treasure. This is not mine, for I only bargained for the land, and not for any treasure that might be concealed beneath it; and yet the former owner of the land will not receive it."

The defendant answered,

"I hope I have a conscience, as well as my fellow-citizen. I sold him the land with all its contingent, as well as existing advantages, and consequently, the treasure inclusively."

The chief, who was at the same time their supreme judge, recapitulated their words, in order that the parties might see whether or not he understood them aright. Then, after some reflection, said,

"Thou hast a son, friend, I believe?"

"Yes."

"And thou," addressing the other, "a daughter?"

"Yes."

"Well, then, let thy son marry *thy* daughter, and bestow the treasure on the young couple for a marriage portion."

Alexander seemed surprised and perplexed.

"Think you my sentence unjust?" the chief asked him.

"Oh, no!" replied Alexander, "but it astonishes me."

"And how, then, would the case have been decided in your country?"

"To confess the truth," said Alexander, "we should have taken both parties into custody, and have seized the treasure for the king's use."

"For the king's use!" exclaimed the chief; "does the sun shine on that country?"

"Oh, yes!"

"Does it rain there?"

"Assuredly."

"Wonderful! But are there tame animals in the country, that live on the grass and green herbs?"

"Very many, and of many kinds."

"Ay, that must, then, be the cause," said the chief, "for the sake of those innocent animals the All-gracious Being continues to let the sun shine, and the rain drop down on your country, since its inhabitants are unworthy of such blessings."

Hadrian and the Aged Planter

While passing near Tiberias in Galilee, the emperor Hadrian observed an old man digging a large trench in order to plant some fig trees.

"If you had properly employed the morning of your life," remarked Hadrian, "you would not have to work so hard in the evening of your days."

"I have well employed the morning of my early days, nor will I neglect the evening of my life; and let God do what he thinks best," replied the man.

"How old are you, good man?"

"A hundred years."

"What!" exclaimed Hadrian, "a hundred years old, and you are still planting trees? Do you hope to enjoy the fruits of your labor?"

"Great king," rejoined the hoary-headed elder, "yes, I do hope so; if God permit, I may even eat the fruit of these very trees; if not, my children will. Did not my forefathers plant trees for me, and shall I not do the same for my children?"

Hadrian, pleased with the old man's reply, said,

"Well, old man, if you ever live to see the fruit of these trees, let me know. Yes, let me know. Do you hear, old fellow?" and with these words he left him.

The old man did live long enough to see the fruits of his labor. The trees flourished, and bore excellent fruit. As soon as they were sufficiently ripe, he gathered the choicest figs, put them in a basket, and marched off toward the emperor's residence. Hadrian happened to be looking out of one of the windows of his palace, and noticed the old man,

Translated by Leo W. Schwarz and published in his anthology, *The Jewish Caravan.* Copyright 1935 by Leo W. Schwarz. Reprinted by permission of Holt, Rinehart and Winston, Inc.

bent with age, with a basket on his shoulders, standing near the gate. He ordered him to be admitted to his court.

"What is your pleasure, old man?"

"May it please your majesty to recollect seeing some years ago a very old man planting some trees; you commanded him, if he ever should gather the fruit, to let you know. I am that old man, and this is the fruit of those very trees. May it please you graciously to accept them as a humble tribute of gratitude for your great condescension."

Hadrian, surprised and gratified to see so extraordinary an example of old age crowned with the full use of all faculties and honest effort, asked the old man to be seated, and ordering the basket to be emptied of fruit, and to be filled with gold, gave it to him as a present. Some courtiers who witnessed this remarkable scene, exclaimed,

"Is it possible that our great emperor should show so much honor to a miserable Jew!"

"Why should I not honor him whom God has honored?" replied Hadrian. "Look at his age, and imitate his example!"

The emperor then very graciously dismissed the old man, who returned home highly pleased and delighted. When he reached his village and exhibited the present he had received, the people were all astonished. Amongst the neighbors whom curiosity had brought to his house, there was a silly covetous woman, who, seeing so much treasure obtained for a few figs, imagined that the emperor must be very fond of this fruit. She therefore hastily ran home, and shouted at her husband,

"You wretch, why are you tarrying here? Have you not heard that Cæsar is very fond of figs? Go, take some to him, and you may become as rich as your neighbor."

The foolish fellow, unable to bear the reproaches of his wife, took a large sack, filled with figs, on his shoulders, and after a strenuous journey, arrived, much fatigued, at the palace-gate, and demanded admittance to the emperor. Being asked what he wanted, he answered that, understanding that his majesty was very fond of figs, he had brought a whole sack full, for which he expected a great reward. The officer on duty reported this to the emperor. Hadrian smiled at the man's folly and impertinence.

"Yes," he said to the officer, "the fellow shall have his reward. Let him remain where he is, and let everyone who enters the gate take one of his figs and throw it at his face until they are all gone: then let him depart."

The order was immediately executed. The wretched man, abused, pelted, derided, instead of wishing for gold, prayed only to see the bottom of his bag. After much patience, and still more pain, his prayer was answered. The bag being empty, the poor fellow was dismissed. Dejected and sorrowful, he hastened home. His wife, who was all the while considering how to spend the unexpected treasure, how many fine gowns and cloaks and jewels she would purchase and relishing the thought of how attractive she would look, how the neighbors would stare to see her dressed in silk and gold—most impatiently awaited her husband's return. He came finally, and though she saw the bag was empty, she imagined that his pockets at least were full. Without even greeting him, or permitting him to take breath, she hastily asked him what good luck he had.

"Have patience," replied the enraged husband, "have patience, and I will tell you. I have both great and good luck. My great luck was that I took to the emperor figs and not peaches, else I should have been stoned to death. And my good luck was that the figs were ripe, else I should have left my brains behind me."

NACHMAN OF BRATZLAV

Reb Nachman of Bratzlav (1770-1811) was a descendant of the Baal Shem Tov, the Jewish mystic who founded the Hasidic movement. Nachman was a writer on many subjects, but he was primarily a *tzaddik,* that is, one of the righteous.

The Rabbi's Son

Not long ago there lived a rabbi who in all his life had scarcely lifted his head from the study of the holy books, and who was so strict in his observance of every last dot in the ritual that he would scarcely raise his eyes to heaven without first seeking a law that might tell him whether it was permitted at that moment and hour to raise one's eyes to heaven. And in all the world there was nothing that angered him so much as the practices of those who were called Hasidim, for in their wild prayer, in their miracles of healing, and in their carelessness of the strictures of the law, he saw the hand of the evil one. And when he found men in his own village going over to the ways of the Hasidim, the rabbi became bitter against them, and he fought with all his strength to prevent another soul from being lost to the erring ones, and he thought, "After I am dead, there will be none to prevent them, and they will all go and become followers of the mad, howling Zaddikim, who disgrace the Sabbath with their loud singing and lusty dancing,

Translated by Meyer Levin. From *The Golden Mountain,* published by Robert O. Ballou. Reprinted by permission of Mr. Levin.

and who scarcely know how to read in the holy books." The rabbi longed for a son who would continue after him to keep the people to the observance of the holy law.

When a son was born to him in his old age, he took it joyfully as a sign from above that his way was the only path to heaven, and that the way would not be left without a guide. The rabbi thought, "My son will be a great light against the Hasidim; he will destroy them entirely, with their ignorant Zaddikim, their mad chanting in the woods, and their magic tricks of healing." He was watchful over the boy every instant of day and night, that the child might not touch even the shadow of an impurity.

The youth that grew was remarkable in learning. He sat on a high stool near the table, and studied the books that were before him. But as the young boy sat on the stool, he would sometimes lift his eyes from the pages of the holy books, and his gaze would reach through the window out into the fields, into the distance that was yellow and green with leaves; then his soul would glide forth upon the path of his gaze, and his soul would hover like a bird in the free air.

At those moments the boy felt himself drawn as toward a singing voice, and he was very happy. But then he would remember his books, and force his eyes back upon the page, and hold his head down with both his hands, that he might not err.

More often the longing came upon him, and his soul went out to the call of a song, as a bird answering the song of its mate. And in that time the boy was alight with a holiness that made bright the entire room, and joy was all about him. But when he returned to his books he felt himself dragged down to listen to the mouths of the dead, and there was a yearning and a longing in him for he knew not what.

The flame and the yearning consumed him, his body became weak, and he was as a trembling candle-flame that may die with every puff of the wind. Still he did not know what he desired, but his yearning was as that of the unborn souls that await their embodiment on earth.

The rabbi saw that his son was becoming weak, and he

spoke with him of all the wonders of the law's myriad commands, and of his life that was needed to combat the Hasidim on earth. But in all the things that the rabbi said, there was no help for the boy; only when his father spoke of the evil of the Hasidim, only then he felt a trembling within him, and a sudden warmth.

Among the young scholars with whom he sometimes studied, there were two who went secretly among the Hasidim; and when they saw the rabbi's son become so pale, and losing his heart for learning, they said, "What is it that is ill with you?"

He told them, "I feel a longing for something, and I cannot tell what it is."

Then they said to him, "Only one man can help you, and he is the great Zaddik who lives one day's journey from here. You must go to him, for he has the power to release your soul to its destiny."

"Is he pure?" asked the rabbi's son.

"We do not know whether he is pure," they told him, "for he does not keep himself from contact with the sinful. But we do know that he never leaves anyone until he has taken his burden from him."

"Is he learned?" asked the rabbi's son.

"We do not know whether he is learned," they answered, "for he lives in a hut in the forest, and works as a woodcutter. But he knows the song that the sparrow sings to heaven."

Then the boy went to his father the rabbi and said, "Let me go to see a Zaddik who lives in a little town a day's journey away."

The rabbi was deeply pained at his son's words, for he knew that the Zaddik was but a simple man, a leader of the Hasidim. "What help can he be to you, my son," the rabbi asked, "when you yourself have more learning than he?"

The boy returned to his studies, but again he felt the terrible longing come over his soul and his eyes lifted, and he looked into the distance. Then he went to his father and begged him, "Let me go."

The rabbi saw his son become more frail and wan each day, until when the boy asked him a third time, the rabbi said, "You may not go alone to him, for it may be the evil one who is drawing you on this way. But I will go with you to this ignorant man, that you may see him and forget him."

When they had put the horses to the cart, the rabbi said, "Let us see whether there will be a sign from heaven upon this journey. If nothing happens to delay the journey, it is a sign that this is a true pilgrimage; but if we should be stopped on our way, it is a sign that we must turn back, and we will return."

So they rode forth, and all went well until they came to a shallow brook, but as the cart was crossing the brook, one of the horses slipped and fell and overturned the cart, so that the rabbi and his son were thrown into the water.

When they had come out of the water, and righted the cart, the rabbi said: "You see, my son, heaven has sent us a sign to turn back, for this is an evil journey." So they returned home, and the boy sat again over his books. But soon the heaviness returned to his heart, and he felt the call of the distance. He feared to speak to his father, for he remembered the omen on their journey. Days passed, and each day the boy became weaker, until he was as a dying man who no longer fears what may be said on earth. "Father," he cried, "I must go and speak with the Zaddik!"

Once more the rabbi consented, and they rode on their way. But when they had ridden two-thirds of a day, the cart went over a great stone, and both axles of the cart were broken.

"This Zaddik must surely be an impostor," the rabbi declared, "for we have had another omen, and our journey to him is barred." They mended the wagon, and returned home.

But the boy's soul was more than ever unquiet, until he prevailed upon the rabbi to set out for a third time upon the journey. "But, father," he begged, "let us not take what may befall by chance as an omen from heaven. If the horse slips, or the wagon breaks, have we proof that the Zaddik is sinful?"

The rabbi said, "But if there is a sign of sin against him alone, will you obey?"

"I will obey, and return home, and never ask to go to him again."

They set out on their third journey. All went well; at night they came to an inn not far from the village of the Zaddik. As they sat over their evening meal, the boy dreamy and lost in awaited happiness, the rabbi began to speak with a merchant who sat at a near-by table.

"Where does a rabbi travel?" the merchant enquired.

"On his way," said the rabbi, for he was ashamed to say that he was going to consult a man of no learning. "And you?" he asked.

"I am a merchant; I have just been to a village," said the stranger. And he spoke the name of the Zaddik's place.

Then, as one who remembers the sounds of a name, the rabbi said: "I have heard that many people come to consult with a wonder-worker who lives in that same village."

At this, the merchant laughed out loud. "Don't speak of him!" he shouted. "I have just come from that very man's house!"

The boy raised his head, as one who listens in a dream, and his wide eyes pierced the stranger.

"Is it indeed true," the rabbi asked, "that he is a holy man?"

"A holy man!" the stranger laughed. "He is an impostor and an agent of the evil one! I myself saw him defile the Sabbath!"

Then the rabbi turned to his son and said, "You have heard what the stranger has told us, in all innocence, not knowing where we were bound."

"I have heard," the boy replied, and his voice was as the voice of the dead.

They returned home.

Soon after, the boy died.

One night, as the grieving rabbi slept, his son appeared to him in a dream; the youth was wrapped in anger, and as the rabbi asked him, "My son, why are you angry?" the boy cried, "Go to that Zaddik to whom I longed to go!" The rabbi awoke, and remembered his dream, and said to himself, "Perhaps it was a chance dream," and did not go.

But again his son appeared to him as he slept, and the boy wore the form of the Angel of Wrath. And he cried, "Go to the Zaddik! Go!" This time the rabbi thought, "The dream is the work of the evil one." But when his son appeared to him a third time, the rabbi knew that he must go.

And as he came to that same inn where he had stopped with his son, he entered, to pass the night. He sat alone in the room, and did not touch the food that was placed before him; his heart was heavy. Then a voice spoke, a voice of laughter, saying, "Ah, the rabbi is here again."

The rabbi looked up and saw the same merchant whom he had met that other night when he had stopped at the inn.

"The rabbi is here again," the merchant said, "and this time he is alone!"

"Are you not that merchant whom I met here once before?" the rabbi asked.

"Indeed I am!" said the stranger, and laughing, he opened wide his mouth and cried, "If you like, I'll swallow you alive."

The rabbi started with fright. "Who are you!" he murmured, trembling.

"Do you remember," the stranger said, "how you and your son once rode to see the Zaddik, and on the way your horse tripped and fell in the brook? Yet your son made you go again on the way to that holy man, but the second time the axles of your wagon were broken? And the third time you met me here, and I told you that the man was not holy, but an impostor who sinned on Sabbath? Then you turned back once more, and so your son died of loneliness and grief? Go, rabbi! now that I have got rid of your son you may go on your way to the Hasid; for know that in your son there lived the power of the lesser flame, and the power of the greater flame was in the Zaddik, and if they two had come together on this earth, Messiah would have descended! But I placed obstacles in your way, until your son was dead; and now, rabbi, you can go to see the Zaddik!"

With these words, the stranger vanished.

And the rabbi continued on his journey, and came to the hut of the Hasid. And there he wept, "Alas, for him who is lost unto us, and cannot be found again!"

MARTIN BUBER

Martin Buber, the eminent Jewish philosopher and theologian, was one of those who informed the modern world of the meaning of Hasidic mysticism. He has published many volumes of Hasidic legends as well as historical and philosophical studies. His best known work, *I and Thou,* introduces into modern thought the idea that between man and man, and between man and God, there can be, and indeed must be, a "dialogue."

The Judgment

It happened once—it was on the fourth day of the week and about the first hour of evening, when the sun has just vanished from our sight—that the Baal-Shem left his house to make a journey. He had not spoken of where he was going to any person, either disciple or friend, so that the goal and meaning of this trip remained a mystery for all his followers, even for those who accompanied him. This time too he drove a great stretch of the way in a short space of time; for it is known to all, indeed, that place and time were not fetters to the will of the master as to one of us.

About midnight the Baal-Shem stopped in a strange village before the house of a tax-collector and innkeeper, in order to rest there for the hours of the night which remained to him. It became apparent that the host knew neither the Baal-Shem nor any of his followers, but, as is

Translated by Maurice Friedman. From *The Legend of the Baal-Shem* by Martin Buber. Copyright 1955 by Harper & Brothers. Used by permission.

not seldom the case among people of this profession, he was
nonetheless curious to know to what station his guest belonged and to what end he had undertaken this trip. While
he offered the master and the others a late meal and made
their beds for them, he exchanged questions and answers
with them. In reply to the innkeeper's inquiries the Baal-
Shem gave him to understand that he was a preacher and
that, having been informed that on the coming Sabbath the
wedding of a rich and distinguished man was going to take
place in Berlin, he wished to be there at that time in order
to officiate at the ceremony.

When the host heard this, he remained silent and perplexed for awhile and then said, "Sir, you mock my inquisi-
tiveness! How can you travel that stretch of road in the
time which remains to you! Indeed, if you did not spare
horse and man, you might perhaps be able to be there for
another Sabbath, but never for this one."

The Baal-Shem smiled a little and replied, "Do not concern yourself about that, friend; I am sure of my horses.
They have already done many good pieces of work for me."

Soon after that he lay down to rest along with his followers. But the host remained awake in his bed the whole
night long, for the strange man and his business appeared
to him all too remarkable. Yet there was something in the
glance of the man which did not allow the innkeeper to believe that he was a joker or even a fool. The longing came
over him to see this thing through to the end. He therefore
thought of a clever pretext to offer the strange preacher his
company. In fact, a great deal of business occurred to him
that he might take care of to some advantage in Berlin.
Then he decided to talk this over with his guest in the
morning.

When the master and his followers had risen from bed,
the host went to him and reported his wish, and the Baal-
Shem agreed. On the other hand, he showed no especial
hurry to be on his way, looked around the house tranquilly,
spoke a prayer with his followers, and finally bid the host
prepare still another large meal. This they ate and remained

then in conversation while the innkeeper ran up and down out of unrest and curiosity.

When the day had already descended, the master commanded that the wagon be made ready and the horses hitched to it. They travelled away, and soon the night came over them. The Baal-Shem and his followers sat silent. This appeared rare and strange to the mind of the innkeeper, and it seemed to him that this was a trip the like of which he had never yet taken. There was nothing else but darkness. At times it felt to him as if they rolled deep underneath the streets of men through mysterious passages in the earth, and then again the way that they took felt to him so light and transparent that it seemed as if they floated in the air. They encountered no noise, no people, no animals, no places. The innkeeper could not control his thoughts. Everything in him and around him appeared to have dissolved into something fleeting and transitory.

Suddenly it seemed to him as if the air around him became denser, the first light dawned, he felt beneath him again the shaking of the wagon on the floor of the earth, a dog barked in the distance, a rooster crowed, a hut lay to one side in the dawn light. They travelled thus for awhile, the morning became clear, and when the last mists vanished before the sun, the innkeeper saw before him a great city. Barely a quarter of an hour passed by before they reached Berlin.

The master selected a modest inn which stood on the outskirts of the city, in that neighbourhood where low houses lay in their little gardens almost as in the country. Then he sat down with his disciples to breakfast in an arbour in front of the house. After they had eaten, they remained together in prayer and speech. The innkeeper who had made the trip with them thought of the statement of the preacher that he was travelling to Berlin to the wedding of a great man and that to-day was the day of the ceremony, and he could not understand how the Baal-Shem could remain so tranquil instead of going to associate with the guests in the house of the bridegroom. Still perplexed by the events of the night and yet already pricked by this new question, he approached the master. But when he prepared to open his mouth, the Baal-Shem raised a cheerful countenance, and the innkeeper saw thereon the merry mockery with which the latter, in great kindness, smiled at his restless soul. Then the courage for the question deserted him, and he took leave in order to wander about a little in the strange city.

He was not under way more than an hour when he saw that on every side the people stood together in order to share a piece of news with one another and to discuss it. So he went up to one of them and asked what might have happened to cause the people to forget their affairs. He received this information: in the house of a rich Jew, whose wedding was to have taken place that very day, the bride had suddenly passed away in the morning after she had worked with great joy until midnight getting her finery ready, had made the preparations for the feast, and had spent the rest of the night in restful sleep. Also she had in no way been sick or weakly, but was known to all as a beautiful and strong young creature.

The house of the bridegroom was pointed out to the innkeeper. He entered there and found the wedding guests standing in distress and confusion around the dead girl, who lay on the bed, pale but undeformed. The doctors, who appeared to be still troubled about her, were just now taking their leave of the master of the house, expressing with some embarrassment the opinion that she who was dead must now remain dead. The bridegroom stood motionless; his face wrapped round with grief as with a grey veil. This and that one among the guests came up to him and whispered words meant to comfort him, but the man remained mute as if he had not heard. Then the innkeeper also ventured to go up to him, and he told him of the unusual manner in which he had travelled such a great way that night with the strange preacher. He gave it as his opinion that the wonder-worker who could make this journey would probably also know how to do much more that was out of the ordinary, and he advised the master of the house to go to him and confide his suffering to him. The bridegroom gripped his hand, held it fast and requested to be conducted to the inn of the Baal-Shem. He went before the master, told him the whole of the painful event, and bade him come to the bed of the dead. The Baal-Shem went with him immediately to the lifeless bride and gazed long at her silent face.

Everyone grew still and waited for his word. But he turned from the waiting men and said to the women, "Prepare quickly the winding sheet for the dead and carry out your customs without delay." To the bridegroom he said, "Bid men go to the cemetery where you bring the dead of your house to rest and prepare an abode for this one too." Then the bridegroom sent there and had a grave dug. "I shall go with you in the funeral procession," the master said. "But take the wedding clothes and the gown that you yourself have selected for this day and bring them to the grave." When everything was arranged, they laid the corpse in an open shrine and carried it out. The Baal-Shem walked first after the coffin, and many people followed him with bated breath.

Before the grave the Baal-Shem commanded that the dead should be laid in the grave in the uncovered coffin so that her face looked up freely to heaven and could be seen by all. He also ordered that no earth should be thrown on her. He gave instructions to two men to stand near him and await his orders. Then he stepped up to the open grave, leaned on his staff, and let his eyes rest on the face of the dead. Thus he stood without moving, and those who saw him observed that he was like one without life, as if he had sent his spirit forth to another place. Everyone stood in a wide circle around the grave. After awhile he motioned to the two men. They drew near and saw that the countenance of the departed had reddened with the breath of life and that breath came and went out of her mouth. The Baal-Shem bade them lift her out of the grave. It then happened that she stood up and looked around her. Then the master stepped back and commanded the bridegroom that he should instantly and without speech clothe the bride in her veil and that he should lead her to the bridal canopy and not recall the incident by any word. The bridegroom, however, asked that it be the master who should bless the marriage.

So they led the veiled girl into the house under the canopy. But when the Baal-Shem raised his voice and spoke the marriage blessing over the pair, the bride tore the veil from her face, looked at him and cried, "This is the man who acquitted me!"

"Be silent!" the Baal-Shem rebuked her. The bride grew still, and before the people could realize what was happening, the master had left the house.

Later, when all the wedding guests sat at the meal and the shadow of the past event began to fade, the bride herself arose to tell her story.

Her bridegroom had already been married once, and it was as a widower that he had desired her for a wife. However, the first, dead wife had been her aunt who had taken her in and cared for her as an orphan and allowed her to grow up near her in the house. Then it happened that the wife became ill and there was no help for her, and she herself knew well that her time had now come to an end. It weighed heavily on her spirit that when she should have been dead for a little while, her husband, who was not yet old, might possibly raise up another in her place. And as she thought about this, she realized his choice would fall on her young relative, who knew all the affairs of the great house so well and was pleasant to behold and who would be before his eyes every hour of the day. And because she herself had loved her husband very much and was disquieted over the short time which had been granted her to be at his side, she was very envious of the young creature. As she felt her last hour slip away, she called both of them to her bedside. And when they who loved her saw her pining away so, their souls overflowed with sorrow. She exacted a solemn promise from them never to marry each other. To the two of them, who suffered over the dying woman, this promise did not seem difficult and they gladly gave it.

But then the dead woman was carried away, and her

place was empty. Even her shadow faded from the room, and there were now only the living, and all around them was life. They looked in each other's eyes every hour, and soon they understood that they could not let each other go. Then they broke their oath and pledged themselves to each other.

But on the morning of the wedding, when the house was full of joy and no one thought of the dark days when one now dead had dwelt there in sadness, the will of the dead woman came back to its abode, demanded that its violated rights be restored, and sought to kill the fortunate woman. Now, at the bidding of the strange power, the life of the bride was torn away from her body, which lay there stiff. Then her soul struggled mightily over the bridegroom with the soul of the dead.

When she was carried to the grave, both of their souls came before the judgment. It was the voice of a man which administered justice over them, and they fought before him over the decision. The voice gave the verdict, "You dead, who no longer have a share in the earth, let go of her. For behold, justice is with the living. This woman and this man bear no guilt. They must do what they did not want to do in order to still the need of their souls." And since the dead would not desist from oppressing the bride, the voice cried out to her, "Let go of her! Do you not see that she must go to the wedding? The canopy is waiting!" Then the bride awakened to life, allowed herself to be lifted out of the grave and clothed in her veil, and still slightly stunned, she followed the women to the canopy.

"But," she said to the bridegroom and to the guests when she had finished her tale, "when the preacher spoke the blessing over us, I recognized the voice which had pronounced judgment over me."

HEINRICH HEINE

On his deathbed in Paris, in the year 1856, Heine, speaking of Divine forgiveness is reported to have said, "Naturally, He will forgive me. C'est son métier." Born in 1797, Heine was in some degree a child of the Enlightenment. A Jew, a German, something of a Frenchman as well, a philosopher, a critic, a storyteller, he was principally a poet. Like many German Jews of his time, he was baptized and received into the Lutheran Church, but unlike the majority of these he did not remain a practicing convert. We may see plainly in *The Rabbi of Bacherach* that it would not have been easy for Heine to embrace Christianity without reservations. He wrote in one of his Italian travel sketches that the lizards on a certain hillside had reported that the stones expected God to manifest Himself amongst them in the form of a stone.

The late Lion Feuchtwanger is said to have attempted to finish this unfinished novella. His proposed ending has never to my knowledge been translated into English.

The Rabbi of Bacherach

Chapter 1

Above the Rhineland, where the great river's banks cease to smile, where mountain and cliff, with their romantic ruined castles, show a bolder bearing, and a wilder, sterner majesty arises—there, like a fearful tale of olden times, lies the gloomy, ancient town of Bacherach. But these walls with the toothless battlements and blind lookouts, in whose gaps the wind blows and the sparrows nest, were not always so broken-down and crumbling. In the ugly unpaved alleys seen through the ruined gate there did not always reign that dreary silence broken only now and then by screaming children, bickering women, and lowing cows. These walls were proud and strong once, and through these alleys moved a fresh, free life, power and pomp, joy and sorrow, plenty of love, and plenty of hate.

Bacherach was once one of those municipalities which the Romans founded when they ruled along the Rhine. And, although subsequent times were stormy and the inhabitants later came under the overlordship of the Hohenstaufen and finally that of the Wittelsbachs, nevertheless they knew, after the example of other towns on the Rhine, how to maintain a fairly free commonwealth. It consisted of a combination of several corporate bodies, with those of the old patriciate and those of the guilds—which again were subdivided according to their different trades—both striving for sole power. So that while outwardly they all stood firmly together, bound to common vigilance and defense against the neighboring robber barons, internally their divergent interests kept them in constant dissension. There was therefore little neighborliness and much mistrust; even overt outbursts of passion were not infrequent. The Lord Warden sat on the high tower of Sareck; and, like his falcon, he swooped down whenever called for—and sometimes uncalled for. The clergy ruled in darkness by darkening the souls. One of the most isolated and helpless of bodies, gradually crushed by the civil law, was the small Jewish community which had first settled in Bacherach in Roman days, and later, during the Great Persecution, had taken in whole flocks of fugitive brothers in the faith.

The Great Persecution of the Jews began with the Crusades and raged most grimly about the middle of the fourteenth century, at the end of the Great Plague which, like any other public disaster, was blamed on the Jews. It was asserted that they had brought down the wrath of God, and that they had poisoned the wells with the aid of the lepers.

The enraged rabble, especially the hordes of the Flagellants —half-naked men and women who, lashing themselves for penance and chanting a mad song to the Virgin Mary, swept through the Rhineland and South Germany—murdered many thousands of Jews, tortured them, or baptized them by force. Another accusation, which even before that time, and throughout the Middle Ages until the beginning of the past century, cost them much blood and anguish, was the absurd tale, repeated *ad nauseam* in chronicle and legend, that the Jews would steal the consecrated wafer, stabbing it with knives until the blood ran from it, and that they would slay Christian children at their feast of the Passover, in order to use the blood for their nocturnal rite.

The Jews—sufficiently hated for their faith, their wealth, and their ledgers—were on this holiday entirely in the hands of their enemies, who could encompass their destruction with ease by spreading rumors of such an infanticide, perhaps even sneaking the bloody corpse of a child into a Jewish outcast's house, and then setting upon the Jews at their prayers. There would be murder, plunder, and baptism; and great miracles would be wrought by the dead child, whom the Church might even canonize in the end. Saint Werner is one of these saints; and it was in his honor that at Oberwesel the great abbey was founded which is now one of the most beautiful ruins on the Rhine, and delights us so much with the Gothic splendor of its long, ogival windows, proudly soaring pillars, and stone-carvings, when we pass it on a gay, green summer day and do not know its origin. In honor of this saint, three more great churches were built along the Rhine and innumerable Jews abused or murdered. This happened in the year 1287; and in Bacherach, where one of Saint Werner's churches arose, the Jews also underwent many trials and tribulations. For two centuries afterwards they were spared such attacks of mob fury, although they were still harassed and threatened enough.

However, the more they were beset with hate from without, the more fond and tender grew the Bacherach Jews' domestic life, and the more profound their piety and fear of

God. A model of godly conduct was the local rabbi, called Rabbi Abraham; a young man still, but famed far and wide for his learning. He was born in the town, and his father, who had been the rabbi there before him, had charged him in his last will to devote himself to the same calling and never leave Bacherach unless in deadly peril. This word, and a cabinet full of rare books, was all that was left him by his father, who had lived in poverty and learning. Nevertheless, Rabbi Abraham was a very wealthy man now, being married to the only daughter of his late paternal uncle who had been a dealer in jewelry, and whose riches he had inherited. A few sly gossips kept hinting at that—as if the Rabbi had married his wife just for the money. But the women, contradicting in unison, had old stories to tell: how the Rabbi had been in love with Sarah—she was commonly called Lovely Sarah—long before he went to Spain, and how she had to wait seven years till he returned after he wed her against her father's will, and even without her consent, by means of the "betrothal ring." For every Jew can make a Jewish girl his lawful wife if he succeeds in putting a ring on her finger and saying at the same time: "I take thee for my wife, according to the law of Moses and Israel!"

At the mention of Spain the sly ones used to smile in a knowing way; probably because of a dark rumor that while Rabbi Abraham had studied the holy law zealously enough at the Academy of Toledo, he had also copied Christian customs and absorbed ways of free thinking, like the Spanish Jews who at that time had attained to an extraordinary height of culture. In their hearts, though, those gossips hardly believed their own insinuations. For the Rabbi's life, after his return from Spain, had been extremely pure, pious, and earnest; he observed the most trivial rites with painful conscientiousness, fasted each Monday and Thursday, abstained from meat and wine except on the Sabbath and other holidays, and spent his days in study and in prayer. By day, he expounded the Law to the students whom his fame had drawn to Bacherach; and by night he gazed on the stars in the sky, or into the eyes of Lovely Sarah. The Rabbi's

marriage was childless, yet there was about him no lack of
life or gaiety. The great hall in his house, which adjoined
the synagogue, was open to the whole community. Here one
came and went without ceremony, offered quick prayers,
traded news, or took common counsel in hard times. Here
the children played on Sabbath mornings while in the synagogue the weekly chapter was read; here one met for wedding and funeral processions, quarreled, and was reconciled; here those that were cold found a warm stove, and the
hungry a well-spread table. Besides, there was a multitude
of relatives surrounding the Rabbi; brothers and sisters with
their wives and husbands and children, as well as both his
and his wife's uncles and aunts and countless other kin—all
of whom regarded him as the head of the family—made
themselves at home in his house from dawn to dusk, and
never failed to dine there in full force on the high holidays.
In particular, such grand family dinners took place in the
Rabbi's house at the annual celebration of the Passover, an
age-old, wondrous festival which Jews all over the world
still observe on the eve of the fourteenth day of the month
of Nisan, in eternal memory of their redemption from
Egyptian slavery, and in the following manner:

As soon as night falls, the mistress of the house lights the
lamps, spreads the tablecloth, puts three pieces of the flat
unleavened bread in its midst, covers them with a napkin,
and on the pile places six little dishes containing symbolical
food: an egg, lettuce, horse-radish, the bone of a lamb, and
a brown mixture of raisins, cinnamon, and nuts. At this
table, the head of the house then sits down with all relations
and friends, and reads to them from a very curious book
called the Haggadah, the contents of which are a strange
mixture of ancestral legends, miraculous tales of Eygpt, odd
narratives, disputations, prayers, and festive songs. A huge
supper is brought in halfway through this celebration; and
even during the reading, at certain times, one tastes of the
symbolical dishes, eats pieces of unleavened bread, and
drinks four cups of red wine. This nocturnal festival is mel-
ancholically gay in character, gravely playful, and mysterious as a fairy tale. And the traditional singsong in which the

Haggadah is read by the head of the house, and now and then repeated by the listeners in chorus, sounds at the same time so awesomely intense, maternally gentle, and suddenly awakening, that even those Jews who have long forsaken the faith of their fathers and pursued foreign joys and honors are moved to the depths of their hearts when the old, familiar sounds of the Passover happen to strike their ears.

And so Rabbi Abraham once sat in the great hall of his house with his relations, disciples, and other guests, to celebrate the eve of the Passover. Everything in the hall was brighter than usual; over the table hung a gaily embroidered silk spread whose gold fringes touched the floor; the plates with the symbolic foods shone appealingly, as did the tall, wine-filled goblets adorned with the embossed images of many holy stories. The men sat in their black cloaks and black, flat hats and white ruffs; the women, in strangely glittering garments made of cloths from Lombardy, wore their diadems and necklaces of gold and pearls; and the silver Sabbath lamp cast its most festive light on the devoutly merry faces of old and young. Reclining, as custom enjoins, on the purple velvet cushions of a chair raised above the others, Rabbi Abraham sat reading and chanting the Haggadah, while the mixed choir fell in or responded in the prescribed places. The Rabbi wore his black holiday garb. His noble, somewhat austere features seemed milder than usual; his lips were smiling out of the dark beard as if they had something fair to tell; and in his eyes was a light as of happy memories and visions of the future.

Lovely Sarah, seated beside him on a similar high velvet chair, wore none of her jewelry, being the hostess; only white linen enclosed her slender form and pious face. It was a touchingly beautiful face, just as always the beauty of Jewesses is of a peculiarly moving kind—a consciousness of the deep misery, the bitter scorn, and the evil chances wherein their kindred and friends live, brings to their lovely features a certain aching tenderness and observant loving apprehension that strangely charm our hearts. So, on this evening, Lovely Sarah sat looking constantly into her husband's eyes. But every now and then she also glanced at the

quaint parchment book of the Haggadah which lay before
her, bound in gold and velvet: an old heirloom with wine
stains of many years on it, which had come down from her
grandfather's time and in which were many bold and
brightly-colored pictures that even as a little girl she had so
loved to look at on Passover evenings. They represented all
kinds of biblical stories, such as Abraham smashing his father's idols with a hammer; the angels coming to him; Moses
killing the Mizri; and Pharaoh sitting in state on his throne,
with the frogs giving him no rest even at table. Also she saw
how Pharaoh drowned, thank God! and how the children of
Israel went cautiously through the Red Sea; how they stood
openmouthed before Mount Sinai, with their sheep, cows,
and oxen; how pious King David played the harp; and finally, how Jerusalem, with the towers and battlements of
its Temple, shone in the glory of the sun!

The second cup of wine was poured, the faces and the
voices of the guests grew brighter, and the Rabbi, taking a
piece of the unleavened bread and raising it in a gay greeting, read these words from the Haggadah: "Behold, this is
the bread our fathers ate in Egypt. Whoever is hungry, let
him come and share it! Whoever is in want, let him come
and celebrate the Passover! This year we are here; the coming year, in the land of Israel! This year we are slaves; the
coming year, free men!"

At this moment, the door of the hall opened and two tall,
pale men entered, wrapped in very wide cloaks, and one of
them said: "Peace be with you; we are men of your faith,
on a journey, and wish to celebrate the Passover with you."
And the Rabbi, quickly and kindly, replied, "Peace be with
you. Sit down here by me." The two strangers promptly sat
down at the table, and the Rabbi read on. Sometimes, while
the others were saying the responses, he would throw an
endearing word to his wife: alluding to the old joke that on
this evening the head of a Jewish house considers himself a
king, he said to her, "Be happy, my Queen!" But she, smiling sadly, replied, "We have no Prince"—by which she
meant the son of the house, whom a passage in the Haggadah requires to question his father in certain prescribed

words about the meaning of the festival. The Rabbi said nothing, only pointing with his finger to a picture just turned up in the Haggadah, on which was shown very charmingly how the three angels came to Abraham, to announce to him that he would have a son by his wife Sarah, who with feminine cunning was listening to their talk from behind the tent door. This little hint sent a threefold blush to the beautiful woman's cheeks; she cast her eyes down, and then lovingly raised them again to her husband, who went on chanting the wondrous story of Rabbi Joshua, Rabbi Eliezer, Rabbi Azariah, Rabbi Akiba, and Rabbi Tarfon, who sat reclining in B'ne B'rak and talked all night long of the Children of Israel's exodus from Egypt, until their disciples came to tell them that it was daylight and the great morning prayer was being recited in the synagogue.

Now, as Lovely Sarah was thus devoutly listening and continually looking at her husband, she noticed that his face suddenly froze in horrible distortion, the blood left his cheeks and lips, and his eyes stood out like balls of ice. But almost at the same instant she saw his features returning to their former calm and cheerfulness, his cheeks and lips growing red again, his eyes circling merrily—in fact, his whole being seemed seized by a mad gaiety that otherwise was quite foreign to his nature. Lovely Sarah was frightened as never before in her life. A chilling dread rose in her, due less to the signs of rigid terror which for a moment she had seen in her husband's countenance than to his present merriment, which gradually turned into rollicking exultation. The Rabbi moved his cap from one ear to the other, pulled and twisted his beard comically, sang the text of the Haggadah as if it were a catch; and in the enumeration of the Egyptian plagues, when it is the custom to dip the forefinger in the full cup and shake the clinging drop of wine to the ground, the Rabbi sprinkled the younger girls with red wine and there was much wailing over spoiled collars, and ringing laughter. An ever more eerie feeling overcame Lovely Sarah at this convulsively bubbling gaiety of her husband's; seized by nameless qualms, she gazed on the humming swarm of brightly illumined people, comfortably rocking to and fro, nibbling the thin Passover bread or sipping wine or gossiping or singing aloud, in the very happiest of moods.

The time for supper came and all rose to wash, and Lovely Sarah brought a great silver basin covered with embossed gold figures, which she held before each guest while water was poured over his hands. When she thus served the Rabbi, he winked at her significantly and quietly slipped out of the door. Lovely Sarah followed on his heels; hastily, the Rabbi grasped her hand and quickly drew her away through the dark alleys of Bacherach, quickly through the town gate, out onto the highway leading along the Rhine, toward Bingen.

It was one of those nights in spring which, though soft enough and starry, raise strange shivers in the soul. The fragrance of the flowers was deathly. The birds chirped as if glad to vex someone and yet vexed themselves. The moon cast malicious yellow stripes of light over the darkly murmuring river. The tall, bulky rocks of the cliffs looked like menacingly wagging giants' heads. The watchman on the tower of Castle Strahleck blew a melancholy tune, and with it, jealously chiming, tolled the little death bell of Saint Werner's. Lovely Sarah still held the silver ewer in her right hand; her left was held by the Rabbi, and she felt that his fingers were icy and his arm was trembling. But she followed in silence, perhaps because she had long been accustomed to obey her husband blindly and without questioning—perhaps, too, because fear sealed her lips from within.

Below Castle Sonneck, opposite Lorch—about where the hamlet of Niederrheinbach stands now—a high cliff arches out over the bank of the Rhine. This Rabbi Abraham ascended with his wife, looked all about him, and stared up at the stars. Lovely Sarah, trembling and chilled by fears of death, stood with him and regarded the pale face on which pain, dread, piety, and rage seemed to flash back and forth in the ghostly light of the moon. But when the Rabbi suddenly tore the silver ewer from her hand and hurled it clanking down into the Rhine, she could no longer bear the awful anxiety—and crying out, "Merciful Shaddai!" she threw herself at his feet and implored him to reveal the dark secret.

The Rabbi moved his lips soundlessly a few times, unable to speak; but finally he called out, "Do you see the Angel of Death? Down there he hovers over Bacherach. Yet we have escaped his sword. Praised be the Lord!" And in a voice still shaking with fright he told how, reclining happily and chanting the Haggadah, he had chanced to look under the table and there, at his feet, had seen the bloody corpse of a child. "Then I knew," added the Rabbi, "that our two late guests were not of the community of Israel, but of the assembly of the godless whose plan was to bring that corpse into our house by stealth, charge us with the murder, and incite the people to loot and murder us. I could not let on that I saw through the work of darkness; thereby I should have only speeded my destruction. Cunning alone could save our lives. Praised be the Lord! Have no fear, Lovely Sarah; our friends and relatives also will be saved. It was my blood after which the villains lusted; I have escaped them, and they will be content with my silver and gold. Come with me, Lovely Sarah, to another land; we will leave misfortune behind; lest it follow us, I threw the last of my possessions, the silver ewer, to it as a peace offering. The God of our fathers will not forsake us. Come, you are tired. Down there, Silent William stands by his boat; he will row us up the Rhine."

Without a sound and as if her every limb were broken, Lovely Sarah sank into the Rabbi's arms. Slowly, he carried her down to the river bank, to Silent William who, although a deaf-mute, was a handsome lad; he supported his old foster mother, a neighbor of the Rabbi's, as a fisherman, and kept his boat at this point. It seemed, however, as if he sensed the Rabbi's intention or had, in fact, been waiting for him; for playing about his silent lips was the sweetest compassion, and his great blue eyes rested meaningly on Lovely Sarah as he carefully lifted her into the boat.

The glance of the dumb youth stirred Lovely Sarah from her daze. She suddenly realized that all her husband had told her was no mere dream; and streams of bitter tears poured down over her cheeks which now were as white as her garment. She sat in the center of the boat, a weeping marble image, while beside her sat her husband and Silent William, both rowing earnestly.

Now, whether this is due to the oars' monotonous beat, or to the boat's rocking, or to the fragrance of those mountainous banks where joy grows, it always happens that somehow even the saddest will feel strangely calmed, when on a night in spring he is lightly borne in a light boat, on the dear, clear river Rhine. Truly, old, kindhearted Father Rhine cannot bear to see his children weep. Hushing their tears he rocks them in his faithful arms, tells them his loveliest fairy tales and promises them his most golden treasures —perhaps even the hoard of the Nibelungs, sunk ages ago. Lovely Sarah's tears, too, flowed ever more gently; her greatest woes were playfully carried away by the whispering waves. The night grew less darkly awesome, and the native hills greeted her as in the tenderest farewell. Greeting kindlier than all was the Kädrich, her favorite mountain— and in the strange moonlight it seemed as if up there a damsel stood with anxiously outstretched arms, as if quick dwarfs were swarming out of their rock fissures, and a horseman racing up the mountainside at full gallop. Lovely Sarah felt like a little girl again, sitting once more in the lap of her aunt from Lorch and being told the pretty story of the bold knight who freed the poor damsel the dwarfs had kidnapped, and further true stories: of the queer Whispervale beyond, where the birds talk quite sensibly, and of Gingerbread Land, where the good, obedient children go, and of enchanted princesses, singing trees, crystal castles, golden bridges, laughing water sprites. . . . But in between all these pretty tales that were coming to life, ringing and gleaming, Lovely Sarah heard her father's voice angrily scolding poor Aunt for putting so much nonsense into the child's head! Soon it was as if she were being placed on the little stool before her father's velvet-covered chair, and he were smoothing her long hair with gentle fingers, smiling cheerfully, and rocking himself comfortably in his roomy Sabbath dressing gown of blue silk. . . . It must be a Sabbath, for the flowered spread was on the table, all the silver in the room had been polished until it shone like mirror glass, and the white-bearded sexton sat beside her father, chewing raisins and talking in Hebrew. Little Abraham also came in, with a perfectly huge book, and modestly asked his uncle for permission to interpret a chapter from the Holy Scripture, so that the Uncle might convince himself that he had learned a great deal in the past week and thus deserved a great deal of praise and cakes. . . . Then the little fellow put the book on the broad arm of the chair and explained the story of Jacob and Rachel—how Jacob raised his voice and wept aloud when he first saw his little cousin Rachel, how he talked with her so fondly by the well, how he had to serve seven years for her, and how quickly they passed, and how he married Rachel and loved her forever and ever. . . . All at once, Lovely Sarah remembered too that her father then exclaimed in a merry voice, "Won't you marry your cousin Sarah like that?" To which little Abraham gravely replied, "I will, and she shall wait seven years." Dimly, these pictures moved through the woman's soul; she saw how she and her little cousin—now grown so big, and her husband—played childishly together in the tabernacle, where they delighted in the gay wallpapers, flowers, mirrors, and gilded apples; how little Abraham would pet her ever more tenderly until he gradually grew bigger and surlier, and finally quite big and quite surly. . . . And at last she is sitting at home in her room, alone, on a Saturday evening; the moon shines brightly through the window, and the door flies open and her cousin Abraham, in travel clothes and pale as death, storms in and grasps her hand and puts a golden ring on her finger and says solemnly: "I hereby take thee for my wife, according to the law of Moses and Israel!" "But now," he adds, trembling, "now I must go away to Spain. Farewell—seven years you shall wait for me!" And he rushes off, and Lovely Sarah, crying, tells all that to her father. . . . He roars and rages: "Cut off your hair, for you are a married woman!"—and wants to ride after Abraham to force him to write a letter of divorcement. But Abraham is over the hills and far away; the father comes home silently; and when Lovely Sarah helps him pull his boots off and soothingly remarks that Abraham would return after seven years, he curses, "Seven years you shall go begging!" and dies soon after.

So the old stories swept through Lovely Sarah's mind like a hurried shadow play, with the images strangely intermingling; and between them appeared half-strange, half-familiar bearded faces, and great flowers with marvelously broad leaves. Then, too, the Rhine seemed to murmur the melodies of the Haggadah, and its pictures rose out of the water, large as life but distorted—crazy pictures: the forefather Abraham anxiously smashes the idols which always hurriedly put themselves together again; the Mizri defends himself fiercely against an enraged Moses; Mount Sinai flashes and flames; King Pharaoh swims in the Red Sea with his jagged golden crown clutched in his teeth; frogs with human faces swim after him, and the waves foam and roar, and a dark giant's hand emerges from them, threateningly. . . .

That, however, was the Bishop Hatto's Mouse Tower, and the boat was just shooting through the eddy of Bingen. It shook Lovely Sarah somewhat out of her reveries, and she looked at the hills along the shore, with the lights in the castles flickering atop them and moonlit night mists drawing past below. But suddenly she thought she saw there her friends and relatives rushing past in terror, with dead faces and white, flowing shrouds, along the Rhine. . . . Everything turned black before her eyes; a stream of ice poured into her soul, and as though sleeping she could just hear the Rabbi saying the night prayer over her, slowly and anxiously as it is said over people sick unto death, and dreamily she stammered the words: "Ten thousand to the right—ten thousand to the left—to guard the King from the dread of the night. . . ."

But, suddenly, all the invading gloom and terror vanished. The dark curtain was torn away from Heaven, and in view above came the Holy City, Jerusalem, with its towers and gates; the Temple gleamed in golden splendor; in its forecourt Lovely Sarah saw her father in his yellow Sabbath dressing gown, smiling cheerfully; from the round windows of the Temple, all her friends and relatives merrily greeted her; in the Holy of Holies knelt pious King David with purple mantle and glittering crown, and his song and harp rang sweetly. And blissfully smiling, Lovely Sarah fell asleep.

Chapter 2

When she opened her eyes, Lovely Sarah was all but blinded by the rays of the sun. The high towers of a great city rose before her, and Silent William stood erect in the boat, guiding it with his boat hook through the merry whirl of ships gaily decked with bunting, the crews of some looking idly down as they passed, while on others all hands were busy unloading boxes, bales, and barrels into lighters which took them ashore, all amidst a deafening noise from the constant halloos of the boatmen, the shouts of the merchants from the river bank, and the railing of the tollmen skipping from deck to deck in their red coats, with thin white maces and white faces.

"Yes, Lovely Sarah," the Rabbi told his wife, cheerfully smiling, "this is the world-famous Free Imperial and Commercial City of Frankfort on the Main, and it is this very river Main which we are sailing. Over there, those houses beckoning amidst green hills are Sachsenhausen, where Lame Gumpertz goes to get the fine myrrh for us at the time of the Feast of Tabernacles. You also see here the strong Main bridge, with its thirteen arches that plenty of folk, carriages, and horses may safely cross, and in the middle stands the little house of which Auntie Dovey told us, where a baptized Jew lives, and pays sixpence to any man who brings him a dead rat, on behalf of the Jewish community which is supposed to deliver five thousand rats' tails annually to the town council."

Upon hearing of this war which the Jews of Frankfort had to wage against the rats Lovely Sarah could not help laughing; the bright sunlight and the new, gay world rising before her had rid her soul of all the past night's dread and horror and, once lifted out of the boat by her husband and Silent William, a happy sense of safety seemed to pervade her. But Silent William with his beautiful, deep blue eyes looked long at her face, half mournfully, half gaily; then, after another meaningful glance at the Rabbi, he jumped back into his boat and soon was gone with it.

"Silent William does bear a great likeness to my late brother," remarked Lovely Sarah.

"The angels all look alike," the Rabbi lightly replied. He took his wife by the hand and led her through the crowds milling on the shore where now—it being the time of the Easter Fair—a mass of wooden trading booths had been put up. Entering the city by the dark Main Gate, they found the traffic no less noisy. Shops rose side by side in a narrow street, and the houses were, as everywhere in Frankfort, specially equipped for trade: the ground floors all without windows, only with open arches allowing the passers-by to look far inside and plainly to observe the merchandise exhibited. How Lovely Sarah marveled at the wealth of precious goods, at a splendor never yet seen! There were Venetians offering for sale all of the luxury of Italy and the East, and Lovely Sarah seemed as though spellbound at the sight of the piled-up finery and jewels, the colorful caps and bodices, the golden bracelets and necklaces, of all the frippery which women like to admire and in which they like even better to deck themselves out. The richly embroidered velvets and silks seemed to want to speak to Lovely Sarah and to flash all manner of odd things back into her memory, and it really seemed to her as if she were a little girl again and Auntie Dovey had kept her promise and taken her to the Frankfort Fair, and that now she were standing in front of the pretty clothes she had been told so much about. With secret joy she was already pondering what to bring back to Bacherach—which of her two young cousins, Blossom or Birdie, would most like the blue satin sash and whether the green little pants would fit little Gottschalk—when all of a sudden she said to herself, "Oh, God! they have all grown up in the meantime and were killed yesterday!" She wildly started, as the horrible nocturnal images appeared again before her; but the gold-embroidered garments, blinking after her as with a thousand rogue's eyes, coaxed all the gloom out of her mind. And as she looked up at her husband's face it was unclouded, gravely mild as usual. "Close your eyes, Lovely Sarah," said the Rabbi and led his wife on through the milling throng.

What a merry bustle! Mostly there were traders bargaining loudly or talking to themselves as they calculated on their fingers, or having their purchases borne to the inn by several heavily laden porters who ran after them at a dog trot. Other faces indicated that curiosity alone had brought them. By his red cloak and golden chain one recognized the ample alderman. The black, prosperously billowing doublet revealed the proud and honorable burgher. The iron Pickelhaube, the yellow leather jerkin and the huge, rattling spurs heralded the heavy cavalryman. Hiding under the point of the black velvet coif was the brow of a rosy girl's face, and the lads leaping after like hunting dogs on the scent showed themselves to be perfect swells by their dashing, feathered berets, their tinkling peaked buskins and their parti-colored silk raiment, which might be green on the right side and red on the left, or rainbow-striped on one and piebald-checkered on the other, so that the foolish fellows looked as if they were split lengthwise. The human tide swept the Rabbi and his wife to the city's great marketplace, surrounded by tall gables and called "the Römer," after a huge house by that name which had been bought by the municipality and dedicated for use as the city hall. In this building took place the election of Germany's Emperor, and before it knightly tournaments were often held. King Maximilian, an ardent lover of such sports, was present in Frankfort at the time, and it was but a day since a great jousting in his honor had taken place before the Römer. Along the wooden barriers, now being torn down by carpenters, numerous idlers still stood and told each other how yesterday the Duke of Brunswick and the Margrave of Brandenburg had charged one another to the sound of trumpets and drums, how Sir Walter the Knave had so mightily unhorsed the Knight of the Bear that the splinters of his lance flew in the air, and how the lank, blond King Max, ringed by his courtiers, had stood on the balcony and rubbed his hands for joy. The golden carpets still hung on the balustrade and from the ogival windows of the city hall. The other houses on the marketplace also were still festively adorned and decked out in coats-of-arms, especially the Limburg house on whose banner a maiden was painted bearing a hawk on her hand while a monkey held up her mirror. On the balcony of this house many knights and ladies stood in smiling conversation, looking down on the crowd that surged to and fro underneath, crazily grouped and attired. What a host of idlers of all ages and estates had flocked together for curiosity's sake! There was laughing, grousing, pilfering, pinching of buttocks and cheering, and in between rang the shrill trumpet blasts of the red-robed physician who stood on his high scaffolding with his clown and his monkey, quite literally trumpeting his skill, praising his tinctures and miracle ointments, or solemnly regarding the urine glass held up by some old woman, or preparing to pull a poor peasant's wisdom tooth. Two fencing masters, fluttering about in gay ribbons with brandished rapiers, met as if by accident and clashed, feigning anger; after long combat they declared each other invincible, and went to collect a few pennies. Now, with fife and drum, the newly founded archers' guild marched by. Then, preceded by the bailiff with a red flag, came a flock of roving damsels from the Würzburg bawdyhouse, "the Ass," on their way to the Rosental, where the honorable authorities had assigned them quarters for the Fair. "Close your eyes, Lovely Sarah," said the Rabbi. For these fancifully and much too scantily clad wenches, some of them very pretty, were carrying on in the lewdest fashion, brazenly baring white breasts, chaffing the passersby with shameless words and swinging their long walking sticks; and while riding them like hobbyhorses down to St. Catherine's Gate, they stridently intoned the witches' song:

> Where is the goat for the Devil's bride?
> Is there no goat? Then to Old Nick

We're going to ride, we're going to ride,
We're going to ride on the stick!

This singsong, which was still audible at a distance, was
lost in the end in the long-drawn-out cathedral sounds of an
approaching procession. This was a sad train of shorn and
barefooted monks bearing lighted wax candles, or banners
with saints' images, or large silver crucifixes. Walking ahead
of them were red- and white-robed boys with smoking
censers. In the center of the procession, beneath a sumptu-
ous canopy, one saw priests wearing white vestments of
precious lace or colored silk stoles, and one of them held in
his hand a sun-shaped gold vessel, which upon reaching a
saint's shrine at one corner of the marketplace he raised up
high, half shouting and half chanting Latin words. . . . At
the same time a little bell rang, and all the people round-
about fell silent, sank to their knees, and made the sign of
the cross. The Rabbi, however, said to his wife, "Close your
eyes, Lovely Sarah," and hastily drew her away into a narrow side street, through a maze of crooked alleys, and finally across the uninhabited, desolate field that separated
the new Jewish quarter from the rest of the city.

Before that time the Jews had lived between the cathedral and the river bank—that is, from the bridge as far as
the Lumpenbrunnen, and from the Mehlwaage as far as St.
Bartholomew's. But the Catholic clergy obtained a papal
bull forbidding the Jews to live so close to the main church,
and the city assigned them a place on the Wollgraben,
where they built the Jewish quarter of today. This was provided with high walls, and also with iron chains across the
gates, to block any onrushing mob—for here, too, the Jews
lived in fear and oppression, and, more than nowadays, in
the memory of past distress. In the year 1240 the unleashed
populace had wrought a great bloodbath among them,
which was called the first Jew-hunt; and in the year 1349,
when the Flagellants set the town afire in their passage
through and charged the Jews with arson, most of the latter
were killed by the incensed people or died in the flames of
their own homes, and this was called the second Jew-hunt.

Later, the Jews were frequently threatened with similar hunts, and whenever there was internal unrest in Frankfort, notably if the town council was quarreling with the guilds, the Christian rabble would be on the point of storming the Jewish quarter. The latter had two gates, which were closed from the outside on Catholic holidays, and from the inside on Jewish ones, and before each gate was a guardhouse manned by soldiers of the city.

When the Rabbi and his wife came to the gate of the Jewish quarter, they could see through the open windows of the guardhouse the lansquenets sprawling on their cots, and outside the door, in the sunshine, the drummer sat improvising on his big drum. He was a large, heavy figure of a man, the jerkin and trousers of flame-yellow cloth puffed out greatly in the arms and thighs and strewn from top to bottom with tiny red tufts so sewn as to seem as if innumerable human tongues were licking out of the cloth. His chest and back were armored with black cloth cushions from which the drum was suspended; on his head he wore a flat, round black cap; and his face was just as flat and round, of the same orange-yellow and spotted with little red pimples, and twisted in a yawning smile. Thus the fellow sat, drumming the melody of the song which the Flagellants used to chant at the Jew-hunt, and in his rough, beery voice he gargled forth the words:

> Our dear Lady true
> Walked in the morning dew,
> *Kyrie Eleison!*

"Jack, that's a bad tune," a voice cried from behind the locked gate of the Jewish quarter; "a bad song, too, Jack— doesn't suit the drum, doesn't suit it a bit and least of all during the Fair and on Easter morning; a bad song, a dangerous song—Jack, Jackie, little Drum-Jackie, I'm a single individual and if you love me, if you love Stern, the long Stern, long Nosey Stern, then stop it!"

These words were forced out of the unseen speaker

partly in anxious haste, partly in slow sighs, in a tone shifting abruptly from soft drawl to hoarse grating, as it is found among consumptives. The drummer remained unmoved, and drumming on in the melody he continued to sing:

> There came a little child,
> His beard was running wild,
> *Hallelujah!*

"Jack," the above-mentioned speaker's voice cried again, "Jack, I'm a single individual and it's a dangerous song, and I don't like to hear it, and I have my reasons, and if you love me you'll sing something else and tomorrow we'll drink. . . ."

At the word "drink" Jack halted his drumming and singing and said in a virtuous tone, "The devil take the Jews, but you, dear Nosey Stern, you're my friend. I protect you, and if we drink together often enough I'll convert you, too. I'll be your godfather; if you're baptized you will go to Heaven, and if you have genius and study hard under me, you may even get to be a drummer. Yes, Nosey, you may yet go far; I'll drum the whole catechism into you tomorrow, when we drink together—but now open the gate; here stand two strangers and demand admission."

"Open the gate?" screeched Nosey Stern, and his voice all but failed. "That's not so quickly done, my dear Jack; you can't tell, you can never tell, and I'm a single individual. Veitel Rindskopf has the key and he is at the moment standing quietly in the corner mumbling his Eighteen Benedictions; one mustn't be interrupted in that. Jeckel the Fool is here, too, but right now he's passing his water. I'm a single individual."

"The devil take the Jews!" roared Jack the Drummer, and, laughing aloud at his own joke, made for the guardhouse and also lay down on the cot.

Now, while the Rabbi and his wife stood all by themselves before the great locked gate, a rasping, nasal, somewhat mocking drawl was heard behind it: "Sternie, don't dawdle so long, take the keys from little Rindskopf's coat pocket, or take your nose and unlock the gate with that. The people have been standing and waiting a long time."

"The people?" anxiously cried the voice of the man who was called Nosey Stern. "I thought there was only one, and I beg you, fool, dear Jeckel Fool, won't you look out who's there?"

Then a small, well-barred window opened in the gate, and in it there appeared a yellow cap with two horns, and under it the merry, wrinkled jester's face of Jeckel the Fool. In the same instant the window was closed again, with an angry rasp: "Open up, open up, there's no one out there but a man and a woman."

"A man and a woman!" groaned Nosey Stern. "And when the gate is opened, the woman drops her skirt and is another man, and then there are two men and we're only three of us."

"Don't be a rabbit," Jeckel the Fool replied. "Take heart and show some courage."

"Courage!" cried Nosey Stern and laughed, glumly and bitterly. "Rabbit! Rabbit is a bad comparison; the rabbit is an unclean animal. Courage! I wasn't put here on account of my courage but on account of my discretion. If too many come, I'm to yell. But I can't hold them off myself. My arm is weak, I have a fontanel, and I'm a single individual. If I'm shot, I'm dead. Then rich Mendel Reiss will sit down to dinner on the Sabbath and wipe the raisin sauce off his mouth and stroke his belly, and perhaps he'll say, 'That long Nosey Stern was a good little fellow, after all; if it hadn't been for him, they would have forced the gate. He let himself be shot dead for us; he was a good little fellow; it's a pity he's dead. . . .'"

At this point the voice became gradually soft and tearful, but suddenly it reverted to a hasty, almost embittered tone: "Courage! And so that rich Mendel Reiss might wipe the raisin sauce off his mouth and stroke his belly and call me a good little fellow—for that I am to let myself be shot dead? Courage! Take heart! Little Strauss, he took heart and watched the jousting on the Römer yesterday and thought they wouldn't know him because he was wearing a purple coat, of velvet, three guilders a yard, with foxtails, all gold-embroidered, quite splendid—and they dusted his purple coat for him until the color went off and his back turned purple, too, and doesn't look like anything human any more. Courage! Crooked Leser took heart and called our rascally burgomaster a rascal, and they strung him up by his feet between two dogs, and Jack the Drummer was drumming. Courage! Don't be a rabbit! Among many dogs the rabbit's done for. I'm a single individual, and I'm afraid."

"Swear to it!" cried Jeckel.

"I'm really afraid," Nosey Stern repeated with a sigh. "I know, the fear's in my blood and I have it from my late mother. . . ."

"Yes, yes," Jeckel the Fool interrupted him, "and your mother had it from her father, and he in turn had it from his father, and so your ancestors had it one from the other, back to your forefather, who took the field under King Saul against the Philistines and was the first to run away. But look, little Rindskopf is almost through; he has made his fourth bow and is already jumping like a flea at the Holy, Holy, Holy, and now he cautiously reaches into his pocket. . . ."

Indeed, the keys rattled, one creaking wing of the gate opened, and the Rabbi and his wife entered Jew Street, which was completely deserted. The turnkey, however, a little man with a good-natured, sour face, dreamily nodded like one who does not like to be disturbed in his thoughts, and having carefully closed the gate again, shuffled off into a corner behind it without saying a word, incessantly murmuring prayers. Less taciturn was Jeckel the Fool, a thickset, slightly bowlegged fellow with a full, laughing, red face and an inhumanly big ham fist which he extended in welcome from the wide sleeves of his checkered jacket. Showing, or, rather, hiding behind him was a long, lean figure, the scrawny neck white-plumed by a fine cambric ruff, and

the thin, pale face marvelously adorned with an almost incredibly long nose that was moving to and fro in fearful
curiosity.

"God's welcome and a good holiday!" said Jeckel the
Fool. "Don't be surprised that the street is now so empty
and quiet. All our people are in the synagogue now, and
you're just in time to hear the story of the sacrifice of Isaac
read there. I know it; it's an interesting story and if I
hadn't heard it thirty-three times already I'd be glad to hear
it again this year. And it's an important story, for if Abraham had really killed Isaac and not the goat, there would
now be more goats and fewer Jews in the world." And with
madly gay grimaces Jeckel began to chant the following
song from the Haggadah:

"A kiddy, a kiddy, was bought by Daddy who paid two
zuzim—a kiddy, a kiddy!

"There came a kitty and ate the kiddy that was bought by
Daddy who paid two zuzim—a kiddy, a kiddy!

"There came a doggy and bit the kitty that ate the kiddy
that was bought by Daddy who paid two zuzim—a kiddy,
a kiddy!

"There came a little stick and beat the doggy that bit the
kitty that ate the kiddy that was bought by Daddy who paid
two zuzim—a kiddy, a kiddy!

"There came a little fire and burned the little stick that
beat the doggy that bit the kitty that ate the kiddy that was
bought by Daddy who paid two zuzim—a kiddy, a kiddy!

"There came a little water and doused the little fire that
burned the little stick that beat the doggy that bit the kitty
that ate the kiddy that was bought by Daddy who paid two
zuzim—a kiddy, a kiddy!

"There came a little ox and drank the little water that
doused the little fire that burned the little stick that beat
the doggy that bit the kitty that ate the kiddy that was
bought by Daddy who paid two zuzim—a kiddy, a kiddy!

"There came a little butcher and butchered the little ox
that drank the little water that doused the little fire that
burned the little stick that beat the doggy that bit the kitty

that ate the kiddy that was bought by Daddy who paid two zuzim—a kiddy, a kiddy!

"There came the Angel of Death and killed the little butcher that killed the little ox that drank the little water that doused the little fire that burned the little stick that beat the doggy that bit the kitty that ate the kiddy that was bought by Daddy who paid two zuzim—a kiddy, a kiddy!"

"Yes, fair lady," added the singer, "the day will come when the Angel of Death will kill the butcher and all our blood come over Edom, for God is an avenging God. . . ."

But suddenly, forcibly putting off the earnestness which involuntarily had come upon him, Jeckel the Fool plunged back into his buffooneries, and in his rasping jester's voice continued, "Fear not, fair lady—Nosey Stern isn't going to harm you. He is dangerous only for old Schnapper-Elle. She has fallen in love with his nose—but the nose deserves it. It is beautiful as the tower which looks upon Damascus, and lofty as the cedar of Lebanon. Without, it gleams like gold leaf and syrup, and within is sheer music and loveliness. It blossoms in summer and freezes in winter, and both summer and winter it is fondled by Schnapper-Elle's white hands. Yes, Schnapper-Elle is in love with him, madly in love. She looks after him, she feeds him, and as soon as he is fat enough, she will marry him. For her age she is young enough, and whoever comes here to Frankfort in three hundred years' time won't be able to see the sky for the many Nosey Sterns."

"You're Jeckel the Fool," laughed the Rabbi, "I know it by your words. I have heard of you often."

"Yes, yes," the other replied with droll modesty, "yes, yes, that's what fame does. A man is often known far and wide for a greater fool than he knows himself. But I try very hard to be a fool, and jump and shake myself to make the bells ring. Others find it easier. . . . But tell me, Rabbi, why are you traveling on the holiday?"

"My excuse," the Rabbi answered the question, "is written in the Talmud, where it says, 'Danger ousts the Sabbath.' "

"Danger!" long Nosey Stern screamed suddenly, acting as though in mortal terror; "danger! danger! Drummer Jack —drum, drum, danger! danger! Drummer Jack. . . ."

From outside, however, Jack the Drummer bellowed in his thick, beery voice: "Ten thousand thunders! The devil take the Jews. That's the third time you've woke me up today, Nosey Stern. Don't make me mad! When I'm mad I get to be like Satan himself, and then, as sure as I'm a Christian, I'll shoot through the window in the gate with my musket, and then let each man watch out for his nose!"

"Don't shoot! Don't shoot! I'm a single individual," Nosey Stern whimpered in terror, and tightly pressed his face against the nearest wall, a position in which, trembling and softly praying, he remained.

"Say, say, what's happened?" Jeckel the Fool now asked with all that quick curiosity which even then characterized the Frankfort Jews.

But the Rabbi wrested himself loose and walked on with his wife, up Jew Street. "See, Lovely Sarah," he sighed, "how ill-guarded is Israel! False friends watch over its gates from the outside, and its sentinels within are Fear and Folly."

Slowly, the two wandered through the long, empty street, where only now and then a rosy girl's head peered out of a window while the sun festively mirrored itself in the bright panes. For the houses in the Jewish quarter were then still new and neat, also lower than now; it was not until the Jews had greatly multiplied in Frankfort, and yet were not allowed to enlarge their quarter, that they built one storey over the other, crowded together like sardines, and thus were crippled in body and soul. The part of the quarter which had remained standing after the great fire, the so-called Old Lane in whose tall black houses a grinning, damp race haggles, is a horrible memento of the Middle Ages. The older synagogue no longer exists; it was less spacious than the present one which was built later, after the refugees from Nuremberg had been received into the community. It was located farther north. The Rabbi did not need to ask where; he could hear the jumble of extremely loud voices

from far away. In the courtyard of the house of God he
parted from his wife, washed his hands at the fountain, and
entered that lower part of the synagogue where the men
pray, while Lovely Sarah ascended a flight of stairs to reach
the women's section.

This upper section was a kind of gallery with three rows
of wooden, maroon-painted seats, each with a board hanging in back which could conveniently be leveled so as to
support a prayer book. The women here sat gossiping together or stood in reverent prayer; at times they also went
in curiosity to the lattice that ran along the eastern side and
through the thin green bars of which one could look down
upon the lower section of the synagogue. There, at high
prayer desks, the men stood in their black cloaks, the
pointed beards flowing down over white ruffs, and the skull-
capped heads more or less shrouded by a square, white,
sometimes gold-embroidered wool or silk scarf with the
fringes prescribed by the Law. The walls of the synagogue
were plainly white-washed and no kind of ornament was to
be seen, except perhaps the gilded iron railing round the
square dais from which the chapters of the Law are read,
and the Holy Ark, a costly embossed coffer seemingly up-
held by marble pillars with rich capitals whose floral work
and foliation luxuriated delightfully, and covered by a curtain of azure-blue velvet on which a pious legend was
worked in tinsel, pearls, and colorful gems. This was where
the silver memorial lamp hung, and also where an inclosed
platform rose, upon whose balustrade all sorts of sacred
utensils were placed, among them the seven-branched can-
dlestick. And before this, facing the Ark, stood the cantor,
whose song was accompanied as if instrumentally by the
voices of his two assistants, the bass and the soprano. For
the Jews have banished all real instrumental music from
their church, in the belief that hymns of praise to God will
rise more edifyingly from the warm human breast than from
cold organ pipes. Lovely Sarah felt a truly childlike pleasure
when the cantor, an excellent tenor, now raised his voice
and the grave, age-old melodies she knew so well blossomed
forth in young, undreamed-of loveliness, while the bass

growled the deep, dark notes in counterpoint, and the soprano, delicately and sweetly, trilled in the intervals. Lovely Sarah had never heard such singing in the synagogue of Bacherach, where the head of the congregation, David Levi, acted as cantor. When this elderly, tottering man with the crumbled, bleating voice tried to trill like a young girl and in such violent effort feverishly shook his limply drooping arm, he was apt to induce laughter rather than devotion.

A sense of pious comfort mixed with feminine curiosity drew Lovely Sarah to the grille where she could look down into the lower section, the so-called *Männerschule*. She had never seen so large a number of coreligionists as she perceived down there, and a still cozier feeling entered her heart in the midst of so many people so nearly related to her by common descent, bent of mind, and suffering. But the woman's soul was still more deeply moved when three old men reverently stepped before the Holy Ark, drew the glittering curtain aside, unlocked the coffer, and carefully took out the book that God wrote with His own hand, and for whose preservation the Jews have suffered so much, so much misery and hatred, infamy and death—a thousand years of martyrdom. This book, a great roll of parchment, was wrapped like a princely child in a gaily embroidered cloak of red velvet; above, on the two wooden rollers, were two little silver vessels in which all sorts of pomegranates and tiny bells daintily moved and tinkled; and in front, shields of gold incrusted with bright jewels hung on little silver chains. The cantor took the book, and as if it were a real child, a child for whose sake one has suffered much and who is therefore only the more beloved, he rocked it in his arms, pranced about with it, pressed it to his heart—and, shuddering under this touch, he raised his voice to so jubilantly devout a song of thanksgiving that to Lovely Sarah the pillars of the Holy Ark seemed to begin to bloom, and the wondrous flowers and leaves of the capitals to grow higher and higher, and all the sounds of the soprano to turn into nightingales, and the dome of the synagogue to burst under the powerful sounds of the bass, and the joy of God to pour down out of the blue sky. That was a beautiful psalm. The congregation repeated the final verse in chorus, and walking slowly toward the raised platform in the center of the synagogue was the cantor with the holy book, while men and boys hastily pressed forward to kiss its velvet covering, or even just to touch it. On the platform the little velvet cloak was removed from the holy book, as were the wrappings inscribed with colored letters, and from the opened parchment roll, in that singing tone which on the Feast of the Passover is still more peculiarly modulated, the cantor read the edifying story of Abraham's temptation.

Lovely Sarah had modestly withdrawn from the grille, and an ample, jewel-bedecked woman of middle age and rather affectedly benevolent demeanor had with a silent nod permitted her to look into her prayer book. The woman seemed to be no great scriptural scholar; for, as she murmured the prayers to herself in the manner of the women, who must not sing aloud, Lovely Sarah noticed that she took excessive liberties with the pronunciation of many words and dropped many a good line altogether. After a while, though, the good woman's limpid eyes rose languidly, an insipid smile passed over her face that was red and white as porcelain, and, in a voice that sought to melt as aristocratically as possible, she said to Lovely Sarah, "He sings very well. But in Holland I've still heard much better singing. You are a stranger and don't know perhaps that he is the cantor from Worms, and that they want to keep him here if he will be content with four hundred guilders a year. He's a dear man, and his hands are like alabaster. I think a great deal of a beautiful hand. A beautiful hand adorns the whole person." With that, the good woman complacently laid her hand, which really was still beautiful, on the back of the prayer desk, and, indicating by a graceful bow of her head that she did not like to be interrupted while talking, she added, "The little singer is just a child and looks quite emaciated. The basso is far too ugly, and our Stern once said very wittily, 'The basso is a bigger fool than one has to demand of a basso.' All three of them eat at my restaurant—but you don't know, perhaps, that I'm Elle Schnapper."

Lovely Sarah thanked her for this information, and Schnapper-Elle in turn related to her in detail how she had once been in Amsterdam and there had been exposed to many base designs on account of her beauty, how three days before Pentecost she had come to Frankfort and married Schnapper, how he had died at last, and on his deathbed said the most touching things, and how hard it was for a restaurant-keeper to keep her hands pretty. Now and then she would cast scornful side glances, probably at some irreverent young women who scrutinized her dress. It was unusual enough: a vast, billowing, white satin skirt with all the animals of Noah's Ark embroidered on it in gaudy colors; a waist of gold cloth like a cuirass; sleeves of red velvet, slit yellow; on the head a tremendously tall cap; around the neck an almighty ruff of stiff white linen, as well as a silver chain from which all sorts of memorial coins, cameos, and curios—among others, a large picture of the city of Amsterdam—hung down over her bosom. But the dress of the other women was just as odd and probably compounded of the fashions of different times, and there was many a little lady strewn with gold and diamonds who rather resembled a walking jeweler's shop. To be sure, the law at that time prescribed a certain garb for the Frankfort Jews: to distinguish them from the Christians, the men were supposed to wear yellow patches on their cloaks, and the women high, blue-striped veils on their headgear. In the Jewish quarter, however, not much attention was paid to this municipal ordinance; and on holidays especially, and above all in the synagogue, the women sought to outdo one another in splendor of raiment, partly so as to be envied, and partly to show the wealth and credit-standing of their spouses.

In the synagogue, while the chapters of the Law are read from the Books of Moses, there usually occurs a slight lull in devotion. The worshippers make themselves comfortable and sit down, whisper with their neighbors about secular affairs, or go out into the courtyard to catch a breath of

fresh air. Little boys meanwhile make bold to visit their
mothers in the women's section, and there, by then, devotion may well have receded even further: there will be chattering, scandal-mongering, laughing, and as everywhere else
the younger women will jest about the old ones, who will in
turn complain of frivolous youth and the degeneration of
the times. And just as there was a chief singer on the ground
floor of the Frankfort synagogue, the upper section had its
chief gossip. This was Puppy Reiss, a flat-chested, greenish
female who sniffed every bit of trouble and always had a
scandal on the tip of her tongue. The usual target of her
barbs was poor Schnapper-Elle, and she could be very
funny aping the other's forced gentility as well as the lan-
guishing decorum with which she would accept the mocking compliments of youth.

"Do you know," cried Puppy Reiss, "what Schnapper-
Elle said yesterday? 'If I weren't beautiful and clever and
beloved, I wouldn't want to be alive.' "

There was loud tittering and Schnapper-Elle, standing
nearby and noticing that it was at her expense, contemptuously lifted her nose and sailed off like a proud galleon, to a
more distant place. Birdie Ochs, a rotund, somewhat clumsy
woman, pityingly remarked that if Schnapper-Elle was vain
and obtuse, she also was kind of heart and doing a lot of
good for people who needed it.

"Especially for Nosey Stern," hissed Puppy Reiss. And
all who knew about the tender liaison laughed all the louder.

"Do you know," the venomous Puppy added, "that Nosey
even sleeps at Schnapper-Elle's house now . . . ? But look,
down there—Susie Flörsheim is wearing the necklace that
Daniel Fläsch gave to her husband in pawn. Fläsch's wife is
furious. . . . Now she's talking to Susie. . . . How amiably
they shake hands, and yet hate each other like Midian and
Moab! Those sweet smiles! Just see that you don't eat one
another for love! I want to hear that conversation."

And like a stalking beast of prey Puppy Reiss sneaked
up and heard the two women exchange feeling lamentations
about the hard work they had done in the past week, cleaning up at home and scouring all the kitchenware—which has

to be done before the Feast of the Passover—lest some tiny crumb of leavened bread still cling to it. They also talked of the laborious baking of the unleavened bread. Mrs. Fläsch in particular could complain of her trouble at the community bakery, for by the order of lots she had not been able to start baking until late afternoon on the very eve of the holiday, and then old Hannah had kneaded the dough all wrong, and the maids had rolled it much too thin, half the breads had burned in the oven, and finally it had rained so hard that water constantly dripped through the boarded roof of the bakery, and thus wet and weary they had been obliged to work far into the night.

"And that, my dear Mrs. Flörsheim," Mrs. Fläsch added, with a considerate kindliness which was anything but genuine, "that was a little bit your fault, too, because you didn't send your people over to help me with the baking."

"Oh, I'm sorry," the other replied. "My people were too busy; the merchandise for the Fair has to be packed, we have so much to do now, my husband. . . ."

"I know," Mrs. Fläsch broke in quickly, bitingly, "I know you have much to do—many pledges and good business and necklaces. . . ."

A poisoned word was about to leave her lips and Mrs. Flörsheim had turned lobster-red already, when suddenly Puppy Reiss screeched, "For God's sake, the strange woman lies dying—water! water!"

Pale as death, Lovely Sarah lay in a faint, and crowding about her was a swarm of bustling, wailing women. One of them held her head, another her arm; a few old crones sprinkled her with water from the little glasses that hung behind their prayer desks so that they might wash their hands in case they should accidentally touch their own bodies; others got an old lemon stuffed with spices—left over from the last fast day, when it had served for nerve-strengthening sniffs—and held it under the unconscious woman's nose. Finally, with a deep sigh of exhaustion, Lovely Sarah opened her eyes. Her silent glances gave thanks for the kindly care. But ringing up from below now was the solemn sound of the Eighteen Benedictions, which no one is allowed to miss, and the busy women scurried back to their seats to offer this prayer as prescribed—standing, and with their faces turned toward the East, in the direction of Jerusalem. Birdie Ochs, Schnapper-Elle, and Puppy Reiss stayed the longest with Lovely Sarah, the first two eagerly offering aid, and the last inquiring once more why she had so suddenly fainted.

Lovely Sarah's faint had a very special cause. It is the custom in the synagogue for anyone who has escaped from great danger to stand up after the reading of the chapters of the Law and publicly to thank Divine Providence for his salvation. And as Rabbi Abraham rose in the synagogue below for such thanksgiving and Lovely Sarah recognized her husband's voice, she noted how its tone gradually changed to the dark murmurs of the prayer for the dead; she heard the names of her relatives and friends, accompanied by that word of blessing which is reserved for the departed; and the last hope left Lovely Sarah's soul, and her soul was torn by the certainty that her friends and relatives had really been killed—that her little niece was dead, that her two little cousins, Blossom and Birdie, were dead, that little Gottschalk also was dead—all murdered and dead! The agony of this realization might have killed her, too, if a merciful faint had not enveloped her senses.

Chapter 3

As Lovely Sarah descended after the end of the services, the Rabbi stood in the courtyard of the synagogue, awaiting his wife. With a cheery nod he ushered her out into the street, where the former quiet had completely vanished and a noisy, milling throng was seen instead. Bearded black-coats recalling an ant heap; women fluttering resplendently like rose chafers; young girls who were not allowed to enter the synagogue and now came bounding out of houses to meet their parents, bowing curly heads to receive their blessing— all were cheerful and gay, and strolled up and down the street in blissful anticipation of a good dinner, whose delicious aroma already made mouths water as it rose from the black, chalk-marked pots which laughing maids had just fetched out of the big community oven.

Especially notable in this jumble was the figure of a Spanish knight whose youthful features showed that intriguing pallor which women usually blame on an unlucky love affair, and men on a lucky one. His walk, though insouciantly sauntering, was of a somewhat studied elegance; the feathers on his beret moved not so much in the breeze as from the aristocratic sway of his head; more than just the necessary clatter issued from his golden spurs and sword-chain. He seemed to be carrying his sword on his arm, and its jeweled hilt sparkled out of the white cavalier's cloak that enveloped his slender limbs with apparent nonchalance and yet betrayed the most careful arrangement of the folds. Now and then, partly with curiosity and partly with the air of the connoisseur, he would approach the passing members of the fair sex, calmly look straight into their eyes, prolong the inspection whenever a face seemed worth while, throw a few quick words of flattery to many a pretty child, and be on his carefree way without waiting for the effect. He had circled Lovely Sarah several times, and every time had been repulsed by her commanding gaze or by the enigmatically smiling mien of her husband; but finally, proudly throwing diffidence to the winds, he boldly blocked the couple's path, and with foppish assurance and honeyed gallantry delivered the following address:

"Señora, I swear! Hear me, Señora: I swear by the roses of the two Castiles, by the hyacinths of Aragon and the pomegranate blossoms of Andalusia! By the sun which illuminates all Spain, with all its flowers, onions, pea soups, forests, mountains, mules, goats, and Old Christians! By the canopy of heaven, on which this sun is merely a golden tassel! And by the God who sits upon the canopy of heaven and day and night ponders the creation of new lovely feminine forms—I swear, Señora, you are the most beautiful woman I've seen in German lands, and should it please you to accept my services, I beg of you the favor, grace, and permission to call myself your knight, and in mock and earnest wear your colors."

A blushing pain passed over Lovely Sarah's face. With one of those glances that are most cutting from the gentlest eye, in a tone most withering if struck by a soft, trembling voice, the deeply hurt woman answered:

"My noble lord—if you wish to be my knight you must fight whole nations, and in this fight there is little thanks to be won, and less honor. If you wish to wear my colors you must sew yellow patches on your cloak or don a blue-striped scarf—for these are my colors, the colors of my house, the house which is called Israel and is most wretched, and which the sons of fortune mock in the streets."

The Spaniard's cheeks turned purple, and infinite embarrassment spread over all his features. "Señora," he said, almost stuttering, "you misunderstood me. . . . An innocent jest, but, by God! no mockery, no mockery of Israel. . . . I myself come from the House of Israel; my grandfather was a Jew, perhaps my father even. . . ."

"And most assuredly, Señor, your uncle is a Jew," suddenly broke in the Rabbi who had calmly watched the scene, and with a merry, bantering glance he added, "and I will personally vouch for it that Don Isaac Abarbanel, the great rabbi's nephew, has sprung from the best blood in Israel, if not in fact from the royal race of David."

Now the sword-chain clattered under the Spaniard's cloak and his cheeks blanched again, assuming an ashen pallor; his upper lip twitched as if scorn were wrestling with pain; the deadliest anger grinned out of his eyes, and in an utterly changed, ice-cold, sharp-edged voice he said, "Señor Rabbi! You know me. Well, then you know who I am. And if the fox knows that I am of the lion's brood, he will take care not to endanger his fox's beard and not to stir my wrath. How should the fox judge the lion? Only he who feels like the lion can see his failings."

"Oh, I see quite well," replied the Rabbi and a pensive gravity darkened his brow, "I see quite well how pride makes the proud lion doff his princely skin and wrap himself in the bright scaly armor of the crocodile, because it is fashionable to be a voracious, cunning, grinning crocodile. What are the lesser animals to do when the lion denies himself? But beware, Don Isaac: you were not made for the element of the crocodile. Water—you well know what I mean—water is your misfortune and you will sink. Your kingdom is not of water; the feeblest trout can do better in it than the king of the forest. Do you recall the currents of the Tagus seeking to devour you . . . ?"

All at once Don Isaac burst into loud laughter, hugged the Rabbi, closed his mouth with kisses, and leaped high for joy, with his spurs clattering so as to frighten the passing Jews. Then, in his natural gay and hearty voice, he shouted, "Faith, you're Abraham of Bacherach! And it was a good joke and also an act of friendship when you jumped into the water from Toledo's Alcantara Bridge and grabbed your friend, a better drinker than swimmer, by the scruff of the neck and pulled him up on dry land. I was on the threshold of some very thorough research on whether gold nuggets might really be found on the bottom of the Tagus, and whether the Romans were right to call it the Golden River. I tell you, I still catch cold from the mere memory of that water party."

With these words the Spaniard gestured as if to shake off drops of water clinging to him. But to the Rabbi's face good cheer had returned, and he repeatedly pressed the hand of his friend, each time saying, "I'm glad!"

"And so am I," said the other. "We haven't seen each other for seven years; at our farewell I was still a young sprig, and you, you were so sedate and serious already. . . . But what became of the fair donna who drew so many sighs from you at the time, well-rhymed sighs that you accompanied on the lute?"

"Hush, hush, the donna can hear us. She is my wife, and today you've furnished her with a sample of your own taste and poetic talent."

It was not without some aftertaste of his earlier embarrassment that the Spaniard greeted the beautiful woman who now, with charming kindness, regretted having grieved her husband's friend by her expressions of displeasure.

"Oh, Señora," Don Isaac replied, "the man who reached with a clumsy hand for a rose must not complain if the thorns scratch. When the evening star gold-sparklingly mirrors itself in the blue tide. . . ."

"For God's sake," the Rabbi broke in, "I beg you to stop it. If we are to wait till the evening star gold-sparklingly mirrors itself in the blue tide, my wife will starve. She has not eaten since yesterday, and in the meantime has suffered much distress and hardship."

"Well, then I'll take you to the best restaurant in Israel," Don Isaac exclaimed, "to the house of my friend Schnapper-Elle, which is near here. I can smell the bewitching fragrance—the restaurant's, of course. Oh, Abraham, if you knew how this fragrance attracts me! It is what has so often lured me to the tents of Jacob, ever since I began my sojourn in this town. Otherwise I have no special liking for the company of God's people, and verily, it is not to pray but to eat that I visit Jew Street. . . ."

"You've never loved us, Don Isaac."

"Yes," continued the Spaniard, "I love your cooking much better than your faith. *It* lacks the proper sauce. And your own selves I never could quite stomach. Even in your best days, in the reign of my ancestor David, who was king over Judah and Israel, I doubt that I could have lasted it among you. Early one morning I should certainly have escaped from the fortress of Zion and emigrated to Phoenicia, or to Babylon, where the joy of life was foaming in the temple of the gods. . . ."

"You're blaspheming, Isaac," darkly muttered the Rabbi. "You are far worse than a Christian. You are a heathen, an idolator."

"Yes, I'm a heathen. And as obnoxious to me as the arid, joyless Hebrews are the gloomy, self-tormenting Nazarenes. May our dear Lady of Sidon, holy Astarte, forgive me for kneeling and praying before the sorrowed Mother of the Crucified. My knee and tongue alone pay homage to death, my heart has remained true to life.

"Don't look so glum, though," went on the Spaniard with his speech, as he saw how little it appeared to edify the Rabbi, "don't look at me with loathing. My nose has kept the faith. When chance brought me into this street one day about noon and I smelled the well-known odors from the Jews' kitchens—than the same longing seized me which our forefathers felt in thinking back to the fleshpots of Egypt; tasty childhood memories awoke in me; before my mind's eye there reappeared the carp in brown raisin sauce which my aunt knew how to prepare so edifyingly each Friday evening; I saw the steamed mutton with garlic and horse-radish again, fit to revive the dead, and the soup with the rapturously swimming dumplings—and my soul melted like the song of a nightingale in love, and ever since that day I have been eating at the restaurant of my friend Donna Schnapper-Elle."

This establishment had meanwhile been reached. Schnapper-Elle herself stood in the doorway of her house, amiably greeting the hungry strangers who crowded in from the Fair. Behind her, peering over her shoulder, long Nosey Stern stood anxiously yet curiously scrutinizing the arrivals. With exaggerated dignity Don Isaac approached our hostess, who answered his waggishly deep bows with endless curt-sies; then he removed his right glove, wrapped his hand in a corner of his cloak, and thus took the hand of Schnapper-Elle which he drew slowly across his mustache and said:

"Señora! Your eyes vie with the fires of the sun; but while an egg grows the harder, the more you boil it, my heart keeps softening the longer it is boiled by the flaming rays of your eyes. Out of the yolk of my heart flutters Amor, the winged god, and seeks a cozy nest in your bosom —this bosom, Señora, with what am I to compare it? In all creation there is no flower, no fruit, resembling it. This plant is unique of its kind. Though the storm strips the tenderest rose, your bosom is a winter rose defying every gale. Though age merely yellows and shrinks the sour lemon, your bosom rivals the sweetest pineapple for tenderness and color. Oh, Señora, even though the city of Amsterdam may be as fair as you told me yesterday, and the day before and every day, the ground on which it rests is a thousand times fairer. . . ."

The knight uttered these last words with feigned timidity and languorous squints at the big picture suspended from Schnapper-Elle's neck; Nosey Stern looked searchingly down from above, and the lauded bosom began to heave so that the city of Amsterdam rocked to and fro.

"Oh," Schnapper-Elle sighed, "virtue is worth more than beauty. What good is beauty to me? My youth will pass, and since Schnapper is dead—he had beautiful hands, at least— what help is beauty to me?" Then she sighed once more, and like an echo, almost inaudibly, Nosey Stern sighed behind her.

"What good is beauty to you?" cried Don Isaac. "Oh, Donna Schnapper-Elle, don't sin against the bounty of creative Nature! Don't abuse her loveliest gifts! She would take fearful vengeance. These enrapturing eyes would become fatuously glazed; these winsome lips would flatten to the point of tastelessness; this chaste, love-seeking body would turn into an unwieldy tallow keg; the city of Amsterdam would come to rest on a murky morass. . . ."

And so, item by item, he pictured Schnapper-Elle's present appearance until the poor woman came to feel strangely perturbed and tried to escape from the knight's eerie conversation. She was doubly glad when she caught sight of Lovely Sarah at this moment and could make the most urgent inquiries whether the lady had quite recovered from her fainting spell, and she promptly plunged into a lively discourse in which all her spurious gentility and genuine kindness of heart came to the fore. With more circumstance than circumspection, she told the sad story of how she herself had almost fainted with horror when the canal boat brought her to Amsterdam, a total stranger, and the rascal carrying her trunk took her not to a respectable inn but to a brazen bawdyhouse, as she had soon found out by the heavy brandy-drinking and the immoral propositions. And, as said before, she would have actually fainted if she could have dared to close her eyes for one instant in the six weeks she spent in that suspicious house. . . .

"On account of my virtue," she closed, "I couldn't dare it. And it all happened to me on account of my beauty. But virtue will last when beauty has passed."

Luckily—for Don Isaac was just about to launch into a critical analysis of the details of this story—squinty-eyed Aaron Hirschkuh of Homburg on the Lahn came out of the house with a white napkin in his teeth, and angrily complained that the soup was long on the table and the guests were seated and the hostess was missing. . . .

(The conclusion and the succeeding chapters have been lost through no fault of the author's.)

SHOLOM ALEICHEM

Sholom Aleichem (1850-1916), born Sholem Rabinowitz
in Russia, became self-supporting at an early age. At
seventeen he gave Russian lessons and at twenty-one was
appointed government Rabbi, under rather peculiar
Czarist regulations, in a small town. This dignity did not
detain him long. He went into business, at which he was
not very successful. He wrote at first in Hebrew, the language of the learned Jewish community, but soon abandoned it for the "jargon," as Yiddish, the language of
the common people, was called. At the age of fifty he
gave up every last pretense of being a businessman. He
already enjoyed a considerable reputation as a chronicler
of Jewish village life in the Pale. He left Russia after the
disturbances of 1905, appalled by the well-organized and
officially sanctioned pogroms and by the infamous Beilis
trial. During the next years he lectured before Jewish
audiences in the United States and Europe. The outbreak
of the First World War brought him to New York where
he died in 1916. During a career that lasted some thirty-
five years he brought out forty volumes of stories and
novels. Adored, and deservedly adored, throughout the
Yiddish-speaking world, Sholom Aleichem was a man of
great charm, and the wittiest of Jewish writers.

On Account of a Hat

"Did I hear you say absent-minded? Now, in our town, that
is, in Kasrilevke, we've really got someone for you—do you

Translated by Isaac Rosenfeld. From *A Treasury of Yiddish Stories*,
edited by Irving Howe and Eliezer Greenberg. Copyright 1954 by The
Viking Press, Inc., and reprinted by their permission.

hear what I say? His name is Sholem Shachnah, but we call him Sholem Shachnah Rattlebrain, and is he absent-minded, is this a distracted creature, Lord have mercy on us! The stories they tell about him, about this Sholem Shachnah—bushels and baskets of stories—I tell you, whole crates full of stories and anecdotes! It's too bad you're in such a hurry on account of the Passover, because what I could tell you, Mr. Sholom Aleichem—do you hear what I say?—you could go on writing it down forever. But if you can spare a moment I'll tell you a story about what happened to Sholem Shachnah on a Passover eve—a story about a hat, a true story, I should live so, even if it does sound like someone made it up."

These were the words of a Kasrilevke merchant, a dealer in stationery, that is to say, snips of paper. He smoothed out his beard, folded it down over his neck, and went on smoking his thin little cigarettes, one after the other.

I must confess that this true story, which he related to me, does indeed sound like a concocted one, and for a long time I couldn't make up my mind whether or not I should pass it on to you. But I thought it over and decided that if a respectable merchant and dignitary of Kasrilevke, who deals in stationery and is surely no *litterateur*—if he vouches for a story, it must be true. What would he be doing with fiction? Here it is in his own words. I had nothing to do with it.

This Sholem Shachnah I'm telling you about, whom we call Sholem Shachnah Rattlebrain, is a real-estate broker—you hear what I say? He's always with landowners, negotiating transactions. Transactions? Well, at least he hangs around the landowners. So what's the point? I'll tell you. Since he hangs around the landed gentry, naturally some of their manner has rubbed off on him, and he always has a mouth full of farms, homesteads, plots, acreage, soil, threshing machines, renovations, woods, timber, and other such terms having to do with estates.

One day God took pity on Sholem Shachnah, and for the first time in his career as a real-estate broker—are you listening?—he actually worked out a deal. That is to say, the work itself, as you can imagine, was done by others, and when the time came to collect the fee, the big rattler turned out to be not Sholem Shachnah Rattlebrain, but Drobkin, a Jew from Minsk province, a great big fearsome rattler, a real-estate broker from way back—he and his two brothers, also brokers and also big rattlers. So you can take my word for it, there was quite a to-do. A Jew has contrived and connived and has finally, with God's help, managed to cut himself in—so what do they do but come along and cut him out! Where's Justice? Sholem Shachnah wouldn't stand for it—are you listening to me? He set up such a holler and an outcry—"Look what they've done to me!"—that at last they gave in to shut him up, and good riddance it was too.

When he got his few cents Sholem Shachnah sent the greater part of it home to his wife, so she could pay off some debts, shoo the wolf from the door, fix up new outfits for the children, and make ready for the Passover holidays. And as for himself, he also needed a few things, and besides he had to buy presents for his family, as was the custom.

Meanwhile the time flew by, and before he knew it, it was almost Passover. So Sholem Shachnah—now listen to this—ran to the telegraph office and sent home a wire: *Arriving home Passover without fail.* It's easy to say "arriving" and "without fail" at that. But you just try it! Just try riding out our way on the new train and see how fast you'll arrive. Ah, what a pleasure! Did they do us a favor! I tell you, Mr. Sholom Aleichem, for a taste of Paradise such as this you'd gladly forsake your own grandchildren! You see how it is: until you get to Zlodievka there isn't much you can do about it, so you just lean back and ride. But at Zlodievka the fun begins, because that's where you have to change, to get onto the new train, which they did us such a favor by running out to Kasrilevke. But not so fast. First, there's the little matter of several hours' wait, exactly as announced in the schedule—provided, of course, that you don't pull in after the Kasrilevke train has left. And at what time of night may you look forward to this treat? The very middle, thank you, when you're dead tired and disgusted, without a friend in the world except sleep—and there's not one single place in the whole station where you can lay your head, not one. When the wise men of Kasrilevke quote the passage from the Holy Book, *"Tov shem meshemon tov,"* they know what they're doing. I'll translate it for you: We were better off without the train.

To make a long story short, when our Sholem Shachnah arrived in Zlodievka with his carpetbag he was half dead; he had already spent two nights without sleep. But that was nothing at all to what was facing him—he still had to spend the whole night waiting in the station. What shall he do? Naturally he looked around for a place to sit down. Whoever heard of such a thing? Nowhere. Nothing. No place to sit. The walls of the station were covered with soot, the floor was covered with spit. It was dark, it was terrible. He finally discovered one miserable spot on a bench where he had just room enough to squeeze in, and no more than that, because the bench was occupied by an official of some sort in a uniform full of buttons, who was lying there all stretched out and snoring away to beat the band. Who this Buttons was, whether he was coming or going, he hadn't the vaguest idea, Sholem Shachnah, that is. But he could tell that Buttons was no dime-a-dozen official. This was plain by his cap, a military cap with a red band and a visor. He could have been an officer or a police official. Who knows? But surely he had drawn up to the station with a ringing of bells, had staggered in, full to the ears with meat and drink, laid himself out on the bench, as in his father's vineyard, and worked up a glorious snoring.

It's not such a bad life to be a gentile, and an official one at that, with buttons, thinks he, Sholem Shachnah, that is, and he wonders, dare he sit next to this Buttons, or hadn't he better keep his distance? Nowadays you never can tell whom you're sitting next to. If he's no more than a plain inspector, that's still all right. But what if he turns out to be a district inspector? Or a provincial commander? Or even higher than that? And supposing this is even Purishkevitch himself, the famous anti-Semite, may his name perish? Let someone else deal with him and Sholem Shachnah turns cold at the mere thought of falling into such a fellow's hands. But then he says to himself—now listen to this—Buttons, he says, who the hell is Buttons? And who gives a hang for Purishkevitch? Don't I pay my fare the same as Purishkevitch? So why should he have all the comforts of life and I none? If Buttons is entitled to a delicious night's sleep, then doesn't he, Sholem Shachnah that is, at least have a nap coming? After all, he's human too, and besides, he's already gone two nights without a wink. And so he sits down, on a corner of the bench, and leans his head back, not, God forbid, to sleep, but just like that, to snooze. But all of a sudden he remembers—he's supposed to be home for Passover, and tomorrow is Passover eve! What if, God have mercy, he should fall asleep and miss his train? But that's why he's got a Jewish head on his shoulders—are you listening to me or not?—so he figures out the answer to that one too, Sholem Shachnah, that is, and goes looking for the porter, a certain Yeremei, he knows him well, to make a deal with him. Whereas he, Sholem Shachnah, is already on his third sleepless night and is afraid, God forbid, that he may miss his train, therefore let him, Yeremei, that is, in God's name, be sure to wake him, Sholem Shachnah, because tomorrow night is a holiday, Passover. "Easter," he says to him in Russian and lays a coin in Yeremei's mitt. "Easter, Yeremei, do you understand, *goyisher kop?* Our Easter." The peasant pockets the coin, no doubt about that, and promises to wake him at the first sign of the train—he can sleep soundly and put his mind at rest. So Sholem Shachnah sits down in his corner of the bench, gingerly, pressed up against the wall, with his carpetbag curled around him so that no one should steal it. Little by little he sinks back, makes himself comfortable, and half shuts his eyes—no more than forty winks, you understand. But before long he's got one foot propped up on the bench and then the other; he stretches out and drifts off to sleep. Sleep? I'll say sleep, like God commanded us: with his head thrown back and his hat rolling away on the floor, Sholem Shachnah is snoring like an eight-day wonder. After all, a human being, up two nights in a row—what would you have him do?

He had a strange dream. He tells this himself, that is, Sholem Shachnah does. He dreamed that he was riding home for Passover—are you listening to me?—but not on the train, in a wagon, driven by a thievish peasant, Ivan Zlodi we call him. The horses were terribly slow, they barely dragged along. Sholem Shachnah was impatient, and he poked the peasant between the shoulders and cried, "May you only drop dead, Ivan darling! Hurry up, you lout! Passover is coming, our Jewish Easter!" Once he called out to him, twice, three times. The thief paid him no mind. But all of a sudden he whipped his horses to a gallop and they went whirling away, up hill and down, like demons. Sholem Shachnah lost his hat. Another minute of this and he would have lost God knows what. "Whoa, there, Ivan old boy! Where's the fire? Not so fast!" cried Sholem Shachnah. He covered his head with his hands—he was worried, you see, over his lost hat. How can he drive into town bareheaded? But for all the good it did him, he could have been hollering at a post. Ivan the Thief was racing the horses as if forty devils were after him. All of a sudden—tppprrru!—they came to a dead stop, right in the middle of the field—you hear me?—a dead stop. What's the matter? Nothing. "Get up," said Ivan, "time to get up."

Time? What time? Sholem Shachnah is all confused. He wakes up, rubs his eyes, and is all set to step out of the wagon when he realizes he has lost his hat. Is he dreaming or not? And what's he doing here? Sholem Shachnah finally comes to his senses and recognizes the peasant—this isn't Ivan Zlodi at all but Yeremei the porter. So he concludes that he isn't on the high road after all, but in the station at Zlodievka, on the way home for Passover, and that if he means to get there he'd better run to the window for a ticket, but fast. Now what? No hat. The carpetbag is right where he left it, but his hat? He pokes around under the bench, reaching all over, until he comes up with a hat—not his own, to be sure, but the official's, with the red band and the visor. But Sholem Shachnah has no time for details and he rushes off to buy a ticket. The ticket window is jammed, everybody and his cousins are crowding in. Sholem Shach-

nah thinks he won't get to the window in time, perish the
thought, and he starts pushing forward, carpetbag and all.
The people see the red band and the visor and they make
way for him. "Where to, Your Excellency?" asks the ticket
agent. What's this Excellency, all of a sudden? wonders
Sholem Shachnah, and he rather resents it. Some joke, a
gentile poking fun at a Jew. All the same he says, Sholem
Shachnah, that is, "Kasrilevke." "Which class, Your Excellency?" The ticket agent is looking straight at the red band
and the visor. Sholem Shachnah is angrier than ever. I'll give
him an Excellency, so he'll know how to make fun of a poor
Jew! But then he thinks, Oh, well, we Jews are in Diaspora
—do you hear what I say?—let it pass. And he asks for a
ticket third class. "Which class?" The agent blinks at him,
very much surprised. This time Sholem Shachnah gets good
and sore and he really tells him off. "Third!" says he. All
right, thinks the agent, third is third.

In short, Sholem Shachnah buys his ticket, takes up his
carpetbag, runs out onto the platform, plunges into the
crowd of Jews and gentiles, no comparison intended, and
goes looking for the third-class carriage. Again the red band
and the visor work like a charm, everyone makes way for
the official. Sholem Shachnah is wondering, What goes on
here? But he runs along the platform till he meets a conductor carrying a lantern. "Is this third class?" asks Sholem
Shachnah, putting one foot on the stairs and shoving his
bag into the door of the compartment. "Yes, Your Excellency," says the conductor, but he holds him back. "If you
please, sir, it's packed full, as tight as your fist. You couldn't
squeeze a needle into that crowd." And he takes Sholem
Shachnah's carpetbag—you hear what I'm saying?—and
sings out, "Right this way, Your Excellency, I'll find you a
seat." "What the Devil!" cries Sholem Shachnah. "Your
Excellency and Your Excellency!" But he hasn't much time
for the fine points; he's worried about his carpetbag. He's
afraid, you see, that with all these Excellencies he'll be
swindled out of his belongings. So he runs after the conductor with the lantern, who leads him into a second-class
carriage. This is also packed to the rafters, no room even to

yawn in there. "This way please, Your Excellency!" And again the conductor grabs the bag and Sholem Shachnah lights out after him. "Where in blazes is he taking me?" Sholem Shachnah is racking his brains over this Excellency business, but meanwhile he keeps his eye on the main thing— the carpetbag. They enter the first-class carriage, the conductor sets down the bag, salutes, and backs away, bowing. Sholem Shachnah bows right back. And there he is, alone at last.

Left alone in the carriage, Sholem Shachnah looks around to get his bearings—you hear what I say? He has no idea why all these honors have suddenly been heaped on him— first class, salutes, Your Excellency. Can it be on account of the real-estate deal he just closed? That's it! But wait a minute. If his own people, Jews, that is, honored him for this, it would be understandable. But gentiles! The conductor! The ticket agent! What's it to them? Maybe he's dreaming. Sholem Shachnah rubs his forehead, and while passing down the corridor glances into the mirror on the wall. It nearly knocks him over! He sees not himself but the official with the red band. That's who it is! "All my bad dreams on Yeremei's head and on his hands and feet, that lug! Twenty times I tell him to wake me and I even give him a tip, and what does he do, that dumb ox, may he catch cholera in his face, but wake the official instead! And me he leaves asleep on the bench! Tough luck, Sholem Shachnah old boy, but this year you'll spend Passover in Zlodievka, not at home."

Now get a load of this. Sholem Shachnah scoops up his carpetbag and rushes off once more, right back to the station where he is sleeping on the bench. He's going to wake himself up before the locomotive, God forbid, lets out a blast and blasts his Passover to pieces. And so it was. No sooner had Sholem Shachnah leaped out of the carriage with his carpetbag than the locomotive did let go with a blast— do you hear me?—one followed by another, and then, good night!

The paper dealer smiled as he lit a fresh cigarette, thin as a straw. "And would you like to hear the rest of the story?

The rest isn't so nice. On account of being such a rattle-brain, our dizzy Sholem Shachnah had a miserable Passover, spending both Seders among strangers in the house of a Jew in Zlodievka. But this was nothing—listen to what happened afterward. First of all, he has a wife, Sholem Shachnah, that is, and his wife—how shall I describe her to you? *I* have a wife, *you* have a wife, we all have wives, we've had a taste of Paradise, we know what it means to be married. All I can say about Sholem Shachnah's wife is that she's A Number One. And did she give him a royal welcome! Did she lay into him! Mind you, she didn't complain about his spending the holiday away from home, and she said nothing about the red band and the visor. She let that stand for the time being; she'd take it up with him later. The only thing she complained about was—the telegram! And not so much the telegram—you hear what I say?—as the one short phrase, *without fail*. What possessed him to put that into the wire: *Arriving home Passover without fail*. Was he trying to make the telegraph company rich? And besides, how dare a human being say "without fail" in the first place? It did him no good to answer and explain. She buried him alive. Oh, well, that's what wives are for. And not that she was altogether wrong—after all, she had been waiting so anxiously. But this was nothing compared with what he caught from the town, Kasrilevke, that is. Even before he returned the whole town—you hear what I say?—knew all about Yeremei and the official and the red band and the visor and the conductor's Your Excellency—the whole show. He himself, Sholem Shachnah, that is, denied everything and swore up and down that the Kasrilevke smart-alecks had invented the entire story for lack of anything better to do. It was all very simple—the reason he came home late, after the holidays, was that he had made a special trip to inspect a wooded estate. Woods? Estate? Not a chance—no one bought *that!* They pointed him out in the streets and held their sides, laughing. And everybody asked him, 'How does it feel, Reb Sholem Shachnah, to wear a cap with a red band and a visor?' 'And tell us,' said others, 'what's it like to travel first class?' As for the chil-

dren, this was made to order for them—you hear what I
say? Wherever he went they trooped after him, shouting,
'Your Excellency! Your excellent Excellency! Your most
excellent Excellency!'

"You think it's so easy to put one over on Kasrilevke?"

Hodel

You look, Mr. Sholom Aleichem, as though you were surprised that you hadn't seen me for such a long time. You're
thinking that Tevye has aged all at once, his hair has turned
gray.

Ah, well, if you only knew the troubles and heartaches he
has endured of late! How is it written in our Holy Books?
"Man comes from dust, and to dust he returns." Man is
weaker than a fly, and stronger than iron. Whatever plague
there is, whatever trouble, whatever misfortune—it never
misses me. Why does it happen that way? Maybe because
I am a simple soul who believes everything that everyone
says. Tevye forgets that our wise men have told us a thousand times: "Beware of dogs . . ."

But I ask you, what can I do if that's my nature? I am,
as you know, a trusting person, and I never question God's
ways. Whatever He ordains is good. Besides, if you do complain, will it do you any good? That's what I always tell my
wife. "Golde," I say, "you're sinning. We have a *midrash*—"

"What do I care about a *midrash*?" she says. "We have a
daughter to marry off. And after her two more are almost
ready. And after these two, three more—may the evil eye
spare them!"

"Tut," I say. "What's that? Don't you know, Golde, that
our sages have thought of that also? There is a *midrash* for
that too—"

From *The Old Country*, translated by Julius and Frances Butwin.
Copyright 1946 by Crown Publishers, Inc. Used by permission of the
publisher.

But she doesn't let me finish. "Daughters to be married off," she says, "are a stiff *midrash* in themselves."

Try to explain something to a woman!

Where does that leave us? Oh yes, with a houseful of daughters, bless the Lord, each one prettier than the next. It may not be proper for me to praise my own children, but I can't help hearing what the whole world calls them, can I? Beauties, every one of them! And especially Hodel, the one that comes after Tzeitl, who, you remember, fell in love with the tailor. And Hodel—how can I describe her to you? Like Esther in the Bible, "of beautiful form and fair to look upon." And as if that weren't bad enough, she has to have brains too. She can write and she can read—Yiddish and Russian both. And books she swallows like dumplings. You may be wondering how a daughter of Tevye happens to be reading books when her father deals in butter and cheese? That's what I'd like to know myself.

But that's the way it is these days. Look at these lads who haven't got a pair of pants to their name, and still they want to study! Ask them, "What are you studying? Why are you studying?" They can't tell you. It's their nature, just as it's a goat's nature to jump into gardens. Especially since they aren't even allowed in the schools. "Keep off the grass!" read all the signs as far as they're concerned. And yet you ought to see how they go after it! And who are they? Workers' children. Tailors' and cobblers', so help me God! They go away to Yehupetz or to Odessa, sleep in garrets, eat what Pharaoh ate during the plagues—frogs and vermin—and for months on end do not see a piece of meat before their eyes. Six of them can make a banquet on a loaf of bread and a herring. Eat, drink, and be merry! That's the life!

Well, one of that band had to lose himself in our corner of the world. I used to know his father—he was a cigarette-maker and as poor as a man could be. But that is nothing against the young fellow. For if Rabbi Jochanan wasn't too proud to mend boots, what is wrong with having a father who makes cigarettes? There is only one thing I can't understand: why should a pauper like that be so anxious to study? True, to give the devil his due, the boy has a good

head on his shoulders, an excellent head. Pertschik, his name
was, but we called him Feferel—Peppercorn. And he looked
like a peppercorn, little, dark, dried up, and homely, but full
of confidence and with a quick, sharp tongue.

Well, one day I was driving home from Boiberik, where
I had got rid of my load of milk and butter and cheese, and
as usual I sat lost in thought, dreaming of many things, of
this and that, and of the rich people of Yehupetz who had
everything their own way while Tevye, the *shlimazel,* and
his wretched little horse slaved and hungered all their days.
It was summer, the sun was hot, the flies were biting, on all
sides the world stretched endlessly. I felt like spreading out
my arms and flying!

I lift up my eyes, and there on the road ahead of me I see
a young man trudging along with a package under his arm,
sweating and panting. "Rise, O Yokel the son of Flekel, as
we say in the synagogue," I called out to him. "Climb into
my wagon and I'll give you a ride. I have plenty of room.
How is it written? 'If you see the ass of him that hateth thee
lying under its burden, thou shalt forbear to pass it by.'
Then how about a human being?"

At this the *shlimazel* laughs and climbs into the wagon.

"Where might the young gentleman be coming from?" I
ask.

"From Yehupetz."

"And what might a young gentleman like you be doing in
Yehupetz?" I ask.

"A young gentleman like me is getting ready for his ex-
aminations."

"And what might a young gentleman like you be studying?"

"I only wish I knew!"

"Then why does a young gentleman like you bother his
head for nothing?"

"Don't worry, Reb Tevye. A young gentleman like me
knows what he's doing."

"So, if you know who *I* am, tell me who *you* are!"

"Who am I? I'm a man."

"I can see that you're not a horse. I mean, as we Jews say, *whose* are you?"

"Whose should I be but God's?"

"I know that you're God's. It is written, 'All living things are His.' I mean, whom are you descended from? Are you from around here or from Lithuania?"

"I am descended," he says, "from Adam, our father. I *come* from right around here. You know who we are."

"Well then, who is your father? Come, tell me."

"My father," he says, "was called Pertschik."

I spat with disgust. "Did you have to torture me like this all that time? Then you must be Pertschik the cigarette-maker's son!"

"Yes, that's who I am. Pertschik the cigarette-maker's son."

"And you go to the university?"

"Yes, the university."

"Well," I said, "I'm glad to hear it. Man and fish and fowl —you're all trying to better yourselves! But tell me, my lad, what do you live on, for instance?"

"I live on what I eat."

"That's good," I say. "And what do you eat?"

"I eat anything I can get."

"I understand," I say. "You're not particular. If there is something to eat, you eat. If not, you bite your lip and go to bed hungry. But it's all worth while as long as you can attend the university. You're comparing yourself to those rich people of Yehupetz—"

At these words Pertschik bursts out, "Don't you dare compare me to them! They can go to hell as far as I care!"

"You seem to be somewhat prejudiced against the rich," I say. "Did they divide your father's inheritance among themselves?"

"Let me tell you," says he, "it may well be that you and I and all the rest of us have no small share in *their* inheritance."

"Listen to me," I answer. "Let your enemies talk like that. But one thing I can see: you're not a bashful lad. You know what a tongue is for. If you have the time, stop at my house tonight and we'll talk a little more. And if you come early, you can have supper with us too."

Our young friend didn't have to be asked twice. He arrived at the right moment—when the borscht was on the table and the knishes were baking in the oven. "Just in time!" I said. "Sit down. You can say grace or not, just as you please. I'm not God's watchman; I won't be punished for your sins." And as I talk to him I feel myself drawn to the fellow somehow; I don't know why. Maybe it's because I like a person one can talk to, a person who can understand a quotation and follow an argument about philosophy or this or that or something else. That's the kind of person I am.

And from that evening on our young friend began coming to our house almost every day. He had a few private students, and when he was through giving his lessons he'd come to our house to rest up and visit for a while. What the poor fellow got for his lessons you can imagine for yourself, if I tell you that the very richest people used to pay their tutors three rubles a month; and besides their regular duties they were expected to read telegrams for them, write out addresses, and even run errands at times. Why not? As the passage says, "If you eat bread you have to earn it." It was lucky for him that most of the time he ate with us. For this he used to give my daughters lessons too. One good turn deserves another. And in this way he almost became a member of the family. The girls saw to it that he had enough to eat and my wife kept his shirts clean and his socks mended. And it was at this time that we changed his Russian name of Pertschik to Feferel. And it can truthfully be said that we all came to love him as though he were one of us, for by nature he was a likable young man, simple, straightforward, generous. Whatever he had he shared with us.

There was only one thing I didn't like about him, and that was the way he had of suddenly disappearing. Without warning he would get up and go off; we would look around: no Feferel. When he came back I would ask, "Where were you, my fine-feathered friend?" And he wouldn't say a word. I don't know how you are, but as for me, I dislike a person with secrets. I like a person to be willing to tell what he's been up to. But you can say this for him: when he did start talking, you couldn't stop him. He poured out everything. What a tongue he had! "Against the Lord and against His anointed; let us break their bands asunder." And the main thing was to break the bands. He had the wildest notions, the most peculiar ideas. Everything was upside down, topsy-turvy. For instance, according to his way of thinking, a poor man was far more important than a rich one, and if he happened to be a worker too, then he was really the brightest jewel in the diadem! He who toiled with his hands stood first in his estimation.

"That's good," I say, "but will that get you any money?"

At this he becomes very angry and tries to tell me that money is the root of all evil. Money, he says, is the source of all falsehood, and as long as money amounts to something, nothing will ever be done in this world in the spirit of justice. And he gives me thousands of examples and illustrations that make no sense whatever.

"According to your crazy notions," I tell him, "there is no justice in the fact that my cow gives milk and my horse draws a load." I didn't let him get away with anything. That's the kind of man Tevye is. But my Feferel can argue too. And how he can argue! If there is something on his mind he comes right out with it.

One evening we were sitting on my stoop talking things over, discussing philosophic matters, when he suddenly says, "Do you know, Reb Tevye, you have very fine daughters."

"Is that so?" say I. "Thanks for telling me. After all, they have someone to take after."

"The oldest one especially is a very bright girl. She's all there!"

"I know without your telling me," say I. "The apple never falls very far from the tree."

I glowed with pride. What father isn't happy when his children are praised? How should I have known that from such an innocent remark would grow such fiery love?

Well, one summer twilight I was driving through Boi-

berik, going from villa to villa with my goods, when someone stopped me. I looked up and saw that it was Ephraim
the matchmaker. And Ephraim, like all matchmakers, was
concerned with only one thing—arranging marriages. So
when he saw me here in Boiberik he stopped me.

"Excuse me, Reb Tevye," he says, "I'd like to tell you
something."

"Go ahead," I say, stopping my horse, "as long as it's
good news."

"You have," says he, "a daughter."

"I have," I answer, "seven daughters."

"I know," says he. "I have seven too."

"Then together," I tell him, "we have fourteen."

"But joking aside," he says, "here is what I have to tell
you. As you know, I am a matchmaker; and I have a young
man for you to consider, the very best there is, a regular
prince. There's not another like him anywhere."

"Well," I say, "that sounds good enough to me. But what
do you consider a prince? If he's a tailor or a shoemaker
or a teacher, you can keep him. I'll find my equal or I won't
have anything. As the *midrash* says—"

"Ah, Reb Tevye," says he, "you're beginning with your
quotations already! If a person wants to talk to you he has
to study up first. But better listen to the sort of match
Ephraim has to offer you. Just listen and be quiet."

And then he begins to rattle off all his client's virtues.
And it really sounds like something. First of all, he comes
from a very fine family. And that is very important to me,
for I am not just a nobody either. In our family you will
find all sorts of people—spotted, striped, and speckled, as
the Bible says. There are plain, ordinary people, there are
workers, and there are property owners. Secondly, he is a
learned man who can read small print as well as large; he
knows all the commentaries by heart. And that is certainly
not a small thing either, for an ignorant man I hate even
worse than pork itself. To me an unlettered man is worse,
a thousand times worse, than a hoodlum. You can go around
bareheaded, you can even walk on your head if you like,
but if you know what Rashi and the others have said, you

are a man after my own heart. And on top of everything, Ephraim tells me, this man of his is as rich as can be. He has his own carriage drawn by two horses so spirited that you can see a vapor rising from them. And that I don't object to either. Better a rich man than a poor one! God Himself must hate a poor man, for if He did not, would He have made him poor?

"Well," I ask, "what more do you have to say?"

"What more can I say? He wants me to arrange a match with you. He is dying, he's so eager. Not for you, naturally, but for your daughter. He wants a pretty girl."

"He is dying? Then let him go on dying. And who is this treasure of yours? What is he? A bachelor? A widower? Is he divorced? What's wrong with him?"

"He is a bachelor," said Ephraim. "Not so young any more, but he's never been married."

"And what is his name, may I ask?"

But this he wouldn't tell me. "Bring the girl to Boiberik, and then I'll tell you."

"Bring her? That's the way one talks about a horse or a cow that's being brought to market. Not a girl!"

Well, you know what these matchmakers are. They can talk a stone wall into moving. So we agreed that early next week I would bring my daughter to Boiberik. And, driving home, all sorts of wonderful thoughts came to me, and I imagined my Hodel riding in a carriage drawn by spirited horses. The whole world envied me, not so much for the carriage and horses as for the good deeds I accomplished through my wealthy daughter. I helped the needy with money—let this one have twenty-five rubles, that one fifty, another a hundred. How do we say it? "Other people have to live too." That's what I think to myself as I ride home in the evening, and I whip my horse and talk to him in his own language.

"Hurry, my little horse," I say, "move your legs a little faster and you'll get your oats that much sooner. As the Bible says, 'If you don't work, you don't eat.'"

Suddenly I see two people coming out of the woods—a man and a woman. Their heads are close together and they are whispering to each other. Who could they be? I wonder, and I look at them through the dazzling rays of the setting sun. I could swear the man was Feferel. But whom was he walking with so late in the day? I put up my hand and shield my eyes and look closely. Who was the damsel? Could it be Hodel? Yes, that's who it was! Hodel! So? So that's how they'd been studying their grammar and reading their books together? Oh, Tevye, what a fool you are!

I stop the horse and call out, "Good evening! And what's the latest news of the war? How do you happen to be out here this time of the day? What are you looking for, the day before yesterday?"

At this they stop, not knowing what to do or say. They stand there, awkward and blushing, with their eyes lowered. Then they look up at me, I look at them, and they look at each other.

"Well," I say, "you look as if you hadn't seen me in a long time. I am the same Tevye as ever; I haven't changed by a hair."

I speak to them half angrily, half jokingly. Then my daughter, blushing harder than ever, speaks up.

"Father, you can congratulate us."

"Congratulate you?" I say. "What's happened? Did you find a treasure buried in the woods? Or were you just saved from some terrible danger?"

"Congratulate us," says Feferel this time. "We're engaged."

"What do you mean, engaged?"

"Don't you know what engaged means?" says Feferel, looking me straight in the eyes. "It means that I'm going to marry her and she's going to marry me."

I look him back in the eyes and say, "When was the contract signed? And why didn't you invite me to the ceremony? Don't you think I have a slight interest in the matter?" I joke with them and yet my heart is breaking. But Tevye is not a weakling. He wants to hear everything out. "Getting married," I say, "without matchmakers, without an engagement feast?"

"What do we need matchmakers for?" says Feferel. "We arranged it between ourselves."

"So?" I say. "That's one of God's wonders! But why were you so silent about it?"

"What was there to shout about?" says he. "We wouldn't have told you now either, but since we have to part soon, we decided to have the wedding first."

This really hurt. How do they say it? It hurt to the quick. Becoming engaged without my knowledge—that was bad enough, but I could stand it. He loves her, she loves him—that I'm glad to hear. But getting married? That was too much for me.

The young man seemed to realize that I wasn't too well pleased with the news. "You see, Reb Tevye," he offered, "this is the reason: I am about to go away."

"When are you going?"

"Very soon."

"And where are you going?"

"That I can't tell you. It's a secret."

What do you think of that? A secret! A young man named Feferel comes into our lives—small, dark, homely, disguises himself as a bridegroom, wants to marry our daughter and then leave her—and he won't even say where he's going! Isn't that enough to drive you crazy?

"All right," I say. "A secret is a secret. But explain this to me, my friend. You are a man of such—what do you call it?—integrity; you wallow in justice. So tell me, how does it happen that you suddenly marry Tevye's daughter and then leave her? Is that integrity? Is that justice? It's lucky that you didn't decide to rob me or burn my house down!"

"Father," says Hodel, "you don't know how happy we are now that we've told you our secret. It's like a weight off our chests. Come, Father, kiss me."

And they both grab hold of me, she on one side, he on the other, and they begin to kiss and embrace me, and I to kiss them in return. And in their great excitement they begin to kiss each other. It was like going to a play. "Well," I say at last, "maybe you've done enough kissing already? It's time to talk about practical things."

"What, for instance?" they ask.

"For instance," I say, "the dowry, clothes, wedding expenses, this, that, and the other—"

"We don't need a thing," they tell me. "We don't need anything. No this, no that, no other."

"Well then, what do you need?" I ask.

"Only the wedding ceremony," they tell me.

What do you think of that! Well, to make a long story short, nothing I said did any good. They went ahead and had their wedding, if you want to call it a wedding. Naturally it wasn't the sort that I would have liked. A quiet little wedding—no fun at all. And besides, there was a wife I had to do something about. She kept plaguing me: what were they in such a hurry about? Go try to explain their haste to a woman. But don't worry. I invented a story—"great, powerful, and marvelous," as the Bible says, about a rich aunt in Yehupetz, an inheritance, all sorts of foolishness.

And a couple of hours after this wonderful wedding I hitched up my horse and wagon and the three of us got in, that is, my daughter, my son-in-law, and I, and off we went to the station at Boiberik. Sitting in the wagon, I steal a look at the young couple, and I think to myself, What a great and powerful Lord we have and how cleverly He rules the world. What strange and fantastic beings He has created. Here you have a new young couple, just hatched; he is going off, the Good Lord alone knows where, and is leaving her behind—and do you see either one of them shed a tear, even for appearance's sake? But never mind—Tevye is not a curious old woman. He can wait. He can watch and see.

At the station I see a couple of young fellows, shabbily dressed, down at the heels, coming to see my happy bridegroom off. One of them is dressed like a peasant and wears his blouse like a smock over his trousers. The two whisper together mysteriously for several minutes. Look out, Tevye, I say to myself. You have fallen among a band of horse thieves, pickpockets, housebreakers, or counterfeiters.

Coming home from Boiberik, I can't keep still any longer

and tell Hodel what I suspect. She bursts out laughing and tries to assure me that they are very honest young men, honorable men, who were devoting their lives to the welfare of humanity; their own private welfare meant nothing to them. For instance, the one with his blouse over his trousers was a rich man's son. He had left his parents in Yehupetz and wouldn't take a penny from them.

"Oh," said I, "that's just wonderful. An excellent young man! All he needs, now that he has his blouse over his trousers and wears his hair long, is a harmonica, or a dog to follow him, and then he would really be a beautiful sight!" I thought I was getting even with her for the pain she and this new husband of hers had caused me. But did she care? Not at all! She pretended not to understand what I was saying. I talked to her about Feferel and she answered me with "the cause of humanity" and "workers" and other such talk.

"What good is your humanity and your workers," I say, "if it's all a secret? There is a proverb: 'Where there are secrets, there is knavery.' But tell me the truth now. Where did he go, and why?"

"I'll tell you anything," she says, "but not that. Better don't ask. Believe me, you'll find out yourself in good time. You'll hear the news—and maybe very soon—and good news at that."

"Amen," I say. "From your mouth into God's ears! But may our enemies understand as little about it as I do."

"That," says she, "is the whole trouble. You'll never understand."

"Why not?" say I. "Is it so complicated? It seems to me that I can understand even more difficult things."

"These things you can't understand with your brain alone," she says. "You have to feel them, you have to feel them in your heart."

And when she said this to me, you should have seen how her face shone and her eyes burned. Ah, those daughters of mine! They don't do anything halfway. When they become involved in anything it's with their hearts and minds, their bodies and souls.

Well, a week passed, then two weeks—five—six—seven
—and we heard nothing. There was no letter, no news of
any kind. "Feferel is gone for good," I said and glanced
over at Hodel. There wasn't a trace of color in her face. And
at the same time she didn't rest at all; she found something
to do every minute of the day, as though trying to forget
her troubles. And she never once mentioned his name, as if
there never had been a Feferel in the world.

But one day when I came home from work I found Hodel
going about with her eyes swollen from weeping. I made a
few inquiries and found out that someone had been to see
her, a long-haired young man who had taken her aside and
talked to her for some time. Ah! That must have been the
young fellow who had disowned his rich parents and pulled
his blouse down over his trousers.

Without further delay I called Hodel out into the yard and
bluntly asked her, "Tell me, daughter, have you heard from
him?"

"Yes."

"Where is he, your predestined one?"

"He is far away."

"What is he doing there?"

"He is serving time."

"Serving time?"

"Yes."

"Why? What did he do?"

She doesn't answer me. She looks me straight in the eyes
and doesn't say a word.

"Tell me, dear daughter," I say, "according to what I can
understand, he is not serving for a theft. So if he is neither
a thief nor a swindler, why is he serving? For what good
deeds?"

She doesn't answer. So I think to myself, If you don't
want to, you don't have to. He is your headache, not mine.
But my heart aches for her. No matter what you say, I'm
still her father.

Well, it was the evening of *Hashono Rabo*. On a holiday
I'm in the habit of resting, and my horse rests too. As it is
written in the Bible: "Thou shalt rest from thy labors and

so shall thy wife and thine ass." Besides, by that time of the year there is very little for me to do in Boiberik. As soon as the holidays come and the *shofar* sounds, all the summer villas close down and Boiberik becomes a desert. At that season I like to sit at home on my own stoop. To me it is the finest time of the year. Each day is a gift from heaven. The sun no longer bakes like an oven but caresses with a heavenly softness. The woods are still green, the pines give out a pungent smell. In my yard stands the *succeh*—the booth I have built for the holiday, covered with branches, and around me the forest looks like a huge *succeh* designed for God himself. Here, I think, God celebrates His holiday, here and not in town, in the noise and tumult where people run this way and that, panting for breath as they chase after a small crust of bread, and all you hear is money, money, money.

As I said, it is the evening of *Hashono Rabo*. The sky is a deep blue and myriads of stars twinkle and shine and blink. From time to time a star falls through the sky, leaving behind it a long green band of light. This means that someone's luck has fallen. I hope it isn't my star that is falling, and somehow Hodel comes to mind. She has changed in the last few days, has come to life again. Someone, it seems, has brought her a letter from him, from over there. I wish I knew what he had written, but I won't ask. If she won't speak, I won't either. Tevye is not a curious old woman. Tevye can wait.

And as I sit thinking of Hodel, she comes out of the house and sits down near me on the stoop. She looks cautiously around and then whispers, "I have something to tell you, Father. I have to say good-by to you, and I think it's for always."

She spoke so softly that I could barely hear her, and she looked at me in a way that I shall never forget.

"What do you mean, good-by for always?" I say to her and turn my face aside.

"I mean I am going away early tomorrow morning, and possibly we shall never see each other again."

"Where are you going, if I may be so bold as to ask?"

"I am going to him."

"To him? And where is he?"

"He is still serving, but soon they'll be sending him away."

"And you're going there to say good-by to him?" I ask, pretending not to understand.

"No. I am going to follow him," she says. "Over there."

"There? Where is that? What do they call the place?"

"We don't know the exact name of the place, but we know that it's far—terribly, terribly far."

And she speaks, it seems to me, with great joy and pride, as though he had done something for which he deserved a medal. What can I say to her? Most fathers would scold a child for such talk, punish her, even beat her maybe. But Tevye is not a fool. To my way of thinking, anger doesn't get you anywhere. So I tell her a story.

"I see, my daughter, as the Bible says, 'Therefore shalt thou leave thy father and mother'—for a Feferel you are ready to forsake your parents and go off to a strange land, to some desert across the frozen wastes, where Alexander of Macedon, as I once read in a storybook, once found himself stranded among savages . . ."

I speak to her half in fun and half in anger, and all the time my heart weeps. But Tevye is no weakling; I control myself. And Hodel doesn't lose her dignity either; she answers me word for word, speaking quietly and thoughtfully. And Tevye's daughters can talk.

And though my head is lowered and my eyes are shut, still I seem to see her—her face is pale and lifeless like the moon, but her voice trembles. Shall I fall on her neck and plead with her not to go? I know it won't help. Those daughters of mine—when they fall in love with somebody, it is with their heads and hearts, their bodies and souls.

Well, we sat on the doorstep a long time—maybe all night. Most of the time we were silent, and when we did speak it was in snatches, a word here, a word there. I said to her, "I want to ask you only one thing: did you ever hear of a girl marrying a man so that she could follow him to the ends of the earth?" And she answered, "With him I'd go anywhere." I pointed out how foolish that was. And she said, "Father, you will never understand." So I told her a little fable, about a hen that hatched some ducklings. As soon as the ducklings could move they took to the water and swam, and the poor hen stood on shore, clucking and clucking.

"What do you say to that, my daughter?"

"What can I say?" she answered. "I am sorry for the poor hen; but just because she stood there clucking, should the ducklings have stopped swimming?"

There is an answer for you. She's not stupid, that daughter of mine.

But time does not stand still. It was beginning to get light already, and within the house my old woman was muttering. More than once she had called out that it was time to go to bed, but, seeing that it didn't help, she stuck her head out of the window and said to me, with her usual benediction, "Tevye, what's keeping you?"

"Be quiet, Golde," I answered. "Remember what the Psalm says: 'Why are the nations in an uproar, and why do the peoples mutter in vain?' Have you forgotten that it's *Hashono Rabo* tonight? Tonight all our fates are decided and the verdict is sealed. We stay up tonight. Listen to me, Golde, you light the samovar and make some tea while I get the horse and wagon ready. I am taking Hodel to the station in the morning." And once more I make up a story about how she has to go to Yehupetz, and from there farther on, because of the same old inheritance. It is possible, I say, that she may have to stay there through the winter and maybe the summer too, and maybe even another winter; and so we ought to give her something to take along —some linen, a dress, a couple of pillows, some pillow slips, and things like that.

And as I give these orders I tell her not to cry. "It's *Hashono Rabo,* and on *Hashono Rabo* one mustn't weep. It's a law." But naturally they don't pay any attention to me, and when the time comes to say good-by they all start weeping—their mother, the children, and even Hodel herself. And when she came to say good-by to her older sister Tzeitl (Tzeitl and her husband spend their holidays with us), they fell on each other's necks and you could hardly tear them apart.

I was the only one who did not break down. I was firm as steel—though inside I was more like a boiling samovar. All the way to Boiberik we were silent, and when we came near the station I asked her for the last time to tell me what it was that Feferel had really done. If they were sending him away there must have been a reason. At this she became angry and swore by all that was holy that he was innocent. He was a man, she insisted, who cared nothing about himself. Everything he did was for humanity at large, especially for those who toiled with their hands—that is, the workers.

That made no sense to me. "So he worries about the world" I told her. "Why doesn't the world worry a little about him? Nevertheless, give him my regards, that Alexander of Macedon of yours, and tell him I rely on his honor —for he is a man of honor, isn't he?—to treat my daughter well. And write to your old father sometimes."

When I finish talking she falls on my neck and begins to weep. "Good-by, Father," she cries. "Good-by! God alone knows when we shall see each other again."

Well, that was too much for me. I remembered this Hodel when she was still a baby and I carried her in my arms, I carried her in my arms. . . . Forgive me, Mr. Sholom Aleichem, for acting like an old woman. If you only knew what a daughter she is! If you could only see the letters she writes! Oh, what a daughter . . .

And now let's talk about more cheerful things. Tell me, what news is there about the cholera in Odessa?

ISAAC LOEB PERETZ

Isaac Loeb Peretz (1851-1915), a Polish Jew who wrote in
Yiddish, was born one year later than Sholom Aleichem
and died one year earlier. A cultivated man, he knew
French, German, and Russian literature as well as Hebrew. He belonged to that generation of Eastern European Jews which found it necessary to leave the Ghetto
and become familiar with a larger world. He managed a
flour mill, practiced law, taught Hebrew and took an
active part in the affairs of the Polish-Jewish community.
He was a liberal reformer and educator. To write in Yiddish rather than in Hebrew was considered a sign of lib-
eralism, a break with the orthodoxy of the Ghetto, and a
declaration of solidarity with the uneducated, with arti-
sans, craftsmen, laborers and women—with the people.

Cabalists

When times are bad even Torah—that best of merchandise
—finds no takers.

The Lashtchever yeshivah was reduced to Reb Yekel, its
master, and an only student.

Reb Yekel is a thin old man with a long disheveled beard
and eyes dulled with age. His beloved remaining pupil,
Lemech, is a tall thin young man with a pale face, black
curly earlocks, black feverish eyes, parched lips, and a
tremulous, pointed Adam's apple. Both are dressed in rags,

Translated by Shlomo Katz. This and the other stories by I. L. Peretz
are from *A Treasury of Yiddish Stories* by Irving Howe & Eliezer Greenberg. Copyright 1954 by The Viking Press, Inc., and reprinted by their
permission.

and their chests are exposed for lack of shirts. Only with difficulty does Reb Yekel drag the heavy peasant boots he wears; his pupil's shoes slip off his bare feet.

That is all that remained of the once famed yeshivah.

The impoverished town gradually sent less food to the students, provided them with fewer "eating days," and the poor boys went off, each his own way. But Reb Yekel decided that here he would die, and his remaining pupil would place the potsherds on his eyes.

They frequently suffered hunger. Hunger leads to sleeplessness, and night-long insomnia arouses a desire to delve into the mysteries of Cabala.

For it can be considered in this wise: as long as one has to be up all night and suffer hunger all day, let these at least be put to some use, let the hunger be transformed into fasts and self-flagellation, let the gates of the world reveal their mysteries, spirits, and angels.

Teacher and pupil had engaged in Cabala for some time. Now they sat alone at the long table. For other people it was already past lunchtime; for them it was still before breakfast. They were accustomed to this. The master of the yeshivah stared into space and spoke; his pupil leaned his head on both hands and listened.

"In this too there are numerous degrees," the master said. "One man knows a part, another knows a half, a third knows the entire melody. The rabbi, of blessed memory, knew the melody in its wholeness, with musical accompaniment, but I," he added mournfully, "I barely merit a little bit, no larger than this"—and he measured the small degree of his knowledge on his bony finger. "There is melody that requires words: this is of low degree. Then there is a higher degree—a melody that sings of itself, without words, a pure melody! But even this melody requires voicing, lips that should shape it, and lips, as you realize, are matter. Even the sound itself is a refined form of matter.

"Let us say that sound is on the borderline between matter and spirit. But in any case, that melody which is heard by means of a voice that depends on lips is still not pure, not entirely pure, not genuine spirit. The true melody sings without voice, it sings within, in the heart and bowels.

"This is the secret meaning of King David's words: 'All my bones shall recite . . .' The very marrow of the bones should sing. That's where the melody should reside, the highest adoration of God, blessed be He. This is not the melody of man! This is not a composed melody! This is part of the melody with which God created the world; it is part of the soul which He instilled in it.

"This is how the hosts of heaven sing. This is how the rabbi, of blessed memory, sang."

The discourse was interrupted by an unkempt young man girded with a rope about his loins—obviously a porter. He entered the House of Study and placed a bowl of grits and a slice of bread beside the master and said in a coarse voice, "Reb Tevel sends food for the master of the yeshivah." As he turned to leave he added, "I will come for the bowl later."

Shaken out of his reverie by the porter's voice, Reb Yekel rose heavily and, dragging his feet in his big boots, went to wash his hands at the basin. He continued his remarks, which now lacked enthusiasm, and Lemech from his seat followed his voice with great eagerness.

"But I," Reb Yekel's mournful voice trailed, "have not even merited to understand to what degree that melody belongs, through what gate it emerges. See," he added with a smile, "but I do know the fasts and 'combinations' required for this purpose, and I may even reveal them to you today."

The pupil's eyes bulged. His mouth opened in his eagerness not to miss even a word. But the master broke off abruptly. He washed his hands, wiped them, pronounced the benediction, and, returning to the table, recited with trembling lips the blessing over the bread.

With shaking hands he raised the bowl. The warm steam covered his bony face. Then he replaced it on the table and took up the spoon in his right hand, warming his left hand against the bowl. His tongue pressed the first bite of salted bread against his toothless gums.

Having warmed his face with his hands, he wrinkled his

forehead, pursed his thin bluish lips, and blew upon the bowl.

All this time the pupil regarded him intently, and as the master's trembling lips stretched to meet the first spoonful of grits Lemech's heart seemed to contract. He covered his face with both hands and seemed to shrink all over.

Some minutes later another young man came, carrying a second bowl of grits and bread. "Reb Yosef sends dinner for the pupil," he announced. But Lemech did not remove his hands from his face.

The master put down his spoon and approached his pupil. For a moment he looked at him with loving pride; then he wrapped his hand in the wing of his coat and touched his shoulder.

"They brought you dinner," he reminded Lemech gently.

The pupil slowly removed his hands from his face, which was now even paler, and from his eyes, which burned with a still wilder fire.

"I know, *Rebbe,* but I will not eat today."

"The fourth fast in a row?" the master wondered. "And you will fast alone? Without me?" he added with a touch of resentment.

"This is a different kind of fast," the pupil answered. "It is a penitence fast."

"What are you saying? You, a penitence fast?"

"Yes, *Rebbe,* a penitence fast. A moment ago, when you began to eat, a sinful thought flitted through my mind, a covetous thought."

Late that night the pupil woke his master. They slept on facing benches in the House of Study.

"Rebbe, Rebbe!" he called in a weak voice.

"What is it?" The master awoke in fright.

"Just now I attained a high degree . . ."

"How?" the master asked, still not entirely awake.

"Something sang within me."

"How? How?"

"I hardly know myself," the pupil replied in a still weaker voice. "I couldn't sleep and I pondered your words. I wanted to know the melody. I grieved so at not knowing it that I began to weep—everything within me wept, all my limbs wept before the Almighty.

"And even as I wept I made the combinations you had revealed to me. It was strange, I did not recite them by mouth, but somehow deep within me, as if it happened by itself. Suddenly there was a great light. My eyes were closed but I saw light, much great light."

"And then?" The master bent down to him.

"Then I felt so good because of the light; it seemed to me that I had lost all weight, that I could fly."

"And then, then what?"

"Then I felt very gay and cheerful so that I could laugh. My face didn't move, nor my lips, yet I laughed. It was such joyous, good, hearty laughter."

"Yes, yes, from joy."

"Then something within me hummed, like the beginning of a melody."

"Well? And then?"

"Then I heard the melody sing within me."

"What did you feel? What? Tell."

"I felt as if all my senses were deadened and shut off, and that something within me sang, the way it is necessary to sing, but without words, simply melody."

"How? How?"

"No, I can't describe it. I knew it before. Then the song became—became—"

"What became of it? What?"

"A kind of music . . . as if I had a violin within me, or as if Yonah the musician was within me and he was playing as he does at the rabbi's table, except that he played still better, more delicately, with more spirit. And all this time there was no sound, no sound at all, pure spirit."

"You are fortunate! You are fortunate! You are fortunate!"

"Now it's all gone," said the pupil sadly. "My senses are awake again, and I am so tired, so tired . . . so that . . . *Rebbe!*" he shouted suddenly and grasped at his chest. "*Rebbe!* Recite the confession with me! They came after me! A singer is missing in the heavenly host! A white-

winged angel! *Rebbe! Rebbe! Shma Yisroel!* Hear, O Israel!
Shmaaa . . . Yis . . ."

The entire town was unanimous in wishing for themselves
a death such as this. Only the master of the yeshivah was
not satisfied.

"Only a few fasts more," he said, sighing, "and he would
have died with the Divine Kiss!"

Bontsha the Silent

Here on earth the death of Bontsha the Silent made no impression at all. Ask anyone: Who was Bontsha, how did he
live, and how did he die? Did his strength slowly fade, did
his heart slowly give out—or did the very marrow of his
bones melt under the weight of his burdens? Who knows?
Perhaps he just died from not eating—starvation, it's called.

If a horse, dragging a cart through the streets, should fall,
people would run from blocks around to stare, newspapers
would write about this fascinating event, a monument
would be put up to mark the very spot where the horse had
fallen. Had the horse belonged to a race as numerous as
that of human beings, he wouldn't have been paid this
honor. How many horses are there, after all? But human
beings—there must be a thousand million of them!

Bontsha was a human being; he lived unknown, in silence,
and in silence he died. He passed through our world like a
shadow. When Bontsha was born no one took a drink of
wine; there was no sound of glasses clinking. When he was
confirmed he made no speech of celebration. He existed like
a grain of sand at the rim of a vast ocean, amid millions of
other grains of sand exactly similar, and when the wind at
last lifted him up and carried him across to the other shore
of that ocean, no one noticed, no one at all.

During his lifetime his feet left no mark upon the dust of

Translated by Hilde Abel.

the streets; after his death the wind blew away the board that marked his grave. The wife of the gravedigger came upon that bit of wood, lying far off from the grave, and she picked it up and used it to make a fire under the potatoes she was cooking; it was just right. Three days after Bontsha's death no one knew where he lay, neither the gravedigger nor anyone else. If Bontsha had had a headstone, someone, even after a hundred years, might have come across it, might still have been able to read the carved words, and his name, Bontsha the Silent, might not have vanished from this earth.

His likeness remained in no one's memory, in no one's heart. A shadow! Nothing! Finished!

In loneliness he lived, and in loneliness he died. Had it not been for the infernal human racket someone or other might have heard the sound of Bontsha's bones cracking under the weight of his burdens; someone might have glanced around and seen that Bontsha was also a human being, that he had two frightened eyes and a silent trembling mouth; someone might have noticed how, even when he bore no actual load upon his back, he still walked with his head bowed down to earth, as though while living he was already searching for his grave.

When Bontsha was brought to the hospital ten people were waiting for him to die and leave them his narrow little cot; when he was brought from the hospital to the morgue twenty were waiting to occupy his pall; when he was taken out of the morgue forty were waiting to lie where he would lie forever. Who knows how many are now waiting to snatch from him that bit of earth?

In silence he was born, in silence he lived, in silence he died—and in an even vaster silence he was put into the ground.

Ah, but in the other world it was not so! No! In Paradise the death of Bontsha was an overwhelming event. The great trumpet of the Messiah announced through the seven heavens: Bontsha the Silent is dead! The most exalted angels, with the most imposing wings, hurried, flew, to tell

130 ISAAC LOEB PERETZ

one another, "Do you know who has died? Bontsha! Bontsha the Silent!"

And the new, the young little angels with brilliant eyes, with golden wings and silver shoes, ran to greet Bontsha, laughing in their joy. The sound of their wings, the sound of their silver shoes, as they ran to meet him, and the bubbling of their laughter, filled all Paradise with jubilation, and God Himself knew that Bontsha the Silent was at last here.

In the great gateway to heaven Abraham, our father, stretched out his arms in welcome and benediction. "Peace be with you!" And on his old face a deep sweet smile appeared.

What, exactly, was going on up there in Paradise?

There, in Paradise, two angels came bearing a golden throne for Bontsha to sit upon, and for his head a golden crown with glittering jewels.

"But why the throne, the crown, already?" two important saints asked. "He hasn't even been tried before the heavenly court of justice to which each new arrival must submit." Their voices were touched with envy. "What's going on here, anyway?"

And the angels answered the two important saints that, yes, Bontsha's trial hadn't started yet, but it would only be a formality, even the prosecutor wouldn't dare open his mouth. Why, the whole thing wouldn't take five minutes!

"What's the matter with you?" the angels asked. "Don't you know whom you're dealing with? You're dealing with Bontsha, Bontsha the Silent!"

When the young, the singing angels encircled Bontsha in love, when Abraham, our father, embraced him again and again, as a very old friend, when Bontsha heard that a throne waited for him, and for his head a crown, and that when he would stand trial in the court of heaven no one would say a word against him—when he heard all this, Bontsha, exactly as in the other world, was silent. He was silent with fear. His heart shook, in his veins ran ice, and he knew this must all be a dream or simply a mistake.

He was used to both, to dreams and mistakes. How often,

in that other world, had he not dreamed that he was wildly
shoveling up money from the street, that whole fortunes
lay there on the street beneath his hands—and then he
would wake and find himself a beggar again, more miserable than before the dream.

How often in that other world had someone smiled at
him, said a pleasant word—and then, passing and turning
back for another look, had seen his mistake and spat at
Bontsha.

Wouldn't that be just my luck, he thought now, and he
was afraid to lift his eyes, lest the dream end, lest he awake
and find himself again on earth, lying somewhere in a pit
of snakes and loathesome vipers, and he was afraid to make
the smallest sound, to move so much as an eyelash; he trembled and he could not hear the paeans of the angels; he
could not see them as they danced in stately celebration
about him; he could not answer the loving greeting of
Abraham, our father, "Peace be with you!" And when at
last he was led into the great court of justice in Paradise he
couldn't even say "Good morning." He was paralyzed with
fear.

And when his shrinking eyes beheld the floor of the
courtroom of justice, his fear, if possible, increased. The
floor was of purest alabaster, embedded with glittering diamonds. On such a floor stand my feet, thought Bontsha. My
feet! He was beside himself with fear. Who knows, he
thought, for what very rich man, or great learned rabbi, or
even saint, this whole thing's meant? The rich man will
arrive, and then it will all be over. He lowered his eyes; he
closed them.

In his fear he did not hear when his name was called out
in the pure angelic voice: "Bontsha the Silent!" Through
the ringing in his ears he could make out no words, only
the sound of that voice like the sound of music, of a violin.

Yet did he, perhaps, after all, catch the sound of his own
name, "Bontsha the Silent?" And then the voice added, "To
him that name is as becoming as a frock coat to a rich man."

What's that? What's he saying? Bontsha wondered, and
then he heard an impatient voice interrupting the speech of

his defending angel. "Rich man! Frock coat! No metaphors, please! And no sarcasm!"

"He never," began the defending angel again, "complained, not against God, not against man; his eye never grew red with hatred, he never raised a protest against heaven."

Bontsha couldn't understand a word, and the harsh voice of the prosecuting angel broke in once more. "Never mind the rhetoric, please!"

"His sufferings were unspeakable. Here, look upon a man who was more tormented than Job!"

Who? Bontsha wondered. Who is this man?

"Facts! Facts! Never mind the flowery business and stick to the facts, please!" the judge called out.

"When he was eight days old he was circumcised—"

"Such realistic details are unnecessary—"

"The knife slipped, and he did not even try to staunch the flow of blood—"

"—are distasteful. Simply give us the important facts."

"Even then, an infant, he was silent, he did not cry out his pain," Bontsha's defender continued. "He kept his silence, even when his mother died, and he was handed over, a boy of thirteen, to a snake, a viper—a stepmother!"

Hm, Bontsha thought, could they mean me?

"She begrudged him every bite of food, even the moldy rotten bread and the gristle of meat that she threw at him, while she herself drank coffee with cream."

"Irrelevant and immaterial," said the judge.

"For all that, she didn't begrudge him her pointed nails in his flesh—flesh that showed black and blue through the rags he wore. In winter, in the bitterest cold, she made him chop wood in the yard, barefoot! More than once were his feet frozen, and his hands, that were too young, too tender, to lift the heavy logs and chop them. But he was always silent, he never complained, not even to his father—"

"Complain! To that drunkard!" The voice of the prosecuting angel rose derisively, and Bontsha's body grew cold with the memory of fear.

"He never complained," the defender continued, "and he

was always lonely. He never had a friend, never was sent to school, never was given a new suit of clothes, never knew one moment of freedom."

"Objection! Objection!" the prosecutor cried out angrily. "He's only trying to appeal to the emotions with these flights of rhetoric!"

"He was silent even when his father, raving drunk, dragged him out of the house by the hair and flung him into the winter night, into the snowy, frozen night. He picked himself up quietly from the snow and wandered into the distance where his eyes led him.

"During his wanderings he was always silent; during his agony of hunger he begged only with his eyes. And at last, on a damp spring night, he drifted to a great city, drifted there like a leaf before the wind, and on his very first night, scarcely seen, scarcely heard, he was thrown into jail. He remained silent, he never protested, he never asked, Why, what for? The doors of the jail were opened again, and, free, he looked for the most lowly filthy work, and still he remained silent.

"More terrible even than the work itself was the search for work. Tormented and ground down by pain, by the cramp of pain in an empty stomach, he never protested, he always kept silent.

"Soiled by the filth of a strange city, spat upon by unknown mouths, driven from the streets into the roadway, where, a human beast of burden, he pursued his work, a porter, carrying the heaviest loads upon his back, scurrying between carriages, carts, and horses, staring death in the eyes every moment, he still kept silent.

"He never reckoned up how many pounds he must haul to earn a penny; how many times, with each step, he stumbled and fell for that penny. He never reckoned up how many times he almost vomited out his very soul, begging for his earnings. He never reckoned up his bad luck, the other's good luck. No, never. He remained silent. He never even demanded his own earnings; like a beggar, he waited at the door for what was rightfully his, and only in the depths of his eyes was there an unspoken longing. 'Come back later!'

they'd order him; and, like a shadow, he would vanish, and then, like a shadow, would return and stand waiting, his eyes begging, imploring, for what was his. He remained silent even when they cheated him, keeping back, with one excuse or another, most of his earnings, or giving him bad money. Yes, he never protested, he always remained silent.

"Once," the defending angel went on, "Bontsha crossed the roadway to the fountain for a drink, and in that moment his whole life was miraculously changed. What miracle happened to change his whole life? A splendid coach, with tires of rubber, plunged past, dragged by runaway horses; the coachman, fallen, lay in the street, his head split open. From the mouths of the frightened horses spilled foam, and in their wild eyes sparks struck like fire in a dark night, and inside the carriage sat a man, half alive, half dead, and Bontsha caught at the reins and held the horses. The man who sat inside and whose life was saved, a Jew, a philanthropist, never forgot what Bontsha had done for him. He handed him the whip of the dead driver, and Bontsha, then and there, became a coachman—no longer a common porter! And what's more, his great benefactor married him off, and what's still more, this great philanthropist himself provided a child for Bontsha to look after."

"And still Bontsha never said a word, never protested."

They mean me, I really do believe they mean me, Bontsha encouraged himself, but still he didn't have the gall to open his eyes, to look up at his judge.

"He never protested. He remained silent even when that great philanthropist shortly thereafter went into bankruptcy without ever having paid Bontsha one cent of his wages.

"He was silent even when his wife ran off and left him with her helpless infant. He was silent when, fifteen years later, that same helpless infant had grown up and become strong enough to throw Bontsha out of the house."

They mean me, Bontsha rejoiced, they really mean me.

"He even remained silent," continued the defending angel, "when that same benefactor and philanthropist went out of bankruptcy, as suddenly as he'd gone into it, and still didn't pay Bontsha one cent of what he owed him. No, more than that. This person, as befits a fine gentleman who has gone through bankruptcy, again went driving the great coach with the tires of rubber, and now, now he had a new coachman, and Bontsha, again a porter in the roadway, was run over by coachman, carriage, horses. And still, in his agony, Bontsha did not cry out; he remained silent. He did not even tell the police who had done this to him. Even in the hospital, where everyone is allowed to scream, he remained silent. He lay in utter loneliness on his cot, abandoned by the doctor, by the nurse; he had not the few pennies to pay them—and he made no murmur. He was silent in that awful moment just before he was about to die, and he was silent in that very moment when he did die. And never one murmur of protest against man, never one murmur of protest against God!"

Now Bontsha begins to tremble again. He senses that after his defender has finished, his prosecutor will rise to state the case against him. Who knows of what he will be accused? Bontsha, in that other world on earth, forgot each present moment as it slipped behind him to become the past. Now the defending angel has brought everything back to his mind again—but who knows what forgotten sins the prosecutor will bring to mind?

The prosecutor rises. "Gentlemen!" he begins in a harsh and bitter voice, and then he stops. "Gentlemen—" he begins again, and now his voice is less harsh, and again he stops. And finally, in a very soft voice, that same prosecutor says, "Gentlemen, he was always silent—and now I too will be silent."

The great court of justice grows very still, and at last from the judge's chair a new voice rises, loving, tender. "Bontsha my child, Bontsha"—the voice swells like a great harp—"my heart's child . . ."

Within Bontsha his very soul begins to weep. He would like to open his eyes, to raise them, but they are darkened with tears. It is so sweet to cry. Never until now has it been sweet to cry.

"My child, my Bontsha . . ."

Not since his mother died has he heard such words, and spoken in such a voice.

"My child," the judge begins again, "you have always suffered, and you have always kept silent. There isn't one secret place in your body without its bleeding wound; there isn't one secret place in your soul without its wound and blood. And you never protested. You always were silent.

"There, in that other world, no one understood you. You never understood yourself. You never understood that you need not have been silent, that you could have cried out and that your outcries would have brought down the world itself and ended it. You never understood your sleeping strength. There in that other world, that world of lies, your silence was never rewarded, but here in Paradise is the world of truth, here in Paradise you will be rewarded. You, the judge can neither condemn nor pass sentence upon. For you there is not only one little portion of Paradise, one little share. No, for you there is everything! Whatever you want! Everything is yours!"

Now for the first time Bontsha lifts his eyes. He is blinded by light. The splendor of light lies everywhere, upon the walls, upon the vast ceiling, the angels blaze with light, the judge. He drops his weary eyes.

"Really?" he asks, doubtful, and a little embarrassed.

"Really!" the judge answers. "Really! I tell you, everything is yours. Everything in Paradise is yours. Choose! Take! Whatever you want! You will only take what is yours!"

"Really?" Bontsha asks again, and now his voice is stronger, more assured.

And the judge and all the heavenly host answer, "Really! Really! Really!"

"Well then"—and Bontsha smiles for the first time—"well then, what I would like, Your Excellency, is to have, every morning for breakfast, a hot roll with fresh butter."

A silence falls upon the great hall, and it is more terrible than Bontsha's has ever been, and slowly the judge and the angels bend their heads in shame at this unending meekness they have created on earth.

Then the silence is shattered. The prosecutor laughs aloud, a bitter laugh.

If Not Higher

Early every Friday morning, at the time of the Penitential Prayers, the Rabbi of Nemirov would vanish.

He was nowhere to be seen—neither in the synagogue nor in the two Houses of Study nor at a *minyan*. And he was certainly not at home. His door stood open; whoever wished could go in and out; no one would steal from the rabbi. But not a living creature was within.

Where could the rabbi be? Where should he be? In heaven, no doubt. A rabbi has plenty of business to take care of just before the Days of Awe. Jews, God bless them, need livelihood, peace, health, and good matches. They want to be pious and good, but our sins are so great, and Satan of the thousand eyes watches the whole earth from one end to the other. What he sees he reports; he denounces, informs. Who can help us if not the rabbi!

That's what the people thought.

But once a Litvak came, and he laughed. You know the Litvaks. They think little of the Holy Books but stuff themselves with Talmud and law. So this Litvak points to a passage in the *Gemarah*—it sticks in your eyes—where it is written that even Moses, our Teacher, did not ascend to heaven during his lifetime but remained suspended two and a half feet below. Go argue with a Litvak!

So where can the rabbi be?

"That's not my business," said the Litvak, shrugging. Yet all the while—what a Litvak can do!—he is scheming to find out.

Translated by Marie Syrkin.

That same night, right after the evening prayers, the Litvak steals into the rabbi's room, slides under the rabbi's bed, and waits. He'll watch all night and discover where the rabbi vanishes and what he does during the Penitential Prayers.

Someone else might have got drowsy and fallen asleep, but a Litvak is never at a loss; he recites a whole tractate of the Talmud by heart.

At dawn he hears the call to prayers.

The rabbi has already been awake for a long time. The Litvak has heard him groaning for a whole hour.

Whoever has heard the Rabbi of Nemirov groan knows how much sorrow for all Israel, how much suffering, lies in each groan. A man's heart might break, hearing it. But a Litvak is made of iron; he listens and remains where he is. The rabbi, long life to him, lies on the bed, and the Litvak under the bed.

Then the Litvak hears the beds in the house begin to creak; he hears people jumping out of their beds, mumbling a few Jewish words, pouring water on their fingernails, banging doors. Everyone has left. It is again quiet and dark; a bit of light from the moon shines through the shutters.

(Afterward the Litvak admitted that when he found himself alone with the rabbi a great fear took hold of him. Goose pimples spread across his skin, and the roots of his earlocks pricked him like needles. A trifle: to be alone with the rabbi at the time of the Penitential Prayers! But a Litvak is stubborn. So he quivered like a fish in water and remained where he was.)

Finally the rabbi, long life to him, arises. First he does what befits a Jew. Then he goes to the clothes closet and takes out a bundle of peasant clothes: linen trousers, high boots, a coat, a big felt hat, and a long wide leather belt studded with brass nails. The rabbi gets dressed. From his coat pocket dangles the end of a heavy peasant rope.

The rabbi goes out, and the Litvak follows him.

On the way the rabbi stops in the kitchen, bends down, takes an ax from under the bed, puts it in his belt, and leaves the house. The Litvak trembles but continues to follow.

The hushed dread of the Days of Awe hangs over the dark streets. Every once in a while a cry rises from some *minyan* reciting the Penitential Prayers, or from a sickbed. The rabbi hugs the sides of the streets, keeping to the shade of the houses. He glides from house to house, and the Litvak after him. The Litvak hears the sound of his heartbeats mingling with the sound of the rabbi's heavy steps. But he keeps on going and follows the rabbi to the outskirts of the town.

A small wood stands behind the town.

The rabbi, long life to him, enters the wood. He takes thirty or forty steps and stops by a small tree. The Litvak, overcome with amazement, watches the rabbi take the ax out of his belt and strike the tree. He hears the tree creak and fall. The rabbi chops the tree into logs and the logs into sticks. Then he makes a bundle of the wood and ties it with the rope in his pocket. He puts the bundle of wood on his back, shoves the ax back into his belt, and returns to the town.

He stops at a back street beside a small broken-down shack and knocks at the window.

"Who is there?" asks a frightened voice. The Litvak recognizes it as the voice of a sick Jewish woman.

"I," answers the rabbi in the accent of a peasant.

"Who is I?"

Again the rabbi answers in Russian. "Vassil."

"Who is Vassil, and what do you want?"

"I have wood to sell, very cheap." And, not waiting for the woman's reply, he goes into the house.

The Litvak steals in after him. In the gray light of early morning he sees a poor room with broken, miserable furnishings. A sick woman, wrapped in rags, lies on the bed. She complains bitterly, "Buy? How can I buy? Where will a poor widow get money?"

"I'll lend it to you," answers the supposed Vassil. "It's only six cents."

"And how will I ever pay you back?" said the poor woman, groaning.

"Foolish one," says the rabbi reproachfully. "See, you are a poor sick Jew, and I am ready to trust you with a little wood. I am sure you'll pay. While you, you have such a great and mighty God and you don't trust him for six cents."

"And who will kindle the fire?" said the widow. "Have I the strength to get up? My son is at work."

"I'll kindle the fire," answers the rabbi.

As the rabbi put the wood into the oven he recited, in a groan, the first portion of the Penitential Prayers.

As he kindled the fire and the wood burned brightly, he recited, a bit more joyously, the second portion of the Penitential Prayers. When the fire was set he recited the third portion, and then he shut the stove.

The Litvak who saw all this became a disciple of the rabbi.

And ever after, when another disciple tells how the Rabbi of Nemirov ascends to heaven at the time of the Penitential Prayers, the Litvak does not laugh. He only adds quietly, "If not higher."

The Golem

Great men were once capable of great miracles.

When the ghetto of Prague was being attacked, and they were about to rape the women, roast the children, and slaughter the rest; when it seemed that the end had finally come, the great Rabbi Loeb put aside his *Gemarah*, went into the street, stopped before a heap of clay in front of the teacher's house, and molded a clay image. He blew into the nose of the *golem*—and it began to stir; then he whispered the Name into its ear, and our *golem* left the ghetto. The rabbi returned to the House of Prayer, and the *golem* fell upon our enemies, threshing them as with flails. Men fell on all sides.

Prague was filled with corpses. It lasted, so they say, through Wednesday and Thursday. Now it is already Fri-

Translated by Irving Howe.

day, the clock strikes twelve, and the *golem* is still busy at its work.

"Rabbi," cries the head of the ghetto, "the *golem* is slaughtering all of Prague! There will not be a gentile left to light the Sabbath fires or take down the Sabbath lamps."

Once again the rabbi left his study. He went to the altar and began singing the psalm "A song of the Sabbath."

The *golem* ceased its slaughter. It returned to the ghetto, entered the House of Prayer, and waited before the rabbi. And again the rabbi whispered into its ear. The eyes of the *golem* closed, the soul that had dwelt in it flew out, and it was once more a *golem* of clay.

To this day the *golem* lies hidden in the attic of the Prague synagogue, covered with cobwebs that extend from wall to wall. No living creature may look at it, particularly women in pregnancy. No one may touch the cobwebs, for whoever touches them dies. Even the oldest people no longer remember the *golem*, though the wise man Zvi, the grandson of the great Rabbi Loeb, ponders the problem: may such a *golem* be included in a congregation of worshipers or not?

The *golem*, you see, has not been forgotten. It is still here! But the Name by which it could be called to life in a day of need, the Name has disappeared. And the cobwebs grow and grow, and no one may touch them.

What are we to do?

SAMUEL JOSEPH AGNON

Samuel Joseph Agnon is the oldest and most highly respected of modern Hebrew writers. A native of Galicia in
the old Austro-Hungarian Empire, he was born in 1888.
He lives now in a house that looks into ancient Jerusalem across the barrier separating the Israeli and Jor-
danian sections of the city. Agnon has lived in Palestine
since 1907, with the exception of an eleven-year period
spent in Germany, from 1913 to 1924. A great Hebraist he
is also a student of Ghetto traditions. Two of his novels
have been translated into English—*The Bridal Canopy*
and *In the Heart of the Seas*. Entirely immersed in Hebrew and Yiddish literature, he apparently has little
interest in Western literary traditions.

The Kerchief

1

Every year my father of blessed memory used to visit the
Lashkowitz fair to do business with the merchants. Lashkowitz is a small town of no more consequence than any of
the other small towns in the district, except that once a year
merchants gather together there from everywhere and offer
their wares for sale in the streets of the town; and whoever
needs goods comes and buys them. In earlier times, two or
three generations ago, more than a hundred thousand people

Translated by I. M. Lask. From *The Jewish Caravan*, edited by Leo W.
Schwarz. Copyright 1935 by Leo W. Schwarz. Reprinted by permission of
Holt, Rinehart and Winston, Inc.

used to gather together there; and even now, when Lashkowitz is in its decline, they come to it from all over the country. You will not find a single merchant in the whole of Galicia who does not keep a shop in Lashkowitz during the fair.

2

For us the week in which my father went to the market was just like the week of the Ninth of Ab. During those days there was not a smile to be seen on mother's lips, and the children also refrained from laughing. Mother, may she rest in peace, used to cook light meals with milk and vegetables, and all sorts of things which children do not dislike. If we caused her trouble she would quiet us, and did not rebuke us even for things which deserved a beating. I often used to find her sitting at the window with moist lashes. And why should my mother sit at the window; did she wish to watch the passersby? Why, she, may her memory be blessed, never concerned herself with other people's affairs, and would only half hear the stories her neighbors might tell her; but it was her custom, ever since the first year in which my father had gone to Lashkowitz, to stand at the window and look out. When my father of blessed memory went to the fair at Lashkowitz for the first time, my mother was once standing at the window when she suddenly cried out, "Oh, they're strangling him!" Folk asked her, "What are you saying?" She answered, "I see a robber taking him by the throat"; and before she had finished her words she had fainted. They sent to the fair and found my father injured, for at the very time that my mother had fainted, somebody had attacked my father for his money and had taken him by the throat; and he had been saved by a miracle. In after years, when I found in the *Book of Lamentations* the words, "She is become as a widow," and I read Rashi's explanation, "As a woman whose husband has gone to a distant land and who intends to return to her," it brought to mind my mother, may she rest in peace, as she used to sit at the window with her tears upon her cheeks.

3

All the time that father was in Lashkowitz I used to sleep in his bed. As soon as I had said the night prayer I used to undress and stretch my limbs in his long bed, cover myself up to my ears and keep them pricked up and ready so that in case I heard the Trumpet of Messiah I might rise at once. It was a particular pleasure for me to meditate on Messiah the King. Sometimes I used to laugh myself when I thought of the consternation which would come about in the whole world when our Righteous Messiah would reveal himself. Only yesterday he was bandaging his wounds and his bruises, and today he's a king! Yesterday he sat among the beggars and they did not recognize him, but sometimes even abused him and treated him with disrespect; and now suddenly the Holy and Blest One has remembered the oath He swore to redeem Israel, and gave him permission to reveal himself to the world. Another in my place might have been angered at the beggars who treated Messiah the King with disrespect; but I honored and revered them, since Messiah the King had desired to dwell in their quarters. In my place another might have treated the beggars without respect, as they eat black bread even on the Sabbaths, and wear dirty clothes. But I honored and revered them, since among them were those who had dwelt together with Messiah.

4

Those were fine nights in which I used to lie on my bed and think of Messiah the King, who would reveal himself suddenly in the world. He would lead us to the land of Israel where we would dwell, every man under his own vine and his own fig tree. Father would not go to fairs and I would not go to school but would walk about all day long in the

Courts of the House of our God. And while lying and medi-
tating thus, my eyes would close of their own accord; and
before they closed entirely I would take my *zizith* and knot
the fringes according to the number of days my father still
had to stay in Lashkowitz. Then all sorts of lights, green,
white, black, red and blue, used to come toward me, like the
lights seen by wayfarers in fields and woods and valleys and
streams, and all kinds of precious things would be gleaming
and glittering in them; and my heart danced for joy at all
the good stored away for us in the future, in the day that
our righteous Messiah would reveal himself, may it be
speedily and in our days, Amen. While I rejoiced so, a great
bird would come and peck at the light. Once I took my
fringes and tied myself to his wings and said, "Bird, bird,
bring me to father." The bird spread its wings and flew with
me to a city called Rome. I looked down and saw a group
of poor men sitting at the gates of the city, and one beggar
among them bandaging his wounds. I turned my eyes away
from him in order not to see his sufferings. When I turned
my eyes away there grew a great mountain with all kinds of
thorns and thistles upon it and evil beasts grazing there, and
impure birds and creeping abominations crawling about it,
and a great wind blew all of a sudden and flung me onto the
mountain, and the mountain began quaking under me and
my limbs felt as though they would fall asunder; but I
feared to cry out lest the creeping abominations should enter my mouth and the impure birds should peck at my
tongue. Then father came and wrapped me in his tallith and
brought me back to my bed. I opened my eyes to gaze at his
face and found that it was day. At once I knew that the
Holy and Blest One had rolled away another night of the
nights of the fair. I took my fringes and made a fresh knot.

5

Whenever father returned from the fair he brought us many
gifts. He was very clever, was father, knowing what each of
us would want most and bringing it to us. Or maybe the

Master of Dreams used to tell father what he showed us in dream, and he would bring it for us.

There were not many gifts that survived long. As is the way of the valuables of this world, they were not lasting. Yesterday we were playing with them, and today they were already thrown away. Even my fine prayer-book was torn, for whatever I might have had to do, I used to open it and ask its counsel; and finally nothing was left of it but a few dog-eared printed scraps.

But one present which father brought mother remained whole for many years. And even after it was lost it did not vanish from my heart, and I still think of it as though it were yet there.

6

That day, when father returned from the fair, it was Friday after the noon hour, when the children are freed from school. Those Friday afternoon hours were the best time of the week, because all the week round a child is bent over his book and his eyes and heart are not his own; as soon as he raises his head he is beaten. On Friday afternoon he is freed from study, and even if he does whatever he wants to, nobody objects. Were it not for the noon meal the world would be like Paradise. But mother had already summoned me to eat and I had no heart to refuse.

Almost before we had begun eating my little sister put her right hand to her ear and set her ear to the table. "What are you doing?" mother asked her. "I'm trying to listen," she answered. Mother asked, "Daughter, what are you trying to listen to?" Then she began clapping her hands with joy and crying, "Father's coming, father's coming." And in a little while we heard the wheels of a wagon. Very faint at first, then louder and louder. At once we threw our spoons down while they were still half full, left our plates on the table and ran out to meet father coming back from the fair. Mother, may she rest in peace, also let her apron fall and stood erect, her arms folded on her bosom, until father entered the house.

How big father was then! I knew my father was bigger than all the other fathers. All the same I used to think there must be someone taller than he—but now even the chandelier hanging from the ceiling in our house seemed to be lower.

Suddenly father bent down, caught me to him, kissed me and asked me what I had learnt. Is it likely that father did not know which portion of the week was being read? But he only asked to try me out. Before I could answer he had caught my brother and sisters, raised them on high and kissed them.

I look about me now to try and find something to which to compare my father when he stood together with his tender children on his return from afar, and I can think of many comparisons, each one finer than the next; yet I can find nothing pleasant enough. But I hope that the love haloing my father of blessed memory may wrap us round whenever we come to embrace our little children, and that joy which possessed us then will be possessed by our children all their lives.

7

The wagoner entered bringing two trunks, one large and the other neither large nor small but medium; and that second trunk seemed to have eyes and smile with them.

Father took his bunch of keys from his pocket and said, "We'll open the trunk and take out my tallith and tefillin." Father was just speaking for fun, since who needs tefillin on Friday afternoon, and even if you think of the tallith, my father had a special tallith for Sabbath, but he only said it in order that we should not be too expectant and not be too anxious for presents.

But we went and undid the straps of the trunk and watched his every movement while he took one of the keys and examined it, smiling affectionately. The key also smiled at us; that is, gleams of light sparkled on the key and it seemed to be smiling. Finally he pressed the key into the lock, opened the trunk, put his hand inside and felt among his possessions. Suddenly he looked at us and became silent. Had father forgotten to place the presents there? Or had he been lodging at an inn where the inn people rose and took out the presents? As happened with the sage by whose hands they sent a gift to Cæsar, a chest full of jewels and pearls, and when he lodged one night at the inn, the inn folk opened the chest and took out everything that was in it and filled it with dust. Then I prayed that just as a miracle was done to that sage so that that dust should be the dust of Abraham our father, which turned into swords when it was thrown into the air, so should the Holy and Blest One perform a miracle with us in order that the things with which the inn keepers had filled father's trunk should be better than all presents. Before my prayer was at an end father brought out all kinds of fine things. There was not a single one among his gifts which we had not longed for all the year round. And that is why I said that the Master of Dreams must have revealed to father what he had shown us in dream.

The gifts of my father deserve to be praised at length, but who is going to praise things that have vanished and are lost? All the same, one fine gift which my father brought my mother on the day that he returned from the fair, deserves to be mentioned in particular.

8

It was a silk brocaded kerchief adorned with flowers and blossoms. On the one side it was brown and they were white, while on the other they were brown and it was white. That was the gift which father of blessed memory brought to mother, may she rest in peace.

Mother opened up the kerchief, stroked it with her fingers and peeped at father; he peeped back at her and both of them remained silent. Finally she folded it again, rose,

put it in the cupboard and said to father, "Wash your hands
and eat." As soon as father sat down to his meal I went out
to my friends in the street and showed them the presents I
had received, and was busy outside with them until the Sabbath began and I went to pray with father.

How pleasant that Sabbath was when we returned from
the synagogue! The skies were full of stars, the houses full
of lamps and candles, people were wearing their Sabbath
clothes and walking quietly beside father in order not to
disturb the Sabbath angels who accompany one home from
the synagogue on Sabbath Eves: candles were alight in the
house and the table prepared and the fine smell of white
bread, and a white table-cloth spread and two Sabbath
loaves on it, covered by a small napkin out of respect; so
that they should not feel ashamed when the blessing is said
first over the wine.

Father bowed and entered and said, "A peaceful and
blessed Sabbath," and mother answered, "Peaceful and
blessed." Father looked at the table and began singing,
"Peace be unto you, angels of peace," while mother sat at
the table, her prayer-book in hand, and the big chandelier
with the ten candles one for each of the Ten Commandments, hanging from the ceiling, gave light. They were answered back by the rest of the candles, one for father, one
for mother, one for each of the little ones; and although we
were smaller than father and mother, all the same our candles were as big as theirs. Then I looked at mother and saw
that her face had changed and her forehead had grown
smaller because of the kerchief wound round her head and
covering her hair, while her eyes seemed much larger and
were shining towards father who went on singing, "A
woman of valor who shall find?"; and the ends of her kerchief which hung down below her chin were quivering very
gently, because the Sabbath angels were moving their wings
and making a wind. It must have been so, for the windows
were closed and where could the wind have come from if
not from the wings of the angels? As it says in the Psalms,
"He maketh his messengers the winds." I held back my
breath in order not to confuse the angels and looked at my

mother, may she rest in peace, and wondered at the Sabbath Day, which is given us for an honor and a glory. Suddenly I felt how my cheeks were being patted. I do not know whether the wings of the angels or the corners of the kerchief were caressing me. Happy is he who merits to have good angels hovering over his head, and happy is he whose mother has stroked his head on the Sabbath Eve.

9

When I awakened from sleep it was already day. The whole world was full of the Sabbath morning. Father and mother were about to go out, he to his little synagogue, and she to the House of Study of my grandfather, may he rest in peace. Father was wearing a black satin robe and a round shtreimel of sable on his head, and mother wore a black dress and a hat with feathers. In the House of Study of my grandfather, where mother used to pray, they did not spend too much time singing, and so she could return early. When I came back with father from the small synagogue she was already seated at the table wearing her kerchief, and the table was prepared with wine and brandy and cakes, large and small, round and doubled over. Father entered, said, "A Sabbath of peace and blessing," put his tallith on the bed, sat down at the head of the table, said, "The Lord is my shepherd, I shall not want," blessed the wine, tasted the cake and began, "A Psalm of David; The earth is the Lord's and the fulness thereof." When the Ark is opened on the New Year's Eve and this Psalm is said there is a great stirring among the congregation. There was a similar stirring in my heart then. Had my mother not taught me that you do not stand on chairs and do not clamber on to the table and do not shout, I would have climbed onto the table and shouted out, "The earth is the Lord's and the fulness thereof"; like that child in the Gemara (Talmud) who used to be seated in the middle of a gold table which was a load for sixteen men, with sixteen silver chains attached, and dishes and glasses and bowls and platters fitted, and with all kinds of food and sweetmeats and spices of all that was created in the Six Days of Creation; and he used to proclaim, "The earth is the Lord's and the fulness thereof."

Mother cut the cake giving each his or her portion; and the ends of her kerchief accompanied her hands. While doing so a cherry fell out of the cake and stained her apron; but it did not touch her kerchief, which remained as clean as it had been when father took it out of his trunk.

10

A woman does not put on a silken kerchief every day or every Sabbath. When a woman stands at the oven what room is there for ornament? Every day is not Sabbath, but on the other hand there are Festivals. The Holy and Blest One took pity on His creatures and gave them times of gladness, holidays and appointed seasons. On festivals mother used to put on a feather hat and go to the synagogue, and at home she would don her kerchief. But on the New Year and the Day of Atonement she kept the kerchief on all day long; similarly on the morning of Hoshana Rabba, the seventh day of Tabernacles. I used to look at mother on the Day of Atonement, when she wore her kerchief and her eyes were bright with prayer and fasting. She seemed to me like a presented prayer-book bound in silk.

The rest of the time the kerchief lay folded in the cupboard, and on Sabbaths and festivals mother would take it out. I never saw her washing it, although she was very particular about cleanliness. When Sabbaths and festivals are properly kept the Sabbath and festival clothes are preserved. But for me she would have kept the kerchief all her life long.

What happened was as follows. On the day I became thirteen years old and a member of the congregation, my mother, may she rest in peace, bound her kerchief round my neck. Blessed be He who is everywhere, who has given His word to guardians. There was not a spot of dirt to be found on the kerchief. But sentence had been passed already on the kerchief, that it was to be lost through me. This kerchief, which I had observed so much and so long, would vanish because of me.

11

Now I shall pass from one theme to another until I return to my original theme. At that time there came a beggar to our town who was sick with running sores; his hands were swollen, his clothes were rent and tattered, his shoes were cracked, and when he showed himself in the street the children threw earth and stones at him. And not only the children but even the grownups and householders turned angry faces on him. Once when he went to the market to buy bread or onions the stall-women drove him away. Not that the stall-women in our town were cruel; indeed, they were tender-hearted. Some would give the food from their mouths to orphans, others went to the forest, gathered twigs, made charcoal of them and shared them free among the beggars and poor folk. But every beggar has his own luck. When he fled from them and entered the House of Study, the beadle shouted at him and pushed him out. And when on the Sabbath Eve he crept into the House of Study, nobody invited him to come home with them and share the Sabbath meal. God forbid that the sons of our father Abraham do not perform works of charity; but the ministers of Satan used to accompany that beggar and pull a veil over Jewish eyes so that they should not perceive his dire needs. As to where he heard the blessing over wine, and where he ate his three Sabbath meals—if he was not sustained by humankind he must have been sustained by the Grace of God.

Hospitality is a great thing, since buildings are erected and wardens appointed for the sake of it and to support the poor. But I say it in praise of our townsfolk, that although they did not establish any poorhouse or elect any wardens, every man who could do so used to find a place for a poor man in his own house, thus seeing the troubles of his brother and aiding him and supporting him at the hour of his need; and his sons and daughters who saw this would learn from his deeds. When trouble would befall a man he would groan; the walls of his house would groan with him because of the mighty groaning of the poor; and he would know that there are blows even greater than that which had befallen him. And as he comforted the poor, so would the Holy and Blest One in the future comfort him.

12

Now I leave the beggars and shall tell only of my mother's kerchief, which she tied round my neck when I grew old enough to perform all the commandments and be counted a member of the congregation. On that day, when I returned from the House of Study to eat the midday meal, I was dressed like a bridegroom and was very happy and pleased with myself because I was now donning tefillin. On the way I found that beggar sitting on a heap of stones, changing the bandages of his sores, his clothes rent and tattered, nothing but a bundle of rags which did not even hide his sores. He looked at me as well. The sores on his face seemed like eyes of fire. My heart stopped, my knees began shaking, my eyes grew dim and everything seemed to be in a whirl. But I took my heart in my hand, nodded to the beggar, wished him peace, and he wished me peace back.

Suddenly my heart began thumping, my ears grew hot and a sweetness such as I had never experienced in all my days took possession of all my limbs; my lips and my tongue were sweet with it, my mouth fell agape, my two eyes were opened and I stared before me as a man who sees in waking what has been shown him in dream. And so I stood staring in front of me. The sun stopped still in the sky, not a creature was to be seen in the street; but the merciful sun looked down upon the earth and its light shone bright on the sores of the beggar. I began loosening my kerchief to breathe more freely, for tears stood in my throat. Before I could loosen it, my heart began racing with wonder, and the

sweetness, which I had already felt, doubled and redoubled.
I took off the kerchief and gave it to the beggar. He took it
and wound it round his sores. The sun came and stroked
my neck.

I looked around. There was not a creature in the market,
but a pile of stones lay there and reflected the sun's light.
For a little while I stood there without thinking. Then I
moved my feet and returned home.

13

When I reached the house I walked round it on all four
sides. Suddenly I stopped at mother's window, the one from
which she used to look out. The place was strange; the sun's
light upon it did not dazzle but warmed, and there was perfect rest there. Two or three people passing slowed their
paces and lowered their voices; one of them wiped his brow
and sighed deeply. It seems to me that that sigh must still be
hanging there, until the end of all generations.

I stood there awhile, a minute or two minutes or more.
Finally I moved from thence and entered the house. When I
entered I found mother sitting in the window as was her
way. I greeted her and she returned my greeting. Suddenly
I felt that I had not treated her properly; she had had a fine
kerchief which she used to bind round her head on Sabbaths
and festivals, and I had taken it and given it to a beggar to
bind up his feet with. Ere I had ended begging her to forgive me she was gazing at me with love and affection. I
gazed back at her, and my heart was filled with the same
gladness as I had felt on that Sabbath when my mother had
set the kerchief about her head for the first time.

The end of the story of the kerchief of my mother, may
she rest in peace.

STEFAN ZWEIG

Stefan Zweig was born in 1881 in Austria. Brilliant and
versatile he studied philosophy in Vienna, wrote fiction
and biography. The First World War interrupted his literary activities. He went to Switzerland and joined in
the pacifist activities led by Romain Rolland. His interests were very wide; he wrote on psychology and religion,
politics and history. Self-exiled for many years in Switzerland, England and South America, he died in Brazil at
the age of sixty. Among his books are *Amok, Joseph
Fouché,* and *Adepts in Self-Portraiture.*

Buchmendel

Having just got back to Vienna, after a visit to an out-of-
the-way part of the country, I was walking home from the
station when a heavy shower came on, such a deluge that
the passers-by hastened to take shelter in doorways, and I
myself felt it expedient to get out of the downpour. Luckily
there is a café at almost every street-corner in the metropo-
lis, and I made for the nearest, though not before my hat
was dripping wet and my shoulders were drenched to the
skin. An old-fashioned suburban place, lacking the attrac-
tions (copied from Germany) of music and a dancing-floor
to be found in the centre of the town; full of small shopkeepers and working folk who consumed more newspapers
than coffee and rolls. Since it was already late in the evening, the air, which would have been stuffy anyhow, was

From *Kaleidoscope* by Stefan Zweig. Copyright 1934 by The Viking Press,
Inc., and reprinted by their permission.

thick with tobacco-smoke. Still, the place was clean and brightly decorated, had new satin-covered couches, and a shining cash-register, so that it looked thoroughly attractive. In my haste to get out of the rain, I had not troubled to read its name—but what matter? There I rested, warm and comfortable, though looking rather impatiently through the blue-tinted window panes to see when the shower would be over, and I should be able to get on my way.

Thus I sat unoccupied, and began to succumb to that inertia which results from the narcotic atmosphere of the typical Viennese café. Out of this void, I scanned various individuals whose eyes, in the murky room, had a greyish look in the artificial light; I mechanically contemplated the young woman at the counter as, like an automaton, she dealt out sugar and a teaspoon to the waiter for each cup of coffee; with half an eye and a wandering attention I read the uninteresting advertisements on the walls—and there was something agreeable about these dull occupations. But suddenly, and in a peculiar fashion, I was aroused from what had become almost a doze. A vague internal movement had begun; much as a toothache sometimes begins, without one's being able to say whether it is on the right side or the left, in the upper jaw or the lower. All I became aware of was a numb tension, an obscure sentiment of spiritual unrest. Then, without knowing why, I grew fully conscious. I must have been in this café once before, years ago, and random associations had awakened memories of the walls, the tables, the chairs, the seemingly unfamiliar smoke-laden room.

The more I endeavoured to grasp this lost memory, the more obstinately did it elude me; a sort of jellyfish glistening in the abysses of consciousness, slippery and unseizable. Vainly did I scrutinize every object within the range of vision. Certainly when I had been here before the counter had had neither marble top nor cash-register; the walls had not been panelled with imitation rosewood; these must be recent acquisitions. Yet I had indubitably been here, more than twenty years back. Within these four walls, as firmly fixed as a nail driven up to the head in a tree, there clung a part of my ego, long since overgrown. Vainly I explored, not only the room, but my own inner man, to grapple the lost links. Curse it all, I could not plumb the depths!

It will be seen that I was becoming vexed, as one is always out of humour when one's grip slips in this way, and reveals the inadequacy, the imperfections, of one's spiritual powers. Yet I still hoped to recover the clue. A slender thread would suffice, for my memory is of a peculiar type, both good and bad; on the one hand stubbornly untrustworthy, and on the other incredibly dependable. It swallows the most important details, whether in concrete happenings or in faces, and no voluntary exertion will induce it to regurgitate them from the gulf. Yet the most trifling indication—a picture postcard, the address on an envelope, a newspaper cutting—will suffice to hook up what is wanted as an angler who has made a strike and successfully imbedded his hook reels in a lively, struggling, and reluctant fish. Then I can recall the features of a man seen once only, the shape of his mouth and the gap to the left where he had an upper eye-tooth knocked out, the falsetto tone of his laugh, and the twitching of the moustache when he chooses to be merry, the entire change of expression which hilarity effects in him. Not only do these physical traits rise before my mind's eye, but I remember, years afterwards, every word the man said to me, and the tenor of my replies. But if I am to see and feel the past thus vividly, there must be some material link to start the current of associations. My memory will not work satisfactorily on the abstract plane.

I closed my eyes to think more strenuously, in the attempt to forge the hook that would catch my fish. In vain! In vain! There was no hook, or the fish would not bite. So fierce waxed my irritation with the inefficient and mulish thinking apparatus between my temples that I could have struck myself a violent blow on the forehead, much as an irascible man will shake and kick a penny-in-the-slot machine which, when he has inserted his coin, refuses to render him his due.

So exasperated did I become at my failure that I could no longer sit quiet, but rose to prowl about the room. The instant I moved, the glow of awakening memory began. To the right of the cash-register, I recalled, there must be a doorway leading into a windowless room, where the only light was artificial. Yes, the place actually existed. The decorative scheme was different, but the proportions were unchanged. A square box of a place, behind the bar—the card-room. My nerves thrilled as I contemplated the furniture, for I was on the track, I had found the clue, and soon I should know all. There were two small billiard-tables, looking like silent ponds covered with green scum. In the corners, card-tables, at one of which two bearded men of professorial type were playing chess. Beside the iron stove, close to a door labelled "Telephone," was another small table. In a flash I had it! That was Mendel's place, Jacob Mendel's. That was where Mendel used to hang out, Buchmendel. I was in the Café Gluck! How could I have forgotten Jacob Mendel? Was it possible that I had not thought about him for ages, a man so peculiar as well-nigh to belong to the Land of Fable, the eighth wonder of the world, famous at the university and among a narrow circle of admirers, magician of book-fanciers, who had been wont to sit there from morning till night, an emblem of bookish lore, the glory of the Café Gluck? Why had I had so much difficulty in hooking my fish? How could I have forgotten Buchmendel?

I allowed my imagination to work. The man's face and form pictured themselves vividly before me. I saw him as he had been in the flesh, seated at the table with its grey marble top, on which books and manuscripts were piled. Motionless he sat, his spectacled eyes fixed upon the printed page. Yet not altogether motionless, for he had a habit (acquired at school in the Jewish quarter of the Galician town from which he came) of rocking his shiny bald pate backwards and forwards and humming to himself as he read. There he studied catalogues and tomes, crooning and rocking, as Jewish boys are taught to do when reading the Talmud. The rabbis believe that, just as a child is rocked to sleep in its cradle, so are the pious ideas of the holy text better instilled by this rhythmical and hypnotizing movement of head and body. In fact, as if he had been in a trance, Jacob Mendel

saw and heard nothing while thus occupied. He was oblivious
to the click of billiard-balls, the coming and going of waiters, the ringing of the telephone bell; he paid no heed when
the floor was scrubbed and when the stove was refilled. Once
a red-hot coal fell out of the latter, and the flooring began to
blaze a few inches from Mendel's feet; the room was full of
smoke, and one of the guests ran for a pail of water to extin-
guish the fire. But neither the smoke, the bustle, nor the
stench diverted his attention from the volume before him.
He read as others pray, as gamblers follow the spinning of
the roulette board, as drunkards stare into vacancy; he read
with such profound absorption that ever since I first watched
him the reading of ordinary mortals has seemed a pastime.
This Galician second-hand book dealer, Jacob Mendel, was
the first to reveal to me in my youth the mystery of absolute
concentration which characterizes the artist and the scholar,
the sage and the imbecile; the first to make me acquainted
with the tragical happiness and unhappiness of complete
absorption.

A senior student introduced me to him. I was studying the
life and doings of a man who is even today too little known,
Mesmer the magnetizer. My researches were bearing scant
fruit, for the books I could lay my hands on conveyed
sparse information, and when I applied to the university
librarian for help he told me, uncivilly, that it was not his
business to hunt up references for a freshman. Then my college friend suggested taking me to Mendel.

"He knows everything about books, and will tell you
where to find the information you want. The ablest man in
Vienna, and an original to boot. The man is a saurian of the
book-world, an antediluvian survivor of an extinct species."

We went, therefore, to the Café Gluck, and found Buchmendel in his usual place, bespectacled, bearded, wearing a
rusty black suit, and rocking as I have described. He did not
notice our intrusion, but went on reading, looking like a
nodding mandarin. On a hook behind him hung his ragged
black overcoat, the pockets of which bulged with manuscripts, catalogues, and books. My friend coughed loudly, to
attract his attention, but Mendel ignored the sign. At length

Schmidt rapped on the table-top, as if knocking at a door, and at this Mendel glanced up, mechanically pushed his spectacles on to his forehead, and from beneath his thick and untidy ashen-grey brows there glared at us two dark, alert little eyes. My friend introduced me, and I explained my quandary, being careful (as Schmidt had advised) to express great annoyance at the librarian's unwillingness to assist me. Mendel leaned back, laughed scornfully, and answered with a strong Galician accent:

"Unwillingness, you think? Incompetence, that's what's the matter with him. He's a jackass. I've known him (for my sins) twenty years at least, and he's learned nothing in the whole of that time. Pocket their wages—that's all such fellows can do. They should be mending the road, instead of sitting over books."

This outburst served to break the ice, and with a friendly wave of the hand the bookworm invited me to sit down at his table. I reiterated my object in consulting him; to get a list of all the early works on animal magnetism, and of contemporary and subsequent books and pamphlets for and against Mesmer. When I had said my say, Mendel closed his left eye for an instant, as if excluding a grain of dust. This was, with him, a sign of concentrated attention. Then, as though reading from an invisible catalogue, he reeled out the names of two or three dozen titles, giving in each case place and date of publication and approximate price. I was amazed, though Schmidt had warned me what to expect. His vanity was tickled by my surprise, for he went on to strum the keyboard of his marvellous memory, and to produce the most astounding bibliographical marginal notes. Did I want to know about sleepwalkers, Perkins's metallic tractors, early experiments in hypnotism, Braid, Gassner, attempts to conjure up the devil, Christian Science, theosophy, Madame Blavatsky? In connexion with each item there was a hailstorm of book-names, dates, and appropriate details. I was beginning to understand that Jacob Mendel was a living lexicon, something like the general catalogue of the British Museum Reading Room, but able to walk about on two legs. I stared dumbfounded at this bibliographical phe-

nomenon, which masqueraded in the sordid and rather unclean domino of a Galician second-hand book dealer, who,
after rattling off some eighty titles (with assumed indiffer-
ence, but really with the satisfaction of one who plays an
unexpected trump), proceeded to wipe his spectacles with a
handkerchief which might long before have been white.

Hoping to conceal my astonishment, I inquired:

"Which among these works do you think you could get
for me without too much trouble?"

"Oh, I'll have a look round," he answered. "Come here
tomorrow and I shall certainly have some of them. As for
the others, it's only a question of time, and of knowing
where to look."

"I'm greatly obliged to you," I said; and then, wishing to
be civil, I put my foot in it, proposing to give him a list of
the books I wanted. Schmidt nudged me warningly, but too
late. Mendel had already flashed a look at me—such a look,
at once triumphant and affronted, scornful and overwhelm-
ingly superior—the royal look with which Macbeth answers
Macduff when summoned to yield without a blow. He
laughed curtly. His Adam's apple moved excitedly. Obviously he had gulped down a choleric and insulting epithet.

Indeed he had good reason to be angry. Only a stranger,
an ignoramus, could have proposed to give him, Jacob Mendel, a memorandum, as if he had been a bookseller's assistant or an underling in a public library. Not until I knew
him better did I fully understand how much my would-be
politeness must have galled this aberrant genius—for the
man had, and knew himself to have, a titanic memory,
wherein, behind a dirty and undistinguished-looking forehead, was indelibly recorded a picture of the title-page of
every book that had been printed. No matter whether it had
issued from the press yesterday, or hundreds of years ago,
he knew its place of publication, its author's name, and its
price. From his mind, as if from the printed page, he could
read off the contents, could reproduce the illustrations;
could visualize, not only what he had actually held in his
hands, but also what he had glanced at in a bookseller's
window; could see it with the same vividness as an artist

sees the creations of fancy which he has not yet reproduced upon canvas. When a book was offered for six marks by a Regensburg dealer, he could remember that, two years before, a copy of the same work had changed hands for four crowns at a Viennese auction, and he recalled the name of the purchaser. In a word, Jacob Mendel never forgot a title or a figure; he knew every plant, every infusorian, every star, in the continually revolving and incessantly changing cosmos of the book-universe. In each literary specialty, he knew more than the specialists; he knew the contents of the libraries better than the librarians; he knew the book-lists of most publishers better than the heads of the firms concerned—though he had nothing to guide him except the magical powers of his inexplicable but invariably accurate memory.

True, this memory owed its infallibility to the man's limitations, to his extraordinary power of concentration. Apart from books, he knew nothing of the world. The phenomena of existence did not begin to become real for him until they had been set in type, arranged upon a composing stick, collected and, so to say, sterilized in a book. Nor did he read books for their meaning, to extract their spiritual or narrative substance. What aroused his passionate interest, what fixed his attention, was the name, the price, the format, the title-page. Though in the last analysis unproductive and uncreative, this specifically antiquarian memory of Jacob Mendel, since it was not a printed book-catalogue but was stamped upon the grey matter of a mammalian brain, was, in its unique perfection, no less remarkable a phenomenon than Napoleon's gift for physiognomy, Mezzofanti's talent for languages, Lasker's skill at chess-openings, Busoni's musical genius. Given a public position as teacher, this man with so marvellous a brain might have taught thousands and hundreds of thousands of students, have trained others to become men of great learning and of incalculable value to those communal treasure-houses we call libraries. But to him, a man of no account, a Galician Jew, a book-pedlar whose only training had been received in a Talmudic school, this upper world of culture was a fenced precinct he could never enter; and his amazing faculties could only find application at the marble-topped table in the inner room of the Café Gluck. When, some day, there arises a great psychologist who shall classify the type of that magical power we term memory as effectively as Buffon classified the genera and species of animals, a man competent to give a detailed description of all the varieties, he will have to find a pigeon-hole for Jacob Mendel, forgotten master of the lore of book-prices and book-titles, the ambulatory catalogue alike of incunabula and the modern commonplace.

In the book-trade and among ordinary persons, Jacob Mendel was regarded as nothing more than a second-hand book-dealer in a small way of business. Sunday after Sunday, his stereotyped advertisement appeared in the "Neue Freie Presse" and the "Neues Wiener Tagblatt." It ran as follows: "Best prices paid for old books, Mendel, Obere Alserstrasse." A telephone number followed, really that of the Café Gluck. He rummaged every available corner for his wares, and once a week, with the aid of a bearded porter, conveyed fresh booty to his headquarters and got rid of old stock—for he had no proper bookshop. Thus he remained a petty trader, and his business was not lucrative. Students sold him their textbooks, which year by year passed through his hands from one "generation" to another; and for a small percentage on the price he would procure any additional book that was wanted. He charged little or nothing for advice. Money seemed to have no standing in his world. No one had ever seen him better dressed than in the threadbare black coat. For breakfast and supper he had a glass of milk and a couple of rolls, while at midday a modest meal was brought him from a neighbouring restaurant. He did not smoke; he did not play cards; one might almost say he did not live, were it not that his eyes were alive behind his spectacles, and unceasingly fed his enigmatic brain with words, titles, names. The brain, like a fertile pasture, greedily sucked in this abundant irrigation. Human beings did not interest him, and of all human passions perhaps one only moved him, the most universal—vanity.

When someone, wearied by a futile hunt in countless

other places, applied to him for information, and was instantly put on the track, his self-gratification was overwhelming; and it was unquestionably a delight to him that in Vienna and elsewhere there existed a few dozen persons who respected him for his knowledge and valued him for the services he could render. In every one of these monstrous aggregates we call towns, there are here and there facets which reflect one and the same universe in miniature —unseen by most, but highly prized by connoisseurs, by brethren of the same craft, by devotees of the same passion. The fans of the book-market knew Jacob Mendel. Just as anyone encountering a difficulty in deciphering a score would apply to Eusebius Mandyczewski of the Musical Society, who would be found wearing a grey skull-cap and seated among multifarious musical MSS, ready, with a friendly smile, to solve the most obstinate crux; and just as, today, anyone in search of information about the Viennese theatrical and cultural life of earlier times will unhesitatingly look up the polyhistor Father Glossy; so, with equal confidence did the bibliophiles of Vienna, when they had a particularly hard nut to crack, make a pilgrimage to the Café Gluck and lay their difficulty before Jacob Mendel.

To me, young and eager for new experiences, it became enthralling to watch such a consultation. Whereas ordinarily, when a would-be seller brought him some ordinary book, he would contemptuously clap the cover to and mutter, "Two crowns"; if shown a rare or unique volume, he would sit up and take notice, lay the treasure upon a clean sheet of paper; and, on one such occasion, he was obviously ashamed of his dirty, ink-stained fingers and mourning finger-nails. Tenderly, cautiously, respectfully, he would turn the pages of the treasure. One would have been as loath to disturb him at such a moment as to break in upon the devotions of a man at prayer; and in very truth there was a flavour of solemn ritual and religious observance about the way in which contemplation, palpation, smelling and weighing in the hand followed one another in orderly succession. His rounded back waggled while he was thus engaged, he muttered to himself, exclaimed "Ah" now and again to express wonder or admiration, or "Oh, dear" when a page was missing or another had been mutilated by the larva of a book-beetle. His weighing of the tome in his hand was as circumspect as if books were sold by the ounce, and his snuffling at it as sentimental as a girl's smelling of a rose. Of course it would have been the height of bad form for the owner to show impatience during this ritual of examination.

When it was over, he willingly, nay, enthusiastically, tendered all the information at his disposal, not forgetting relevant anecdotes, and dramatized accounts of the prices which other specimens of the same work had fetched at auctions or in sales by private treaty. He looked brighter, younger, more lively at such times, and only one thing could put him seriously out of humour. This was when a novice offered him money for his expert opinion. Then he would draw back with an affronted air, looking for all the world like the skilled custodian of a museum gallery to whom an American traveller has offered a tip—for to Jacob Mendel contact with a rare book was something sacred, as is contact with a woman to a young man who has not had the bloom rubbed off. Such moments were his platonic love-nights. Books exerted a spell on him, never money. Vainly, therefore, did great collectors (among them one of the notables of Princeton University) try to recruit Mendel as buyer or librarian. The offer was declined with thanks. He could not forsake his familiar headquarters at the Café Gluck. Thirty-three years before, an awkward youngster with black down sprouting on his chin and black ringlets hanging over his temples, he had come from Galicia to Vienna, intending to adopt the calling of rabbi; but ere long he forsook the worship of the harsh and jealous Jehovah to devote himself to the more lively and polytheistic cult of books. Then he happened upon the Café Gluck, by degrees making it his workshop, headquarters, post-office—his world. Just as an astronomer, alone in an observatory, watches night after night through a telescope the myriads of stars, their mysterious movements, their changeful medley, their extinction and their flaming-up anew, so did Jacob Mendel, seated at his table in the Café Gluck, look through his spectacles into the universe of books, a universe that lies above the world of our everyday life, and, like the stellar universe, is full of changing cycles.

It need hardly be said that he was highly esteemed in the Café Gluck, whose fame seemed to us to depend far more upon his unofficial professorship than upon the godfathership of the famous musician, Christoph Willibald Gluck, composer of *Alcestis* and *Iphigenia*. He belonged to the outfit quite as much as did the old cherrywood counter, the two billiard-tables with their cloth stitched in many places, and the copper coffee-urn. His table was guarded as a sanctuary. His numerous clients and customers were expected to take a drink "for the good of the house," so that most of the profit of his far-flung knowledge flowed into the big leathern pouch slung round the waist of Deubler, the waiter. In return for being a centre of attraction, Mendel enjoyed many privileges. The telephone was at his service for nothing. He could have his letters directed to the café, and his parcels were taken in there. The excellent old woman who looked after the toilet brushed his coat, sewed on buttons, and carried a small bundle of underlinen every week to the wash. He was the only guest who could have a meal sent in from the restaurant; and every morning Herr Standhartner, the proprietor of the café, made a point of coming to his table and saying, "Good morning!"—though Jacob Mendel, immersed in his books, seldom noticed the greeting. Punctually at half-past seven he arrived, and did not leave till the lights were extinguished. He never spoke to the other guests, never read a newspaper, noticed no changes; and once, when Herr Standhartner civilly asked him whether he did not find the electric light more agreeable to read by than the malodorous and uncertain kerosene lamps they had replaced, he stared in astonishment at the new incandescents. Although the installation had necessitated several days' hammering and bustle, the introduction of the glow-lamps had escaped his notice. Only through the two round apertures of the spectacles, only through these two shining and sucking lenses, did the milliards of black infusorians which were the letters filter into his brain. What-

ever else happened in his vicinity was disregarded as un-
meaning noise. He had spent more than thirty years of his
waking life at this table, reading, comparing, calculating, in
a continuous waking dream, interrupted only by intervals
of sleep.

A sense of horror overcame me when, looking into the
inner room behind the bar at the Café Gluck, I saw that
the marble-top of the table where Jacob Mendel used to
deliver his oracles was now as bare as a tombstone. Grown
older since those days, I understood how much disappears
when such a man drops out of his place in the world, were
it only because amid the daily increase in hopeless monot-
ony, the unique grows continually more precious. Besides,
in my callow youth a profound intuition had made me ex-
ceedingly fond of Buchmendel. It was through the observation of him that I had first become aware of the enigmatic
fact that supreme achievement and outstanding capacity are
only rendered possible by mental concentration, by a su-
blime monomania that verges on lunacy. Through the
living example of this obscure genius of a second-hand book
dealer, far more than through the flashes of insight in the
works of our poets and other imaginative writers, had been
made plain to me the persistent possibility of a pure life of
the spirit, of complete absorption in an idea, an ecstasy as
absolute as that of an Indian yogi or a medieval monk; and
I had learned that this was possible in an electric-lighted
café and adjoining a telephone box. Yet I had forgotten
him, during the war years, and through a kindred immersion
in my own work. The sight of the empty table made me
ashamed of myself, and at the same time curious about the
man who used to sit there.

What had become of him? I called the waiter and inquired.

"No, Sir," he answered. "I'm sorry, but I never heard of
Herr Mendel. There is no one of that name among the fre-
quenters of the Café Gluck. Perhaps the head-waiter will
know."

"Herr Mendel?" said the head-waiter, dubiously, after a
moment's reflection. "No, Sir, never heard of him. Unless

you mean Herr Mandl, who has a hardware store in the Florianigasse?"

I had a bitter taste in the mouth, the taste of an irrecoverable past. What is the use of living, when the wind obliterates our footsteps in the sand directly we have gone by? Thirty years, perhaps forty, a man had breathed, read, thought, and spoken within this narrow room; three or four years had elapsed, and there had arisen a new king over Egypt, which knew not Joseph. No one in the Café Gluck had ever heard of Jacob Mendel, of Buchmendel. Somewhat pettishly I asked the head-waiter whether I could have a word with Herr Standhartner, or with one of the old staff.

"Herr Standhartner, who used to own the place? He sold it years ago, and has died since. . . . The former head-waiter? He saved up enough to retire, and lives upon a little property at Krems. No, Sir, all of the old lot are scattered. All except one, indeed, Frau Sporschil, who looks after the toilet. She's been here for ages, worked under the late owner, I know. But she's not likely to remember your Herr Mendel. Such as she hardly know one guest from another."

I dissented in thought.

"One does not forget a Jacob Mendel so easily!"

What I said was:

"Still I should like to have a word with Frau Sporschil, if she has a moment to spare."

The "Toilettenfrau" (known in the Viennese vernacular as the "Schocoladefrau") soon emerged from the basement, white-haired, run to seed, heavy-footed, wiping her chapped hands upon a towel as she came. She had been called away from her task of cleaning up, and was obviously uneasy at being summoned into the strong light of the guest-rooms—for common folk in Vienna, where an authoritative tradition has lingered on after the revolution, always think it must be a police matter when their "superiors" want to question them. She eyed me suspiciously, though humbly. But as soon as I asked her about Jacob Mendel, she braced up, and at the same time her eyes filled with tears.

"Poor Herr Mendel . . . so there's still someone who bears him in mind?"

Old people are commonly much moved by anything which recalls the days of their youth and revives the memory of past companionships. I asked if he was still alive.

"Good Lord, no. Poor Herr Mendel must have died five or six years ago. Indeed, I think it's fully seven since he passed away. Dear, good man that he was; and how long I knew him, more than twenty-five years; he was already sitting every day at his table when I began to work here. It was a shame, it was, the way they let him die."

Growing more and more excited, she asked if I was a relative. No one had ever inquired about him before. Didn't I know what had happened to him?

"No," I replied, "and I want you to be good enough to tell me all about it."

She looked at me timidly, and continued to wipe her damp hands. It was plain to me that she found it embarrassing, with her dirty apron and her tousled white hair, to be standing in the full glare of the café. She kept looking round anxiously, to see if one of the waiters might be listening.

"Let's go into the card-room," I said. "Mendel's old room. You shall tell me your story there."

She nodded appreciatively, thankful that I understood and led the way to the inner room, a little shambling in her gait. As I followed, I noticed that the waiters and the guests were staring at us as a strangely assorted pair. We sat down opposite one another at the marble-topped table, and there she told me the story of Jacob Mendel's ruin and death. I will give the tale as nearly as may be in her own words, supplemented here and there by what I learned afterwards from other sources.

"Down to the outbreak of war, and after the war had begun, he continued to come here every morning at half-past seven, to sit at this table and study all day just as before. We had the feeling that the fact of a war going on had never entered his mind. Certainly he didn't read the newspapers, and didn't talk to anyone except about books. He paid no attention when (in the early days of the war, before the authorities put a stop to such things) the newspaper-vendors ran through the streets shouting, 'Great Battle on the East-

ern Front' (or wherever it might be), 'Horrible Slaughter,'
and so on; when people gathered in knots to talk things
over, he kept himself to himself; he did not know that Fritz,
the billiard-marker, who fell in one of the first battles, had
vanished from this place; he did not know that Herr Standhartner's son had been taken prisoner by the Russians at
Przemysl; never said a word when the bread grew more
and more uneatable and when he was given bean-coffee to
drink at breakfast and supper instead of hot milk. Once
only did he express surprise at the changes, wondering why
so few students came to the café. There was nothing in the
world that mattered to him except his books.

"Then disaster befell him. At eleven one morning, two
policemen came, one in uniform, and the other a plain-
clothes man. The latter showed the red rosette under the
lapel of his coat and asked whether there was a man named
Jacob Mendel in the house. They went straight to Herr
Mendel's table. The poor man, in his innocence, supposed
they had books to sell, or wanted some information; but
they told him he was under arrest, and took him away at
once. It was a scandal for the café. All the guests flocked
round Herr Mendel, as he stood between the two police
officers, his spectacles pushed up under his hair, staring
from each to the other bewildered. Some ventured a protest, saying there must be a mistake—that Herr Mendel was a
man who wouldn't hurt a fly; but the detective was furious
and told them to mind their own business. They took him
away, and none of us at the Café Gluck saw him again for
two years. I never found out what they had against him,
but I would take my dying oath that they must have made a
mistake. Herr Mendel could never have done anything
wrong. It was a crime to treat an innocent man so harshly."

The excellent Frau Sporschil was right. Our friend Jacob
Mendel had done nothing wrong. He had merely (as I sub-
sequently learned) done something incredibly stupid, only
explicable to those who knew the man's peculiarities. The
military censorship board, whose function it was to super-
vise correspondence passing into and out of neutral lands,
one day got its clutches upon a postcard written and signed

by a certain Jacob Mendel, properly stamped for transmission abroad. This postcard was addressed to Monsieur Jean Labourdaire, Libraire, Quai de Grenelle, Paris—to an enemy country, therefore. The writer complained that the last eight issues of the monthly "Bulletin bibliographique de la France" had failed to reach him, although his annual subscription had been duly paid in advance. The jack-in-office who read this missive (a high-school teacher with a bent for the study of the Romance languages, called up for "war-service" and sent to employ his talents at the censorship board instead of wasting them in the trenches) was astonished by its tenor. "Must be a joke," he thought. He had to examine some two thousand letters and postcards every week, always on the alert to detect anything that might savour of espionage, but never yet had he chanced upon anything so absurd as that an Austrian subject should unconcernedly drop into one of the imperial and royal letterboxes a postcard addressed to someone in an enemy land, regardless of the trifling detail that since August 1914 the Central Powers had been cut off from Russia on one side and from France on the other by barbed-wire entanglements and a network of ditches in which men armed with rifles and bayonets, machine-guns and artillery, were doing their utmost to exterminate one another like rats. Our schoolmaster enrolled in the Landsturm did not treat this first postcard seriously, but pigeon-holed it as a curiosity not worth talking about to his chief. But a few weeks later there turned up another card, again from Jacob Mendel, this time to John Aldridge, Bookseller, Golden Square, London, asking whether the addressee could send the last few numbers of the "Antiquarian" to an address in Vienna which was clearly stated on the card.

The censor in the blue uniform began to feel uneasy. Was his "class" trying to trick the schoolmaster? Were the cards written in cipher? Possible, anyhow; so the subordinate went over to the major's desk, clicked his heels together, saluted, and laid the suspicious documents before "properly constituted authority." A strange business, certainly. The police were instructed by telephone to see if there actually was a

Jacob Mendel at the specified address, and, if so, to bring the fellow along. Within the hour, Mendel had been arrested, and (still stupefied by the shock) brought before the major, who showed him the postcards and asked him with drill-sergeant roughness whether he acknowledged their authorship. Angered at being spoken to so sharply, and still more annoyed because his perusal of an important catalogue had been interrupted, Mendel answered tartly:

"Of course I wrote the cards. That's my handwriting and signature. Surely one has a right to claim the delivery of a periodical to which one has subscribed?"

The major swung half-round in his swivel-chair and exchanged a meaning glance with the lieutenant seated at the adjoining desk.

"The man must be a double-distilled idiot," was what they mutely conveyed to one another.

Then the chief took counsel within himself whether he should discharge the offender with a caution, or whether he should treat the case more seriously. In all offices, when such doubts arise, the usual practice is, not to spin a coin, but to send in a report. Thus Pilate washes his hands of responsibility. Even if the report does no good, it can do no harm, and is merely one useless manuscript or typescript added to a million others.

In this instance, however, the decision to send in a report did much harm, alas, to an inoffensive man of genius, for it involved asking a series of questions, and the third of them brought suspicious circumstances to light.

"Your full name?"

"Jacob Mendel."

"Occupation?"

"Book-pedlar" (for, as already explained, Mendel had no shop, but only a pedlar's license).

"Place of birth?"

Now came the disaster. Mendel's birthplace was not far from Petrikau. The major raised his eyebrows. Petrikau, or Piotrkov, was across the frontier, in Russian Poland.

"You were born a Russian subject. When did you acquire Austrian nationality? Show me your papers."

"Papers? Identification papers? I have nothing but my hawker's license."

"What's your nationality, then? Was your father Austrian or Russian?"

Undismayed, Mendel answered:

"A Russian, of course."

"What about yourself?"

"Wishing to evade Russian military service, I slipped across the frontier thirty-three years ago, and ever since I have lived in Vienna."

The matter seemed to the major to be growing worse and worse.

"But didn't you take steps to become an Austrian subject?"

"Why should I?" countered Mendel. "I never troubled my head about such things."

"Then you are still a Russian subject?"

Mendel, who was bored by this endless questioning, answered simply:

"Yes, I suppose I am."

The startled and indignant major threw himself back in his chair with such violence that the wood cracked protestingly. So this was what it had come to! In Vienna, the Austrian capital, at the end of 1915, after Tarnow, when the war was in full blast, after the great offensive, a Russian could walk about unmolested, could write letters to France and England, while the police ignored his machinations. And then the fools who wrote in the newspapers wondered why Conrad von Hotzendorf had not advanced in seven-leagued boots to Warsaw, and the general staff was puzzled because every movement of the troops was immediately blabbed to the Russians.

The lieutenant had sprung to his feet and crossed the room to his chief's table. What had been an almost friendly conversation took a new turn, and degenerated into a trial.

"Why didn't you report as an enemy alien directly the war began?"

Mendel, still failing to realize the gravity of his position, answered in his singing Jewish jargon:

"Why should I report? I don't understand."

The major regarded this inquiry as a challenge, and asked threateningly:

"Didn't you read the notices that were posted up everywhere?"

"No."

"Didn't you read the newspapers?"

"No."

The two officers stared at Jacob Mendel (now sweating with uneasiness) as if the moon had fallen from the sky into their office. Then the telephone buzzed, the typewriters clacked, orderlies ran hither and thither, and Mendel was sent under guard to the nearest barracks, where he was to await transfer to a concentration camp. When he was ordered to follow the two soldiers, he was frankly puzzled, but not seriously perturbed. What could the man with the gold-lace collar and the rough voice have against him? In the upper world of books, where Mendel lived and breathed and had his being, there was no warfare, there were no misunderstandings, only an ever-increasing knowledge of words and figures, of book-titles and authors' names. He walked good-humouredly enough downstairs between the soldiers, whose first charge was to take him to the police station. Not until, there, the books were taken out of his overcoat pockets, and the police impounded the portfolio containing a hundred important memoranda and customers' addresses, did he lose his temper, and begin to resist and strike blows. They had to tie his hands. In the struggle, his spectacles fell off, and these magical telescopes, without which he could not see into the wonderworld of books, were smashed into a thousand pieces. Two days later, insufficiently clad (for his only wrap was a light summer cloak), he was sent to the internment camp for Russian civilians at Komorn.

I have no information as to what Jacob Mendel suffered during these two years of internment, cut off from his beloved books, penniless, among roughly nurtured men, few of whom could read or write, in a huge human dunghill. This must be left to the imagination of those who can grasp the torments of a caged eagle. By degrees, however, our world, grown sober after its fit of drunkenness, has become aware that, of all the cruelties and wanton abuses of power during the war, the most needless and therefore the most inexcusable was this herding together behind barbed-wire fences of thousands upon thousands of persons who had outgrown the age of military service, who had made homes for themselves in a foreign land, and who (believing in the good faith of their hosts) had refrained from exercising the sacred right of hospitality granted even by the Tunguses and Araucanians—the right to flee while time permits. This crime against civilization was committed with the same un-thinking hardihood in France, Germany and Britain, in every belligerent country of our crazy Europe.

Probably Jacob Mendel would, like thousands as innocent as he, have perished in this cattle-pen, have gone stark mad, have succumbed to dysentery, asthenia, softening of the brain, had it not been that before the worst happened, a chance (typically Austrian) recalled him to the world in which a spiritual life became again possible. Several times after his disappearance, letters from distinguished customers were delivered for him at the Café Gluck. Count Schönberg, sometime lord-lieutenant of Styria, an enthusiastic collector of works on heraldry; Siegenfeld, the former dean of the theological faculty, who was writing a commentary on the works of St. Augustine; Edler von Pisek, an octogenarian admiral on the retired list, engaged in writing his memoirs—these and other persons of note, wanting information from Buchmendel, had repeatedly addressed communications to him at his familiar haunt, and some of these were duly forwarded to the concentration camp at Komorn. There they fell into the hands of the commanding officer, who happened to be a man of humane disposition, and was astonished to find what notables were among the correspondents of this dirty little Russian Jew, who, half-blind now that his spectacles were broken and he had no money to buy new ones, crouched in a corner like a mole, grey, eyeless, and dumb. A man who had such patrons must be a person of importance, whatever he looked like. The C.O. therefore read the letters to the short-sighted Mendel, and penned answers for him to sign—answers which were mainly requests that influence should be exercised on his behalf. The spell worked, for these correspondents had the solidarity of collectors. Joining forces and pulling strings they were able (giving guarantees for the "enemy alien's" good behaviour) to secure leave for Buchmendel's return to Vienna in 1917, after more than two years at Komorn— on the condition that he should report daily to the police. The proviso mattered little. He was a free man once more, free to take up his quarters in his old attic, free to handle books again, free (above all) to return to his table in the Café Gluck. I can describe the return from the underworld of the camp in the good Frau Sporschil's own words:

"One day—Jesus, Mary, Joseph, I could hardly believe my eyes—the door opened (you remember the way he had) little wider than a crack, and through this opening he sidled, poor Herr Mendel. He was wearing a tattered and much-darned military cloak, and his head was covered by what had perhaps once been a hat thrown away by the owner as past use. No collar. His face looked like a death's head, so haggard it was, and his hair was pitifully thin. But he came in as if nothing had happened, went straight to his table, and took off his cloak, not briskly as of old, for he panted with the exertion. Nor had he any books with him. He just sat there without a word, staring straight in front of him with hollow, expresionless eyes. Only by degrees, after we had brought him the big bundle of printed matter which had arrived for him from Germany, did he begin to read again. But he was never the same man."

No, he was never the same man, not now the miraculum mundi, the magical walking book-catalogue. All who saw him in those days told me the same pitiful story. Something had gone irrecoverably wrong he was broken, the blood-red comet of the war had burst into the remote, calm atmosphere of his bookish world. His eyes, accustomed for decades to look at nothing but print, must have seen terrible sights in the wire-fenced human stockyard, for the eyes that had formerly been so alert and full of ironical gleams were now almost completely veiled by the inert lids, and looked sleepy and red-bordered behind the carefully repaired spec-tacle-frames. Worse still, a cog must have broken somewhere in the marvellous machinery of his memory, so that the working of the whole was impaired; for so delicate is the structure of the brain (a sort of switchboard made of the most fragile substances, and as easily jarred as are all instru-ments of precision) that a blocked arteriole, a congested bundle of nerve-fibres, a fatigued group of cells, even a displaced molecule, may put the apparatus out of gear and make harmonious working impossible. In Mendel's mem-ory, the keyboard of knowledge, the keys were stiff, or—to use psychological terminology—the associations were im-paired. When, now and again, someone came to ask for information, Jacob stared blankly at the inquirer, failing to understand the question, and even forgetting it before he had found the answer. Mendel was no longer Buchmendel, just as the world was no longer the world. He could not now become wholly absorbed in his reading, did not rock as of old when he read, but sat bolt upright, his glasses turned mechanically towards the printed page, but perhaps not read-ing at all, and only sunk in a reverie. Often, said Frau Sporschil, his head would drop on to his book and he would fall asleep in the daytime, or he would gaze hour after hour at the stinking acetylene lamp which (in the days of the coal famine) had replaced the electric lighting. No, Mendel was no longer Buchmendel, no longer the eighth wonder of the world, but a weary, worn-out, though still breathing, useless bundle of beard and ragged garments, which sat, as futile as a potato-bogle, where of old the Pythian oracle had sat; no longer the glory of the Café Gluck, but a shameful scare-crow, evil-smelling, a parasite.

That was the impression he produced upon the new pro-prietor, Florian Gurtner from Retz, who (a successful profiteer in flour and butter) had cajoled Standhartner into selling him the Café Gluck for eighty thousand rapidly depreciating paper crowns. He took everything into his hard peasant grip, hastily arranged to have the old place redec-orated, bought fine-looking satin-covered seats, installed a marble porch, and was in negotiation with his next-door neighbor to buy a place where he could extend the café into a dancing hall. Naturally while he was making these embellishments, he was not best pleased by the parasitic encumbrance of Jacob Mendel, a filthy old Galician Jew, who had been in trouble with the authorities during the war, was still to be regarded as an "enemy alien," and, while occupying a table from morning till night, consumed no more than two cups of coffee and four or five rolls. Standhartner, indeed, had put in a word for this guest of long standing, had explained that Mendel was a person of note, and, in the stock-taking, had handed him over as having a permanent lien upon the establishment, but as an asset rather than a liability. Florian Gurtner, however, had brought into the café, not only new furniture, and an up-to-date cash register, but also the profit-making and hard temper of the post-war era, and awaited the first pretext for ejecting from his smart coffee-house the last troublesome vestige of suburban shabbiness.

The good excuse was not slow to present itself. Jacob Mendel was impoverished to the last degree. Such banknotes as had been left to him had crumbled away to nothing during the inflation period; his regular clientele had been killed, ruined, or dispersed. When he tried to resume his early trade of book-pedlar, calling from door to door to buy and to sell, he found that he lacked strength to carry books up and down stairs. A hundred little signs showed him to be a pauper. Seldom, now, did he have a midday meal sent in from the restaurant, and he began to run up a score at the Café Gluck for his modest breakfast and supper. Once his payments were as much as three weeks overdue. Were it only for this reason, the head-waiter wanted Gurtner to "give Mendel the sack." But Frau Sporschil intervened, and stood surety for the debtor. What was due could be stopped out of her wages!

This staved off disaster for a while, but worse was to come. For some time the head-waiter had noticed that rolls were disappearing faster than the tally would account for. Naturally suspicion fell upon Mendel, who was known to be six months in debt to the tottering old porter whose services he still needed. The head-waiter, hidden behind the stove, was able, two days later, to catch Mendel red-handed. The unwelcome guest had stolen from his seat in the card-room, crept behind the counter in the front room, taken two rolls from the bread-basket, returned to the card-room, and hungrily devoured them. When settling-up at the end of the day, he said he had only had coffee; no rolls. The source of wastage had been traced, and the waiter reported his discovery to the proprietor. Herr Gurtner, delighted to have so good an excuse for getting rid of Mendel, made a scene, openly accused him of theft, and declared that nothing but the goodness of his own heart prevented his sending for the police.

"But after this," said Florian, "you'll kindly take yourself off for good and all. We don't want to see your face again at the Café Gluck."

Jacob Mendel trembled, but made no reply. Abandoning his poor belongings, he departed without a word.

"It was ghastly," said Frau Sporschil. "Never shall I forget the sight. He stood up, his spectacles pushed on to his forehead, and his face white as a sheet. He did not even stop to put on his cloak, although it was January, and very cold. You'll remember that severe winter, just after the war. In his fright, he left the book he was reading open upon the table. I did not notice it at first, and then, when I wanted to pick it up and take it after him, he had already stumbled out through the doorway. I was afraid to follow him into the street, for Herr Gurtner was standing at the door and shouting at him, so that a crowd had gathered. Yet I felt ashamed to the depths of my soul. Such a thing would never have happened under the old master. Herr Standhartner would not have driven Herr Mendel away for pinching one or two rolls when he was hungry, but would have let him have as many as he wanted for nothing, to the end of his days. Since the war, people seem to have grown heartless. Drive away a man who had been a guest daily for so many, many years. Shameful! I should not like to have to answer before God for such cruelty!"

The good woman had grown excited, and, with the pas-

180 STEFAN ZWEIG

sionate garrulousness of old age, she kept on repeating how
shameful it was, and that nothing of the sort would have
happened if Herr Standhartner had not sold the business. In
the end I tried to stop the flow by asking her what had happened to Mendel, and whether she had ever seen him again.
These questions excited her yet more.

"Day after day, when I passed his table, it gave me the
creeps, as you will easily understand. Each time I thought
to myself: 'Where can he have got to, poor Herr Mendel?'
Had I known where he lived, I would have called and taken
him something nice and hot to eat—for where could he get
the money to cook food and warm his room? As far as I
knew, he had no kinsfolk in the wide world. When, after a
long time, I had heard nothing about him, I began to believe that it must be all up with him, and that I should never
see him again. I had made up my mind to have a mass said
for the peace of his soul, knowing him to be a good man,
after twenty-five years' acquaintance.

"At length one day in February, at half-past seven in the
morning, when I was cleaning the windows, the door
opened, and in came Herr Mendel. Generally, as you know,
he sidled in, looking confused, and not 'quite all there'; but
this time, somehow, it was different. I noticed at once the
strange look in his eyes; they were sparkling, and he rolled
them this way and that, as if to see everything at once; as
for his appearance, he seemed nothing but beard and skin
and bone. Instantly it crossed my mind: 'He's forgotten all
that happened last time he was here; it's his way to go about
like a sleepwalker noticing nothing; he doesn't remember
about the rolls, and how shamefully Herr Gurtner ordered
him out of the place, half in mind to set the police on him.'
Thank goodness, Herr Gurtner hadn't come yet, and the
head-waiter was drinking coffee. I ran up to Herr Mendel,
meaning to tell him he'd better make himself scarce, for
otherwise that ruffian" (she looked round timidly to see if
we were overheard, and hastily amended her phrase), "Herr
Gurtner, I mean, would only have him thrown into the
street once more. 'Herr Mendel,' I began. He started, and
looked at me. In that very moment (it was dreadful), he

must have remembered the whole thing, for he almost collapsed, and began to tremble, not his fingers only, but to shiver and shake from head to foot. Hastily he stepped back into the street, and fell in a heap on the pavement as soon as he was outside the door. We telephoned for the ambulance and they carried him off to hospital, the nurse who came saying he had high fever directly she touched him. He died that evening. 'Double pneumonia,' the doctor said, and that he never recovered consciousness—could not have been fully conscious when he came to the Café Gluck. As I said, he had entered like a man walking in his sleep. The table where he had sat day after day for thirty-six years drew him back to it like a home."

Frau Sporschil and I went on talking about him for a long time, the two last persons to remember this strange creature, Buchmendel: I to whom in youth the book-pedlar from Galicia had given the first revelation of a life wholly devoted to the things of the spirit; she, the poor old woman who was caretaker of a café-toilet, who had never read a book in her life, and whose only tie with this strangely matched comrade in her subordinate, poverty-stricken world had been that for twenty-five years she had brushed his overcoat and had sewn on buttons for him. We, too, might have been considered strangely assorted, but Frau Sporschil and I got on very well together, linked, as we sat at the forsaken marble-topped table, by our common memories of the shade our talk had conjured up—for joint memories and, above all, loving memories, always establish a tie. Suddenly, while in the full stream of talk, she exclaimed:

"Lord Jesus, how forgetful I am. I still have the book he left on the table the evening Herr Gurtner gave him the key of the street. I didn't know where to take it. Afterwards, when no one appeared to claim it, I ventured to keep it as a souvenir. You don't think it wrong of me, Sir?"

She went to a locker where she stored some of the requisites for her job, and produced the volume for my inspection. I found it hard to repress a smile, for I was face to face with one of life's little ironies. It was the second volume of Hayn's *Bibliotheca Germanorum erotica et curiosa,* a compendium of gallant literature known to every book-collector. "Habent sua fata libelli!" This scabrous publication, as legacy of the vanished magician, had fallen into toil-worn hands which had perhaps never held any other printed work than a prayer-book. Maybe I was not wholly successful in controlling my mirth, for the expression of my face seemed to perplex the worthy soul, and once more she said:

"You don't think it wrong of me to keep it, Sir?"

I shook her cordially by the hand.

"Keep it, and welcome," I said. "I am absolutely sure that our old friend Mendel would be only too delighted to know that someone among the many thousand he has provided with books, cherishes his memory."

Then I took my departure, feeling a trifle ashamed when I compared myself with this excellent old woman, who, so simply and so humanely, had fostered the memory of the dead scholar. For she, uncultured though she was, had at least preserved a book as a memento; whereas I, a man of education and a writer, had completely forgotten Buchmendel for years—I, who at least should have known that one only makes books in order to keep in touch with one's fellows after one has ceased to breathe, and thus to defend oneself against the inexorable fate of all that lives—transitoriness and oblivion.

JOSEPH OPATOSHU

Joseph Opatoshu, born in Poland in 1887, received a
Jewish education and also attended a commercial
school in Warsaw. He came to America in 1907, worked
in a factory and taught Hebrew in New York City. He
attended Cooper Union at night and graduated with
the degree of Civil Engineer. A novelist and short story
writer, he became an important figure in the Yiddish
literary world. His best known book is *In Polish Woods*.

Horse Thief

1

Morning. . . . Tirzeh cooked some schav, beat several eggs
into it, boiled a pot of potatoes and put the food on the
table to cool. She sat down and lost herself in thought:
"Solomon ought to be back from prayers soon. Guess it's
about time to wake Zanvl. Runs around night after night,
God only knows where."

Tirzeh looked at Zanvl, who was sleeping near the door,
his mop of hair sprawling over his gleaming forehead.

"Some young one I've raised! Strong as a bull. With such
a son another mother would be delighted. And I? This very
day—God forbid—they may catch him." She sighed dis-
consolately. "It's no easy matter taking fifty horses across
the border. And who's to blame if not that fine father of his!

Translated by A. B. Magil. Copyright 1928 by *The Menorah Journal*,
New York City. Reprinted with the permission of the editor and Mrs.
Adele Opatoshu. This short story forms the first two chapters of *The
Romance of a Horse Thief* by Joseph Opatoshu.

Lord knows, I've rowed enough about it. Many's the time I've said: 'Solomon, one horse-dealer in the family is enough. Let the boy learn a trade.' That's all he needed! He'd just measure me off with that thief's eye of his and sing me a tune to bring my mother's milk back to me!"

Tirzeh blew her nose in her apron.

"Never had any joy of my children. Out of twelve there's only three left. Zanvl was always wild. Children never wanted to play with him—he beat them so. Hit even his own rebbi. The neighbors said all along no good would come of him. Just think of it! a child is born with a caul and an ungodly scream! Who ever heard of such a thing? And Sarah—doesn't she give me trouble enough? Always bumming around somewhere. . . . And every day there's some new scandal about her posted on the synagogue wall. Of course, we might marry her off before Hannah, even though she's younger. I only hope to God I have some joy of Hannah. . . ."

Zanvl turned over and opened wide his blue eyes. He folded his arms under his head, stretched himself and yawned.

"Must be late!"

He leaped out of bed, washed himself, put on his polished boots and combed his hair Polish style. He folded his arms round his hips and began doing a dance, shouting:

"Matko, podavay! (Mother, give me something to eat.)"

"You're even worse than a goy," Tirzeh said. "When a goy gets up, the first thing he does is say his paternoster. And you?"

"Not a word, mother," he laughed and, catching the barefoot Tirzeh in his arms, began dancing with her despite her struggles.

"Let go of me, you rascal! Poison is what I'll give you!"

Zanvl roared. He poured out a glass of whiskey and tossed it off, and then sat down to his bowl of schav and potatoes.

Solomon came in, carrying his talith-bag under his arm. He was on the point of saying something, but Tirzeh cut him short with: "A fine specimen you've made of your young saint! Such blessings on all my enemies' heads! He gets up like an animal, says not a word of prayers and gobbles up a bowl of potatoes and schav. You wouldn't listen to me, Solomon. So here you are!"

Solomon's lips drew tight and he turned pale.

"Shut your mouth, you old talking-machine! Who's asking you?"

Zanvl kept on eating and smiled.

"A thief doesn't have to *daven*," he said.

Solomon didn't answer. He began walking up and down the room. He felt that Tirzeh was right, but to admit it was out of the question. And he loved Zanvl dearly and forgave him much.

"He'll get older," Solomon told himself, "and he'll change. I wasn't better myself when I was his age. And besides, Zanvl has strength and nerve, two qualities which every horse thief ought to possess: they make his colleagues look up to him." For Solomon knew that ever since Zanvl had entered his "business," he was looked upon with different eyes.

"Saw Moses 'Kuniarsh' (Horse-Dealer) today," Solomon said.

"Well?"

"He'll be here soon. From the drift of his talk he seems to think he can bargain us down a few roubles. Says he can get it cheaper."

"Cheaper? The devil take him! If it's a penny less, dad, I don't stir from the spot. The old fox! I'll fix him some day."

"All right, all right. Stop hollering, he's coming," Solomon said quickly, and went to the door. A tall, thick-set Jew in a loose rep coat came in.

"Good morning."

"Good year, Reb Moses," Solomon replied and offered him a chair. "Here, have a seat."

Moses let himself down slowly, groaning and panting. He took out cigars and passed them around.

"Well, Zanvl," Moses began with a cough, "are you ready to go tonight?"

"If we'll only come to an agreement, I'm ready at any time."

"What do you mean? Why, I thought your father and I had settled it already."

"What's the use of beating around the bush, Reb Moses? Unless I see two hundred roubles on the table I don't stir from the spot. You say you can get it cheaper? You're welcome to it. I have nothing against you."

"Bah, Zanvl, you've got a little too much pepper in you. You must be doing a flourishing business if you can toss away a hundred and fifty roubles like that. Be sensible for once. The entire thing will take less than an hour, and a hundred and fifty roubles for an hour's work seems fine pay to me. Rothschild himself wouldn't turn it down. Come on, Zanvl, don't make a fool of yourself. Now if I were certain that the horses would get across the border safely, fifty roubles more or less wouldn't matter. But what will I do if, God forbid, they capture the horses? Do you want to stand partner on the loss, ha? You don't answer. That's no way to do business, Zanvl."

Zanvl sat sulkily and said nothing. He knew that Moses would talk him into giving in, the old fox! Nearly all the horses are mine, he thought. Moses got them for a song. And now he wants to bargain us down another fifty roubles. No!

Zanvl arose.

"Reb Moses, you're wasting your breath. It'll do you no good. I won't take anything less than two hundred roubles."

Moses looked straight into Zanvl's eyes and smiled.

"Eh, Zanvl, you seem to be getting rather excited. You and I, Solomon, will settle it between us. Meanwhile, let's have a drink."

Tirzeh brought some brandy and a little light food. With a groan Moses pulled out a thick wallet, counted out two hundred roubles and handed them to Solomon.

They drank each other's health.

As Zanvl approached the woods, he saw his father standing there with two youths. He quickly dismounted and began tying the horses one behind the other. This done, he said goodby to his father and cautiously rode out of the woods, following narrow, winding by-paths, while the two youths rode behind him.

All along the way Zanvl tried to think about the border. But the image of Rachel always interrupted his thoughts. "What if they shoot me tonight?" flashed across his mind.

He smiled broadly to himself and took out a small flat bottle of whiskey from the leg of his boot. He pulled at it several times to drive the thought away.

Soon they came to the edge of the stream. "Halt!" Zanvl called softly, raising his hand. They all stood still.

"We'll wait here till it gets real dark. Now, fellows, take the bottle of whiskey and rub it into the horses' heads to keep them from neighing. But do it all quietly. Don't make a sound, understand?"

The horses soon grew calmer as if they too sensed the danger. They crowded together with lowered heads and remained motionless. Zanvl looked at them standing there, body against body, with their lowered, pensive heads, and a sudden feeling of pity came over him.

All around was still. Now and then a breeze blew, bringing the wet, keen smell of juniper. Slowly, calmly, flowed the stream, its small dark-violet ripples rising and swallowing each other.

Zanvl lay on his belly, watching the dark blue mountains grow out of the water, spread their way into the sky. A reddish strip cut through them, leaving them hanging between water and sky.

Zanvl felt something pouring through all his limbs, filling him with wildness and life. The violet ripples seemed to call to him and he longed to throw off his clothes and leap into the water.

"Let's take a swim, fellows!" he said, turning to the other two. They raised their heads, looked at each other and shrugged their shoulders as if to say, "He must be crazy with the heat."

Zanvl spat contemptuously into the water. "Quitters!" he grunted and began swiftly to undress.

There was a splash as he went in. He swam around several times and came out. "Fools, you don't know a good thing when you see it," he said, and grasping a thick branch of an old tree, began pulling himself up and down.

It grew darker and darker. The horses stood as motionless as if they had been hewn out of stone. Zanvl and the two youths doused them with cold water to rouse them and the party moved on again quietly.

Silence. Only the rhythmic beating of the horses' hoofs and an occasional neigh. A red light appeared in the distance. That marked "the chain." There, Zanvl knew, dangled a long chain from a high block of wood, white with black stripes.

Zanvl led the way into a side-path and they slowed down. He kept patting his stallion, and now and then treated him to a lump of sugar.

Footsteps. . . .

They halted and listened. Again silence and they moved on. Zanvl looked around him. Another fifty paces and they would be in Prussia. Again they turned into a small sandy path and began driving the horses through prickly gooseberry bushes.

Two soldiers came out of a distant clump of trees. For a moment a quiver ran through Zanvl, but recovering at once, he ordered the youths to whip up the horses with all their might. The horses took fright. The youths jumped off and ran off. Zanvl was furious.

"Cowardly dogs! A plague upon you!" he roared and rode to meet the soldiers. They stopped him and began untying the horses. Zanvl argued with them and tried to bribe them, but in vain. A cold sweat covered his body. He gritted his teeth. Suddenly he dug his spurs into his stallion as hard as he could. The horse leaped forward and with his forelegs threw down one of the soldiers. He galloped away with the other horses following. The other soldier, frantic and confused, began shooting. Hit, some of the horses plunged around and dropped. But in another moment Zanvl was on the other side of the border thumbing his nose at the soldiers.

3

Two Germans were waiting for him on the other side. One of them led the horses away and the other invited Zanvl for a glass of beer. Zanvl could see groups of people sitting on the grass not far from the saloon. He knew them as professional smugglers of secondhand clothes; they were waiting for the train from Berlin, due at one in the morning, which brought the old-clothes dealers. The goods unpacked, each of the smugglers would don several garments and ride over into Poland.

A group of elderly Jews in long loose coats were sitting by, enjoying a quiet talk. They envied "Yeke Fool" (so they called the German) and his easy-going life, but most of all they envied the saloonkeeper, who ran the saloon on the highway and did a flourishing trade day and night. For the most part genteel but indigent Chassidim, they had tried all trades, even teaching children, and had failed at them all. Now they made their living wandering over from Prussia, each with three suits or their equivalent on his back.

In another group women in sheitels were gossiping indignantly about some Jewish girls who were sitting a little further on with a group of Gentile boys and girls. The place where the young people were sitting rang with laughter. The boy stretched out a girl on the grass and began wagering that she was wearing nothing under her dress. After a while an old Jewess, unable to control herself any longer, came over and began railing at them. They let the girl go. An impudent young fellow jumped up gaily, hugged the old lady and tried to kiss her. She began to scream while everybody roared with laughter.

A German smoking a thick cigar sauntered by. He stopped and snarled: "Dirty Jews!" and went on.

Zanvl went into the saloon. He emptied several mugs of beer, smoked a cigar, said goodby to the German and went out. The merchants with their bundles of clothes had already arrived and had spread out their merchandise in the middle of a field. The smugglers took off their clothes and stood there in undershirts and drawers, the women blouseless—all of them pushing, straining to get to the merchants, with the stronger ones grabbing most of the clothes. The women fought with the girls and the girls tore off the sheitels from the women's heads. While they were struggling, a half-naked *sheigetz* came over and slyly untied the string of a girl's petticoat. When the girl reached out to get hold of a jacket she found herself standing in a pair of short linen drawers. At which the young *shkotsim* formed a circle and began dancing around her, refusing to let her out.

The "Jewish" guard came by with his gun on his shoulder, joking with the Jews and giving them advice. Soon a sturdy wench came over, took the guard's arm and went off with him into the woods.

A short distance away stood Zanvl, watching it all. He spat vehemently, flung the word "Stinkers!" into the night, and vanished into a side street.

He passed a group of smugglers with packs on their shoulders.

"Ay, Zanvl," cried out a yellow-faced man, "what are you doing here?"

"I had to see a German," replied Zanvl quietly and was walking on.

"Tell it to your granny, Zanvl. We know, all right," leered a small, broad-shouldered fellow.

"You louse! Who's asking you? Is it any of your business?" The smugglers glanced at each other uncertainly.

"Sure." The yellow-face turned to the little fellow. "Always sticking your nose into everything. If he'd punched you in the jaw, do you think I'd have cared? Like hell! You'll put your foot into it one of these days. And you,

Zanvl, why do you go up in the air so quickly? Let the dog bark. Maybe you'd care to take along a package of silks?"

"Sure!" Zanvl said. "How much do I get?"

"Why, a ten-spot, of course."

"Nix, brother. Fifteen."

The yellow-face thought a while.

"All right!" he said.

The smugglers put down their packs, while the yellow-face went off, to return after a few minutes with a large bundle of silks. Zanvl put the straps over his shoulders, lifted the bundle lightly on his back and set out. When they came near the border, they divided into two groups, the yellow-face leading. They took off their shoes, rolled up their trouser-legs and waited. The yellow-face went into the woods to reconnoitre. Soon he returned accompanied by several soldiers, and at a given signal, the group went across the border. One by one they went through the woods. No one said a word; at the slightest sound they slid into the tall grain with their bundles, lay there a while until it was quiet again, and then went on.

Zanvl was tired. The day's activities had exhausted him and he felt all his limbs ache. He wanted to think of Rachel, but he could not collect his thoughts.

About three in the morning they arrived in the last village just outside the city. They rested their bundles on the ground and sat down to rest in a valley meadow. Suddenly there came the sound of hoofbeats. They grabbed their bundles and scattered in every direction. Zanvl ran away without his cap. Dizzy with fatigue he strode along as swiftly as he could. Shots rang through the air.

"They're chasing us!" Zanvl thought and stood still. Before him stretched the ancient graveyard. He climbed the fence and jumped light as a cat down on the other side. Calmly, quietly, he began to walk among the tombstones. He found a tall hillock, put his bundle on the earth for a pillow, threw himself down and fell fast asleep. . . .

From every part of Poland merchants and peasants thronged to Loivitch, bringing their cattle, horses and swine. The narrow streets were impassable and the roads leading to the city were filled with *britzkas*. From afar it looked as if the city had been besieged by semi-savage foes, who had descended upon it with all their goods and possessions, barring all roads and storming with loud cries into the city.

Zanvl and his companions went out to the fair early in the morning. They wandered about, looking everything over, and late in the afternoon came to the horse market, which looked like a military camp preparing for departure. All around the market were wagons and *britzkas*, while the horses stood unharnessed between the shafts to allow the merchants to inspect them. In the middle of the market were a number of thoroughbreds and alongside stretched a runway on which their speed was being tested.

Zanvl strode through the market, casting glances all around, feeling at home among the horses. A young man came towards him with a basket of toy tin roosters, one of which he held in his mouth and blew. Zanvl bought a rooster and began walking about, crowing loudly. But he soon grew tired of this and threw the toy away.

A broad-shouldered, cross-eyed fellow wearing a cap with a split visor came ambling through the market, his hands thrust into his pockets. He seemed to be looking for someone.

"Well, I'll be damned! Look who's here! What are you doing here, Zanvl?"

"Yay!" Zanvl shouted and jumped at Kishke joyously. "I thought you were doing time behind 'the gates of mercy'!"

Kishke did not answer. He looked Zanvl's companions up and down, spat curtly and taking Zanvl by the arm, led him aside.

"Do you want to be in on something soft?" he asked.

"I'll say!"

"Well, listen," said Kishke in a low voice. "Just a little way from here there's a peasant with five colts that are beauties. If everything goes as it should, the mazuma will be in our pockets by ten tonight."

Zanvl called over Gradul and Moshele and they began to work out a plan.

Alongside a *britzka* stood a young peasant tearing chunks from a loaf of bread under his arm and stuffing them into his mouth. Behind him were five beautiful horses. Zanvl brushed against the peasant as if by accident and stepped with all his might upon his foot. The peasant seized Zanvl with both hands and flung him away. Zanvl spat on his hands, clenched his fists and hurled himself at the fellow. One blow and the peasant was stretched out. He tried to get up, but Zanvl smashed him between the eyes and he rolled over.

Soon a crowd of peasants and Jews gathered from all sides. Cries rang through the air: "Kill the Jew! The unbelieving dog, kill him!"

Meanwhile Gradul and Kishke had untied the horses and led three of them unobtrusively away. The others Moshele guarded until after the fight, and when the peasants were on the point of making peace, he sent the horses galloping away. The peasants began chasing the runaways and Moshele and Zanvl took the opportunity to beat a retreat.

5

Night. A large room. Solomon "Kradnik" (Thief) took a loaded revolver out of a chest. He put several pairs of shoes into a bag and looked at the large clock on the wall.

"Hm, twelve. Still have a whole hour."

In bed under the large down quilt lay Tirzeh, snoring tumultuously.

"Blowing that old bugle of hers!" Kradnik grunted and spat testily.

Solomon looked at his daughter Sarah, who lay on a sleeping-couch with her right eye open. "Other girls like her are already mothers," he sighed.

Solomon felt that he was to blame for Sarah's spinster-hood. He might have had half a dozen grandchildren.

"We've seen better times. A person earned his roubles easier than he does now. Matchmakers used to knock at the door constantly and young men would act as their own matchmakers. They were crazy about Sarah. And now?"

The mottled gander that slept under the stove suddenly awoke, stretched himself on his thin legs, and began beating his wings against the cage. He snatched some oat-grains with his beak and then stuck his head into a bowl of water. He stretched his neck, rolled his eyes, and swallowed deeply.

"Yes," thought Solomon, "if it please God that this business turn out successfully, then first of all a dowry for Sarah. It'll be a burden lifted from my mind. And after all, why should she wait any longer?"

Solomon opened his tobacco pouch and rolled himself a cigarette. He opened the door of the stove, shoved out a glowing coal, and lit the cigarette. He glanced at the window, blowing thick smoke through his mouth. The dark walls veiled in shadows filled him with melancholy. Outside the wind whistled. He shivered. It was cold.

He placed himself with his back against the warm stove and returned to his thoughts. On the road to the woods his son Zanvl was now walking. If everything turned out as it should, they would cut through the woods, quietly lead out the two mares, walk them to the hill and—away to Moses Kuniarsh. That little job would bring in over two hundred roubles. The thought of the money put Solomon into better spirits.

"And on my word of honor, if with God's help I only get the roubles, then first of all I'll marry off Sarah."

A smile lit up his face and tears came into his gray eyes. He sat down, reached into the leg of his boot for the flat bottle of whiskey, and took several pulls at it. He went to the cupboard and stopped his hunger with a piece of cheese.

Out on the street arose the long whistle of the night-

watchman, then the howling of a homeless dog. Solomon
gazed at the window and saw the frost creeping over it. He
took several bricks of peat, shoved them into the fire, and
again stood with his back to the stove, lost in thought. "And
suppose we get caught?" His old thin body trembled. Not
so long since he was caught with the officer's nags. He could
still feel the sticks beating his body, cutting his skin, drawing
the blood. So badly they beat him he had to lie in bed a
whole month.

That mischance had made Solomon begin thinking of
turning to another trade. And every time some new little job
came his way, he vowed it would be the last.

"A dog's life. I've lived over fifty years and what have I
got for my pains? Nothing but fear all the time. Money? A
pauper's wealth!"

Solomon took hold of his sparse beard and held it out
straight from his chin. He noticed several gray hairs. "Hm,
a summons—they're calling me to the other world."

Solomon recalled how once on a Saturday afternoon he
was sitting in the old Beth Hamidrash listening to a Lithu-
anian *maggid* describe the other world—paradise and hell.
Soon after death there comes the Angel of the Realm of the
Dead, knocks three times at your grave, and asks your
name. If the dead one is a pious man, he answers immediately; a sinner forgets and is lost.

Solomon imagined himself dead. The Angel of the Realm
of the Dead, a tall, bony Jew with thick eyebrows—just like
Simchah Greber—asks him his name. And he—he has forgotten. . . .

Solomon felt a sinking at the heart. He pressed heavily
against the stove and scratched his head. He suddenly felt a
fierce hatred for Moses Kuniarsh. Thirty years ago they
were both stealing horses together, and now—Solomon is
the thief and Moses the merchant. Moses is now a fine, respectable member of the community, a *gabbai* in the old
Beth Hamidrash, and last year presented a Scroll of the Law
to the synagogue. He gives his daughters dowries of two
thousand roubles and supports his sons-in-law. And he? He
spends sleepless nights, busy making Moses richer.

Solomon could see Moses sleeping in his Viennese bed
with the carved headpieces, his long, broad beard spread
luxuriantly over his pudgy breast. The quilt rises up and
down: he must be dreaming that he has been chosen to be
supervisor in the city. And he, Solomon, a thin old man, sits
here in the small hours of the night and gets ready to steal
a couple of horses for which he will get half and Moses half.
And who can tell whether he won't be caught?

Solomon sighed dully and looked at the clock. "Time to
be going." He put on a warm shirt, tied a green belt around
him, and stuck a pair of woolen one-fingered mittens into
the belt. He pulled on his long boots, turned down the lamp,
and went out.

On the outskirts of the city, near the woods, Solomon
lifted the bag from his shoulders and waited. He extended
his long thin neck and with staring eyes listened like an old
hungry wolf to the silence. Then he put two fingers into his
mouth and whistled. From the other side of the woods came
an answering whistle.

"A clever fellow!" Solomon thought. "If he only weren't
so wild and would listen to his father—I'd be fixed in my
old age all right."

Zanvl emerged from the woods and called: "Come on,
dad, it's late."

Solomon grabbed his bag and hurried over. "How are the
horses getting along?" he asked.

"How should they? They're asleep in the stable."

Solomon and Zanvl strode on determinedly. Neither
spoke. They looked like two wolves stealing out of the
forest into the broad highway. The old man kept feeling at
his breast to make sure the revolver was there and mumbling to himself: "Bay horse. Roan. Chestnut horse. Roan.
Cholera. Moses Kuniarsh. . . ."

Every now and then he would grab Zanvl by the arm:
"Somebody's coming!"

Zanvl would halt, prick his ears and stare around him.
No one. He would smile—the old boy was getting shaky—
and stride on.

Solomon felt a sharp chill go through his bones. He

thought of his Tirzeh lying now under the warm quilt, snoring. "A dog's life. About time I retired from this fine business."

A dog barked. "Damn the dogs!" Solomon muttered. "A vile death on them! Why the devil did God ever create them?"

Scattered houses appeared on the hill. Zanvl took the bag with the shoes and went into the village. A black shaggy dog jumped at him, barking loudly. Zanvl drew back, but the dog came after him. He leaped at the dog, grabbed him with his hands by the throat and began choking him. The dog struggled only briefly; he rolled his eyes glassily, stuck out his long pointed tongue, and remained lifeless in Zanvl's hands.

Zanvl stood up and looked at the dog stretched out at his feet, the long red tongue hanging from his mouth. He spat sharply and looked around: the old man had disappeared.

At the bottom of the hill stood Solomon, his teeth chattering with terror. The sight of Zanvl choking the dog had been too much for him, and he had run away to the bottom of the hill.

Zanvl took hold of the bag; then with the swiftness of a young gypsy he lifted the door off the hinges. Warm steam beat into his face. He took out the whiskey, made the horses drunk, and put shoes on their feet. Then he led them softly out of the stable.

At the foot of the hill Solomon put the shoes into a bag that was tied to his shoulder. They mounted their horses and rode away into the gray night.

ISRAEL JOSHUA SINGER

The late Israel Joshua Singer, brother of Isaac Bashevis
Singer, was born in Poland in 1893. His best known
work, *The Brothers Ashkenazi,* is probably the finest example of a family chronicle in Yiddish literature. With
the possible exception of Sholem Asch he is the best of
the Jewish social novelists. There is nothing at all provincial or parochial about his understanding of twentieth century Jewish life in the first two decades of this
century. In 1933 a dramatization of his novel *Yoshe Kalb*
was presented with great success on the Yiddish stage in
New York. He settled here in 1937 and became a con-
tributor to the Jewish *Daily Forward.* He died in New
York City in 1944.

Repentance

Rabbi Ezekiel of Kozmir and his followers were great be-
lievers in the divine principle of joyousness.

Reb Ezekiel himself was a giant of a man, standing a full
head above his Chasidic followers, and broader in the
shoulders than any two of them placed side by side. On
Holy Days the court of Reb Ezekiel was jammed with visiting Chasidim, and in their synagogue the mighty head of

From *The River Breaks Up* by I. J. Singer, translated by Maurice
Samuel. Copyright 1938 by Alfred A. Knopf, Inc., and reprinted by permission of the publisher.

Reb Ezekiel, swathed in the silver-worked headpiece of his prayer-shawl, swam above all others, a banner and a crown, an adornment to the gathering and the symbol of its glory.

Reb Ezekiel is no more than a memory today, but there are still extant two of his possessions: an ivory walking-stick and a white satin gaberdine which fastens at the front not with buttons but with silver hooks and eyes. The grip of the stick is so high that no man is able to use it for walking-purposes. A certain grandson of Reb Ezekiel, inheritor of the dynastic rights of this rabbinic line, puts on Reb Ezekiel's gaberdine once a year, on the New Year, when the ram's horn is to be blown for the opening of the heavenly gates; but if he tries to take a step in this mantle of his grandfather, he stumbles over the ends, which trail along the floor. To protect him not less than the illustrious garment, the followers of the grandson put down a carpet of straw on the floor of the synagogue for the two days of the New Year.

Rabbi Ezekiel and his followers believed not only in joyousness, but in the virtue of good food.

Of the fast-days which are sprinkled throughout the sacred calendar, Reb Ezekiel and his followers observed only the Day of Atonement. Even on the Ninth Day of Ab, the Black Fast which commemorates the tremendous calamity of the storming of the Temple, Reb Ezekiel and his followers ate. If it came to pass once in a while that a fool of a Chasid, having had a bad dream, insisted on fasting, he had to leave the court and go across the Vistula to the village opposite Kozmir.

At the court of Rabbi Ezekiel there were always dancing and singing; there was perpetual drinking of wine and mead. It was a common saying with the Rabbi, his children, the Chasidic followers and visitors:

"It is not the study of the Law that matters, but the melody which goes with the studying; it is not the praying that matters, but the sweet chanting of the prayer."

One day a strange thing happened. Rabbi Naphthali Aphter, the greatest opponent and critic of Reb Ezekiel, actually came on a visit to the town of Kozmir, for the Sabbath of Repentance.

Rabbi Naphthali Aphter was the exact opposite of Reb Ezekiel of Kozmir. He was a weakling, a pygmy of a Jew, skin and bones, something that a moderate wind could carry away. He fasted every day of the week, from Sabbath to Sabbath, that is. He broke his fast evenings with a plate of soup, nothing more; and lest he should derive from the soup anything more than the barest sustenance, lest he should take pleasure in the taste of food, he would throw into the plate of soup a fistful of salt. On Saturdays he permitted himself meat and fish, in honour of the sanctity of the Sabbath; he ate the eye of a fish and a sinew of flesh. When he ate, every swallow of food could be traced in its passage down his slender, stringy throat. Further to mortify his body, Rabbi Naphthali slept no more than two hours a night; the rest of the time he sat before the sacred books. And when he studied he did not follow the traditional custom, which bids the student set his repetitions to a sweet chant; this he considered a sinful concession to the lust of his ears. He muttered the words dryly under his breath. In the night he held the candle in his right hand, to be certain that he did not doze. His hand trembled, and the drops of grease fell on the yellow pages of the pious books, which he turned with his left hand. The tears ran down his withered, parchment-like cheeks and fell side by side with the drops of grease on the ancient pages, which smelt of wax, tears, hair, and mildew.

He repeated for the thousandth time, in the harsh mutter of his study: "*Shivoh medurei gehinom,* there are seven chambers in the courts of hell. The fire of the first chamber is sixty times as hot as the fire we know on earth; the fire of the second chamber is sixty times as hot as the fire of the first chamber; the fire of the third chamber is sixty times as hot . . . and thus it follows that the fire of the seventh chamber is hotter by sixty times sixty to the seventh time than the fire which we know on earth.

He continued: "Therefore happy are those who are only

transformed into fish and animals, into trees and grasses. And there are also human souls which wander in the wildness of space, and there are others which are flung about as with slings, and their plight is bitterest of all."

Rabbi Naphthali had sundered himself completely from the things of this world. He had even separated himself from his wife and knew her no more. But wicked thoughts, evil visitations, tormented him, especially in the nights, and gave him no peace.

And this was not only when he lay down for the two hours of slumber which he permitted himself. Even while he sat at his sacred books shapes and phantoms in the likeness of females surrounded him. It was useless to close his eyes on them, for with closed eyes he only saw them better. They penetrated his ears, also. They shook down great masses of black hair, they sang with voices of piercing sweetness, they danced immodestly, and they flung their arms round him. They caressed his sparse little beard, they played with his stiff, flat earlocks, twining these round their fingers.

He fled from these visions and voices to the ritual bath, which lay in a corner of the yard of his house. He tore off his clothes, stumbled down the cold, slippery stone steps, and flung his weak body into the black, icy water. But even then it seemed to him that he struck with his head not against the harsh water, but against soft, silky cushions; and his body lay on down, tempting and exciting.

A naked woman, irresistibly beautiful, held him close in the hot bands of her arms. . . . He fled from the water and took vows to be harsher with his rebellious and pampered body. He halved his allowance of soup at the end of the day and doubled the salt with which he spoiled its taste. He wept day and night, and his eyes were never dry. But the Evil Inclination, the Wicked One, whispered mockingly in his ear:

"Fool that you are! You have separated yourself from your wife, who is a pure and good woman, to sin in secret with abominations of the night; you have left your simple couch of straw and feathers to loll on divans of silk and down. . . ."

Rabbi Naphthali wept so long and so hard that at last the well of his tears dried up and his eyes gave out only a thin rheum. He longed to become blind, so that he might look no more on the sinful world. But the Evil One read his thoughts and continued to whisper mockery into his ear:

"Fool that you are! Why do you seek to rid yourself of the eyes of the flesh? Is it not because you know that with the eyes of the spirit and the imagination you can see sweet visions a thousand times more sinful?"

Then, in the end, Rabbi Naphthali decided to visit the rabbinic court of Kozmir.

"If fasting and mortification of the flesh will not help, perhaps Reb Ezekiel has better counsel," he thought.

He slung a sack over his shoulders, took his prayer-shawl and phylacteries under his arm, and set out for Kozmir, planning to arrive there for the Sabbath of Repentance.

When they learned in the court of the Kozmir Rabbi that Naphthali himself, the bitterest opponent and critic of Rabbi Ezekiel, had arrived on a visit, there was great rejoicing. Reb Mottye Godel, the chief beadle and grand vizier of the Kozmir Rabbi, stroked his beard proudly and said to all the Chasidim:

"This is a great victory. If Reb Naphthali himself comes here, the others will follow, and soon all the Jews will acknowledge our Rabbi. I tell you, we will live to see that day."

Rabbi Naphthali arrived, of course, not on the Sabbath itself, but on the preceding day; and he asked at once to be admitted to the presence of Reb Ezekiel. But the Kozmir Rabbi could not receive him. He was going, he declared, to the baths, to purify himself for the Sabbath. He remained in the baths longer than was his wont. In the steam-room he climbed up to the highest and hottest level of the stairs and shouted joyously to the attendants to pour more water on the heated stones and to fill the room with more steam. His followers, who would accompany him to the highest steps, fled from him this time, unable to endure the heat. The Rabbi laughed loudly at them.

"Fools," he cried, "how will you learn to endure the flames of hell?"

When he returned from the baths, Reb Ezekiel lay down on the well-stuffed, leather-covered couch on which he rested in the day-time, and he seemed to have forgotten entirely about Reb Naphthali. After he had taken a nap he commanded that the Sabbath fish be brought in to him to taste, and then he remembered Reb Naphthali.

"Mottye," he said, "bring in the fish prepared for the Sabbath—and Reb Naphthali too."

It was a custom with Reb Ezekiel to taste the Sabbath fish the evening before. He said: "They that taste thereof have merited life, as the holy word says."

It was also a custom with him to sharpen the pearl-handled bread-knife himself, and himself to slice the onions which were served with the fish on the Sabbath.

When Rabbi Naphthali entered, conducted by the chief beadle, Reb Ezekiel greeted him joyously:

"Welcome, and blessed be thy coming," he exclaimed in a thundering voice which sent tremors through Reb Naphthali. He put out his hand, seized Reb Naphthali's, and squeezed it so hard that Reb Naphthali doubled up.

"What good tidings have you for me, Reb Naphthali?" he asked happily.

"I have come to ask you counsel on the matter of repentance," answered Reb Naphthali, trembling.

"Repentance?" shouted Reb Ezekiel, and his voice was as gay as if he had heard the sweetest tidings. "Repentance? Assuredly! Take a glass of whisky. What is the meaning of the word 'repentance'? It is: to turn! And when a Jew takes a glass of whisky he turns it upside down, which is to say that he performs an act of repentance."

And without waiting, Reb Ezekiel filled two silver beakers with brandy in which floated spices and little leaves.

"Good health and life, Reb Naphthali," he said, and pushed one beaker forward.

Reb Ezekiel emptied his own beaker at a gulp. Reb Naphthali broke into a stuttering cough with the mere smell of the drink, but Reb Ezekiel would not let him put it down.

"Reb Naphthali, you have come for my counsel. The first thing, then, which I will teach you will be the mystery of eating and drinking."

He forced Reb Naphthali to swallow the brandy and then pushed toward him a huge piece of stuffed carp, highly seasoned.

"This," he said with a smile, "comes from the hand of my wife. She is a valiant woman, a pearl of price, and her stuffed fish have in them not less than one sixtieth of the virtue and taste of Leviathan himself."

The first piece Reb Naphthali tried to swallow stuck in his throat. But Reb Ezekiel would not be put off, and he compelled Reb Naphthali to eat.

"Rabbi Naphthali, the road of repentance is not an easy one, as you see. But there is no turning back on it."

When it was impossible to make Rabbi Naphthali eat another bite, Reb Ezekiel took him by the hand, led him into the other room, and bade him stretch himself out on the well-stuffed leather-covered couch.

Rabbi Naphthali refused to lie down.

"What?" he said; "lie down and sleep in the middle of the day? And with the Sabbath approaching?"

"It is better to sleep two days than to entertain one thought," said Reb Ezekiel, and closed the door on him.

During the Ten Penitential Days which stretch from the New Year to the Day of Atonement Reb Ezekiel taught Reb Naphthali the mystery of food and the inner significance of joyousness. Every day there was another banquet in the rabbinic court, and wine and mead were consumed in barrelfuls. The singing in the court was heard throughout the whole townlet of Kozmir; it echoed in the surrounding hills and carried across the Vistula.

"Well, Reb Naphthali, are you visited by thoughts, by fantasies?" Reb Ezekiel asked him every day.

"Less now," answered Reb Naphthali.

"In that case here's another glass of mead," said Reb

Ezekiel, and took care that Reb Naphthali drank it all down.

And every day, when the banquet was over, he led his guest into his own room and made him sleep on his leather-covered couch.

"Sleep!" he said. "Ordinary, unknowing Jews are permitted to sleep in the day-time only on Sabbaths. But good and pious Jews who are followers of a Chasidic rabbi are enjoined to sleep by daylight every day in the week."

When they all sat at the dinner which precedes the eve of the Day of Atonement, Reb Ezekiel kept closer watch than ever on the visitor. Not a minute passed but what he pressed on him another tidbit.

"Reb Naphthali, eat, I say. Every mouthful you swallow is written down in your heavenly account as a meritorious deed. Eat heartily and swell the account."

In the court of Kozmir the Day of Atonement was the merriest day of the year.

The Rabbi himself stood at the pulpit and conducted the prayers. He did not let anyone replace him, but led the congregation from morning till evening, through all the divisions of devotion. He did not sit down for a minute, and his voice never ceased from singing.

All prayers were set to a happy chant in Kozmir, even the most doleful, even the martyrologies. The House of Prayer was jammed with Jews in prayer-shawls and white robes. Above them all towered the Rabbi, his head adorned with a skull-cap wrought with gold embroidery, the crown and glory of the congregation. His voice rang as loudly in the closing prayer of the Day of Atonement as it had done in the opening prayer of the evening before, though he had not tasted food or drink for twenty-four hours. Around him stood his dynasty, his sons and grandsons, all in silk and white satin, and their voices sustained him throughout the whole service. The melodious tumult of this choir was heard in town, in the hills, and in the village across the river; the congregation helped to swell it, and the day was observed with dancing as well as singing. Round the door of the House of Prayer stood the feminine half of the dynasty, the Rabbi's wife, his daughters, his daughters-in-law, his grand-daughters. They, too, were dressed in silk and satin; on their bosoms shone gold-embroidered coverings; on their heads wimples glittered with precious stones; and their lips moved piously in whispered prayer.

Reb Naphthali bent down to the earth in the fervour of his devotions. He longed to squeeze at least one tear from his sinful eyes, but all his efforts availed him nothing. The riot of song all about him deafened him, and he could not concentrate on one miserable thought.

When the Day of Atonement was over, the congregants took the stubs of the burning candles from the boxes of sand and went out into the synagogue yard to the Benediction of the Moon. The moon swam luminously in a clear sky, and the congregants rejoiced in her light.

"Welcome," they cried to her, dancing joyously. "Be thou a good sign and a bringer of good luck."

Reb Ezekiel stood in the midst of his Chasidim, radiant as the moon in the midst of the stars.

"Welcome!" he cried thunderously to Reb Naphthali, and took him by the hand as if he were about to draw him into a dance. But in that instant Reb Naphthali was seized with a violent trembling, and before anyone could take hold of him he had slipped to the ground.

The Chasidim dropped on the ground beside him, but when they felt his hands and face, these were as cold as the damp grass on which he lay. There was no sign of breath in the frail body.

Panic descended on the assembly. Hundreds of congregants tried to touch the body where it lay, wrapped in prayer-shawl and white robe. But those that were at the centre lifted up the body of Reb Naphthali, carried it into the House of Prayer, and laid it down on the pulpit, where the Scroll is laid for the reading of the Law. Those that could not get into the House did not go to their homes, but remained standing, petrified, and some of them began to weep audibly.

The panic lasted only a minute or two.

The door of the Rabbi's room opened, and the Rabbi, his face as radiant as when he had stretched out his hand to Reb Naphthali and the latter had fallen to the ground, looked out above the congregation. He had withdrawn for a moment and he was back with the congregation. His voice rang out:

"If anyone wants to weep, let him take a row-boat and pass to the other side of the Vistula. There is no weeping in Kozmir."

Amazed, silent, the Chasidim followed the gesture of the Rabbi and filed into his room.

The table sparkled with gold and silver in the light of a hundred candles. Ranged along its centre were dusty bottles of wine and mead, each surrounded by a heap of grapes and pears and pomegranates.

The Chasidim seated themselves. The Rabbi drank, sang happily, and distributed morsels to his favourites. This night he was more generous than ever before. Children and grandchildren sat at the head of the table, snatched his gifts, and followed him in song.

The feasting lasted through the night, and only when the morning star was peeping in through the window did Mottye, the chief beadle, give the signal that the Rabbi was now prepared to make an utterance. The Chasidim crowded close to him, their hands upon one another's shoulders.

Many minutes passed before the Rabbi came to his utterance. He sat playing with the silver watch which lay in front of him on the table. He picked up a heavy bunch of grapes and moved it up and down as if he were estimating its weight. And throughout all this he chanted a Chasidic melody to himself.

When he had finished the melody and had let all the echoes die down about him, he opened his mouth and spoke:

"I wanted to teach him the great mystery of joyousness, but he was unable to grasp it."

He looked out of the window toward the House of Prayer, where the little body of Reb Naphthali, wrapped in prayer-shawl and white robe, lay on the pulpit, and he ended his utterance:

"He had sunk too far into habits of gloom, and there was no saving him."

ISAAC BABEL

Isaac Babel was the son of a Jewish household in Odessa. In 1915, at the age of twenty-one, he moved to St. Petersburg, where like many Jews he resided illegally. His first work was published by Maxim Gorky, who esteemed him greatly as a writer. Babel participated actively in the Revolution and the Civil War. In the twenties he resumed writing. One of his books, *Red Cavalry*, appeared in the United States in his lifetime, but failed to attract much notice. The critic and translator Raymond Rosenthal did much to revive his reputation in the late forties. Babel disappeared during the Stalin purges of the thirties. It is not known whether he was shot or died in one of the concentration camps.

Gedali

On Sabbath eves I am oppressed by the dense melancholy of memories. In bygone days on these occasions my grandfather would stroke the volumes of Ibn Ezra with his yellow beard. His old woman in her lace cap would trace fortunes with her knotty fingers over the Sabbath candles, and sob softly to herself. On those evenings my child's heart was rocked like a little ship upon enchanted waves. O the rotted Talmuds of my childhood! O the dense melancholy of memories!

I roam through Zhitomir in search of a shy star. By the

ancient synagogue, by its yellow and indifferent walls, old Jews with prophets' beards and passionate rags on their sunken chests sell chalk and wicks and bluing.

Here before me is the market, and the death of the market. Gone is the fat soul of plenty. Dumb padlocks hang upon the booths, and the granite paving is as clean as a skull. My shy star blinks, and fades from sight.

Success came to me later on; success came just before sunset. Gedali's little shop was hidden away in a row of others, all hermetically closed. Where was your kindly shade that evening, Dickens? In that little old curiosity shop you would have seen gilt slippers, ship's cables, an ancient compass, a stuffed eagle, a Winchester with the date 1810 engraved upon it, a broken saucepan.

Old Gedali, the little proprietor in smoked glasses and a green frock coat down to the ground, meandered around his treasures in the roseate void of evening. He rubbed his small white hands, plucked at his little gray beard, and listened, head bent, to the mysterious voices wafting down to him.

The shop was like the box of an important and knowledge-loving little boy who will grow up to be a professor of botany. There were buttons in it, and a dead butterfly, and its small owner went by the name of Gedali. All had abandoned the market; but Gedali had remained. He wound in and out of a labyrinth of globes, skulls, and dead flowers, waving a bright feather duster of cock's plumes and blowing dust from the dead flowers.

And so we sat upon small beer-barrels, Gedali twisting and untwisting his narrow beard. Like a little black tower, his hat swayed above us. Warm air flowed past. The sky changed color. Blood, delicate-hued, poured down from an overturned bottle up there, and a vague odor of corruption enfolded me.

"The Revolution—we will say 'yes' to it, but are we to say 'no' to the Sabbath?" began Gedali, winding about me the straps of his smoke-hidden eyes. "Yes, I cry to the Revolution. Yes, I cry to it, but it hides its face from Gedali and sends out on front nought but shooting . . ."

"The sunlight doesn't enter eyes that are closed," I answered the old man. "But we will cut open those closed eyes . . ."

"A Pole closed my eyes," whispered the old man, in a voice that was barely audible. "The Poles are bad-tempered dogs. They take the Jew and pluck out his beard, the curs! And now they are being beaten, the bad-tempered dogs. That is splendid, that is the Revolution. And then those who have beaten the Poles say to me: 'Hand your phonograph over to the State, Gedali . . .' 'I am fond of music, Pani,' I say to the Revolution. 'You don't know what you are fond of, Gedali. I'll shoot and then you'll know. I cannot do without shooting, because I am the Revolution.' "

"She cannot do without shooting, Gedali," I told the old man, "because she is the Revolution."

"But the Poles, kind sir, shot because they were the Counter-Revolution. You shoot because you are the Revolution. But surely the Revolution means joy. And joy does not like orphans in the house. Good men do good deeds. The Revolution is the good deed of good men. But good men do not kill. So it is bad people that are making the Revolution. But the Poles are bad people too. Then how is Gedali to tell which is Revolution and which is Counter-Revolution? I used to study the Talmud, I love Rashi's Commentaries and the books of Maimonides. And there are yet other understanding folk in Zhitomir. And here we are, all of us learned people, falling on our faces and crying out in a loud voice: 'Woe unto us, where is the joy-giving Revolution?' "

The old man fell silent. And we saw the first star pierce through the Milky Way.

"The Sabbath has begun," Gedali stated solemnly; "Jews should be going to the synagogue. Pan comrade," he said, rising, his top hat like a little black tower swaying on his head, "bring a few good people to Zhitomir. Oh, there's a scarcity of good people in our town. Oh, what a scarcity! Bring them along and we will hand over all our phonographs to them. We are not ignoramuses. The International —we know what the International is. And I want an International of good people. I would like every soul to be listed and given first-category rations. There, soul, please eat and enjoy life's pleasures. Pan comrade, you don't know what the International is eaten with . . ."

"It is eaten with gunpowder," I answered the old man, "and spiced with best-quality blood."

And then, from out of the blue gloom, the young Sabbath came to take her seat of honor.

"Gedali," I said, "today is Friday, and it's already evening. Where are Jewish biscuits to be got, and a Jewish glass of tea, and a little of that pensioned-off God in a glass of tea?"

"Not to be had," Gedali replied, hanging the padlock on his little booth. "Not to be had. Next door is a tavern, and they were good people who served in it; but nobody eats there now, people weep there."

He buttoned his green frock coat on three bone buttons, flicked himself with the cock's feathers, sprinkled a little water on his soft palms, and departed, a tiny, lonely visionary in a black top hat, carrying a big prayerbook under his arm.

The Sabbath is coming. Gedali, the founder of an impossible International, has gone to the synagogue to pray.

The Story of My Dovecot

To M. GORKY

When I was a kid I longed for a dovecot. Never in all my life have I wanted a thing more. But not till I was nine did father promise the wherewithal to buy the wood to make one and three pairs of pigeons to stock it with. It was then 1904, and I was studying for the entrance exam to the preparatory class of the secondary school at Nikolayev in the Province of Kherson, where my people were at that time living. This province of course no longer exists, and our town has been incorporated in the Odessa Region.

I was only nine, and I was scared stiff of the exams. In both subjects, Russian language and arithmetic, I couldn't afford to get less than top marks. At our secondary school the *numerus clausus* was stiff: a mere five percent. So that out of forty boys only two that were Jews could get into the preparatory class. The teachers used to put cunning questions to Jewish boys; no one else was asked such devilish questions. So when father promised to buy the pigeons he demanded top marks with distinction in both subjects. He absolutely tortured me to death. I fell into a state of permanent daydream, into an endless, despairing, childish reverie. I went to the exam deep in this dream, and nevertheless did better than everybody else.

I had a knack for book-learning. Even though they asked cunning questions, the teachers could not rob me of my intelligence and my avid memory. I was good at learning, and got top marks in both subjects. But then everything went wrong. Khariton Efrussi, the corn-dealer who exported wheat to Marseille, slipped someone a 500-rouble bribe. My mark was changed from A to A—, and Efrussi Junior went to the secondary school instead of me. Father took it very badly. From the time I was six he had been cramming me with every scrap of learning he could, and that A— drove him to despair. He wanted to beat Efrussi up, or at least bribe two longshoremen to beat Efrussi up, but mother talked him out of the idea, and I started studying for the second exam the following year, the one for the lowest class. Behind my back my people got the teacher to take me in one year through the preparatory and first-year courses simultaneously, and conscious of the family's despair, I got three whole books by heart. These were Smirnovsky's *Russian Grammar,* Yevtushevsky's *Problems,* and Putsykovich's *Manual of Early Russian History.* Children no longer cram from these books, but I learned them by heart line upon line, and the following year in the Russian exam Karavayev gave me an unrivaled A+.

This Karavayev was a red-faced, irritable fellow, a graduate of Moscow University. He was hardly more than thirty. Crimson glowed in his manly cheeks as it does in

the cheeks of peasant children. A wart sat perched on one
cheek, and from it there sprouted a tuft of ash-colored cat's
whiskers. At the exam, besides Karavayev, there was the
Assistant Curator Pyatnitsky, who was reckoned a big
noise in the school and throughout the province. When the
Assistant Curator asked me about Peter the Great a feeling of complete oblivion came over me, an awareness that
the end was near: an abyss seemed to yawn before me, an
arid abyss lined with exultation and despair.

About Peter the Great I knew things by heart from
Putsykovich's book and Pushkin's verses. Sobbing, I recited
these verses, while the faces before me suddenly turned upside down, were shuffled as a pack of cards is shuffled.
This card-shuffling went on, and meanwhile, shivering,
jerking my back straight, galloping headlong, I was shouting Pushkin's stanzas at the top of my voice. On and on I
yelled them, and no one broke into my crazy mouthings.
Through a crimson blindness, through the sense of absolute freedom that had filled me, I was aware of nothing but
Pyatnitsky's old face with its silver-touched beard bent toward me. He didn't interrupt me, and merely said to
Karavayev, who was rejoicing for my sake and Pushkin's:

"What a people," the old man whispered, "those little
Jews of yours! There's a devil in them!"

And when at last I could shout no more, he said:

"Very well, run along, my little friend."

I went out from the classroom into the corridor, and
there, leaning against a wall that needed a coat of white-
wash, I began to awake from my trance. About me Russian
boys were playing, the school bell hung not far away above
the stairs, the caretaker was snoozing on a chair with a
broken seat. I looked at the caretaker, and gradually woke
up. Boys were creeping toward me from all sides. They
wanted to give me a jab, or perhaps just have a game, but
Pyatnitsky suddenly loomed up in the corridor. As he
passed me he halted for a moment, the frock coat flowing
down his back in a slow heavy wave. I discerned embarrassment in that large, fleshy, upper-class back, and got
closer to the old man.

"Children," he said to the boys, "don't touch this lad."
And he laid a fat hand tenderly on my shoulder.

"My little friend," he went on, turning me towards him,
"tell your father that you are admitted to the first class."

On his chest a great star flashed, and decorations jin-
gled in his lapel. His great black uniformed body started to
move away on its stiff legs. Hemmed in by the shadowy
walls, moving between them as a barge moves through a
deep canal, it disappeared in the doorway of the head-
master's study. The little servingman took in a tray of tea,
clinking solemnly, and I ran home to the shop.

In the shop a peasant customer, tortured by doubt, sat
scratching himself. When he saw me my father stopped
trying to help the peasant make up his mind, and without
a moment's hesitation believed everything I had to say.
Calling to the assistant to start shutting up shop, he dashed
out into Cathedral Street to buy me a school cap with a
badge on it. My poor mother had her work cut out getting
me away from the crazy fellow. She was pale at that moment, she was experiencing destiny. She kept smoothing
me, and pushing me away as though she hated me. She
said there was always a notice in the paper about those
who had been admitted to the school, and that God would
punish us, and that folk would laugh at us if we bought a
school cap too soon. My mother was pale; she was experiencing destiny through my eyes. She looked at me with
bitter compassion as one might look at a little cripple boy,
because she alone knew what a family ours was for misfortunes.

All the men in our family were trusting by nature, and
quick to ill-considered actions. We were unlucky in everything we undertook. My grandfather had been a rabbi
somewhere in the Belaya Tserkov region. He had been
thrown out for blasphemy, and for another forty years he
lived noisily and sparsely, teaching foreign languages. In
his eightieth year he started going off his head. My Uncle
Leo, my father's brother, had studied at the Talmudic
Academy in Volozhin. In 1892 he ran away to avoid doing
military service, eloping with the daughter of someone

serving in the commissariat in the Kiev military district.
Uncle Leo took this woman to California, to Los Angeles,
and there he abandoned her, and died in a house of ill fame
among Negroes and Malays. After his death the American
police sent us a heritage from Los Angeles, a large trunk
bound with brown iron hoops. In this trunk there were
dumbbells, locks of women's hair, uncle's talith, horse-
whips with gilt handles, scented tea in boxes trimmed with
imitation pearls. Of all the family there remained only crazy
Uncle Simon-Wolf, who lived in Odessa, my father, and I.
But my father had faith in people, and he used to put them
off with the transports of first love. People could not forgive him for this, and used to play him false. So my father
believed that his life was guided by an evil fate, an inexplicable being that pursued him, a being in every respect
unlike him. And so I alone of all our family was left to my
mother. Like all Jews I was short, weakly, and had headaches from studying. My mother saw all this. She had never
been dazzled by her husband's pauper pride, by his incom-
prehensible belief that our family would one day be richer
and more powerful than all others on earth. She desired no
success for us, was scared of buying a school jacket too
soon, and all she would consent to was that I should have
my photo taken.

On September 20, 1905, a list of those admitted to the
first class was hung up at the school. In the list my name
figured too. All our kith and kin kept going to look at this
paper, and even Shoyl, my granduncle, went along. I loved
that boastful old man, for he sold fish at the market. His
fat hands were moist, covered with fish-scales, and smelt of
worlds chill and beautiful. Shoyl also differed from ordinary folk in the lying stories he used to tell about the Polish
Rising of 1861. Years ago Shoyl had been a tavern-keeper
at Skvira. He had seen Nicholas I's soldiers shooting Count
Godlevski and other Polish insurgents. But perhaps he
hadn't. *Now* I know that Shoyl was just an old ignoramus
and a simple-minded liar, but his cock-and-bull stories I
have never forgotten: they were good stories. Well now,
even silly old Shoyl went along to the school to read the list

with my name on it, and that evening he danced and
pranced at our pauper ball.

My father got up the ball to celebrate my success, and
asked all his pals—grain-dealers, real-estate brokers, and
the traveling salesmen who sold agricultural machinery in
our parts. These salesmen would sell a machine to anyone.
Peasants and landowners went in fear of them: you couldn't
break loose without buying something or other. Of all Jews,
salesmen are the widest-awake and the jolliest. At our party
they sang Hasidic songs consisting of three words only but
which took an awful long time to sing, songs performed
with endless comical intonations. The beauty of these intonations may only be recognized by those who have had
the good fortune to spend Passover with the Hasidim or who
have visited their noisy Volhynian synagogues. Besides the
salesmen, old Lieberman who had taught me the Torah and
ancient Hebrew honored us with his presence. In our circle
he was known as Monsieur Lieberman. He drank more
Bessarabian wine than he should have. The ends of the traditional silk tassels poked out from beneath his waistcoat,
and in ancient Hebrew he proposed my health. In this toast
the old man congratulated my parents and said that I had
vanquished all my foes in single combat: I had vanquished
the Russian boys with their fat cheeks, and I had vanquished the sons of our own vulgar parvenus. So too in
ancient times David King of Judah had overcome Goliath,
and just as I had triumphed over Goliath, so too would our
people by the strength of their intellect conquer the foes
who had encircled us and were thirsting for our blood.
Monsieur Lieberman started to weep as he said this, drank
more wine as he wept, and shouted *"Vivat!"* The guests
formed a circle and danced an old-fashioned quadrille with
him in the middle, just as at a wedding in a little Jewish
town. Everyone was happy at our ball. Even mother took a
sip of vodka, though she neither liked the stuff nor understood how anyone else could—because of this she considered all Russians cracked, and just couldn't imagine how
women managed with Russian husbands.

But our happy days came later. For mother they came

when of a morning, before I set off for school, she would
start making me sandwiches; when we went shopping to
buy my school things—pencil box, money box, satchel, new
books in cardboard bindings, and exercise books in shiny
covers. No one in the world has a keener feeling for new
things than children have. Children shudder at the smell of
newness as a dog does when it scents a hare, experiencing
the madness which later, when we grow up, is called inspiration. And mother acquired this pure and childish sense
of the ownership of new things. It took us a whole month
to get used to the pencil box, to the morning twilight as I
drank my tea on the corner of the large, brightly-lit table
and packed my books in my satchel. It took us a month to
grow accustomed to our happiness, and it was only after the
first half-term that I remembered about the pigeons.

I had everything ready for them: one rouble fifty and
a dovecot made from a box by Grandfather Shoyl, as we
called him. The dovecot was painted brown. It had nests for
twelve pairs of pigeons, carved strips on the roof, and a special grating that I had devised to facilitate the capture of
strange birds. All was in readiness. On Sunday, October 20,
I set out for the bird market, but unexpected obstacles arose
in my path.

The events I am relating, that is to say my admission to
the first class at the secondary school, occurred in the autumn of 1905. The Emperor Nicholas was then bestowing
a constitution on the Russian people. Orators in shabby
overcoats were clambering onto tall curbstones and ha-
ranguing the people. At night shots had been heard in the
streets, and so mother didn't want me to go to the bird
market. From early morning on October 20 the boys next
door were flying a kite right by the police station, and our
water carrier, abandoning all his buckets, was walking
about the streets with a red face and brilliantined hair.
Then we saw baker Kalistov's sons drag a leather vaulting-
horse out into the street and start doing gym in the middle
of the roadway. No one tried to stop them: Semernikov the
policeman even kept inciting them to jump higher. Semernikov was girt with a silk belt his wife had made him, and

his boots had been polished that day as they had never been polished before. Out of his customary uniform, the policeman frightened my mother more than anything else. Because of him she didn't want me to go out, but I sneaked out by the back way and ran to the bird market, which in our town was behind the station.

At the bird market Ivan Nikodimych, the pigeon-fancier, sat in his customary place. Apart from pigeons, he had rabbits for sale too, and a peacock. The peacock, spreading its tail, sat on a perch moving a passionless head from side to side. To its paw was tied a twisted cord, and the other end of the cord was caught beneath one leg of Ivan Nikodimych's wicker chair. The moment I got there I bought from the old man a pair of cherry-colored pigeons with luscious tousled tails, and a pair of crowned pigeons, and put them away in a bag on my chest under my shirt. After these purchases I had only forty copecks left, and for this price the old man was not prepared to let me have a male and female pigeon of the Kryukov breed. What I liked about Kryukov pigeons was their short, knobbly, good-natured beaks. Forty copecks was the proper price, but the fancier insisted on haggling, averting from me a yellow face scorched by the unsociable passions of bird-snarers. At the end of our bargaining, seeing that there were no other customers, Ivan Nikodimych beckoned me closer. All went as I wished, and all went badly.

Toward twelve o'clock, or perhaps a bit later, a man in felt boots passed across the square. He was stepping lightly on swollen feet, and in his worn-out face lively eyes glittered.

"Ivan Nikodimych," he said as he walked past the bird-fancier, "pack up your gear. In town the Jerusalem aristocrats are being granted a constitution. On Fish Street Grandfather Babel has been constitutioned to death."

He said this and walked lightly on between the cages like a barefoot ploughman walking along the edge of a field.

"They shouldn't," murmured Ivan Nikodimych in his wake. "They shouldn't!" he cried more sternly. He started collecting his rabbits and his peacock, and shoved the

Kryukov pigeons at me for forty copecks. I hid them in my bosom and watched the people running away from the bird market. The peacock on Ivan Nikodimych's shoulder was last of all to depart. It sat there like the sun in a raw autumnal sky; it sat as July sits on a pink riverbank, a white-hot July in the long cool grass. No one was left in the market, and not far off shots were rattling. Then I ran to the station, cut across a square that had gone topsy-turvy, and flew down an empty lane of trampled yellow earth. At the end of the lane, in a little wheeled armchair, sat the legless Makarenko, who rode about town in his wheel-chair selling cigarettes from a tray. The boys in our street used to buy smokes from him, children loved him, I dashed toward him down the lane.

"Makarenko," I gasped, panting from my run, and I stroked the legless one's shoulder, "have you seen Shoyl?"

The cripple did not reply. A light seemed to be shining through his coarse face built up of red fat, clenched fists, chunks of iron. He was fidgeting on his chair in his excitement, while his wife Kate, presenting a wadded behind, was sorting out some things scattered on the ground.

"How far have you counted?" asked the legless man, and moved his whole bulk away from the woman, as though aware in advance that her answer would be unbearable.

"Fourteen pair of leggings," said Kate, still bending over, "six undersheets. Now I'm a-counting the bonnets."

"Bonnets!" cried Makarenko, with a choking sound like a sob, "it's clear, Catherine, that God has picked on me, that I must answer for all. People are carting off whole rolls of cloth, people have everything they should, and we're stuck with bonnets."

And indeed a woman with a beautiful burning face ran past us down the lane. She was clutching an armful of fezzes in one arm and a piece of cloth in the other, and in a voice of joyful despair she was yelling for her children, who had strayed. A silk dress and a blue blouse fluttered after her as she flew, and she paid no attention to Makarenko who was rolling his chair in pursuit of her. The

legless man couldn't catch up. His wheels clattered as he
turned the handles for all he was worth.

"Little lady," he cried in a deafening voice, "where did
you get that striped stuff?"

But the woman with the fluttering dress was gone. Round
the corner to meet her leaped a rickety cart in which a
peasant lad stood upright.

"Where've they all run to?" asked the lad, raising a red
rein above the nags jerking in their collars.

"Everybody's on Cathedral Street," said Makarenko
pleadingly, "everybody's there, sonny. Anything you happen to pick up, bring it along to me. I'll give you a good
price."

The lad bent down over the front of the cart and
whipped up his piebald nags. Tossing their filthy croups
like calves, the horses shot off at a gallop. The yellow lane
was once more yellow and empty. Then the legless man
turned his quenched eyes upon me.

"God's picked on me, I reckon," he said lifelessly, "I'm
a son of man, I reckon."

And he stretched a hand spotted with leprosy toward me.

"What's that you've got in your sack?" he demanded, and
took the bag that had been warming my heart.

With his fat hand the cripple fumbled among the tum-
bler pigeons and dragged to light a cherry-colored she-bird.
Jerking back its feet, the bird lay still on his palm.

"Pigeons," said Makarenko, and squeaking his wheels he
rode right up to me. "Damned pigeons," he repeated, and
struck me on the cheek.

He dealt me a flying blow with the hand that was clutching the bird. Kate's wadded back seemed to turn upside
down, and I fell to the ground in my new overcoat.

"Their spawn must be wiped out," said Kate, straightening up over the bonnets. "I can't a-bear their spawn, nor
their stinking menfolk."

She said more things about our spawn, but I heard nothing of it. I lay on the ground, and the guts of the crushed
bird trickled down from my temple. They flowed down my

cheek, winding this way and that, splashing, blinding me. The tender pigeon-guts slid down over my forehead, and I closed my solitary unstopped-up eye so as not to see the world that spread out before me. This world was tiny, and it was awful. A stone lay just before my eyes, a little stone so chipped as to resemble the face of an old woman with a large jaw. A piece of string lay not far away, and a bunch of feathers that still breathed. My world was tiny, and it was awful. I closed my eyes so as not to see it, and pressed myself tight into the ground that lay beneath me in soothing dumbness. This trampled earth in no way resembled real life, waiting for exams in real life. Somewhere far away Woe rode across it on a great steed, but the noise of the hoofbeats grew weaker and died away, and silence, the bitter silence that sometimes overwhelms children in their sorrow, suddenly deleted the boundary between my body and the earth that was moving nowhither. The earth smelled of raw depths, of the tomb, of flowers. I smelled its smell and started crying, unafraid. I was walking along an unknown street set on either side with white boxes, walking in a getup of bloodstained feathers, alone between the pavements swept clean as on Sunday, weeping bitterly, fully and happily as I never wept again in all my life. Wires that had grown white hummed above my head, a watchdog trotted on in front, in the lane on one side a young peasant in a waistcoat was smashing a window frame in the house of Khariton Efrussi. He was smashing it with a wooden mallet, striking out with his whole body. Sighing, he smiled all around with the amiable grin of drunkenness, sweat, and spiritual power. The whole street was filled with a splitting, a snapping, the song of flying wood. The peasant's whole existence consisted in bending over, sweating, shouting queer words in some unknown, non-Russian language. He shouted the words and sang, shot out his blue eyes; till in the street there appeared a procession bearing the Cross and moving from the Municipal Building. Old men bore aloft the portrait of the neatly-combed Tsar, banners with graveyard saints swayed above their heads, inflamed old women flew on in front. Seeing the procession, the peasant pressed his mallet to his chest and dashed off in pursuit of the banners, while I, waiting till the tail-end of the procession had passed, made my furtive way home. The house was empty. Its white doors were open, the grass by the dovecot had been trampled down. Only Kuzma was still in the yard. Kuzma the yardman was sitting in the shed laying out the dead Shoyl.

"The wind bears you about like an evil wood-chip," said the old man when he saw me. "You've been away ages. And now look what they've done to granddad."

Kuzma wheezed, turned away from me, and started pulling a fish out of the rent in grandfather's trousers. Two pike perch had been stuck into grandfather: one into the rent in his trousers, the other into his mouth. And while grandfather was dead, one of the fish was still alive, and struggling.

"They've done grandfather in, but nobody else," said Kuzma, tossing the fish to the cat. "He cursed them all good and proper, a wonderful damning and blasting it was. You might fetch a couple of pennies to put on his eyes."

But then, at ten years of age, I didn't know what need the dead had of pennies.

"Kuzma," I whispered, "save us."

And I went over to the yardman, hugged his crooked old back with its one shoulder higher than the other, and over this back I saw grandfather. Shoyl lay in the sawdust, his chest squashed in, his beard twisted upwards, battered shoes on his bare feet. His feet, thrown wide apart, were dirty, lilac-colored, dead. Kuzma was fussing over him. He tied the dead man's jaws and kept glancing over the body to see what else he could do. He fussed as though over a newly-purchased garment, and only cooled down when he had given the dead man's beard a good combing.

"He cursed the lot of 'em right and left," he said, smiling, and cast a loving look over the corpse. "If Tartars had crossed his path he'd have sent them packing, but Russians came, and their women with them, Rooski women. Russians just can't bring themselves to forgive, I know what Rooskis are."

The yardman spread some more sawdust beneath the body, threw off his carpenter's apron, and took me by the hand.

"Let's go to father," he mumbled, squeezing my hand tighter and tighter. "Your father has been searching for you since morning, sure as fate you was dead."

And so with Kuzma I went to the house of the tax-inspector, where my parents, escaping the pogrom, had sought refuge.

Awakening

All the folk in our circle—brokers, shopkeepers, clerks in banks and steamship offices—used to have their children taught music. Our fathers, seeing no other escape from their lot, had thought up a lottery, building it on the bones of little children. Odessa more than other towns was seized by the craze. And in fact, in the course of ten years or so our town supplied the concert platforms of the world with infant prodigies. From Odessa came Mischa Elman, Zimbalist, Gabrilowitsch. Odessa witnessed the first steps of Jascha Heifetz.

When a lad was four or five, his mother took the puny creature to Zagursky's. Mr. Zagursky ran a factory of infant prodigies, a factory of Jewish dwarfs in lace collars and patent-leather pumps. He hunted them out in the slums of the Moldavanka, in the evil-smelling courtyards of the Old Market. Mr. Zagursky charted the first course, then the children were shipped off to Professor Auer in St. Petersburg. A wonderful harmony dwelt in the souls of those wizened creatures with their swollen blue hands. They became famous virtuosi. My father decided that I should emulate them. Though I had, as a matter of fact, passed the age limit set for infant prodigies, being now in my fourteenth year, my shortness and lack of strength made it possible to pass me off as an eight-year-old. Herein lay father's hope.

I was taken to Zagursky's. Out of respect for my grand-father, Mr. Zagursky agreed to take me on at the cut rate of a rouble a lesson. My grandfather Leivi-Itzkhok was the laughingstock of the town, and its chief adornment. He used to walk about the streets in a top hat and old boots, dissipating doubt in the darkest of cases. He would be asked what a Gobelin was, why the Jacobins betrayed Robespierre, how you made artificial silk, what a Caesarean section was. And my grandfather could answer these questions. Out of respect for his learning and craziness, Mr. Zagursky only charged us a rouble a lesson. And he had the devil of a time with me, fearing my grandfather, for with me there was nothing to be done. The sounds dripped from my fiddle like iron filings, causing even me excruciating agony, but father wouldn't give in. At home there was no talk save of Mischa Elman, exempted by the Tsar himself from military service. Zimbalist, father would have us know, had been presented to the King of England and had played at Buckingham Palace. The parents of Gabrilowitsch had bought two houses in St. Petersburg. Infant prodigies brought wealth to their parents, but though my father could have reconciled himself to poverty, fame he must have.

"It's not possible," people feeding at his expense would insinuate, "it's just not possible that the grandson of such a grandfather . . ."

But what went on in my head was quite different. Scraping my way through the violin exercises, I would have books by Turgenev or Dumas on my music stand. Page after page I devoured as I deedled away. In the daytime I would relate impossible happenings to the kids next door; at night I would commit them to paper. In our family, composition was a hereditary occupation. Grandfather Leivi-Itzkhok, who went cracked as he grew old, spent his whole life writing a tale entitled "The Headless Man." I took after him.

Three times a week, laden with violin case and music, I made my reluctant way to Zagursky's place on Witte (formerly Dvoryanskaya) Street. There Jewish girls aflame

with hysteria sat along the wall awaiting their turn,
pressing to their feeble knees violins exceeding in dimen-
sions the exalted persons they were to play to at Buckingham Palace.

The door to the sanctum would open, and from Mr.
Zagursky's study there would stagger big-headed, freckled
children with necks as thin as flower stalks and an epileptic
flush on their cheeks. The door would bang to, swallowing
up the next dwarf. Behind the wall, straining his throat, the
teacher sang and waved his baton. He had ginger curls and
frail legs, and sported a big bow tie. Manager of a monstrous lottery, he populated the Moldavanka and the dark
culs-de-sac of the Old Market with the ghosts of pizzicato
and cantilena. Afterward old Professor Auer lent these
strains a diabolical brilliance.

In this crew I was quite out of place. Though like them
in my dwarfishness, in the voice of my forebears I perceived inspiration of another sort.

The first step was difficult. One day I left home laden
like a beast of burden with violin case, violin, music, and
twelve roubles in cash—payment for a month's tuition. I
was going along Nezhin Street; to get to Zagursky's I
should have turned into Dvoryanskaya, but instead of that
I went up Tiraspolskaya and found myself at the harbor.
The alloted time flew past in the part of the port where
ships went after quarantine. So began my liberation. Zagursky's saw me no more: affairs of greater moment occupied
my thoughts. My pal Nemanov and I got into the habit of
slipping aboard the S.S. *Kensington* to see an old salt
named Trottyburn. Nemanov was a year younger than I.
From the age of eight onward he had been doing the most
ingenious business deals you can imagine. He had a wonderful head for that kind of thing, and later on amply fulfilled his youthful promise. Now he is a New York mil-
lionaire, director of General Motors, a company no less
powerful than Ford. Nemanov took me along with him
because I silently obeyed all his orders. He used to buy
pipes smuggled in by Mr. Trottyburn. They were made in
Lincoln by the old sailor's brother.

"Gen'lemen," Mr. Trottyburn would say to us, "take my word, the pets must be made with your own hands. Smoking a factory-made pipe—might as well shove an enema in your mouth. D'you know who Benvenuto Cellini was? He was a grand lad. My brother in Lincoln could tell you about him. Live and let live is my brother's motto. He's got it into his head that you just has to make the pets with your own hands, and not with no one else's. And who are we to say him no, gen'lemen?"

Nemanov used to sell Trottyburn's pipes to bank-managers, foreign consuls, well-to-do Greeks. He made a hundred percent on them.

The pipes of the Lincolnshire master breathed poetry. In each one of them thought was invested, a drop of eternity. A little yellow eye gleamed in their mouthpieces, and their cases were lined with satin. I tried to picture the life in Old England of Matthew Trottyburn, the last master-pipemaker, who refused to swim with the tide.

"We can't but agree, gen'lemen, that the pets has to be made with your own hands."

The heavy waves by the sea wall swept me further and further away from our house, impregnated with the smell of leeks and Jewish destiny. From the harbor I migrated to the other side of the breakwater. There on a scrap of sandspit dwelt the boys from Primorskaya Street. Trouserless from morn till eve, they dived under wherries, sneaked coconuts for dinner, and awaited the time when boats would arrive from Kherson and Kamenka laden with watermelons, which melons it would be possible to break open against moorings.

To learn to swim was my dream. I was ashamed to confess to those bronzed lads that, born in Odessa, I had not seen the sea till I was ten, and at fourteen didn't know how to swim.

How slow was my acquisition of the things one needs to know! In my childhood, chained to the Gemara, I had led the life of a sage. When I grew up I started climbing trees.

But swimming proved beyond me. The hydrophobia of my ancestors—Spanish rabbis and Frankfurt money-changers—dragged me to the bottom. The waves refused to support me. I would struggle to the shore pumped full of salt water and feeling as though I had been flayed, and return to where my fiddle and music lay. I was fettered to the instruments of my torture, and dragged them about with me. The struggle of rabbis versus Neptune continued till such time as the local water-god took pity on me. This was Yefim Nikitich Smolich, proofreader of the *Odessa News*. In his athletic breast there dwelt compassion for Jewish children, and he was the god of a rabble of rickety starvelings. He used to collect them from the bug-infested joints on the Moldavanka, take them down to the sea, bury them in the sand, do gym with them, dive with them, teach them songs. Roasting in the perpendicular sunrays, he would tell them tales about fishermen and wild beasts. To grownups Nikitich would explain that he was a natural philosopher. The Jewish kids used to roar with laughter at his tales, squealing and snuggling up to him like so many puppies. The sun would sprinkle them with creeping freckles, freckles of the same color as lizards.

Silently, out of the corner of his eye, the old man had been watching my duel with the waves. Seeing that the thing was hopeless, that I should simply never learn to swim, he included me among the permanent occupants of his heart. That cheerful heart of his was with us there all the time; it never went careering off anywhere else, never knew covetousness and never grew disturbed. With his sunburned shoulders, his superannuated gladiator's head, his bronzed and slightly bandy legs, he would lie among us on the other side of the mole, lord and master of those melon-sprinkled, paraffin-stained waters. I came to love that man, with the love that only a lad suffering from hysteria and headaches can feel for a real man. I was always at his side, always trying to be of service to him.

He said to me:

"Don't you get all worked up. You just strengthen your nerves. The swimming will come of itself. How d'you mean, the water won't hold you? Why shouldn't it hold you?"

Seeing how drawn I was to him, Nikitich made an exception of me alone of all his disciples. He invited me to visit the clean and spacious attic where he lived in an ambience of straw mats, showed me his dogs, his hedgehog, his tortoise, and his pigeons. In return for this wealth I showed him a tragedy I had written the day before.

"I was sure you did a bit of scribbling," said Nikitich. "You've the look. You're looking in *that* direction all the time; no eyes for anywhere else."

He read my writings, shrugged a shoulder, passed a hand through his stiff gray curls, paced up and down the attic.

"One must suppose," he said slowly, pausing after each word, "one must suppose that there's a spark of the divine fire in you."

We went out into the street. The old man halted, struck the pavement with his stick, and fastened his gaze upon me.

"Now what is it you lack? Youth's no matter—it'll pass with the years. What you lack is a feeling for nature."

He pointed with his stick at a tree with a reddish trunk and a low crown.

"What's that tree?"

I didn't know.

"What's growing on that bush?"

I didn't know this either. We walked together across the little square on the Alexandrovsky Prospect. The old man kept poking his stick at trees; he would seize me by the shoulder when a bird flew past, and he made me listen to the various kinds of singing.

"What bird is that singing?"

I knew none of the answers. The names of trees and birds, their division into species, where birds fly away to, on which side the sun rises, when the dew falls thickest—all these things were unknown to me.

"And you dare to write! A man who doesn't live in nature, as a stone does or an animal, will never in all his life write two worthwhile lines. Your landscapes are like descriptions of stage props. In heaven's name, what have your parents been thinking of for fourteen years?"

What *had* they been thinking of? Of protested bills of exchange, of Mischa Elman's mansions. I didn't say anything to Nikitich about that, but just kept mum.

At home, over dinner, I couldn't touch my food. It just wouldn't go down.

"A feeling for nature," I thought to myself. "Goodness, why did that never enter my head? Where am I to find someone who will tell me about the way birds sing and what trees are called? What do *I* know about such things? I might perhaps recognize lilac, at any rate when it's in bloom. Lilac and acacia—there are acacias along De Ribas and Greek Streets."

At dinner father told a new story about Jascha Heifetz. Just before he got to Robinat's he had met Mendelssohn, Jascha's uncle. It appeared that the lad was getting eight hundred roubles a performance. Just work out how much that comes to at fifteen concerts a month!

I did, and the answer was twelve thousand a month. Multiplying and carrying four in my head, I glanced out of the window. Across the cement courtyard, his cloak swaying in the breeze, his ginger curls poking out from under his soft hat, leaning on his cane, Mr. Zagursky, my music teacher, was advancing. It must be admitted he had taken his time in spotting my truancy. More than three months had elapsed since the day when my violin had grounded on the sand by the breakwater.

Mr. Zagursky was approaching the main entrance. I dashed to the back door, but the day before it had been nailed up for fear of burglars. Then I locked myself in the privy. In half an hour the whole family had assembled outside the door. The women were weeping. Aunt Bobka, exploding with sobs, was rubbing her fat shoulder against the door. Father was silent. Finally he started speaking, quietly and distinctly as he had never before spoken in his life.

"I am an officer," said my father. "I own real estate. I go hunting. Peasants pay me rent. I have entered my son in the Cadet Corps. I have no need to worry about my son."

He was silent again. The women were sniffling. Then a

terrible blow descended on the privy door. My father was hurling his whole body against it, stepping back and then throwing himself forward.

"I am an officer," he kept wailing. "I go hunting. I'll kill him. This is the end."

The hook sprang from the door, but there was still a bolt hanging onto a single nail. The women were rolling about on the floor, grasping father by the legs. Crazy, he was trying to break loose. Father's mother came over, alerted by the hubbub.

"My child," she said to him in Hebrew, "our grief is great. It has no bounds. Only blood was lacking in our house. I do not wish to see blood in our house."

Father gave a groan. I heard his footsteps retreating. The bolt still hung by its last nail.

I sat it out in my fortress till nightfall. When all had gone to bed, Aunt Bobka took me to grandmother's. We had a long way to go. The moonlight congealed on bushes unknown to me, on trees that had no name. Some anonymous bird emitted a whistle and was extinguished, perhaps by sleep. What bird was it? What was it called? Does dew fall in the evening? Where is the constellation of the Great Bear? On what side does the sun rise?

We were going along Post Office Street. Aunt Bobka held me firmly by the hand so that I shouldn't run away. She was right to. I was thinking of running away.

ISAAC BASHEVIS SINGER

Isaac Bashevis Singer, born in 1904 in Poland, has lived in the United States since 1935. During the twenties he was a journalist for the Yiddish press in Warsaw. A fertile and productive writer, he has produced a great volume of work, much of it as yet untranslated. Mr. Singer published in *Forwards* which maintained the European tradition of the *feuilleton*. The last of the important Yiddish writers in America (the language is dying out here), he is considered by many to be the most gifted. *The Family Moskat,* the first of his novels to be translated into English, was a chronicle novel. As Mr. Singer grows older, his writing becomes increasingly unconventional and original. His recent books are *Satan in Goray, The Magician of Lublin, The Spinoza of Market Street,* and *The Slave* (1962).

Gimpel the Fool

1

I am Gimpel the fool. I don't think myself a fool. On the contrary. But that's what folks call me. They gave me the name while I was still in school. I had seven names in all: imbecile, donkey, flax-head, dope, glump, ninny, and fool. The last name stuck. What did my foolishness consist of? I was easy to take in. They said, "Gimpel, you know the

Translated by Saul Bellow. This story and the next one are from *Gimpel the Fool.* Copyright © 1953, by The Viking Press, Inc., copyright © 1957 by Isaac Bashevis Singer, and reprinted by permission of Farrar, Straus & Cudahy, Inc.

rabbi's wife has been brought to childbed?" So I skipped school. Well, it turned out to be a lie. How was I supposed to know? She hadn't had a big belly. But I never looked at her belly. Was that really so foolish? The gang laughed and hee-hawed, stomped and danced and chanted a good-night prayer. And instead of the raisins they give when a woman's lying in, they stuffed my hand full of goat turds. I was no weakling. If I slapped someone he'd see all the way to Cracow. But I'm really not a slugger by nature. I think to myself: Let it pass. So they take advantage of me.

I was coming home from school and heard a dog barking. I'm not afraid of dogs, but of course I never want to start up with them. One of them may be mad, and if he bites there's not a Tartar in the world who can help you. So I made tracks. Then I looked around and saw the whole market place wild with laughter. It was no dog at all but Wolf-Leib the Thief. How was I supposed to know it was he? It sounded like a howling bitch.

When the pranksters and leg-pullers found that I was easy to fool, every one of them tried his luck with me. "Gimpel, the Czar is coming to Frampol; Gimpel, the moon fell down in Turbeen; Gimpel, little Hodel Furpiece found a treasure behind the bathhouse." And I like a golem believed everyone. In the first place, everything is possible, as it is written in the Wisdom of the Fathers, I've forgotten just how. Second, I had to believe when the whole town came down on me! If I ever dared to say, "Ah, you're kidding!" there was trouble. People got angry. "What do you mean! You want to call everyone a liar?" What was I to do? I believed them, and I hope at least that did them some good.

I was an orphan. My grandfather who brought me up was already bent toward the grave. So they turned me over to a baker, and what a time they gave me there! Every woman or girl who came to bake a batch of noodles had to fool me at least once. "Gimpel, there's a fair in heaven; Gimpel, the rabbi gave birth to a calf in the seventh month; Gimpel, a cow flew over the roof and laid brass eggs." A student from the yeshiva came once to buy a roll, and he

said, "You, Gimpel, while you stand here scraping with
your baker's shovel the Messiah has come. The dead have
arisen." "What do you mean?" I said. "I heard no one
blowing the ram's horn!" He said, "Are you deaf?" And all
began to cry, "We heard it, we heard!" Then in came Rietze
the Candle-dipper and called out in her coarse voice, "Gimpel, your father and mother have stood up from the grave.
They're looking for you."

To tell the truth, I knew very well that nothing of the
sort had happened, but all the same, as folks were talking,
I threw on my wool vest and went out. Maybe something
had happened. What did I stand to lose by looking? Well,
what a cat music went up! And then I took a vow to believe nothing more. But that was no go either. They confused me so that I didn't know the big end from the small.

I went to the rabbi to get some advice. He said, "It is
written, better to be a fool all your days than for one hour
to be evil. You are not a fool. They are the fools. For he
who causes his neighbor to feel shame loses Paradise himself." Nevertheless the rabbi's daughter took me in. As I
left the rabbinical court she said, "Have you kissed the wall
yet?" I said, "No; what for?" She answered, "It's the law;
you've got to do it after every visit." Well, there didn't
seem to be any harm in it. And she burst out laughing. It
was a fine trick. She put one over on me, all right.

I wanted to go off to another town, but then everyone
got busy matchmaking, and they were after me so they
nearly tore my coat tails off. They talked at me and talked
until I got water on the ear. She was no chaste maiden, but
they told me she was virgin pure. She had a limp, and they
said it was deliberate, from coyness. She had a bastard, and
they told me the child was her little brother. I cried,
"You're wasting your time. I'll never marry that whore."
But they said indignantly, "What a way to talk! Aren't you
ashamed of yourself? We can take you to the rabbi and
have you fined for giving her a bad name." I saw then that
I wouldn't escape them so easily and I thought: They're set
on making me their butt. But when you're married the hus-

band's the master, and if that's all right with her it's agreeable to me too. Besides, you can't pass through life unscathed, nor expect to.

I went to her clay house, which was built on the sand, and the whole gang, hollering and chorusing, came after me. They acted like bear-baiters. When we came to the well they stopped all the same. They were afraid to start anything with Elka. Her mouth would open as if it were on a hinge, and she had a fierce tongue. I entered the house. Lines were strung from wall to wall and clothes were drying. Barefoot she stood by the tub, doing the wash. She was dressed in a worn hand-me-down gown of plush. She had her hair put up in braids and pinned across her head. It took my breath away, almost, the reek of it all.

Evidently she knew who I was. She took a look at me and said, "Look who's here! He's come, the drip. Grab a seat."

I told her all; I denied nothing. "Tell me the truth," I said, "are you really a virgin, and is that mischievous Yechiel actually your little brother? Don't be deceitful with me, for I'm an orphan."

"I'm an orphan myself," she answered, "and whoever tries to twist you up, may the end of his nose take a twist. But don't let them think they can take advantage of me. I want a dowry of fifty guilders, and let them take up a collection besides. Otherwise they can kiss my you-know-what." She was very plainspoken. I said, "It's the bride and not the groom who gives a dowry." Then she said, "Don't bargain with me. Either a flat 'yes' or a flat 'no'—Go back where you came from."

I thought: No bread will ever be baked from *this* dough. But ours is not a poor town. They consented to everything and proceeded with the wedding. It so happened that there was a dysentery epidemic at the time. The ceremony was held at the cemetery gates, near the little corpse-washing hut. The fellows got drunk. While the marriage contract was being drawn up I heard the most pious high rabbi ask, "Is the bride a widow or a divorced woman?" And the sex-

ton's wife answered for her, "Both a widow and divorced."
It was a black moment for me. But what was I to do, run
away from under the marriage canopy?

There was singing and dancing. An old granny danced
opposite me, hugging a braided white *chalah*. The master of
revels made a "God 'a mercy" in memory of the bride's
parents. The schoolboys threw burrs, as on Tishe b'Av fast
day. There were a lot of gifts after the sermon: a noodle
board, a kneading trough, a bucket, brooms, ladles, household articles galore. Then I took a look and saw two
strapping young men carrying a crib. "What do we need
this for?" I asked. So they said, "Don't rack your brains
about it. It's all right, it'll come in handy." I realized I was
going to be rooked. Take it another way though, what did I
stand to lose? I reflected: I'll see what comes of it. A whole
town can't go altogether crazy.

2

At night I came where my wife lay, but she wouldn't let
me in. "Say, look here, is this what they married us for?" I
said. And she said, "My monthly has come." "But yesterday they took you to the ritual bath, and that's afterward,
isn't it supposed to be?" "Today isn't yesterday," said she,
"and yesterday's not today. You can beat it if you don't
like it." In short, I waited. ·

Nor four months later she was in childbed. The townsfolk hid their laughter with their knuckles. But what could
I do? She suffered intolerable pains and clawed at the walls.
"Gimpel," she cried, "I'm going. Forgive me!" The house
filled with women. They were boiling pans of water. The
screams rose to the welkin.

The thing to do was to go to the House of Prayer to repeat Psalms, and that was what I did.

The townsfolk liked that, all right. I stood in a corner
saying Psalms and prayers, and they shook their heads at
me. "Pray, pray!" they told me. "Prayer never made any

woman pregnant." One of the congregation put a straw to
my mouth and said, "Hay for the cows." There was something to that too, by God!

She gave birth to a boy. Friday at the synagogue the sexton stood up before the Ark, pounded on the reading table,
and announced, "The wealthy Reb Gimpel invites the congregation to a feast in honor of the birth of a son." The
whole House of Prayer rang with laughter. My face was
flaming. But there was nothing I could do. After all, I *was*
the one responsible for the circumcision honors and rituals.

Half the town came running. You couldn't wedge another soul in. Women brought peppered chick-peas, and
there was a keg of beer from the tavern. I ate and drank as
much as anyone, and they all congratulated me. Then there
was a circumcision, and I named the boy after my father,
may he rest in peace. When all were gone and I was left
with my wife alone, she thrust her head through the bed-
curtain and called me to her.

"Gimpel," said she, "why are you silent? Has your ship
gone and sunk?"

"What shall I say?" I answered. "A fine thing you've
done to me! If my mother had known of it she'd have died
a second time."

She said, "Are you crazy, or what?"

"How can you make such a fool," I said, "of one who
should be the lord and master?"

"What's the matter with you?" she said. "What have you
taken it into your head to imagine?"

I saw that I must speak bluntly and openly. "Do you
think this is the way to use an orphan?" I said. "You have
borne a bastard."

She answered, "Drive this foolishness out of your head.
The child is yours."

"How can he be mine?" I argued. "He was born seventeen weeks after the wedding."

She told me then that he was premature. I said, "Isn't he
a little too premature?" She said, she had had a grandmother who carried just as short a time and she resembled

this grandmother of hers as one drop of water does another. She swore to it with such oaths that you would have believed a peasant at the fair if he had used them. To tell the plain truth, I didn't believe her; but when I talked it over next day with the schoolmaster he told me that the very same thing had happened to Adam and Eve. Two they went up to bed, and four they descended.

"There isn't a woman in the world who is not the granddaughter of Eve," he said.

That was how it was; they argued me dumb. But then, who really knows how such things are?

I began to forget my sorrow. I loved the child madly, and he loved me too. As soon as he saw me he'd wave his little hands and want me to pick him up, and when he was colicky I was the only one who could pacify him. I bought him a little bone teething ring and a little gilded cap. He was forever catching the evil eye from someone, and then I had to run to get one of those abracadabras for him that would get him out of it. I worked like an ox. You know how expenses go up when there's an infant in the house. I don't want to lie about it; I didn't dislike Elka either, for that matter. She swore at me and cursed, and I couldn't get enough of her. What strength she had! One of her looks could rob you of the power of speech. And her orations! Pitch and sulphur, that's what they were full of, and yet somehow also full of charm. I adored her every word. She gave me bloody wounds though.

In the evening I brought her a white loaf as well as a dark one, and also poppyseed rolls I baked myself. I thieved because of her and swiped everything I could lay hands on: macaroons, raisins, almonds, cakes. I hope I may be forgiven for stealing from the Saturday pots the women left to warm in the baker's oven. I would take out scraps of meat, a chunk of pudding, a chicken leg or head, a piece of tripe, whatever I could nip quickly. She ate and became fat and handsome.

I had to sleep away from home all during the week, at the bakery. On Friday nights when I got home she always made an excuse of some sort. Either she had heartburn, or a stitch in the side, or hiccups, or headaches. You know what women's excuses are. I had a bitter time of it. It was rough. To add to it, this little brother of hers, the bastard, was growing bigger. He'd put lumps on me, and when I wanted to hit back she'd open her mouth and curse so powerfully I saw a green haze floating before my eyes. Ten times a day she threatened to divorce me. Another man in my place would have taken French leave and disappeared. But I'm the type that bears it and says nothing. What's one to do? Shoulders are from God, and burdens too.

One night there was a calamity in the bakery; the oven burst, and we almost had a fire. There was nothing to do but go home, so I went home. Let me, I thought, also taste the joy of sleeping in bed in mid-week. I didn't want to wake the sleeping mite and tiptoed into the house. Coming in, it seemed to me that I heard not the snoring of one but, as it were, a double snore, one a thin enough snore and the other like the snoring of a slaughtered ox. Oh, I didn't like that! I didn't like it at all. I went up to the bed, and things suddenly turned black. Next to Elka lay a man's form. Another in my place would have made an uproar, and enough noise to rouse the whole town, but the thought occurred to me that I might wake the child. A little thing like that—why frighten a little swallow, I thought. All right then, I went back to the bakery and stretched out on a sack of flour and till morning I never shut an eye. I shivered as if I had had malaria. "Enough of being a donkey," I said to myself. "Gimpel isn't going to be a sucker all his life. There's a limit even to the foolishness of a fool like Gimpel."

In the morning I went to the rabbi to get advice, and it made a great commotion in the town. They sent the beadle for Elka right away. She came, carrying the child. And what do you think she did? She denied it, denied everything, bone and stone! "He's out of his head," she said. "I know nothing of dreams or divinations." They yelled at her, warned her, hammered on the table, but she stuck to her guns: it was a false accusation, she said.

The butchers and the horse-traders took her part. One of the lads from the slaughterhouse came by and said to me, "We've got our eye on you, you're a marked man." Meanwhile the child started to bear down and soiled itself. In the rabbinical court there was an Ark of the Covenant, and they couldn't allow that, so they sent Elka away.

I said to the rabbi, "What shall I do?"

"You must divorce her at once," said he.

"And what if she refuses?" I asked.

He said, "You must serve the divorce. That's all you'll have to do."

I said, "Well, all right, Rabbi. Let me think about it."

"There's nothing to think about," said he. "You mustn't remain under the same roof with her."

"And if I want to see the child?" I asked.

"Let her go, the harlot," said he, "and her brood of bastards with her."

The verdict he gave was that I mustn't even cross her threshold—never again, as long as I should live.

During the day it didn't bother me so much. I thought: It was bound to happen, the abscess had to burst. But at night when I stretched out upon the sacks I felt it all very bitterly. A longing took me, for her and for the child. I wanted to be angry, but that's my misfortune exactly, I don't have it in me to be really angry. In the first place—this was how my thoughts went—there's bound to be a slip sometimes. You can't live without errors. Probably that lad who was with her led her on and gave her presents and what not, and women are often long on hair and short on sense, and so he got around her. And then since she denies it so, maybe I was only seeing things? Hallucinations do happen. You see a figure or a mannikin or something, but when you come up closer it's nothing, there's not a thing there. And if that's so, I'm doing her an injustice. And when I got so far in my thoughts I started to weep. I sobbed so that I wet the flour where I lay. In the morning I went to the rabbi and told him that I had made a mistake. The rabbi wrote on with his quill, and he said that if that were so he would have to reconsider the whole case. Until he had finished I wasn't to go near my wife, but I might send her bread and money by messenger.

3

Nine months passed before all the rabbis could come to an agreement. Letters went back and forth. I hadn't realized that there could be so much erudition about a matter like this.

Meanwhile Elka gave birth to still another child, a girl this time. On the Sabbath I went to the synagogue and invoked a blessing on her. They called me up to the Torah, and I named the child for my mother-in-law—may she rest in peace. The louts and loudmouths of the town who came into the bakery gave me a going over. All Frampol refreshed its spirits because of my trouble and grief. However, I resolved that I would always believe what I was told. What's the good of *not* believing? Today it's your wife you don't believe; tomorrow it's God Himself you won't take stock in.

By an apprentice who was her neighbor I sent her daily a corn or a wheat loaf, or a piece of pastry, rolls or bagels, or, when I got the chance, a slab of pudding, a slice of honeycake, or wedding strudel—whatever came my way. The apprentice was a goodhearted lad, and more than once he added something on his own. He had formerly annoyed me a lot, plucking my nose and digging me in the ribs, but when he started to be a visitor to my house he became kind and friendly. "Hey, you, Gimpel," he said to me, "you have a very decent little wife and two fine kids. You don't deserve them."

"But the things people say about her," I said.

"Well, they have long tongues," he said, "and nothing to do with them but babble. Ignore it as you ignore the cold of last winter."

One day the rabbi sent for me and said, "Are you certain, Gimpel, that you were wrong about your wife?"

I said, "I'm certain."

"Why, but look here! You yourself saw it."

"It must have been a shadow," I said.

"The shadow of what?"

"Just one of the beams, I think."

"You can go home then. You owe thanks to the Yanover rabbi. He found an obscure reference in Maimonides that favored you."

I seized the rabbi's hand and kissed it.

I wanted to run home immediately. It's no small thing to be separated for so long a time from wife and child. Then I reflected: I'd better go back to work now, and go home in the evening. I said nothing to anyone, although as far as my heart was concerned it was like one of the Holy Days. The women teased and twitted me as they did every day, but my thought was: Go on, with your loose talk. The truth is out, like the oil upon the water. Maimonides says it's right, and therefore it is right!

At night, when I had covered the dough to let it rise, I took my share of bread and a little sack of flour and started homeward. The moon was full and the stars were glistening, something to terrify the soul. I hurried onward, and before me darted a long shadow. It was winter, and a fresh snow had fallen. I had a mind to sing, but it was growing late and I didn't want to wake the householders. Then I felt like whistling, but I remembered that you don't whistle at night because it brings the demons out. So I was silent and walked as fast as I could.

Dogs in the Christian yards barked at me when I passed, but I thought: Bark your teeth out! What are you but mere dogs? Whereas I am a man, the husband of a fine wife, the father of promising children.

As I approached the house my heart started to pound as though it were the heart of a criminal. I felt no fear, but my heart went thump! thump! Well, no drawing back. I quietly lifted the latch and went in. Elka was asleep. I looked at the infant's cradle. The shutter was closed, but the moon forced its way through the cracks. I saw the newborn child's face and loved it as soon as I saw it—immediately—each tiny bone.

Then I came nearer to the bed. And what did I see but the apprentice lying there beside Elka. The moon went out all at once. It was utterly black, and I trembled. My teeth chattered. The bread fell from my hands, and my wife waked and said, "Who is that, ah?"

I muttered, "It's me."

"Gimpel?" she asked. "How come you're here? I thought it was forbidden."

"The rabbi said," I answered and shook as with a fever.

"Listen to me, Gimpel," she said, "go out to the shed and see if the goat's all right. It seems she's been sick." I have forgotten to say that we had a goat. When I heard she was unwell I went into the yard. The nannygoat was a good little creature. I had a nearly human feeling for her.

With hesitant steps I went up to the shed and opened the door. The goat stood there on her four feet. I felt her everywhere, drew her by the horns, examined her udders, and found nothing wrong. She had probably eaten too much bark. "Good night, little goat," I said. "Keep well." And the little beast answered with a "Maa" as though to thank me for the good will.

I went back. The apprentice had vanished.

"Where," I asked, "is the lad?"

"What lad?" my wife answered.

"What do you mean?" I said. "The apprentice. You were sleeping with him."

"The things I have dreamed this night and the night before," she said, "may they come true and lay you low, body and soul! An evil spirit has taken root in you and dazzles your sight." She screamed out, "You hateful creature! You moon calf! You spook! You uncouth man! Get out, or I'll scream all Frampol out of bed!"

Before I could move, her brother sprang out from behind the oven and struck me a blow on the back of the head. I thought he had broken my neck. I felt that something about me was deeply wrong, and I said, "Don't make a scandal. All that's needed now is that people should accuse me of raising spooks and *dybbuks*." For that was what she had meant. "No one will touch bread of my baking."

In short, I somehow calmed her.

"Well," she said, "that's enough. Lie down, and be shattered by wheels."

Next morning I called the apprentice aside. "Listen here, brother!" I said. And so on and so forth. "What do you say?" He stared at me as though I had dropped from the roof or something.

"I swear," he said, "you'd better go to an herb doctor or some healer. I'm afraid you have a screw loose, but I'll hush it up for you." And that's how the thing stood.

To make a long story short, I lived twenty years with my wife. She bore me six children, four daughters and two sons. All kinds of things happened, but I neither saw nor heard. I believed, and that's all. The rabbi recently said to me, "Belief in itself is beneficial. It is written that a good man lives by his faith."

Suddenly my wife took sick. It began with a trifle, a little growth upon the breast. But she evidently was not destined to live long; she had no years. I spent a fortune on her. I have forgotten to say that by this time I had a bakery of my own and in Frampol was considered to be something of a rich man. Daily the healer came, and every witch doctor in the neighborhood was brought. They decided to use leeches, and after that to try cupping. They even called a doctor from Lublin, but it was too late. Before she died she called me to her bed and said, "Forgive me, Gimpel."

I said, "What is there to forgive? You have been a good and faithful wife."

"Woe, Gimpel!" she said. "It was ugly how I deceived you all these years. I want to go clean to my Maker, and so I have to tell you that the children are not yours."

If I had been clouted on the head with a piece of wood it couldn't have bewildered me more.

"Whose are they?" I asked.

"I don't know," she said. "There were a lot . . . but they're not yours." And as she spoke she tossed her head to the side, her eyes turned glassy, and it was all up with Elka. On her whitened lips there remained a smile.

I imagined that, dead as she was, she was saying, "I deceived Gimpel. That was the meaning of my brief life."

4

One night, when the period of mourning was done, as I lay dreaming on the flour sacks, there came the Spirit of Evil himself and said to me, "Gimpel, why do you sleep?"

I said, "What should I be doing? Eating *kreplach?*"

"The whole world deceives you," he said, "and you ought to deceive the world in your turn."

"How can I deceive all the world?" I asked him.

He answered, "You might accumulate a bucket of urine every day and at night pour it into the dough. Let the sages of Frampol eat filth."

"What about the judgment in the world to come?" I said.

"There is no world to come," he said. "They've sold you a bill of goods and talked you into believing you carried a cat in your belly. What nonsense!"

"Well then," I said, "and is there a God?"

He answered, "There is no God either."

"What," I said, *"is* there, then?"

"A thick mire."

He stood before my eyes with a goatish beard and horn, long-toothed, and with a tail. Hearing such words, I wanted to snatch him by the tail, but I tumbled from the flour sacks and nearly broke a rib. Then it happened that I had to answer the call of nature, and, passing, I saw the risen dough, which seemed to say to me, "Do it!" In brief, I let myself be persuaded.

At dawn the apprentice came. We kneaded the bread, scattered caraway seeds on it, and set it to bake. Then the apprentice went away, and I was left sitting in the little trench by the oven, on a pile of rags. Well, Gimpel, I thought, you've revenged yourself on them for all the shame they've put on you. Outside the frost glittered, but it was warm beside the oven. The flames heated my face. I bent my head and fell into a doze.

I saw in a dream, at once, Elka in her shroud. She called to me, "What have you done, Gimpel?"

I said to her, "It's all your fault," and started to cry.

"You fool!" she said. "You fool! Because I was false is everything false too? I never deceived anyone but myself. I'm paying for it all, Gimpel. They spare you nothing here."

I looked at her face. It was black; I was startled and waked, and remained sitting dumb. I sensed that everything hung in the balance. A false step now and I'd lose Eternal Life. But God gave me His help. I seized the long shovel and took out the loaves, carried them into the yard, and started to dig a hole in the frozen earth.

My apprentice came back as I was doing it. "What are you doing boss?" he said, and grew pale as a corpse.

"I know what I'm doing," I said, and I buried it all before his very eyes.

Then I went home, took my hoard from its hiding place, and divided it among the children. "I saw your mother to-night," I said. "She's turning black, poor thing."

They were so astounded they couldn't speak a word.

"Be well," I said, "and forget that such a one as Gimpel ever existed." I put on my short coat, a pair of boots, took the bag that held my prayer shawl in one hand, my stock in the other, and kissed the *mezzuzah*. When people saw me in the street they were greatly surprised.

"Where are you going?" they said.

I answered, "Into the world." And so I departed from Frampol.

I wandered over the land, and good people did not neglect me. After many years I became old and white; I heard a great deal, many lies and falsehoods, but the longer I lived the more I understood that there were really no lies. Whatever doesn't really happen is dreamed at night. It happens to one if it doesn't happen to another, tomorrow if not today, or a century hence if not next year. What difference can it make? Often I heard tales of which I said, "Now this is a thing that cannot happen." But before a year had elapsed I heard that it actually had come to pass somewhere.

Going from place to place, eating at strange tables, it

often happens that I spin yarns—improbable things that could never have happened—about devils, magicians, windmills, and the like. The children run after me, calling, "Grandfather, tell us a story." Sometimes they ask for particular stories, and I try to please them. A fat young boy once said to me, "Grandfather, it's the same story you told us before." The little rogue, he was right.

So it is with dreams too. It is many years since I left Frampol, but as soon as I shut my eyes I am there again. And whom do you think I see? Elka. She is standing by the washtub, as at our first encounter, but her face is shining and her eyes are as radiant as the eyes of a saint, and she speaks outlandish words to me, strange things. When I wake I have forgotten it all. But while the dream lasts I am comforted. She answers all my queries, and what comes out is that all is right. I weep and implore, "Let me be with you." And she consoles me and tells me to be patient. The time is nearer than it is far. Sometimes she strokes and kisses me and weeps upon my face. When I awaken I feel her lips and taste the salt of her tears.

No doubt the world is entirely an imaginary world, but it is only once removed from the true world. At the door of the hovel where I lie, there stands the plank on which the dead are taken away. The gravedigger Jew has his spade ready. The grave waits and the worms are hungry; the shrouds are prepared—I carry them in my beggar's sack. Another *shnorrer* is waiting to inherit my bed of straw. When the time comes I will go joyfully. Whatever may be there, it will be real, without complication, without ridicule, without deception. God be praised: there even Gimpel cannot be deceived.

The Old Man

1

At the beginning of the great war, Chaim Sachar of Kroch-malna Street in Warsaw was a rich man. Having put aside dowries of a thousand rubles each for his daughters, he was about to rent a new apartment, large enough to include a Torah-studying son-in-law. There would also have to be additional room for his ninety-year-old father, Reb Moshe Ber, a Turisk hassid, who had recently come to live with him in Warsaw.

But two years later, Chaim Sachar's apartment was almost empty. No one knew where his two sons, young giants, who had been sent to the front, had been buried. His wife and two daughters had died of typhus. He had accompanied their bodies to the cemetery, reciting the memorial prayer for the three of them, pre-empting the most desirable place at the prayer stand in the synagogue, and inviting the enmity of other mourners, who accused him of taking unfair advantage of his multiple bereavement.

After the German occupation of Warsaw, Chaim Sachar, a tall, broad man of sixty who traded in live geese, locked his store. He sold his furniture by the piece, in order to buy frozen potatoes and moldy dried peas, and prepared gritty blackish noodles for himself and his father, who had survived the grandchildren.

Although Chaim Sachar had not for many months been near a live fowl, his large caftan was still covered with goose down, his great broad-brimmed hat glistened with fat, and his heavy, snub-toed boots were stained with slaughter-house blood. Two small eyes, starved and frightened, peered

Translated by Norbert Guterman and Elaine Gottlieb.

from beneath his disheveled eyebrows; the red rims about his eyes were reminiscent of the time when he could wash down a dish of fried liver and hard-boiled eggs with a pint of vodka every morning after prayer. Now, all day long, he wandered through the market place, inhaling butchershop odors and those from restaurants, sniffing like a dog, and occasionally napping on porters' carts. With the refuse he had collected in a basket, he fed his kitchen stove at night; then, rolling the sleeves over his hairy arms, he would grate turnips on a grater. His father, meanwhile, sat warming himself at the open kitchen door, even though it was midsummer. An open Mishna treatise lay across his knees, and he complained constantly of hunger.

As though it were all his son's fault, the old man would mutter angrily, "I can't stand it much longer . . . this gnawing. . . ."

Without looking up from his book, a treatise on impurity, he would indicate the pit of his stomach and resume his mumbling in which the word "impure" recurred like a refrain. Although his eyes were a murky blue, like the eyes of a blind man, he needed no glasses, still retained some of his teeth, yellow and crooked as rusty nails, and awoke each day on the side on which he had fallen asleep. He was disturbed only by his rupture, which nevertheless, did not keep him from plodding through the streets of Warsaw with the help of his pointed stick, his "horse," as he called it. At every synagogue he would tell stories about wars, about evil spirits, and of the old days of cheap and abundant living when people dried sheepskins in cellars and drank spirits directly from the barrel through a straw. In return, Reb Moshe Ber was treated to raw carrots, slices of radish, and turnips. Finishing them in no time, he would then, with a trembling hand, pluck each crumb from his thinning beard —still not white—and speak of Hungary, where more than seventy years before, he had lived in his father-in-law's house. "Right after prayer, we were served a large decanter of wine and a side of veal. And with the soup there were hard-boiled eggs and crunchy noodles."

Hollow-cheeked men in rags, with ropes about their loins,

stood about him, bent forward, mouths watering, digesting
each of his words, the whites of their eyes greedily showing,
as if the old man actually sat there eating. Young yeshiva
students, faces emaciated from fasts, eyes shifty and restless
as those of madmen, nervously twisted their long earlocks
around their fingers, grimacing, as though to suppress stom-
ach-aches, repeating ecstatically, "That was the time. A man
had his share of heaven and earth. But now we have nothing."

For many months Reb Moshe Ber shuffled about searching for a bit of food; then, one night in late summer, on
returning home, he found Chaim Sachar, his first-born, lying in bed, sick, barefoot, and without his caftan. Chaim
Sachar's face was as red as though he had been to a steam
bath, and his beard was crumpled in a knot. A neighbor
woman came in, touched his forehead, and chanted, "Woe
is me, it's that sickness. He must go to the hospital."

Next morning the black ambulance reappeared in the
courtyard. Chaim Sachar was taken to the hospital; his
apartment was sprayed with carbolic acid; and his father
was led to the disinfection center, where they gave him a
long white robe and shoes with wooden soles. The guards,
who knew him well, gave him double portions of bread
under the table and treated him to cigarettes. The Sukkoth
holiday had passed by the time the old man, his shaven chin
concealed beneath a kerchief, was allowed to leave the disinfection center. His son had died long before, and Reb
Moshe Ber said the memorial prayer, *kaddish*, for him. Now
alone in the apartment, he had to feed his stove with paper
and wood shavings from garbage cans. In the ashes he baked
rotten potatoes, which he carried in his scarf, and in an iron
pot, he brewed chicory. He kept house, made his own candles by kneading bits of wax and suet around wicks, laun-
dered his shirt beneath the kitchen faucet, and hung it to
dry on a piece of string. He set the mousetraps each night
and drowned the mice each morning. When he went out he
never forgot to fasten the heavy padlock on the door. No
one had to pay rent in Warsaw at that time. Moreover, he
wore his son's boots and trousers. His old acquaintances in

the Houses of Study, envied him. "He lives like a king!" they said, "He has inherited his son's fortune!"

The winter was difficult. There was no coal, and since several tiles were missing from the stove, the apartment was filled with thick black smoke each time the old man made a fire. A crust of blue ice and snow covered the window panes by November, making the rooms constantly dark or dusky. Overnight, the water on his night table froze in the pot. No matter how many clothes he piled over him in bed, he never felt warm; his feet remained stiff, and as soon as he began to doze, the entire pile of clothes would fall off, and he would have to climb out naked to make his bed once more. There was no kerosene; even matches were at a premium. Although he recited chapter upon chapter of the Psalms, he could not fall asleep. The wind, freely roaming about the rooms, banged the doors; even the mice left. When he hung up his shirt to dry, it would grow brittle and break, like glass. He stopped washing himself; his face became coal black. All day long he would sit in the House of Study, near the red-hot iron stove. On the shelves, the old books lay like piles of rags; tramps stood around the tin-topped tables, nondescript fellows with long matted hair and rags over their swollen feet—men who, having lost all they had in the war, were half-naked or covered only with torn clothes, bags slung over their shoulders. All day long, while orphans recited *kaddish,* women stood in throngs around the Holy Ark, loudly praying for the sick, and filling his ears with their moans and lamentations. The room, dim and stuffy, smelled like a mortuary chamber from the numerous anniversary candles that were burning. Every time Reb Moshe Ber, his head hanging down, fell asleep, he would burn himself on the stove. He had to be escorted home at night, for his shoes were hobnailed, and he was afraid he might slip on the ice. The other tenants in his house had given him up for dead. "Poor thing—he's gone to pieces."

One December day, Reb Moshe Ber actually did slip, receiving a hard blow on his right arm. The young man escorting him, hoisted Reb Moshe Ber on his back, and carried him home. Placing the old man on his bed without undress-

ing him, the young man ran away as though he had committed a burglary. For two days the old man groaned, called
for help, wept, but no one appeared. Several times each day
he said his Confession of Sins, praying for death to come
quickly, pounding his chest with his left hand. It was quiet
outside in the daytime, as though everyone had died; a hazy
green twilight came through the windows. At night he heard
scratching noises as though a cat were trying to climb the
walls; a hollow roar seemed to come repeatedly from under-
ground. In the darkness the old man fancied that his bed
stood in the middle of the room and all the windows were
open. After sunset on the second day he thought he saw the
door open suddenly, admitting a horse with a black sheet on
its back. It had a head as long as a donkey's and innumerable eyes. The old man knew at once that this was the Angel
of Death. Terrified, he fell from his bed, making such a
racket that two neighbors heard it. There was a commotion
in the courtyard; a crowd gathered, and an ambulance was
summoned. When he came to his senses, Reb Moshe Ber
found himself in a dark box, bandaged and covered up. He
was sure this was his hearse, and it worried him that he had
no heirs to say *kaddish,* and that therefore the peace of his
grave would be disturbed. Suddenly he recalled the verses he
would have to say to Duma, the Prosecuting Angel, and his
bruised, swollen face twisted into a corpselike smile:

> What man is he that liveth and shall not see death?
> Shall he deliver his soul from the grave?

2

After Passover, Reb Moshe Ber was discharged from the
hospital. Completely recovered, he once more had a great
appetite but nothing to eat. All his possessions had been
stolen; in the apartment only the peeling walls remained.
He remembered Jozefow, a little village near the border of
Galicia, where for fifty years he had lived and enjoyed great
authority in the Turisk hassidic circle, because he had per-

sonally known the old rabbi. He inquired about the possibilities of getting there, but those he questioned merely shrugged their shoulders, and each said something different. Some assured him Jozefow had been burned to the ground, wiped out. A wandering beggar, on the other hand, who had visited the region, said that Jozefow was more prosperous than ever, that its inhabitants ate the Sabbath white bread even on week days. But Jozefow was on the Austrian side of the border, and whenever Reb Moshe Ber broached the subject of his trip, men smiled mockingly in their beards and waved their hands. "Don't be foolish, Reb Moshe Ber. Even a young man couldn't do it."

But Reb Moshe Ber was hungry. All the turnips, carrots, and watery soups he had eaten in public kitchens had left him with a hollow sensation in his abdomen. All night he would dream of Jozefow knishes stuffed with ground meat and onions, of tasty concoctions of tripe and calf's feet, chicken fat and lean beef. The moment he closed his eyes he would find himself at some wedding or circumcision feast. Large brown rolls were piled up on the long table, and Turisk hassidim in silken caftans with high velvet hats over their skull caps, danced, glasses of brandy in their hands, singing:

> What's a poor man
> Cooking for his dinner?
> Borscht and potatoes!
> Borscht and potatoes!
> Faster, faster, hop-hop-hop!

He was the chief organizer of all those parties; he quarreled with the caterers, scolded the musicians, supervised every detail, and having no time to eat anything, had to postpone it all for later. His mouth watering, he awoke each morning, bitter that not even in his dream had he tasted those wonderful dishes. His heart pounded; his body was covered with a cold perspiration. The light outside seemed brighter every day, and in the morning, rectangular patterns of sunlight would waver on the peeling wall, swirling, as though they mirrored the rushing waves of a river close by. Around the bare hook for a chandelier on the crumbling ceiling, flies hummed. The cool golden glow of dawn illumined the window panes, and the distorted image of a bird in flight was always reflected in them. Beggars and cripples sang their songs in the courtyard below, playing their fiddles and blowing little brass trumpets. In his shirt, Reb Moshe Ber would crawl down from the one remaining bed, to warm his feet and stomach and to gaze at the barefoot girls in short petticoats who were beating red comforters. In all directions feathers flew, like white blossoms, and there were familiar scents of rotten straw and tar. The old man, straightening his crooked fingers, pricking up his long hairy ears as though to hear distant noises, thought for the thousandth time that if he didn't get out of here this very summer, he never would.

"God will help me," he would tell himself. "If he wills it, I'll be eating in a holiday arbor at Jozefow."

He wasted a lot of time at first by listening to people who told him to get a passport and apply for a visa. After being photographed, he was given a yellow card, and then he had to stand with hordes of others for weeks outside the Austrian consulate on a crooked little street somewhere near the Vistula. They were constantly being cursed in German and punched with the butts of guns by bearded, pipe-smoking soldiers. Women with infants in their arms wept and fainted. It was rumored that visas were granted only to prostitutes and to men who paid in gold. Reb Moshe Ber, going there every day at sunrise, sat on the ground and nodded over his Beni Issachar treatise, nourishing himself with grated turnips and moldy red radishes. But since the crowd continued to increase, he decided one day to give it all up. Selling his cotton-padded caftan to a peddler, he bought a loaf of bread, and a bag in which he placed his prayer shawl and phylacteries, as well as a few books for good luck; and planning to cross the border illegally, he set out on foot.

It took him five weeks to get to Ivangorod. During the day, while it was warm, he walked barefoot across the fields, his boots slung over his shoulders, peasant fashion. He fed on unripened grain and slept in barns. German military police often stopped him, scrutinized his Russian passport for a long time, searched him to see that he was not carrying contraband, and then let him go. At various times, as he walked, his intestines popped out of place; he lay on the ground and pushed them back with his hands. In a village near Ivangorod he found a group of Turisk hassidim, most of them young. When they heard where he was going and that he intended to enter Galicia, they gaped at him, blinking, then, after whispering among themselves, they warned him, "You're taking a chance in times like these. They'll send you to the gallows on the slightest pretext."

Afraid to converse with him, lest the authorities grow suspicious, they gave him a few marks and got rid of him. A few days later, in that village, people spoke in hushed voices of an old Jew who had been arrested somewhere on the road and shot by a firing squad. But not only was Reb Moshe alive by then; he was already on the Austrian side of the border. For a few marks, a peasant had taken him across, hidden in a cart under a load of straw. The old man started immediately for Rajowiec. He fell ill with dysentery there and lay in the poorhouse for several days. Everyone thought he was dying, but he recovered gradually.

Now there was no shortage of food. Housewives treated Reb Moshe Ber to brown buckwheat with milk, and on Saturdays he even ate cold calf's foot jelly and drank a glass of brandy. The moment his strength returned, he was off again. The roads were familiar here. In this region, the peasants still wore the white linen coats and quadrangular caps with tassels that they had worn fifty years ago; they had beards and spoke Ukrainian. In Zamosc the old man was arrested and thrown into jail with two young peasants. The police confiscated his bag. He refused gentile food and accepted only bread and water. Every other day he was summoned by the commandant who, as though Reb Moshe Ber were deaf, screamed directly into his ear in a throaty language. Comprehending nothing, Reb Moshe Ber simply nodded his head and tried to throw himself at the commandant's feet. This went on until after Rosh Hashonah; only then did the

Zamosc Jews learn that an old man from abroad was being
held in jail. The rabbi and the head of the community obtained his release by paying the commandant a ransom.

Reb Moshe Ber was invited to stay in Zamosc until after
Yom Kippur, but he would not consider it. He spent the
night there, took some bread, and set out on foot for Bilgorai at daybreak. Trudging across harvested fields, digging
turnips for food, he refreshed himself in the thick pinewoods
with whitish berries, large, sour and watery, which grow in
damp places and are called Valakhi in the local dialect. A
cart gave him a lift for a mile or so. A few miles from Bilgorai, he was thrown to the ground by some shepherds who
pulled off his boots and ran away with them.

Reb Moshe Ber continued barefoot, and for this reason
did not reach Bilgorai until late at night. A few tramps,
spending the night in the House of Study, refused to let him
in, and he had to sit on the steps, his weary head on his
knees. The autumnal night was clear and cold; against the
dark yellow, dull glow of the starry sky, a flock of goats,
silently absorbed, peeled bark from the wood that had been
piled in the synagogue courtyard for winter. As though
complaining of an unforgettable sorrow, an owl lamented in
a womanish voice, falling silent and then beginning again,
over and over. People with wooden lanterns in their hands
came at daybreak to say the *Selichoth* prayers. Bringing the
old man inside, they placed him near the stove and covered
him with discarded prayer shawls from the chest. Later in
the morning they brought him a heavy pair of hobnailed,
coarse-leathered military boots. The boots pinched the old
man's feet badly, but Reb Moshe Ber was determined to
observe the Yom Kippur fast at Jozefow, and Yom Kippur
was only one day off.

He left early. There were no more than about four miles
to travel, but he wanted to arrive at dawn, in time for the
Selichoth prayers. The moment he had left town, however,
his stiff boots began to cause him such pain, that he couldn't
take a step. He had to pull them off and go barefoot. Then
there was a downpour with thunder and lightning. He sank
knee deep in puddles, kept stumbling, and became smeared

with clay and mud. His feet swelled and bled. He spent the night on a haystack under the open sky, and it was so cold that he couldn't sleep. In the neighboring villages, dogs kept barking, and the rain went on forever. Reb Moshe Ber was sure his end had come. He prayed God to spare him until the *Nilah* prayer, so that he might reach heaven purified of all sin. Later, when on the eastern horizon, the edges of clouds began to glow, while the fog grew milky white, Reb Moshe Ber was infused with new strength and once again set off for Jozefow.

He reached the Turisk circle at the very moment when the hassidim had assembled in the customary way, to take brandy and cake. A few recognized the new arrival at once, and there was great rejoicing for he had long been thought dead. They brought him hot tea. He said his prayers quickly, ate a slice of white bread with honey, gefilte fish made of fresh carp, and kreplach, and took a few glasses of brandy. Then he was led to the steam bath. Two respectable citizens accompanied him to the seventh shelf and personally whipped him with two bundles of new twigs, while the old man wept for joy.

Several times during Yom Kippur, he was at the point of fainting, but he observed the fast until it ended. Next morning the Turisk hassidim gave him new clothes and told him to study the Torah. All of them had plenty of money, since they traded with Bosnian and Hungarian soldiers, and sent flour to what had been Galicia in exchange for smuggled tobacco. It was no hardship for them to support Reb Moshe Ber. The Turisk hassidim knew who he was—a hassid who had sat at the table of no less a man than Reb Motele of Chernobel! He had actually been a guest at the famous wonder-rabbi's home!

A few weeks later, the Turisk hassidim, timber merchants, just to shame their sworn enemies, the Sandzer hassidim, collected wood and built a house for Reb Moshe Ber and married him to a spinster, a deaf and dumb village girl of about forty.

Exactly nine months later she gave birth to a son—now he had someone to say *kaddish* for him. As though it were a wedding, musicians played at the circumcision ceremony. Well-to-do housewives baked cakes and looked after the mother. The place where the banquet was held, the assembly room of the Turisk circle, smelled of cinnamon, safron, and the women's best Sabbath dresses. Reb Moshe Ber wore a new satin caftan and a high velvet hat. He danced on the table, and for the first time, mentioned his age:

"And Abraham was a hundred years old," he recited, "when his son Isaac was born unto him. And Sarah said: God hath made me laugh so that all who hear will laugh with me."

He named the boy Isaac.

JACOB PICARD

This story was originally published in Nazi Germany by the Jewish Book Association as *Der Gezeichnete, The Marked Man*. A lawyer, literary critic, and poet, Picard was born in an ancient community of southwestern Germany in which lived the descendants of those Jews who had survived the massacres of the Crusaders and the attacks which occurred at the time of the Black Death. Ludwig Lewisohn, Mr. Picard's translator, says of the characters of *The Marked One* that "they speak the local dialects of Baden, Württemberg, the Black Forest, Alsace," with many Hebrew phrases rather oddly pronounced. The massacres of the twentieth century were fiercer than those of the fourteenth. These old Jewish communities are now extinct.

The Marked One

Had a man deeply aware of the trend of things and happenings been asked at the birth of our good Sender Frank concerning the child's future, he would have foretold that its life would not take a customary or a tranquil course. Yet he would not have been able to foresee what, in fact, happened in the end. For Sender encountered obstacles far more unusual than those which are our general portion to meet and to overcome within the days that are granted us.

From *The Marked One, The Lottery Ticket and Eleven Other Stories*, translated with an introduction by Ludwig Lewisohn. Copyright © 1956 by The Jewish Publication Society of America, and reprinted with their permission.

Strange and uncommon was the very moment in which he was born in the small house of his parents, built of the gray basalt blocks of the Rhone region, in the little village of the sterile mountains, half of whose inhabitants were Jews. It came to pass that his own mother detested the notion of bringing him into the world on what seemed to be the appointed day; for it was the secular New Year's Day, nor was it a random one, but the first day of the new century. But nature took its course and so his eyes first opened to this cold world on the first of January of the year 1800. This circumstance alone set him apart from others. He developed with the century, as people were wont to say and tease him with that observation. It is understandable that his fellow villagers did not forget the day of his birth, for there was none other among them who had been born on that day; in fact there were very few born in that entire first year of the century, which was to be followed by the ninety-nine others and the occurrences which they were to bring forth.

It was, to be sure, not this circumstance alone which marked him from the beginning, but it was this one which produced all the others.

Do you of today remember what was meant for a long time by the appellation of "familiars" in certain territories of German speech, to which the Austrian lands belonged too? Few will remember today. Yet generations of our fore-fathers suffered under these regulations which oppressed them during the whole course of their lives; indeed, they hindered the fulfillment of life in its entirety.

For the issue of these regulations was a matter of life and love and death, because no human being can attain perfection or fulfillment without the love between man and woman and the begetting of children to prolong one's mortality, to please God and to attain blessing both for oneself and one's family. Those, who at that time were permitted to found families, were given the appellation of "familiars," and precisely what that meant in that dark period must be made clear to those who are alive today.

What could this have been? Was not everyone permitted to marry, to follow the native impulse of the heart and of the instincts, to unite with another in holy unity in order to be sheltered and to have a refuge in face of the mysterious powers and uncertainties of the struggle for life? No, not all were permitted to do so. Only those might marry who received permission from the government, and the number of these was always definite and small. And how did all this come about? You must be told that in order to realize what kind of a human being this Sender was in his time.

It came about as follows: the great distrust of the world, which grew out of ignorance of our fathers and of their true character, had inspired in the mighty Empress of Austria a groundless fear of supposedly secret actions by the Jews against her ancient realm. She was deluded into thinking that, by diminishing increase among this small part of the many peoples over whom she ruled, she was protecting the others and guarding them against harm. Hence she issued the decree, renewing it from time to time, that in every Jewish family, wherever Jews lived, whether in city or country, only the oldest son in each family would be permitted to marry. Only one, then, of the often numerous sons of a house, could establish a family in his turn. This law prevailed, as it had done before in older periods, for a century and more. It extended almost to the days of our grandfathers and included the lifetime of this poor Sender Frank, of whom we are speaking.

We need hardly try to prove what everyone can easily imagine, that this harsh edict of the government caused the fates of many men to be difficult and intricate. What strange things could not happen if two young people loved each other and knew that they could never be united; how many other possibilities of strange alliances and separations did not necessarily arise under the harshness of this unnatural law?

Senderle, or Little Sender, as he was sometimes called, although he was by no means small of stature, was the third born of a small family, following a sister and a brother, a child almost of his father's old age. He had been born when the oldest son was mature enough to marry and did, indeed, do so soon after the little boy had been born.

And this too was a consequence of the unusual day of his birth, which really caused all that came over him and pursued him, as we shall see. For no one can avoid the law of the Eternal, blessed be He, nor withdraw from that mighty plan, for whose fulfillment He employs inscrutable means.

Sender had, as it were, slipped in between the ages and their involvements as they were manifest in that poverty stricken village. For soon it grew clear that his fellows, seeing that he was rather homely, thought they could deal with him according to their pleasure. Not long after his birth, he being still a very small boy, his mother and father died after the briefest interval. He came under the care of his almost adolescent sister, Rivke, in the straw-thatched little house near the river, on the roof of which moss grew in furry tufts because it was always in the shadow. His sister had to bring him up and take care of him, because between herself and the elder brother there had arisen an enmity on account of money matters, for the man's wife was greedy after possessions, as well as of an unveracious and vicious tongue. She refused to let her husband perform his sacred duty by his young brother. And so the latter was all alone and without protection. And since the other members of the *kehilla* had an instinctive notion of this fact; and since, to mention it once more, he was totally unprepossessing as well as penniless, it happened that he could offer no resistance to them and also that they imposed on him every duty and obligation which they disliked.

Burdens were imposed on him in his narrow life—since he had no knowledge of anything except the village and its compulsions—from the observances of the Law, which none sought to escape; and it was long before he knew that flight was possible for one who suffers from his fellow men on account of his peculiar character.

We must now explain something for those among us whom the Eternal, blessed be His name, has brought back to us through the sufferings of these latter years, but who are ignorant of His Holy Law and of the old customs, in order that they too might understand the involvements which overwhelmed Sender because he was alone and there was none to take his part.

It is a great honor for the men in Israel to be called up in the House of God in order to pronounce the blessing over the Law before the congregation. The order in which men are called up is dependent on the esteem which is granted a man in the *kehilla*. But there is one *Shabbos* and one *parsha*, or Scriptural portion, which a man is not required to bless. He may refuse to be called up, *mi she-yirtze*, on account of the consequences, which were generally feared and which, even to this day, are here and there attributed to the reading of that passage among the faithful.

The section of the *Tauro* which is read on that *Shabbos*, which is called the *Shabbos Bechukkausai*—it occurs during the period of the *Omer*—is the passage which contains the words of the *Tauchocho*, wherein are written the curses which the Eternal, blessed be His name, threatens to execute in case we do not obey Him and the law He has given us, in order that we set an example of faith among the nations.

All the evils which He may send us from His hands to punish and correct us, are written in that passage of that day and he, who is called to the *Tauro* and stands on the *almemor* to pronounce the blessing, affirms the passage as he proclaims it before the congregation.

Hence from of old and also in this period there was a hesitancy among the men to pronounce the *berocho*, the blessing, over these words. They feared the effect that these curses might have upon them and their families, great as was the honor on all other occasions to be called up to the reading of the *Tauro*.

You may call this the superstition of a dark age. But it arose out of reverent fear of the Eternal and His boundless might. At all events, the custom had arisen in all the congregations to call up for this passage someone, whether he wanted to be called up or not, who was alone in the world, who had neither wife nor children to whom these imprecations might bring hurt, illness, humiliation and even death. And none who was so chosen dared to refuse; he believed

that he must undergo this as a part of his fate and to make
this sacrifice for the others. It happened inevitably that
someone was selected for this duty whom the harsh law of
the secular power kept from marrying, as we have set the
matter forth. Rebellion was impossible, seeing that the individual is always weak and helpless against the majority of
the congregation. This custom had obtained for centuries.

This portion, as we have explained, is read at the time of
the *Omer,* when daily the faithful, at *Maariv,* at dusk between *Pesach* and *Shevuaus,* say the memorial prayers in
memory of the bloody and cruel period, a thousand years
ago, which our ancestors suffered in the German lands for
the sake of their holy faith and which left only those few
in life who begot us.

Thus it was almost inevitable that shortly after he had
become a *Bar-Mitzvo* and was received as a man among the
men of Israel, Sender—especially since Shlaume, his prede-
cessor, a feeble little old man, could no longer perform the
duty—was burdened with this heavy and supposedly humili-
ating burden and duty and was obliged to submit himself to
this supposed sacrifice for his fellow men.

He consented, firstly because he had no way of resisting
and, also, because in the early years he did not know that he
had the right to resist according to the correct interpretation
of the Law.

Thus they all became accustomed to having him perform
this annual service and it seemed inevitable to him too. This
was his job, like the job of the *chazan* and the *schauchet,*
equally necessary for all.

This was the heaviest part of the lot imposed upon him by
the strange day of his birth. It was, in his individual case,
too late a day; as well as too early a one from the point of
view of the history of our people to liberate him from the
shameful compulsions of a previous age. For it is so among
men, that evil always begets more evil if no resistance is
offered against the earlier evils which are dragged on from
age to age.

At first Sender hardly noted the fact that he was less respected by the others and held to be a lesser creature than they. He grew into the precise situation which he occupied among them and was satisfied with it, as we are all apt silently to accept what we behold as customary among our neighbors, until we are mature enough to begin thinking for ourselves. To sum it up: he had no voice among them for himself.

Life was hard enough for him and for his sister who managed the little household in their straw-thatched dwelling with the mosses on the roof, which never the sun shone upon. It is easy enough to imagine that. From their parents they had inherited a milch-goat, which had been the cause of the conflict between themselves and their brother's wife. Every few years they had to buy a new one, one of those kindly animals with the pendant udders. This did not take place too often, for these creatures attained a great age. Thus brother and sister were barely able to exist and their house smelled of the goat. They also had a little garden behind their poor dwelling; there the sister planted every spring cabbages and a few potatoes and leeks and also horseradish for the holidays. A little extra profit arose from a sparse trading in chickens and in old clothes. Almost without noticing it, Sender had slipped into these occupations. It is understandable that all this did not make him respected among the people of the *kehilla*. On the other hand, shepherds were glad to listen to him and to chat with him when he sat with them among their sheep at pasture on the mountain meadows far from the village; so were plowmen when they stopped a little behind their plow or while they were sowing seed and he stood near them, entirely absorbed in their work and occupation and in the fruitage of their fields.

In this way many years passed and his sister Rivke showed the signs of age and sorrow. The winters were full of want and chill; they could hardly find food for the goat which helped to sustain them. The summers were hardly less difficult, when Sender wandered out under the bright sky into the neighboring villages to bring back a few pennies. And it was really only the religious festivals which, according to God's will, brought a little cheer and courage and confidence.

Then, one fine day, Sender awoke and realized the nature of his fate.

Hitherto he had accepted everything as inevitable and had resigned himself to passing a life of loneliness, without wife, without children, without the tranquil joy of home. And yet each member of the *kehilla* took an interest in his life, because they knew that he marked the continuance of the century. This was the strange thing about him; the very children knew his age; they cried it out after him. He seemed to age differently than the other people of the community; he seemed also to belong to it more than any other, because he was always needed on that precise day of every year in order to keep the others free of that curse which might threaten them if they pronounced the blessing over the threats of God.

Annually on that day on which it is necessary to read that portion of Scripture in which God's wisdom threatens us with punishment, all the men of the congregation turned around to look at the place in the last row of the *shul* where Sender stood defenseless and alone. He would stride forward hastily, as though to excuse himself for some wrong in the face of the others, and arrive at the *almemor* to perform the bitter duty imposed upon him.

Yes, Sender awakened on a given day and beheld himself as an accursed one; saw himself suddenly as a stranger would have to see him, objectively and from without, himself and his entire existence.

It was on a certain evening, on *Simchas Tauroh,* on a still warm and summery day of October, filled with the fragrance of the last harvest and of the latest flowers, that this thing took place. The young people of the *kehilla* had gathered in the house of Feivel Baum, the largest in the village; they gathered for the sake of the son, Josel Baum, who had the good luck to be able to get married—and was old enough to be—and also on account of the daughter Gela who had been promised in marriage to Eisig Stein from the neighboring village of Laudenbach. This young man was spending the last days of *Succaus* here. This was the chief reason why this gathering of young people was taking place.

They danced to the tune of a fiddle played by a white-blonde vagrant with a wild beard, such as could be seen wandering about the land in those days after the wars of the mighty French Emperor. And they danced the new dance which was called waltz. The French soldiers who had been in occupation here, or had kept marching through for nearly twenty years, had left the waltz behind them. It was only now that people hereabouts dared again to be gay and festive; several years had now passed since one needed any longer to fear the foreign soldiery. The peasants, too, had calmed themselves in that region between the Spessart and the Rhone, where the war had been followed by sundry years of famine which had driven people to despair and to violent deeds against the Jews, although the latter, as everywhere and always, had been pursued by the same misfortunes and had suffered the same want as their neighbors. But now several abundant harvests had been granted and people began to feel some confidence in a better future.

They had, in fact, not been so cheerful for a long time; the very young did not remember the bitter experiences of their elders, having been born during the years of the war. Eisig Stein, of whom they knew that he had lived for half a year in the great city of Frankfurt and had learned the delicate ways of it, danced every dance. He also wore a short, black coat of the latest fashion. We need hardly say that he and Gela were the center of the celebration.

Others danced with the girl too. But how could Sender have undertaken to ask Feivel Baum's Gela to dance with him? At first he just stood near the door; later he sat down at a table near the exit; no, not even really at the table but just half leaning upon a free edge at the end of the bench. They hardly spoke to him. He smiled to himself between his *paiyes* under his black somewhat greasy and tilted visored cap. It was a somewhat bashful smile with which he surveyed the scene.

Of a sudden it came over him that Gela was blonde, like

the wayfaring fiddler who lured them all with his exciting outlandish tunes and, as it were, symbolized everything strange. He saw that she was different from all the others, the black-haired girls of the *kehilla*. And so he loved her from that moment on, because she had never before revealed herself to his eyes. It never occurred to him to show how he felt or to admit it to her. What deterred him was not the fact that he knew her to be promised in marriage to Eisig Stein of Laudenbach. No, it wasn't that. But how could he, the son of a poor man, who had himself remained so poor, have dared to think of marriage with the daughter of the rich Feivel Baum, the chief man of the *kehilla*? Yet when she walked through the village, which didn't happen too often on weekdays and only in the pursuit of definite errands, Sender often met her. He just passed and saluted her; rarely did he speak. Once, however, he said: "Gelele, you look like a little canary bird."

The girl perceived something of what went on within him and started to run, after she had cried out to him: "Are you *meshuggah?*"

He continued to harbor the love in his heart. And from this arose another attitude. One fine day, as he was wandering from one village to another between the ash trees from which the red tufts hung, he met Josel, Gela's brother: "Well," Josel asked him, "are you doing a big business?"

It did, truly, sound a little arrogant and as though he wanted to show Sender his place.

And so Sender snapped back: "As big as yours or that of your *ovaus avauseinu!*"

Now that was, to put it mildly, an exaggeration. And how did the humble Sender come to say a thing like that concerning the *mishpoche* of Josel Baum, whose preeminent position in the community was universally acknowledged? They were not only rich and prominent, but on the mother's side related to the *Bal Shem*, the great sage of Michelstadt in the forest of Oden, who hadn't been dead so very long. But Sender had determined that this belittling of him should come to an end. He was going to show them.

One day he declared to Rivke, his sister, that he was going

on a long journey into foreign parts. He was fed up. He didn't explain what he meant. The elderly spinster, quite overwhelmed, thought her brother had gone out of his mind and in her helplessness ran for advice to the *Parnes*. The *Parnes* with his long white beard came to their poor house. It was too late. Sender had gone. He had packed an old valise with a few necessaries and had disappeared. They ran after him; they peered along the eastern and western village streets. He was no longer to be seen. For, suspecting that he might be pursued, he had gone across the fields and soon found refuge in a forest of spruces. When, after several hours, he emerged upon the nearest highway, he was already in the neighborhood of a distant village where the peasants regarded him distrustfully.

It was late autumn. The fields were bare. Across the hills the shepherds in their ample cloaks wandered with their slow and patient herds through the wind beside the low juniper bushes.

In his home village the excitement lasted for weeks. A thing like that had never happened before. No one could imagine why Sender had left. His sister Rivke wept when the matter was mentioned to her and pitied herself mightily. And yet one couldn't talk to her about anything else; in fact, she expected the matter to be discussed and consolation to be offered her. Only the blonde girl Gela had a dark monition that perhaps she was the cause of this flight. And the men of the *kehilla* were already worried as to who would pronounce the *berocho* when the *Tauchocho*, the imprecations of God, would have to be read. For, alas, man is so made that each one contemplates another's misfortune in the hope that he be not made to share it.

When Sender had set out from home, he had only a very obscure notion of what he would undertake out in the world. On the first day he passed through a region with which he was still somewhat familiar, even though he knew only the name of the village, in which he decided to spend the first night. A peasant let him sleep in the hay of his barn and also gave him two eggs, which he drank raw and ate with them a morsel of dry bread which he had taken with him from home. The people paid little attention to him; it was quite customary in those days to give wanderers casual refuge, for the various sections of the country were united only by roads and rivers and the fare in vehicles or ships was high. Next day the country grew stranger and stranger to him. Descending from a hill he saw the sparkle of a river. Its silvery band between the red and yellow forests of autumn soon disappeared from sight, but not before it had given the wanderer a moment's feeling of breadth and freedom. Thus several days passed. He always found tolerable shelter and needed not to pass a single night in the open or surreptitiously among the haystacks.

One evening, when he saw from afar two towers and the walls of a little city, he was at first afraid. How would it be among so many people? As he drew nearer and turned the corner of a forest, along which the road now led, he observed ahead of him a little man whom he at once recognized as a fellow Jew, for the latter wore a black visored cap and a long coat and in his left hand held a sack which kept moving and stirring so that it was clear that it contained a living creature. Chickens, probably, Sender reflected. How often had he himself returned home thus with the sparse result of a day's wandering?

When he had come near enough to the other to be sure that he was not mistaken, he said: *"Sholaum alechem."*

The little man turned around. A blonde curly beard surrounded his friendly face.

"Alechem sholaum!" he replied and added: "Where are you going so late?"

"Into the town. Do you live there?"

"Surely! Are you a *Ben-Yisroel?"* asked the little man although he had seen with whom he had to do. "Have you business among us?"

"I just want to stay overnight."

"Just overnight? You are *mochel* with me. If you don't know anybody else, stay with me. I consider it a *koved.* I am Boruch, the *schauchet* here."

"I thank you kindly; I am glad to accept."

The little city was beyond the boundary. It had recently been incorporated in the Duchy of Baden. Here, from of old, Jews had lived among the guild craftsmen and the peasants. When Sender accompanied his host into the house and in the low-ceiled room had been greeted by the skinny Frau Breindel, whose forehead was almost entirely hidden by her smooth, parted wig, Boruch said to him once again: "Be you *mochel* here."

They sat down and partook of a simple meal of fried potatoes and pot roast. By this time, of course, Boruch could no longer repress his curiosity as to the whence and wherefore, the aim and goal of his guest. The answers which Sender gave him were not very clear. From the yard one could hear the cackling of the chickens and the bleating of the goats from their stable. Frau Breindel had already taken the day's booty into the chicken house. All this reminded Sender of the little house at home. It was Thursday evening and so it was fitting that Boruch invite him to stay over *Shabbos*. How happily he consented to stay. He felt so united to these people by blood and by the old holy law and the good customs. And they, for their part, were proud to show the *kehilla* that they had a guest over *Shabbos*.

Next afternoon, after *Minchah,* they stood in front of the house on the irregular flagstones with their neighbors, their hands in their trousers' pockets and their long coats spread out so that their gaily embroidered waistcoats of velvet and of silk could be seen. They discussed various matters and naturally again questioned Sender as to whence he came and whither he would go. But how could he have given them a clear notion of his plans? He had escaped the narrowness and the humiliation which his consciousness had suddenly realized. When he thought of it, it came all over him again. He replied:

"I want to learn something, like a trade, and then go back home."

This had come suddenly into his head; he hadn't thought about it before. And when he had said it, the others looked at each other and shook their heads and lifted their eyebrows, and they didn't pronounce the word which was in their minds, namely, the word *meshuggah*.

Only one of them, a man named Itzig Kallmann, gave it as his opinion that the idea was not so unreasonable nowadays, when Jews had all civic rights and could do what they liked, according to the new laws. The Grand Duke of Baden, their new sovereign, to whom the land now belonged, had, carrying out the will of Napoleon, expressed a benevolent attitude to the Jews. Hence it would not be a bad business if someone started to learn a trade or craft. It happened that at that moment the textile dyer Thomas Walz, Kallmann's neighbor, passed by, slowly and with dignity, as was his wont, his hands in his trousers' pockets under his leather apron. He had just come from working at the great trough next door where he rinsed his textiles in the indigo solution. Kallmann stopped him and asked, half jocularly and yet firmly:

"Could you make use of an apprentice? The fellow is a little mature, but maybe he would understand things more easily."

"Indeed, I could," the dyer replied. "You know very well that I'm looking for one. Who is it?"

All the others laughed. But Itzig Kallmann, a man of character who carried out his intentions, took Sender by the arm and, followed by the master dyer, stepped to one side.

A long consultation took place. The others watched and gradually fell silent.

Walz was a clever and a liberal man. In his youth, moreover, he had worked as a wandering journeyman in the French Republic and had witnessed the Revolution against oppression and exploitation. There he had heard about the rights of all men to live on an equal basis. And so he said:

"Why shouldn't I take a Jew as apprentice or journeyman? If he is a good worker, he is just as useful to me as a Christian. Done! You can come to work on Monday."

And so Sender became an apprentice in the indigo dye works and print works, although at first he really had no notion of what it was all about and to what he had consented and what he would later do with whatever he would learn. For his chief conscious aim was to give his absence from home and his life here some meaning and purpose.

He learned quickly; he was willing and satisfied his master as well as anyone. Soon he learned how to split up the precious cakes of indigo, so that nothing was lost of this rare substance from far away. He learned cleverly how to dilute the substance to a handsome blue color and, above all, how to treat the textiles, whether wool or linen, in such a fashion that their color was homogeneous and that the purchasers were satisfied.

The people of the *kehilla* boarded him among themselves. He ate each day with a different family. And although most of them, not unprosperous cattle dealers, did not quite consider him their equal, yet they were not displeased at the fact that he showed the non-Jews how one of their own could exercise a skilled craft. He soon became known among the burghers of the town as the "Jew apprentice"; for so they called him.

Nevertheless he felt lonely and often thought of his native village. Yet he sent no message home. For it made him melancholy to remember how he had always been rejected by the others there and despised without cause. Here he was a free man, even though these people knew little about him. No one jeered at him on account of the day of his birth. They did not know his age nor, above all, did they force him, on the day on which the *Tauchocho* had to be read in *shul,* to take that curse upon himself. Here this sacrifice was exacted by the others of an old man, who was not anymore wholly master of his senses, as had happened at home before his time.

One day, however, before Sender had worked for quite a year, it came to pass that a strange journeyman entered the employ of the other master dyer of the town. He came from the far north and spoke German in a fashion which no one hereabouts had ever heard and also immediately acted with great self-importance. People listened to him, because he was very clever at his trade; his master, too, was proud of him because he introduced an important new method of imprinting colors and patterns handsomely on the textiles, and, finally, because the strangeness of his being made an impression on the people of the town. Now this chap gave it as his opinion that it was not proper for a Jew to be received into a guild and learn a trade. For this tended to limit the opportunity of Christians and also went counter to all tradition and belief, not to mention the circumstance that, according to the wont of the guilds, this fellow was far too old to be an apprentice.

And so the journeyman and apprentices of the other workshops put their heads together, the tanners and the weavers, the wheelwrights and the smiths; they all yielded to his persuasion and demanded that Master Walz discharge his Jewish apprentice. Although Walz at first refused, he could not in the long run withstand the talk and tumult which arose against him. So one fine day he gave Sender notice, although with kind and consoling words. He also gave him a regular recommendation as one skillful in the craft they practiced.

But what good did that do him? Even the Jewish people who had given him food and lodging during this period had not been without their own doubts, because they clung to the customary; they had often wondered what he would undertake, poor as he was, when his apprenticeship would end without any certainty of being able some day to work as a journeyman. So they advised him to set out once more and to return home.

Winter was approaching and so wandering through the land would soon have to cease. The fruit trees were already almost leafless and only the ash trees on the edges of the river still formed a sere reddish roof, and mornings found fogs on the river. So, on one such morning, he set out on his way, not through the mountains but along the course of the river in the direction from which he had come; and he was both excited and confident. For the oppressive circumstances that had driven him away had faded a little from his mind and his predominant feeling now was that which each human being cherishes for his original home.

In this particular year the cold of winter set in early. One night while the migratory birds were still on their way south, a frost occurred and in the morning, overtaken by the cold, the delicate swallows, frozen to death, lay by hundreds on the road and on the river bank. Many still stirred their little wings in their last breath. Sender, a lonely wanderer, with dust-covered shoes, beheld these little bodies and their misery seemed to him his very own. Again and again he bent over, wherever he perceived a flicker of pitiful life, and carefully took into his hand, in order to give a little warmth to it, one or the other of the birds. But as though this last movement had been harmful to the last manifestation of life under these little feathers, each one died in his hand while from its little beak there came a last drop of blood. Then he placed the dead bird on the grass beside the road. They're dying in alien places on their way home, he reflected, and perhaps it is better so. Only one of the birds remained alive; trembling it nestled between his hollow hands as in a nest. Carefully he held it thus for hours; he even tried to feed it; he took a little caterpillar from the bushes and brown grasses or else a little spider out of its dewy web. Without a definite intention, there was a vague hope in him that he could take the bird home to mitigate his own loneliness. But toward noon when suddenly the sun was warm, the bird slipped out of his hands and in a great circular flight swung itself toward the south.

Sender looked after it and murmured to himself: "Now it's going home." And then he added: "If only it survives one more night," since he felt that, in order to reach a goal, it always needs a last exertion of power and a last help. His heart was downcast, thinking of his own fate; he didn't know how they would receive him in his home village which he had secretly left and to which he was now returning. He was suddenly frightened of the narrowness there and of the false words of those who had always been about him and knew his life from its beginnings; and he had a premonition that flight from one's original and permanent destiny is given to no man.

He intended, however, to tell them what he had learned and could do now and beg them to help him open a shop,

so that he might show them what he could do and bring
profit to them and himself by the work of his hands. He
hardly considered the possibility of the thing and whether,
in that barren region with its sparse population, it might at
all profit to exercise his skill. He thought of plan after plan;
at times hope awakened in him of a new life and of the
possibility of being as well esteemed as the others. Perhaps
he would manage to distinguish himself by his work, by
showing that special ability which people required in order
to regard another as their equal. All this was half-con-
sciously within him.

On the noon of a certain day he was almost amazed to
find the landscape becoming familiar. The fields were no
longer strange to him nor the hills covered with juniper
bushes; he saw patches of forest that he recognized and
soon, standing on a hill, he saw from afar the village of
his birth. He was excited and full of dread at the same time
and shy at the thought of suddenly appearing in the sight
of his fellow villagers. Thus he waited until dusk and then
went slowly and slipped, seen by no one, into the sombre
old house where he had left his sister. When he suddenly
entered by the kitchen door, she cried out: "Sender!" She
rushed toward him and embraced him in that exaggerated
manner which people use whose feeling for another is
mostly a matter of self-pity. Well, she was glad after a
fashion to see him back, although she couldn't help wondering what they would say in the *kehilla,* all those who
had pitied her during the long period of his absence. That
very same evening she ran quickly over to her neighbor,
Perle Schwarz, a widow woman, who lived alone not far
away.

So on the next morning the whole village knew that
Sender Frank was back—Sender, who had run away, bank-
rupt and poor. For this appellation—that of the runaway—
now clung to him among the other unforgotten ones. They
asked him where he had been. He was taciturn and in the
end merely showed those of whom he hoped to gain the
means for the realization of his plan to erect a textile dye

shop the certificate of the master dyer Walz in which it said
that Sender Frank had been an apprentice in his dye shop
and imprinting shop for such and such a period and had
shown himself to be faithful, industrious, and quick in
learning and had comported himself in the proper fashion
of an honest Christian apprentice, so that he, the master
dyer, was able to express his satisfaction with this apprentice's skill and behavior and had therefore been unwilling
to withold from him this evidence of his good behavior
and of his skill, even though according to the principles of
their honorable craft and guild, he had not completed his
apprenticeship, though his interruption of it was due to no
fault of his own.

They laughed because he was called an apprentice—he,
whom they had known so long as an adult; and they treated
him to evil words on account of that expression concerning
"honest Christian apprentice" in the certificate. And it goes
without saying that they did not give him enough to make
even the smallest beginning toward what would have been
necessary for the work he wanted to do. Soon the whole
village gossiped concerning what he had in mind: this
Sender, who marked the century for them, and who pronounced the *berocho* for them over the portion *Tauchocho*
of the imprecations—he was going to found an important
business without a penny! What was it that had gotten into
his head, and what a *chuzpe* it was! They laughed at him,
sometimes openly and sometimes behind his back. There
was none who even tried to understand him. And now that
they knew that they no longer needed to fear the worst for
him, namely, that he might have perished, and so recognized that the compassion they had shown his sister Rivke
had been wasted, their mood changed completely. What
business had anyone to run away and go his own path and
escape the control of the community! And little as Sender
had been esteemed before, they now surpassed themselves
in making him feel how little he amounted to within the
community.

A winter of great severity descended. Cold, storm, ice
and snow whirled through the streets and lay on the thatched

roofs. The small, deep river which came from the hills was frozen early. You could cross it as though it were a street. The people shivered in their little houses if they didn't hug the ovens, and doors and windows were closed tight. They huddled there, each family alone; their hearts, too, grew rigid and forgot that it had ever been summer. A gray sky hung low above them. They saw each other only at the services in the *shul,* especially on *Shabbos.* The *shul* was not heated and so they stood there, changing from one foot to another in order to produce a little warmth and letting their sleeves fall over their hands. And there Sender stood among them as he had always done, and as though he had never been away. Swiftly they ran through their prayers which had become a troublesome duty.

And one day the worst came about. No one knew who had invented it. But the children cried and sang it after him, when they saw him. It was a derisive ditty:

> "Sender, whither away?
> Out of the century
> From place to place goes he.
> Through lands by night and day.
> Sender, whither away?"

This is what they cried out after him wherever he showed himself. There was none to forbid them. He was lonelier than ever! His co-evals, or those who were nearly so, addressed him now and then. But he had grown strange to them and quite alienated from them by the space of months during which he had absented himself and also by the manner in which he had disappeared. We are all so bound to the original circle of our lives and to the community of our birth that none can loosen those bonds unpunished.

As soon as the extreme cold receded, Sender once more took up his skimpy trading in the neighboring villages and farmsteads. But there was hardly any profit; the peasants had no young chickens yet and the old ones were just beginning to lay again. Nor were there any lambs or calves. But it did him good to chat with the peasants. He told them what he had experienced, little as it had been, and what he had heard concerning the unknown world out there. Among other things he told them how many people from Baden were now going overseas to America to live an easier life, since there, as the rumor ran, wealth was accessible to all and easily gained in the freedom which obtained there.

Again and again he nurtured plans to go away once more, farther away, and for a longer time. And when toward spring he walked through the warm sunlight over the thawing roads, now brown with manure and earth, he often forgot the immediate pressure of the day and the bitter scolding words which awaited him when he returned with empty hands to his low hut and to his sister who, after a fashion, loved him within the community of their wretchedness. But when a man's destiny is fixed from the beginning, he must bow down to it. These things upon which he meditated availed him nothing. For when he had returned home he had still found Gela Baum there, since it had come to pass that her *shidduch* with Eisig Stein of Laudenbach had been broken off, because her father, Feivel, had at the last moment insisted on deducting one hundred thaler from the originally promised dowry and had been unwilling to yield to persuasion. What he had told no one was that he simply didn't have the money.

When Sender heard this story, he had become weak all over and his blood had suddenly surged toward his heart, even though in the strange places where he had been for so long he had thought of the girl less and less. He had, in fact, been quite tranquil when he had seen her again for the first time and had greeted her, without knowing how things were. But during the whole winter he had carefully avoided her, remembering that last meeting of theirs before he went away, when he had so wanted to say tender words to her. Then came Purim. And although they still derided him and his vain flight, and although one night, as was customary, masked figures appeared at his and his sister's door, too, singing that derisive song and adding to it other insolent and malicious words, nevertheless Sender went to the festival which was arranged annually in the parlor of the old inn. For a Jew must bear derision and malice and even laugh at them, when it is Purim, when it is that festival when everything that touches the individual must seem of little account compared to the reflection and the joy over the grace through which the Eternal, blessed be His name, once upon a time saved our fathers from slander and persecution.

At first they were all a little shy, embarrassed by the rare fact of being all together and forced to adopt certain conventions. It was always thus. The girls sat together and dared hardly to speak, certainly not to laugh or to peek over at the men; until Leopold, the professional jester, walked up to one of the girls with his amusing gait and, dancing up and down before her, inaugurated the general festivity. Soon they were all dancing. Only Sender sat alone again, although so much had changed within him.

Suddenly Gela caught sight of him and, though she was probably not conscious of it, had compassion on his loneliness. She went up to him, pretending it was a Purim jest, and danced with him. Everyone observed it. She smiled a little, as though she were not taking the thing seriously; nevertheless she nestled against him, as to any other partner. But he was awkward and the others laughed at him. He felt her breath upon his cheek and felt the delicate softness of her womanly body. And this did not so much stir his senses as give him an inkling of that being sheltered by love for which he had always yearned. And this kindliness which Gela had shown him without reflecting upon it, quite finally sealed his fate. Now he knew that he would never get away from the village. She had danced with him; she had singled him out, him, who lived in that dark alley and traded in chickens and goats and could never marry and bore the permanent shame of having to say the *berocho* to the portion *Tauchocho* every year in token of his being a victim and a marked man and whose years increased with the years of the century, as though it, too, would have to cease, were he to die, and who would never be able to escape this coil of circumstance.

After that dance life came into all his gestures; his eyes

were radiant as they had never been; his arms and hands quivered. Now he drank some of the brandy with them which they offered here after they had previously drank the yellow wine from Wuerzburg of which they had caused a whole keg to be brought and which had cheered them all. He laughed and was as merry as anyone. They suspected the reason and began to make fun of him and suddenly one of them, half drunk, began to sing the derisive song which the children had made up:

> "Out of the century
> From place to place goes he.
> Through lands by night and day.
> Sender, whither away?"

Everybody laughed. But Sender seemed by no means angry. Quietly he arose and very slowly approached the man who had sung the song and, when they had all fallen silent, expecting tumult and violence, Sender stood still before the fellow and said:

"Shem yisborach (the Holy one, blessed be He) has made your *lev* (heart) hard and will repudiate you—you stuffy stay-at-homes!"

They did not understand his meaning and talked at random to each other. But he turned around and left the room, not bowed but upright and almost proud.

And Gela, as though driven by an invisible force, followed him. In reality it was still the compassion which she had suddenly felt for his loneliness; in addition, a dim feeling impelled her toward him, the strange one, who went his own way. And perhaps she felt a common element in their fate, because her engagement to Eisig Stein of Laudenbach had been broken off and because people gossiped about her, too.

"Come back in, Sender. Let them talk!"

But he would not go back; he said: "No, not any more. You can go with me, Gelele, if you really want to."

At that Gela realized that she had gone too far and that her action could easily be misinterpreted. For even if she had found it in herself to love Sender, it would have been senseless, since he was not privileged to marry; and so she went back into the parlor of the inn.

"Oi, oi,"—it came to her from the lips of those who had looked through the window and observed the momentary intimacy between her and Sender. And one cried out: "May one say *massel tov?*"

Her brother, Josel, came up to her and said loud enough for all to hear: "What do you mean by running after that pauper? I'll tell Father!"

"He is as good as the rest of you," she replied, not so much in order to protect him, but rather in defiance of the others who were in opposition to her too.

When Sender came home to his sister, who had long given up attending such festivities, she immediately perceived from his bearing that something had happened. Silently he sat down at the kitchen table and stared at its scrubbed and furrowed top.

Rivke asked: "What's the matter with you again?"

He did not answer. She put before him an earthenware plate filled with an enormous pancake fried in fat to a dark brown color and said, as though she knew all about it.

"Let them talk, Senderle, and eat. It's a fine Purim cake!"

He smiled quietly and put his hand on hers, by which she was supporting herself against the table, and ate.

"Why do you go and bother with them?"

"I want to show them. They are to see—!"

No, now he had to stay; now he couldn't leave the village. How could he abandon Gela who, as she had plainly shown, clung to him. Something would have to happen to make it possible for him to marry her. Wasn't it conceivable that his brother might soon die? He kept on coughing and coughing and had remained childless as a punishment for his not doing his duty by his close kin. But Sender tried at once to repel this thought as a wicked and blasphemous one. Wasn't there, however, the faint hope that new laws would be made, seeing that all these years there had been so much talk of civic rights and equality and that, therefore, the marriage laws would be altered? He would have a talk with Gela.

Purim came to an end and they looked forward to spring, even though in this mountainous country it came late enough. But at last they started their preparations for Pesach, and the women of every household were busy scrubbing and making everything ready for the holiday.

And so it was difficult for Sender to meet Gela and have a talk with her. In addition, he was in doubt concerning her answer, deeply as he yearned for a favorable one. He knew well enough what reply she was almost bound to make; but was there no possibility of being liberated from the heavy yoke of that old law? He tried to persuade himself of that again and again. And couldn't Gela, in that case, live with him and his sister in their little house? There would be room enough. He would have it renovated inside and out. Surely the shepherd, Karl, who was a skilled bricklayer whenever his sheep were in their winter folds, would do this work for him for little or nothing. He nursed these dreams for weeks.

Meanwhile the whole village gossiped about him and the girl, as was to be foreseen after that incident on Purim. He, himself, had at first no notion of this, for it all went on behind his back.

It was Gela who suffered under it. At home her parents and her brother reproached her; her girl friends made fun of her; she, herself, became ever more indignant because she had never dreamed of any real relationship between herself and Sender and had, on that occasion, showed him only an apparent feeling out of pity, out of *rachmones,* as she insisted. So now she avoided him.

And so it came to pass that, on the second day of Pesach, Sender, returning from the *Maariv* service in his *Yontef* suit, stood leaning against the basin of the village fountain at the corner of the upper village street, and waited for her because he knew that she would have to pass by there on her return from the house of her friend Channa Loeb. She did come and so out of the depth of his innocent confidence he spoke to her there in the dusk.

"Gelele," he said, "may I go with you? I have so much to say to you."

Recognizing him, she strode on rapidly without a further glance and said:

"Let me have *menuche* (peace)." Stricken to the heart he remained behind when she added: "Am I to share your curse?"

That left him standing. Silently he pondered: Curse? Is everything that happens to me accursed? Dully and almost paralyzed he walked along the houses on the downward street and felt, as never before, that he was a stranger here at home. That was it; that was his guilt. Never would he be able to get rid of it; always would it cling to him, if he did not help himself. And when on the next day, as he was taking a walk in order to forget his misery, he accidentally met Gela in the village street and she looked past him, as though she had never seen him before, it hurt him to the very quick, but he accepted it as necessary until he himself would somehow have conquered his fate. There was a rebellion within him, but he did not know where to turn or whence help would come.

The days of *Yontef* were past. Now the land was green, both the oak forest near the village and the stingy fields of oats; the yellow rape climbed the hills in broad bands; the wild plum bushes looked like islands of blossom and soon the crabapple trees displayed their reddish white loveliness. Sender beheld it all. But already there also shot up the useless nettles near the walls of his house and stood in tall clumps.

And every evening toward sunset the Jewish men hurried to the *shul* for the ceremony of *Omer;* from all the alleys they came hastily and it seemed to them, as it did every year on the occasion of these special hours of prayer, as though they were in flight from dark surrounding forces which threatened them, as they had threatened their ancestors a thousand years ago. Sender joined them on each occasion, oppressed in his soul in a double sense. Rarely did any one of the others address him, for they now considered that he had become arrogant in addition to everything else.

And now there approached that *Shabbos Bechukkausai*, when the Scriptural portion concerning the blessings and the

curses would have to be read, as has been related. And they
were all glad enough that Sender was here again on this day,
for to them it seemed to go without saying that he would
again dedicate himself to the service of the community,
especially since in late summer old Schlaume had died, he
who, during Sender's absence, although he could hardly
speak any more, had necessarily been called up to say the
blessing over the section of the *Tauchocho*. They had been
very conscious of the fact, however, that this could not have
been pleasing to God, since Schlaume had no longer been in
his right mind. And Sender was now lower in their esteem
than ever, on account of all that had taken place since his
return.

It was a brilliant day of early summer. The garden edges
were magnificent with all the flowers of the season, with
roses large and small and with late lilac on the bushes. A
Shabbos in all appropriate beauty and tranquility had arisen.
But its festive light seemed inappropriate to the difficult
sedra which they, as Jews everywhere, were destined to read
according to their Holy Law. Meanwhile they were looking
forward to *Shevuaus,* the happy festival of the Revelation of
the Law. . . .

The *chazan* prayed and sang and the *kehilla* prayed and
sang with him. Upstairs, invisible, stood the women, the old
and the young, in their black and gleaming wigs under
their veils, softly praying, each following the lead of her husband's voice which was recognizable to her from below.

The Torah scroll was lifted out of the Holy Ark and the
men were called up one by one: *Rishaun,* the first; *Sheini,*
the second; *Shelishi,* the third; *Revii,* the fourth; and finally
they came to the point at which the blessing over the section
of the *Tauchocho* would have to be pronounced and it was
fully expected that Sender would arise and go up to the
Holy Ark.

Suddenly the women raised their heads. Why was there
such a long silence? On the instant the silence was broken.
The women in the front row could see how all the men
turned around, first only a few, then all of them. And they
stared at a place in the last row of seats near the door where

Sender stood, his *tallis* over his shoulders, and looked at the floor and did not move.

Then one of the men cried: "Sender!"

But he did not stir. And another cried out: "Sender!" And next several at the same time, and finally there was a great crying and calling in the *shul:* "Go on, Sender, go on!" And again and again they cried out.

But he remained calm and silent and unmoved by their loud demand to sacrifice himself for them, although they despised him and though they were now by their cries desecrating the sacred place. They had all turned around now and gazed upon him and were filled with fear. And also the women upstairs huddled together and pressed forward in order to see what was taking place.

But Sender did not stir. And no one else summoned the courage to say the *berocho* over that passage of imprecations in his place.

And so it remained unsaid on that occasion and they were full of fear that this *avereh* would be a permanent burden on the whole *kehilla.*

Deeply cast down they left the House of God after the Torah scroll had been returned to the Ark and the last prayers had been said. The sun of May warmed the houses. But it seemed to these men and women as though a dark veil lay over this day and over their lives. How could that which had taken place be made as though it had not?

Sender was the last to leave the *shul.* A few still stood near the door. They cried out evil words to him; no one joined him as with slow tread he went toward his little house that stood in the shadow of a lane. But from a swallow's nest above the door under his roof, the young birds twittered at him from their yellow beaks.

When he entered, his sister Rivke, her veil still over her head, sat weeping and did not reply when he wished her a good *Shabbos.* She wept as though someone had died.

"Rivkele," he said, "don't be angry! I had to do that. *Shem yisborach,* the Holy One, blessed be He, will welcome me nevertheless and will forgive me. He sees everything as it is in truth."

But she would not be quieted and for days did not address a word to him.

Nor did all the others from now on ever speak to him. They all avoided him because they considered him guilty of that threat of doom which they felt hovering above them on account of the *avereh,* the great sin, which had been committed.

For it is thus among men that the majority will never admit its own guilt, but seeks to project it upon one who has separated himself from it, because it has forgotten the duty of compassion and takes its empty common words for deed and truth. And it is also so because men apply only their own inner norms by which to judge others, so that the good must suffer through the wicked.

Thus they thrust him further and further into utter loneliness; and, while they had formerly jeered at him or been angry at him, he had now become a mere burden and stumbling block, whether they met him or not. And one day he became aware of the fact that he no longer heard the song of jeering which the children had made up. The *Parnes* had forbidden that it be sung; no one was to show a consciousness of his existence. And on another day when Gela met him on a narrow path outside of the village, she promptly turned around when she caught sight of him and hastened back.

He, himself, walked only in the lanes and alleys in order to meet no one. Soon, too, he felt a change in the attitude of the peasants round about. They, who were strict in the observances of their own faith, had been told that he had refused obedience to his. Only an occasional one would talk to him at all when he met him on the farm or in the stable or on the field. Often he sat in the stable with his neighbor, the cooper, in silence and watched the cattle, the cows and the young calves as they took their food of fresh grass and hay out of the mangers and slowly chewed it. This calmed him. This single friend had some understanding of his fate because he, himself, was nearer than others to the truth of life.

The summer faded. The second harvest had been brought

into the barns and on the empty fields the black ravens gathered the stalks that remained and intoned their wintry cries. Even the last penurious crabapples had been garnered. Clouds and perpetual fog succeeded the first long rains of autumn. If now and then they lifted from the hilltops which now were almost constantly swathed, soaking the meadows and the fields in dampness, then bluish flames were kindled here and there and spread their flags across the countryside. Soon there was no more refuge for the lonely man amid the goings on of earth and growth. . . .

And so one day the rumor went through the village that Sender was gone again. He had not returned home during two whole days. A sense of guilt began to oppress them all once more, but they could not make out what it was that weighed them down. Rivke ceased asking for pity in silence. She scolded and screamed and ran about with disheveled hair and accused everyone.

After a week the serving man of Sender's friend, the cooper, Conrad by name, reported that he had seen Sender from afar on the top of a hill. It had certainly been he. And he had walked around and around a tall nut tree and had caressed the trunk and the bark as though these were living things which belonged to him. But so soon as Conrad, evidently seen by him, had offered to approach, he had turned away and, bare-headed and as though pursued, had taken refuge in a nearby grove.

Never again did they see Sender Frank in that part of the world. They went looking for him in the forest round about; they sent inquiries to that town from which he had returned the year before. They found no trace. But many years later, when Rivke had long died and Gela had married a horse trader in Prussia and the children who had once sung those jeering verses were grown up and had children in their turn, there arose a rumor that in America, whither people now traveled in steamships, there was a Jew named Alexander Frank, who was a German by birth and who had earned immeasurable riches as a manufacturer of precious, many-colored textiles. But all this was vague and uncertain. For on another occasion they heard that in a great city of East-

ern Europe, where men still clung faithfully to their ancestral faith, there lived an old *Rav* who was wise above all
men and rich in good deeds and who bore that name which
had not been forgotten during an entire century, because the
events of long ago continued to be related from generation
to generation. But this, too, was only a rumor.

And so it seemed to remain true as the elders of the congregation had decided, namely, that none dare refuse the
sacrifice demanded of him by the community and that therefore Sender had been punished, even as the section *Tauchocho* threatens the people of the Holy One, blessed be He,
for all time to come.

ALBERT HALPER

Albert Halper, a Chicago naturalist and one of the best representatives of that school of writing, was born in 1904. His books include *Union Square, The Foundry, The Chute, The Little People, The Golden Watch*. The following story is taken from *The Shore*, a collection of memoirs published very early in his career (1934). It first appeared in *The American Mercury* when that magazine was still being edited by H. L. Mencken. Alexander Woollcott described it as the "chronicle of a baffled and a desperate spinster."

My Aunt Daisy

In the late spring, just before the hot weather set in, my mother began receiving letters from Boston, and started to wear a frown. She put the letters in the upper right-hand drawer of the old, scratched-up bureau, because the upper right-hand drawer had had no knob for some time now, and if you wanted to open it you had to pry it from side to side with the ice-pick, or the little screw-driver she kept locked up in the sewing-machine.

Finally, after five or six letters had arrived, my mother began to show her agitation, and to drop, here and there, a hint that her youngest sister Daisy wanted to come to Chicago for a few weeks during the summer. We had heard so much about our aunt Daisy that everybody got excited in the flat and began asking questions—everybody except my father, who sat down to the supper table, chewed his food thoughtfully, and didn't say a word all through the meal. My mother watched him quietly.

"Well," he said at last, "is she as crazy as she used to be?"

He received no answer and went on eating. Later, clearing his throat, reaching over for the sugar-bowl with his short fat arm, he asked the question again, this time scowling a bit.

"She's thirty now," my mother said submissively. "She's no girl any longer. She knows how to act."

"She should get married," said my father, finishing his tea, still frowning. "What she needs is a man!" and he put on his hat and went back to the store, leaving a gloomy feeling in the flat.

He knew my mother's youngest sister, and he did not like her. When he spoke of her he called her a *fitchkhe*, which means a skittish little horse. No, he didn't like her. Before he had come to Chicago to settle down, he had lived for a time in Boston, and he knew Aunt Daisy very well. It was evident, as he left the flat, that he had no strong desire to see her again.

Later on in the evening, when he came back from the store, he took his shoes off and sat for a while in the old rocker in the front room, his heavy face half-cupped in his fist, rocking there for a long time. Finally he yawned, got up tiredly, scratched his head, and went to bed. In the kitchen my mother was putting washing to soak, and her hands fluttered above the tubs.

During the next few weeks the flat was like a powder magazine—everything was tense and silent in the house as soon as my father would come home from the store. If we had been playing in the front room or wrestling on the floor, we stopped as soon as we heard that well-known heavy tread on the stairs, so that when our father opened the door he came into a quiet flat. He'd take his hat off, pull up a chair, and start eating right away, while my mother began serving him.

She was a large woman, almost a full head taller than my

father, but it was he who was boss around the house. When
he complained about the bad business in his little grocery,
when he wailed that the hot weather was spoiling the few
slabs of meat in his dinky ice-box and that the chain-stores,
which had begun to expand rapidly, had already reached
Madison Street, half a mile away, my mother had to contract her face with sympathetic suffering, as if she had a
toothache. And if she didn't, he'd holler out that of course
it made no difference to her where the money came from
just as long as she had a place to eat and sleep in. But
right after he'd say this, he'd feel sorry, and would sit there
frowning, with a low grumble rumbling deep down in his
throat. Then he would go back to the store. My mother
would take the dishes from the table after he was gone and
would stand at the sink for a long while before turning on
the hot water.

Sometimes, late at night, from the dark of their bedroom,
I could hear my mother and father talking in low tones.

"But we haven't got room for her," my father would argue. "And besides, it costs something to board her."

But my mother, who had not seen her youngest sister for
many years, kept at it. The letters piled up.

Toward the end of June my father, worn away, gave in.
My mother wrote to Boston telling her sister to come, and
when the train arrived my oldest brother met Aunt Daisy at
the station. He brought her home. My oldest brother, about
twenty at the time, was somewhat of a dandy, wore a wide
straw sailor with a colored ribbon, and was thus delegated to
be the family's reception committee. I remember we watched
him going up the street toward the trolley on his way to the
station, and when he reached the corner he waved back at us
because he knew that we were looking, though he really
could not see us.

He brought Aunt Daisy home. It was late dusk when they
came. The street lamps had not yet lit up, and from the
windows we could see Milt struggling with two heavy bags
while a little woman walked jauntily at his side. In the fad-
ing light we couldn't see her face, and when they got closer
to the flat we went away from the front windows because

she might look up and see us, so when at last the bell rang we were all excited and her entrance was something of a dramatic event. I could hear the bags bumping as my brother struggled with them up the stairs.

Then we opened the door, Milt set the bags down in the hall, and Aunt Daisy, with a little cry, rushed forward into my mother's arms. My mother couldn't talk for a while; she hadn't seen her sister for over fifteen years.

Milt came inside, shut the door, and dumped the bags in the parlor. "It's dark here!" he shouted. "What's the matter?" and he struck matches and lit the gas-lamps in all the rooms of the flat.

In the sudden light we looked at our mother's sister—we stood there gaping, the whole crew of us, six kids. We saw a small, dark, vivacious woman, who looked to be about twenty, flashing us a smile. There was something vibrant about her, about her nostrils, her eyes and hair, and we fell in love with her at once. On her head she wore a small hat with gray and brown feathers, and she had a way of tilting her chin, of flashing her smile, of looking pertly alert that made me think of a bird. Yes, she was a warm little bird.

She took her hat off right away and stared brightly at us in friendship. My mother's eyes were misty as she saw her sister counting us briskly by placing her forefinger saucily against our foreheads, one by one, and trilling "Tra-la-la-la!"

"I'm your aunt Daisy," she said, then bent down and kissed every one of us while our mother stood by, choking and happy. When she came to my oldest brother, she stopped, flashing us all another smile. "I kissed Milt at the train, but I guess I can kiss him again," and she gave him a real loud smack on the lips. My kid brother, who was about six at the time, jumped up in the air and clapped his hands, so my aunt had to kiss him again also.

Then she breezed through the flat, through the six large gloomy rooms, her heels rapping against the floor, while my mother, middle-aged, gray, tired out by childbearing and household drudgery, walked behind her.

When we reached the front room, we all stood at the windows looking down the darkening street, and at that mo-

ment the arc lamps lit up with a sudden burst of light.
"See!" she cried as glare and shadow cut the pavement
below, and she raised my kid brother in her arms and
kissed his cheek again. She was in love with him right
away.

On the outskirts my sister, thirteen and lonely in a house
of many brothers, edged silently away, and with a sad, lost
look stared down at the shining asphalt. She had been
dreaming and thinking of our aunt for weeks and wanted
so much to have someone to talk to. She stood there with
her soft yellow hair in two long plaits hanging down her
back, and by the set of her small jaw I knew she was hating
her little brother. But Aunt Daisy suddenly turned to her,
cuddled her hand, and brought her over. My sister was awkward at first, but it was evident that she liked Aunt Daisy.

Finally Aunt Daisy said: "Where's Isak?" and the flat
went quiet.

"He's at the store," my oldest brother answered after a
while. "He'll be home pretty soon."

"Maybe you ought to go down and tell him, Milton," my
mother put in, pleading.

"He'll be home," Milt said shortly and stared at his
straw hat on a hook.

While we waited for our father, our mother showed Aunt
Daisy to her room, and I started dragging the heavy bags
across the floor, kicking at the brothers who sprang for the
handles. I was about nine years old at the time, and puffed
from the exertion. My mother told Aunt Daisy that she
could have the whole room to herself. "Can you manage
it?" said our aunt, knowing we were crowded, then changed
the subject.

We were to sleep three in a bed and our sister was to
sleep on the sofa. "On the sofa?" Aunt Daisy said in alarm.
"No, she's to sleep with me!" This made my sister so very
happy that she started crying; she looked at Aunt Daisy as
though at that moment she would have kissed her feet.

Then we heard that well-known heavy tread on the bottom stairs. All of us stood crowded in Aunt Daisy's bedroom, waiting. The door slammed.

"Is there a show going on?" shouted our father when he saw all the lights in the flat burning. "What's the meaning of this?" and he strode through the house, turning off all the gas except the parlor jet. He was grumbling to himself, a short, stocky, testy man.

At the threshold of the bedroom he stopped. "Oh . . ." he said, taken slightly aback, and stood looking at my mother's sister, at the trembling smile she flashed at him. What fine teeth she had! They greeted each other quietly, and he asked if the train ride had been hot and dusty. Then he went into his bedroom.

After he went to bed, all of us sat in the parlor with the gas turned low while Aunt Daisy told our mother about the family in Boston. Milt had a date with the daughter of one of the neighbors down the street, but he ran outside and broke it, and then came back. He didn't want to miss the news. Aunt Daisy, speaking low so as not to disturb our father, gave our hungry mother all of it. At that time my grandmother was still alive and also all five of my mother's sisters, all living in Boston or near-by New England cities. My mother was the oldest and had been the first to leave the little village near the Baltic for America; then all had followed. My father, also from the same town, had sent her passage money.

"And how is Mama? How is she?" asked my mother for the fifth time, and Aunt Daisy said our grandmother was well. Our grandmother ran a little dry-goods store in East Boston and was getting along all right, Aunt Daisy said. Then came talk about relatives we had never seen, strange names and little stories connected with every one of them, with my mother happy and excited and breaking out in her native tongue every so often. We sat up late until all of us began yawning, and then went to bed.

In the days that followed Aunt Daisy and my mother were always talking together in the kitchen, in the bedroom, or on the back porch, reminding each other of various happenings of many years ago. They spoke all day long about relatives in Europe, about the little village near Memel on the Baltic, and my mother suddenly remembered old folk tales, and for the first time in my life I saw her face was beautiful as she talked about the things she knew. My father grew a trifle less grouchy, but did not unbend all the way. He still went to bed as soon as he came back from the store at night.

It was now July, and the mid-summer heat was upon us. It blew in from the plains in huge hot waves which rolled up the streets, stifling the town. In the evenings we sat on the back porch, which overlooked a wide yard below, where all the children of the tenement played ball until full darkness came on, throwing the ball up and back until it looked like a gray streak and you wondered how they caught it. Closer to the wall of the next building the men pitched horse-shoes in pairs, the big shoes ringing hard against the iron stakes, and the losing side had to fork up ten cents for a can of beer, which was drunk slowly, going from mouth to mouth, with the kids begging for a chance to blow off the foam.

After the men got tired of playing horse-shoes in the dark, they sat on the stairs below and sang, slowly at first—sad love songs and ballads of the day. Someone would pull out a mouth-organ, and the men would sing softly. They were laborers and mechanics mostly, with a sprinkling of single railroad men who boarded with the families in the building. They all liked to sing.

The mid-Western twang of their songs was new to Aunt Daisy, and she started calling us Westerners. She herself spoke with a Bostonian accent which sounded brittle and odd at first, until we grew accustomed to it.

For the first week or so the entire life of the flat was keyed up, and my mother's thoughtful face lost some of its quiet look. We stayed up later than usual, and Milt went down to the drug-store for a quart of ice-cream almost every night. Aunt Daisy had come with five or six new summer dresses and wore a different one each night, though she did not go out. I believe that she finally spoke to my mother about it, because at the end of the first week my mother had a talk with Milt and a day later Milt started taking Aunt Daisy out.

She was ten years his senior, but on the street she looked so girlish that people took her for Milt's sweetheart. Milt took her downtown to a couple of shows, introduced her to a few of his friends, and then began to worry because he had heard that his girl in the block had started going with another fellow. He grew nervous, dropped Aunt Daisy right away, and tried to straighten things out with his girl.

But the little sip of Loop night life, the lights and music of the down-town restaurants made Aunt Daisy restless and she began to quarrel with Milt. At first he was polite in his answers, but later on, when she grew quick-tempered and told him he owed her a duty as a nephew to take her around, he flew off the handle and answered sharply. My mother tried to smooth things over, but Milt stalked out of the flat and went striding up the street. Daisy locked herself in her bedroom and cried there a long time.

From then on, her visit was not a happy one. Ben, who was the next to the oldest and eighteen at the time, volunteered to take her out, but he was a quiet fellow and had a youngish face, and lacked the poise and easy manner that Milt possessed.

So the evenings passed, the hot summer nights, and Aunt Daisy remained in the flat. Two weeks went by, and she said nothing about leaving. My father spoke to my mother, but my mother said to wait another week. Now that all the news had been exchanged, now that the first flush of meeting had worn off, there was a sharp letdown. We had grown accustomed to Aunt Daisy's Eastern accent and had heard some of her Boston stories for the second and third time. In the daytime we went swimming in the city ponds or in the playgrounds, and only my sister stayed behind. Aunt Daisy, in her loneliness, would read aloud to her from *Ramona* or *Ivanhoe*, and sometimes she liked to braid my sister's heavy yellow hair.

And all the while my father grew grouchier and grouchier. "When is she going?" he would ask my mother. "We're crowded here, the boys have to sleep three in a bed in such hot weather, and you're setting a better table now, a cake or fruit almost every evening. I can't afford it."

My mother would stand there without answering him until my father went back to the store.

At last, during the middle of the third week, my mother must have spoken to her sister about it, for when I came into the flat one hot afternoon I could hear Aunt Daisy crying in her room. My mother stood there, looking helpless. Daisy sobbed out that she had no friends, that she was tired of being unmarried, and she said she had thought she would meet somebody here. "I was looking forward to it so much," she sobbed.

"But the boys are so young," my mother said. "Milton is only twenty. His friends are boys, too."

Aunt Daisy kept on crying. "Besides, I haven't got the railroad fare back," she confessed. "Every penny I could scrape together went into the dresses I brought with me."

My mother stood aghast. Then she saw me.

"God knows, God knows! . . ." she said, and Daisy, looking up, also saw me and began smiling through her tears, to show me she had not been crying. She called me over, laughing softly, and when I came she strained me to her and kissed my face all over. Her arms were trembling. She kept whispering to me and in the end she mussed my hair, laughing nervously. "What did you see? Was I crying?"

I shook my head.

"There!" she cried and flung her arms out happily. "Tra-la-la-la, tra-la-la-la!" and she went singing through the rooms of the flat. In the kitchen my mother, standing over the stove, stirred the heavy soup slowly with a big ladle.

Another week went by, and still my mother was afraid to ask my father for Aunt Daisy's return railroad fare. She put the matter off from day to day. But out of her own meager savings she gave her sister a few dollars for stockings, face-powder, and other things. Aunt Daisy took the money, drew the new hose snug against her shapely little legs, and tousled our heads harder than ever.

"Tra-la-la-la! Tra-la-la-la!"

Milt went out every night now and on Sundays stayed away all day. He bought a pair of flannels and a blue jacket, and went out sporting. The daughter of the neighbor was more gone on him than ever, and just before he used to leave the flat Aunt Daisy would find something to do in her room until he had gone.

Later on, when she was sure that Milt had left the house and when my father had gone to bed, Aunt Daisy would sit on the back porch and wait for a breeze with the rest of us, while a hundred yards to the south the Lake Street elevated roared and crashed along, hurtling its racket through the summer night like long-range artillery. And to the north, a block behind us, were the Northwestern tracks, with freights that passed all night long, their whistles wailing over the town and the black soot of the soft coal they burned floating down upon the people in a thin, sifted ash. The heat brought out the perspiration, and if you rubbed your face your hand came away dirty from the train soot.

In the hot night, looking to left and right, you could see all the porches of the building loaded with families, the men sitting in their socks, the women in thin cotton house-dresses. Some of the families hauled out mattresses and slept on the porches all night; and in the morning you could see them sprawled out, wearily, and if they were awake they'd pull the sheets over them quickly, wait for you to look away, and then duck inside the house.

No rain fell. In the evenings, when the sun rolled down in the west over the piano factory in Walnut Street, clouds of gray dust rose in the air as the men pitched the horse-shoes. Their trousers bottoms would be powdered and they'd have to step back and wait awhile to let the dust settle before looking at the iron shoes. They rushed the can harder than ever and the kids kept fighting to see who would be chosen to blow off the foam.

Then came the tragedy of the summer. One of the young unmarried railroaders had seen Aunt Daisy sitting on the porch and had fallen for her. He was a big, honest, bashful fellow named Harry O'Callahan, and he had the shoulders of a coal-heaver. He had a fine voice, too, and could play the harmonica.

He spied Aunt Daisy one evening as he was pitching horse-shoes, glancing up at our porch on the second floor.

He saw she was small and dark and was dressed in a yellow summer frock. He fell in love right away. Small as I was, I noticed it at once. He played horse-shoes very badly all evening, and the men bawled him out and none would pair off with him, so he had to play against two of them, walking up and back across the dusty ground, and losing every game.

"What's come over you?" the men asked. "You used to beat us all."

Harry shook his head, forked up another dime, and dropped out of the game. And later on, in the hot dark when the men had grouped themselves on the stairs, someone struck up an old railroad song, a ballad about the sweat of the road and the Iron Horse and the whistles of the round-house early in the morning. I had never heard that song before. Harry O'Callahan was singing it. The men grew quiet while his fine baritone floated toward us. When he finished, hand-clapping and foot-stamping thundered at him from all the porches. They called out to him to sing on.

He sang a few more songs and in the choruses the men hummed bass for him. Then he took out his harmonica and played "Down by the Old Mill Stream," and "By the Light of the Silvery Moon," fluttering his cupped hands over the mouth-organ so that quivering notes issued forth.

"Who is that fellow?" Aunt Daisy whispered, asking me in the dark.

I told her.

"Oh, he works on the railroad?" she said and seemed to lose interest, though the music continued to move her. "Is he the big fellow who threw the horse-shoes so badly?"

I nodded.

She said nothing more.

The next evening, when the men pitched the shoes again, Harry seemed to have found his former stride and tossed with his old form; he threw like a champion, twirling the heavy iron shoes unerringly so that they rang angrily around the metal stakes with a burst of sparks. He stared hard ahead through the dust to see the ringers he had made, smiled, then looked up toward our porch. My mother sat quietly, but her hands were clenched in her lap.

Later on, when the men played singles, I went down in the yard and watched. Harry was playing against another railroader, a big fellow, too, his best friend; the fellow's name was Frank.

Harry and Frank played three games while the families leaned from the porches, watching. Harry won them all. Someone was sent for the beer, and when it came the kids stood around in a pushing circle. As he was the winner, Harry got the first drink. He pointed at me with a grin, held the full can aloft, so I worked myself proudly through the group, gripped the can in my fists and, filling my lungs to the bottom, blew all the foam cleanly from the top. It was a neat job, Harry said, and he slipped me a nickel when the other kids weren't looking.

After that, when full darkness came on, the singing started up again, and Harry gave an entire concert with his harmonica. The neighbors seemed to sense that something was up, for they kept looking toward our porch where Aunt Daisy sat in the gloom, only her summer dress showing, a pink one this time. My father had long since gone to bed and Milt was out sparking, but the rest of the family sat on the porch. In one of the pauses my mother called out softly to me, saying it was getting late, but I pretended I didn't hear.

An hour later, after the can had made many trips to the saloon in Lake Street, the men grew boastful and started bragging about their strength. There would be singing, then shouting, then bragging, then singing again. Things grew noisy.

"I can swing the sixteen-pound hammer harder than any man here," a road man shouted. "I drive stakes in with two blows!"

"Well, where's the hammer, where's the hammer to prove it?" the men shouted back.

"That's your affair!" came the answer and the porches howled with laughter.

But pretty soon, because there was so much bragging and counter-bragging, it was decided that weight-lifting was the best all-around test of strength, and someone went down into the basement for two big buckets, crossed the alley where the foundation work of a factory was under way, and came back with the pails loaded to the top with heavy mixing sand. The janitor of the building, sitting in his socks and smoking on his porch, came forward, hollering that the pails belonged to the owner of the building, but the men pacified him with a long drink of beer. He wiped his mustache and went back to his porch again. Someone got hold of an old broom, broke off the stout handle, and tied the two pails to the ends of it with stout cord. Now they had a weight, all right.

The first fellow to step up couldn't lift the two pails higher than his chest. He grunted and strained, but he had to give up. All the smaller men came forward, also the men over forty, but none of them could lift the heavy buckets over their heads. The pails were very big.

Then the day laborers tried. Three of them were able to lift the twin buckets high over their heads, but couldn't hold the pails up there very long. From the porches the families started calling for Harry O'Callahan to try. He sat back in darkness and did not answer.

Finally his best friend Frank got up and, gripping the wooden handle, raised the weight slowly and gracefully up to his chest, his chin, the top of his head, then high above it, straightening out his arms. Cheering broke out from the porches.

"Anybody can lift the weight up quickly, but the real test is lifting it slowly," Frank said, blowing, looking at the day laborers. He sat down, heaving.

"Well, we know who's the strongest now," came from the porches.

Harry stepped from the shadow. Once, twice, three times he lifted the buckets up to his chin and over his head, as slowly as Frank had done and just as gracefully. Then he sat down. Now the cheering was greater than ever and the kids pressed forward to feel Harry's biceps. On the porches

the women were impressed and leaned over more from
the railings. In the dark I saw a pink blur on our porch
move forward, too, and, turning, I noticed that Harry had
also seen.

"That was nothing," he said quietly, but he couldn't keep
the triumphant ring from his voice.

Frank got up and began thinking of new ways of lifting
the weight, of gripping your hands the other way, knuckles
up. He and Harry tried it. It was harder, but both managed
it.

"Do it with one hand!" someone shouted from the
porches, a short fat man sitting in his underwear who was
married to a pretty young woman rumored to be carrying
on an affair with the neighborhood ice-man.

Everybody laughed. Mr. Moser, besides being short and
flabby, was bald and couldn't lift an egg from the floor—
because he couldn't stoop to pick it up.

At first Frank tried it with one hand. He gripped the
wooden bar with his right hand, strained, grunted, and
wrenched, but couldn't lift it higher than his waist. He tried
his left hand.

The kids started yelling, "Harry, Harry!"

Harry came up. He tried first with his left hand, testing to
see how much energy he'd have to use with his right, not
straining himself. You could see he had been thinking it
out. With his left hand he brought the buckets up to his
thigh, a little higher, then lowered them.

"You can't do it!" fat little Mr. Moser shouted, fanning
his face excitedly. The families laughed.

Then the yard grew quiet. Bending over, gripping the
wooden handle firmly with his right hand, winding his fingers hard around the smooth wood until his fist went white,
Harry started lifting. He had a wrist as thick as my leg
around the calf. The buckets, ascending slowly, swayed
from side to side, went up, up, up, as high as his waist, his
chest, his chin, then came down with a plop against the
ground. Toward the end of the hoist Harry's whole frame
had started to quiver from the strain.

"Take some of the sand from the pails," Moser taunted

him from his porch, but his wife, leaning away over, had her eyes glued on Harry O'Callahan. Harry smiled at the sally. He looked up, heaving like a spent swimmer, and as he turned toward our porch I saw the sweat break out on his forehead. He wiped it away, then bent once more to the buckets. His friend Frank advised him not to try again. "Don't try it," said Frank. "You're tired out, it isn't worth it."

But already Harry had his fingers wound around the smooth wooden broom handle and now his jaw was like a block of concrete, and his whole fine, young Irish face was grimly set as if he were about to rush into a burning building to save his heroine.

Slowly, using his strength carefully, he raised the buckets from the ground to his shins, his knees, his thigh, bracing himself, curving his spinal column as the pails rose to his chest. Up, up, up they went, his whole frame quivering like a leaf in the wind, until he had the pails of sand level with his chin, his nose, his eyes. Then with a hoarse, shouting grunt, with a tremendous distortion of facial muscles and baring of teeth, he heaved the weight aloft, grinning like a maniac, his frame quivering so violently you could count the great pitiful shivers of the fellow's big body. A hush fell upon the whole yard. From the rear windows of the flats the gaslight from the kitchens fell upon the scene in long slanting bright blocks of yellow glare.

But as soon as the buckets shot up after that last tremendous wrench of back and shoulder and leg muscles something seemed to snap inside of Harry and he went limp all of a sudden. The buckets thudded to the ground and Harry followed. He lay there writhing, holding his right side.

On one of the porches someone screamed, then fainted. The men rushed from the stairs and picked Harry up. He seemed to be all right again and smiled weakly in shame as they carried him into one of the flats. The men felt him all over.

"It's nothing," he said and got up a little later. "It's nothing, I tell you."

But the next day, when he went to a doctor, he learned

he had ruptured himself. The doctor advised an operation, but Harry didn't have the money, so he bought himself a truss and said that it didn't bother him. The whole building talked about it the next day. People started looking toward our porch, and Aunt Daisy came inside the flat. There was something hostile in their glances and her being an outsider did not help much.

In the evening, when the men started playing horse-shoes, Harry sat on the stairs, watching. He had been warned against any form of exercise, and of course lunging forward as you tossed the shoes was out of the question for him. He sat there in silence while the men tossed the shoes and watched the dust clouds settling to the yard. Once he looked up toward our porch, but he saw that Aunt Daisy was not there.

She was crying in her room, with my mother sitting on the bed soothing her. It had been Aunt Daisy who had screamed and fainted. She sobbed out to my mother that now she couldn't sit out on the porch on account of the neighbors, that Milt never took her out or spoke to her any more, and she couldn't be expected to sit in the hot flat in the evening when the only place for a breeze was on the porch. My mother didn't answer, but she understood.

So two days later, screwing up her courage, my mother spoke to my father about money for her sister's return fare. She was prepared for rumbling and thunder, she was all set for my father to start shouting and hollering and waited for him to bubble and boil under the collar before his heavy cheeks began quivering in wrath. But nothing of the sort happened.

He went quietly into his bedroom and locked the door behind him. When we heard a ripping of cloth we knew he was slitting the stitches of the mattress to get at his wallet. In a few minutes he came out, handed my mother the money, asked for a needle and thread, and went back into the bedroom, closing the door again. Aunt Daisy, sitting in her own room, was given the money after my father left for the store.

The next day the flat was quiet. Aunt Daisy was going

home. My mother made a fine supper, but little was eaten. Before my father returned to the store, he said good-by to his sister-in-law and walked out as she was in the middle of thanking him for the railroad fare. She sat at the table, her eyes red, staring over our heads at the windows.

When the time came for her to go, she started putting on on her hat, the hat with the gray and brown feathers. She looked into the mirror and saw her reddened face, then put more powder on. In the kitchen my mother was drying and re-drying her hands on a towel, standing there helplessly. Finally she came into the front room. They said good-by, kissing, and as the two heads bent together, my mother's head of gray touching the black vibrant hair half hidden in the little hat of feathers, my nose began tickling and I stared hard at the shiny door knob.

Aunt Daisy kissed us all, trying to choke back her sobs. In a corner of the room my sister started crying. Daisy went over and, when she kissed Rose, both of them began sobbing and hugging each other. My mother blew her nose softly, then put her handkerchief into the pocket of her apron. Finally she said, her voice urging, "The train is leaving right away, you'll miss it."

So Aunt Daisy broke away. She wiped her cheeks with a fine lace handkerchief purchased from the money my mother had given her.

At the door Milt stood waiting. Then Ben put his hat and jacket on and said he was going to the station too. "The bags are heavy, I'll handle one of them."

They swung the door open and carried the grips out into the hall, with Aunt Daisy following, when suddenly she came back into the front room and stood sobbing against my mother's breast. My mother, crying herself, stroked her back soothingly.

Then Aunt Daisy was all set. She wiped her eyes, looked pertly alert, and poked her finger at me.

"What did you see? Was I crying?"

I shook my head vigorously.

"There!" she cried happily and strode out after my brothers, who began going down the stairs. We could hear her singing gaily in the hallway, "Tra-la-la-la, tra-la-la-la!" until the door banged.

Then we went to stand at the front windows where we could watch her going up the street, walking between Ben and Milt, stepping jauntily, turning to one then the other, gossiping light-heartedly. It was evident from her stride that she liked to be walking between two big fellows. They went up the gray dusk of the street.

At the corner my brother Milt must have said something to her, for she turned suddenly and waved at us. We waved back, though we knew she could not see us. My sister kept on waving, moving her hand vaguely even after they had turned the corner, while my kid brother pressed his forehead against the glass. The street lamps lit up, and down the block we could hear a splashing sound as a neighbor played his hose against the walk.

"God knows, God knows! . . ." said my mother in the silence, while my sister came forward, crying, to feel under the apron for my mother's hand.

BERNARD MALAMUD

Bernard Malamud, a native of Brooklyn, was born in 1914. He was educated at the City College of New York and at Columbia University. He is universally considered to be one of our most interesting writers. His novels are *The Natural* (1952), *The Assistant* (1956), and *A New Life* (1961). The following is the title story of his first collection of stories.

The Magic Barrel

Not long ago there lived in uptown New York, in a small, almost meager room, though crowded with books, Leo Finkle, a rabbinical student in the Yeshivah University. Finkle, after six years of study, was to be ordained in June and had been advised by an acquaintance that he might find it easier to win himself a congregation if he were married. Since he had no present prospects of marriage, after two tormented days of turning it over in his mind, he called in Pinye Salzman, a marriage broker whose two-line advertisement he had read in the *Forward.*

The matchmaker appeared one night out of the dark fourth-floor hallway of the graystone rooming house where Finkle lived, grasping a black, strapped portfolio that had been worn thin with use. Salzman, who had been long in the business, was of slight but dignified build, wearing an old hat, and an overcoat too short and tight for him. He

From *The Magic Barrel.* Copyright 1954, 1958 by Bernard Malamud. Reprinted by permission of Farrar, Straus & Cudahy, Inc., and Eyre and Spottiswoode (Publishers) Ltd.

smelled frankly of fish, which he loved to eat, and although he was missing a few teeth, his presence was not displeasing, because of an amiable manner curiously contrasted with mournful eyes. His voice, his lips, his wisp of beard, his bony fingers were animated, but give him a moment of repose and his mild blue eyes revealed a depth of sadness, a characteristic that put Leo a little at ease although the situation, for him, was inherently tense.

He at once informed Salzman why he had asked him to come, explaining that his home was in Cleveland, and that but for his parents, who had married comparatively late in life, he was alone in the world. He had for six years devoted himself almost entirely to his studies, as a result of which, understandably, he had found himself without time for a social life and the company of young women. Therefore he thought it the better part of trial and error—of embarrassing fumbling—to call in an experienced person to advise him on these matters. He remarked in passing that the function of the marriage broker was ancient and honorable, highly approved in the Jewish community, because it made practical the necessary without hindering joy. Moreover, his own parents had been brought together by a matchmaker. They had made, if not a financially profitable marriage—since neither had possessed any worldly goods to speak of—at least a successful one in the sense of their everlasting devotion to each other. Salzman listened in embarrassed surprise, sensing a sort of apology. Later, however, he experienced a glow of pride in his work, an emotion that had left him years ago, and he heartily approved of Finkle.

The two went to their business. Leo had led Salzman to the only clear place in the room, a table near a window that overlooked the lamp-lit city. He seated himself at the matchmaker's side but facing him, attempting by an act of will to suppress the unpleasant tickle in his throat. Salzman eagerly unstrapped his portfolio and removed a loose rubber band from a thin packet of much-handled cards. As he flipped through them, a gesture and sound that physically hurt Leo, the student pretended not to see and gazed steadfastly out the window. Although it was still February, winter was on its last legs, signs of which he had for the first time in years begun to notice. He now observed the round white moon, moving high in the sky through a cloud menagerie, and watched with half-open mouth as it penetrated a huge hen, and dropped out of her like an egg laying itself. Salzman, though pretending through eyeglasses he had just slipped on, to be engaged in scanning the writing on the cards, stole occasional glances at the young man's distinguished face, noting with pleasure the long, severe scholar's nose, brown eyes heavy with learning, sensitive yet ascetic lips, and a certain, almost hollow quality of the dark cheeks. He gazed around at shelves upon shelves of books and let out a soft, contented sigh.

When Leo's eyes fell upon the cards, he counted six spread out in Salzman's hand.

"So few?" he asked in disappointment.

"You wouldn't believe me how much cards I got in my office," Salzman replied. "The drawers are already filled to the top, so I keep them now in a barrel, but is every girl good for a new rabbi?"

Leo blushed at this, regretting all he had revealed of himself in a curriculum vitae he had sent to Salzman. He had thought it best to acquaint him with his strict standards and specifications, but in having done so, felt he had told the marriage broker more than was absolutely necessary.

He hesitantly inquired, "Do you keep photographs of your clients on file?"

"First comes family, amount of dowry, also what kind promises," Salzman replied, unbuttoning his tight coat and settling himself in the chair. "After comes pictures, rabbi."

"Call me Mr. Finkle. I'm not yet a rabbi."

Salzman said he would, but instead called him doctor, which he changed to rabbi when Leo was not listening too attentively.

Salzman adjusted his horn-rimmed spectacles, gently cleared his throat and read in an eager voice the contents of the top card:

"Sophie P. Twenty four years. Widow one year. No children. Educated high school and two years college. Father promises eight thousand dollars. Has wonderful wholesale business. Also real estate. On the mother's side comes teachers, also one actor. Well known on Second Avenue."

Leo gazed up in surprise. "Did you say a widow?"

"A widow don't mean spoiled, rabbi. She lived with her husband maybe four months. He was a sick boy she made a mistake to marry him."

"Marrying a widow has never entered my mind."

"This is because you have no experience. A widow, especially if she is young and healthy like this girl, is a wonderful person to marry. She will be thankful to you the rest of her life. Believe me, if I was looking now for a bride, I would marry a widow."

Leo reflected, then shook his head.

Salzman hunched his shoulders in an almost imperceptible gesture of disappointment. He placed the card down on the wooden table and began to read another:

"Lily H. High school teacher. Regular. Not a substitute. Has savings and a new Dodge car. Lived in Paris one year. Father is successful dentist thirty-five years. Interested in professional man. Well Americanized family. Wonderful opportunity."

"I knew her personally," said Salzman. "I wish you could see this girl. She is a doll. Also very intelligent. All day you could talk to her about books and theyater and what not. She also knows current events."

"I don't believe you mentioned her age?"

"Her age?" Salzman said, raising his brows. "Her age is thirty-two years."

Leo said after a while, "I'm afraid that seems a little too old."

Salzman let out a laugh. "So how old are you, rabbi?"

"Twenty-seven."

"So what is the difference, tell me, between twenty-seven and thirty-two? My own wife is seven years older than me. So what did I suffer?—Nothing. If Rothschild's a daughter wants to marry you, would you say on account her age, no?"

"Yes," Leo said dryly.

Salzman shook off the no in the yes. "Five years don't mean a thing. I give you my word that when you will live with her for one week you will forget her age. What does it mean five years—that she lived more and knows more than somebody who is younger? On this girl, God bless her, years are not wasted. Each one that it comes makes better the bargain."

"What subject does she teach in high school?"

"Languages. If you heard the way she speaks French, you will think it is music. I am in the business twenty-five years, and I recommend her with my whole heart. Believe me, I know what I'm talking, rabbi."

"What's on the next card?" Leo said abruptly.

Salzman reluctantly turned up the third card:

"Ruth K. Nineteen years. Honor student. Father offers thirteen thousand cash to the right bridegroom. He is a medical doctor. Stomach specialist with marvelous practice. Brother in law owns own garment business. Particular people."

Salzman looked as if he had read his trump card.

"Did you say nineteen?" Leo asked with interest.

"On the dot."

"Is she attractive?" He blushed. "Pretty?"

Salzman kissed his finger tips. "A little doll. On this I give you my word. Let me call the father tonight and you will see what means pretty."

But Leo was troubled. "You're sure she's that young?"

"This I am positive. The father will show you the birth certificate."

"Are you positive there isn't something wrong with her?" Leo insisted.

"Who says there is wrong?"

"I don't understand why an American girl her age should go to a marriage broker."

A smile spread over Salzman's face.

"So for the same reason you went, she comes."

Leo flushed. "I am pressed for time."

Salzman, realizing he had been tactless, quickly explained. "The father came, not her. He wants she should have the best, so he looks around himself. When we will locate the right boy he will introduce him and encourage. This makes a better marriage than if a young girl without experience takes for herself. I don't have to tell you this."

"But don't you think this young girl believes in love?" Leo spoke uneasily.

Salzman was about to guffaw but caught himself and said soberly, "Love comes with the right person, not before."

Leo parted dry lips but did not speak. Noticing that Salzman had snatched a glance at the next card, he cleverly asked, "How is her health?"

"Perfect," Salzman said, breathing with difficulty. "Of course, she is a little lame on her right foot from an auto accident that it happened to her when she was twelve years, but nobody notices on account she is so brilliant and also beautiful."

Leo got up heavily and went to the window. He felt curiously bitter and upbraided himself for having called in the marriage broker. Finally, he shook his head.

"Why not?" Salzman persisted, the pitch of his voice rising.

"Because I detest stomach specialists."

"So what do you care what is his business? After you marry her do you need him? Who says he must come every Friday night in your house?"

Ashamed of the way the talk was going, Leo dismissed Salzman, who went home with heavy, melancholy eyes.

Though he had felt only relief at the marriage broker's departure, Leo was in low spirits the next day. He explained it as arising from Salzman's failure to produce a suitable bride for him. He did not care for his type of clientele. But when Leo found himself hesitating whether to seek out another matchmaker, one more polished than Pinye, he wondered if it could be—his protestations to the contrary, and although he honored his father and mother—that he did not, in essence, care for the matchmaking institution? This thought he quickly put out of mind yet found himself still upset. All day he ran around in the woods—missed an important appointment, forgot to give out his laundry, walked out of a Broadway cafeteria without paying and had to run back with the ticket in his hand; had even not recognized his landlady in the street when she passed with a friend and courteously called out, "A good evening to you, Doctor Finkle." By nightfall, however, he had regained sufficient calm to sink his nose into a book and there found peace from his thought.

Almost at once there came a knock on the door. Before Leo could say enter, Salzman, commercial cupid, was standing in the room. His face was gray and meager, his expression hungry, and he looked as if he would expire on his feet. Yet the marriage broker managed, by some trick of the muscles, to display a broad smile.

"So good evening. I am invited?"

Leo nodded, disturbed to see him again, yet unwilling to ask the man to leave.

Beaming still, Salzman laid his portfolio on the table. "Rabbi, I got for you tonight good news."

"I've asked you not to call me rabbi. I'm still a student."

"Your worries are finished. I have for you a first-class bride."

"Leave me in peace concerning this subject." Leo pretended lack of interest.

"The world will dance at your wedding."

"Please, Mr. Salzman, no more."

"But first must come back my strength," Salzman said weakly. He fumbled with the portfolio straps and took out of the leather case an oily paper bag, from which he extracted a hard, seeded roll and a small, smoked white fish. With a quick motion of his hand he stripped the fish out of its skin and began ravenously to chew. "All day in a rush," he muttered.

Leo watched him eat.

"A sliced tomato you have maybe?" Salzman hesitantly inquired.

"No."

The marriage broker shut his eyes and ate. When he had finished he carefully cleaned up the crumbs and rolled up the remains of the fish, in the paper bag. His spectacled eyes roamed the room until he discovered, amid some piles of books, a one-burner gas stove. Lifting his hat he humbly asked, "A glass tea you got, rabbi?"

Conscience-stricken, Leo rose and brewed the tea. He served it with a chunk of lemon and two cubes of lump sugar, delighting Salzman.

After he had drunk his tea, Salzman's strength and good spirits were restored.

"So tell me, rabbi," he said amiably, "you considered some more the three clients I mentioned yesterday?"

"There was no need to consider."

"Why not?

"None of them suits me."

"What then suits you?"

Leo let it pass because he could give only a confused answer.

Without waiting for a reply, Salzman asked, "You remember this girl I talked to you—the high school teacher?"

"Age thirty-two?"

But, surprisingly, Salzman's face lit in a smile. "Age twenty-nine."

Leo shot him a look. "Reduced from thirty-two?"

"A mistake," Salzman avowed. "I talked today with the dentist. He took me to his safety deposit box and showed me the birth certificate. She was twenty-nine years last August. They made her a party in the mountains where she went for her vacation. When her father spoke to me the first time I forgot to write the age and I told you thirty-two, but now I remember this was a different client, a widow."

"The same one you told me about? I thought she was twenty-four?"

"A different. Am I responsible that the world is filled with widows?"

"No, but I'm not interested in them, nor for that matter, in school teachers."

Salzman pulled his clasped hands to his breast. Looking at the ceiling he devoutly exclaimed, "Yiddishe kinder, what can I say to somebody that he is not interested in high school teachers? So what then you are interested?"

Leo flushed but controlled himself.

"In what else will you be interested," Salzman went on, "if you not interested in this fine girl that she speaks four languages and has personally in the bank ten thousand dollars? Also her father guarantees further twelve thousand. Also she has a new car, wonderful clothes, talks on all subjects, and she will give you a first-class home and children. How near do we come in our life to paradise?"

"If she's so wonderful, why wasn't she married ten years ago?"

"Why?" said Salzman with a heavy laugh. "—Why? Because she is *partikiler*. This is why. She wants the *best*."

Leo was silent, amused at how he had entangled himself. But Salzman had aroused his interest in Lily H., and he began seriously to consider calling on her. When the marriage broker observed how intently Leo's mind was at work on the facts he had supplied, he felt certain they would soon come to an agreement.

Late Saturday afternoon, conscious of Salzman, Leo Finkle walked with Lily Hirschorn along Riverside Drive. He walked briskly and erectly, wearing with distinction the black fedora he had that morning taken with trepidation out of the dusty hat box on his closet shelf, and the heavy black Saturday coat he had thoroughly whisked clean. Leo also owned a walking stick, a present from a distant relative, but quickly put temptation aside and did not use it. Lily, petite and not unpretty, had on something signifying the approach of spring. She was au courant, animatedly, with all sorts of subjects, and he weighed her words and found her surprisingly sound—score another for Salzman, whom he uneasily sensed to be somewhere around, hiding perhaps high in a tree along the street, flashing the lady signals with a pocket mirror; or perhaps a cloven-hoofed Pan, piping nuptial ditties as he danced his invisible way before them, strewing wild buds on the walk and purple grapes in their path, symbolizing fruit of a union, though there was of course still none.

Lily startled Leo by remarking, "I was thinking of Mr. Salzman, a curious figure, wouldn't you say?"

Not certain what to answer, he nodded.

She bravely went on, blushing, "I for one am grateful for his introducing us. Aren't you?"

He courteously replied, "I am."

"I mean," she said with a little laugh—and it was all in good taste, or at least gave the effect of being not in bad—"do you mind that we came together so?"

He was not displeased with her honesty, recognizing that she meant to set the relationship aright, and understanding that it took a certain amount of experience in life, and courage, to want to do it quite that way. One had to have some sort of past to make that kind of beginning.

He said that he did not mind. Salzman's function was traditional and honorable—valuable for what it might achieve, which, he pointed out, was frequently nothing.

Lily agreed with a sigh. They walked on for a while and she said after a long silence, again with a nervous laugh, "Would you mind if I asked you something a little bit personal? Frankly, I find the subject fascinating." Although Leo shrugged, she went on half embarrassedly, "How was it that you came to your calling? I mean was it a sudden passionate inspiration?"

Leo, after a time, slowly replied, "I was always interested in the Law."

"You saw revealed in it the presence of the Highest?"

He nodded and changed the subject. "I understand that you spent a little time in Paris, Miss Hirschorn?"

"Oh, did Mr. Salzman tell you, Rabbi Finkle?" Leo winced but she went on, "It was ages ago and almost forgotten. I remember I had to return for my sister's wedding."

And Lily would not be put off. "When," she asked in a trembly voice, "did you become enamored of God?"

He stared at her. Then it came to him that she was talking not about Leo Finkle, but of a total stranger, some mystical figure, perhaps even passionate prophet that Salzman had dreamed up for her—no relation to the living or dead. Leo trembled with rage and weakness. The trickster had obviously sold her a bill of goods, just as he had him, who'd expected to become acquainted with a young lady of twenty-nine, only to behold, the moment he laid eyes upon her strained and anxious face, a woman past thirty-five and aging rapidly. Only his self-control had kept him this long in her presence.

"I am not," he said gravely, "a talented religious person," and in seeking words to go on, found himself possessed by shame and fear. "I think," he said in a strained manner, "that I came to God not because I loved Him, but because I did not."

This confession he spoke harshly because its unexpectedness shook him.

Lily wilted. Leo saw a profusion of loaves of bread go flying like ducks high over his head, not unlike the winged loaves by which he had counted himself to sleep last night. Mercifully, then, it snowed, which he would not put past Salzman's machinations.

He was infuriated with the marriage broker and swore he would throw him out of the room the minute he reappeared. But Salzman did not come that night, and when Leo's anger had subsided, an unaccountable despair grew in its place. At first he thought this was caused by his disappointment in Lily, but before long it became evident that he had involved himself with Salzman without a true knowledge of his own intent. He gradually realized—with an emptiness that seized him with six hands—that he had called in the broker to find him a bride because he was incapable of doing it himself. This terrifying insight he had derived as a result of his meeting and conversation with Lily Hirschorn. Her probing questions had somehow irritated him into revealing—to himself more than her—the true nature of his relationship to God, and from that it had come upon him, with shocking force, that apart from his parents, he had never loved anyone. Or perhaps it went the other way, that he did not love God so well as he might, because he had not loved man. It seemed to Leo that his whole life stood starkly revealed and he saw himself for the first time as he truly was—unloved and loveless. This bitter but somehow not fully unexpected revelation brought him to a point of panic, controlled only by extraordinary effort. He covered his face with his hands and cried.

The week that followed was the worst of his life. He did not eat and lost weight. His beard darkened and grew ragged. He stopped attending seminars and almost never opened a book. He seriously considered leaving the Yeshivah, although he was deeply troubled at the thought of the loss of all his years of study—saw them like pages torn from a book, strewn over the city—and at the devastating effect of this decision upon his parents. But he had lived without knowledge of himself, and never in the Five Books and all the Commentaries—mea culpa—had the truth been revealed to him. He did not know where to turn, and in all this desolating loneliness there was no *to whom*, although he often thought of Lily but not once could bring himself to go downstairs and make the call. He became touchy and irritable, especially with his landlady, who asked him all manner of personal questions; on the other hand, sensing his own disagreeableness, he waylaid her on the stairs and apologized abjectly, until mortified, she ran from him. Out of this, however, he drew the consolation that he was a Jew and that a Jew suffered. But gradually, as the long and terrible week drew to a close, he regained his composure and some idea of purpose in life: to go on as planned. Although he was imperfect, the ideal was not. As for his quest of a bride, the thought of continuing afflicted him with anxiety and heartburn, yet perhaps with this new knowledge of himself he would be more successful than in the past. Perhaps love would now come to him and a bride to that love. And for this sanctified seeking who needed a Salzman?

The marriage broker, a skeleton with haunted eyes, returned that very night. He looked, withal, the picture of frustrated expectancy—as if he had steadfastly waited the week at Miss Lily Hirschorn's side for a telephone call that never came.

Casually coughing, Salzman came immediately to the point: "So how did you like her?"

Leo's anger rose and he could not refrain from chiding the matchmaker: "Why did you lie to me, Salzman?"

Salzman's pale face went dead white, the world had snowed on him.

"Did you not state that she was twenty-nine?" Leo insisted.

"I give you my word—"

"She was thirty-five, if a day. *At least* thirty-five."

"Of this don't be too sure. Her father told me—"

"Never mind. The worst of it was that you lied to her."

"How did I lie to her, tell me?"

"You told her things about me that weren't true. You made me out to be more, consequently less than I am. She had in mind a totally different person, a sort of semi-mystical Wonder Rabbi."

"All I said, you was a religious man."

"I can imagine."

Salzman sighed. "This is my weakness that I have," he confessed. "My wife says to me I shouldn't be a salesman, but when I have two fine people that they would be wonderful to be married, I am so happy that I talk too much." He smiled wanly. "This is why Salzman is a poor man."

Leo's anger left him. "Well, Salzman, I'm afraid that's all."

The marriage broker fastened hungry eyes on him.

"You don't want any more a bride?"

"I do," said Leo, "but I have decided to seek her in a different way. I am no longer interested in an arranged marriage. To be frank, I now admit the necessity of premarital love. That is, I want to be in love with the one I marry."

"Love?" said Salzman, astounded. After a moment he remarked, "For us, our love is our life, not for the ladies. In the ghetto they—"

"I know, I know," said Leo. "I've thought of it often. Love, I have said to myself, should be a by-product of living and worship rather than its own end. Yet for myself I find it necessary to establish the level of my need and fulfill it."

Salzman shrugged but answered, "Listen, rabbi, if you want love, this I can find for you also. I have such beautiful clients that you will love them the minute your eyes will see them."

Leo smiled unhappily. "I'm afraid you don't understand."

But Salzman hastily unstrapped his portfolio and withdrew a manila packet from it.

"Pictures," he said, quickly laying the envelope on the table.

Leo called after him to take the pictures away, but as if on the wings of the wind, Salzman had disappeared.

March came. Leo had returned to his regular routine. Although he felt not quite himself yet—lacked energy—he was making plans for a more active social life. Of course it would cost something, but he was an expert in cutting corners; and when there were no corners left he would make circles rounder. All the while Salzman's pictures had lain on the table, gathering dust. Occasionally as Leo sat studying, or enjoying a cup of tea, his eyes fell on the manila envelope, but he never opened it.

The days went by and no social life to speak of developed with a member of the opposite sex—it was difficult, given the circumstances of his situation. One morning Leo toiled up the stairs to his room and stared out the window at the city. Although the day was bright his view of it was dark. For some time he watched the people in the street below hurrying along and then turned with a heavy heart to his little room. On the table was the packet. With a suddden relentless gesture he tore it open. For a half-hour he stood by the table in a state of excitement, examining the photographs of the ladies Salzman had included. Finally, with a deep sigh he put them down. There were six, of varying degrees of attractiveness, but look at them long enough and they all became Lily Hirschorn: all past their prime, all starved behind bright smiles, not a true personality in the lot. Life, despite their frantic yoohooings, had passed them by; they were pictures in a brief case that stank of fish. After a while, however, as Leo attempted to return the photographs into the envelope, he found in it another, a snapshot of the type taken by a machine for a quarter. He gazed at it a moment and let out a cry.

Her face deeply moved him. Why, he could at first not say. It gave him the impression of youth—spring flowers, yet age—a sense of having been used to the bone, wasted; this came from the eyes, which were hauntingly familiar, yet absolutely strange. He had a vivid impression that he had met her before, but try as he might he could not place her although he could almost recall her name, as if he had read it in her own handwriting. No, this couldn't be; he would have remembered her. It was not, he affirmed, that she had an extraordinary beauty—no, though her face was attractive enough; it was that *something* about her moved him. Feature for feature, even some of the ladies of the photographs could do better; but she leaped forth to his heart—had *lived*, or wanted to—more than just wanted, perhaps regretted how she had lived—had somehow deeply suffered: it could be seen in the depths of those reluctant eyes, and from the way the light enclosed and shone from her, and within her, opening realms of possibility: this was her own. Her he desired. His head ached and eyes narrowed with the intensity of his gazing, then as if an obscure fog had blown up in the mind, he experienced fear of her and was aware that he had received an impression, somehow, of evil. He shuddered, saying softly, it is thus with us all. Leo brewed some tea in a small pot and sat sipping it without sugar, to calm himself. But before he had finished drinking, again with excitement he examined the face and found it good: good for Leo Finkle. Only such a one could understand him and help him seek whatever he was seeking. She might, perhaps, love him. How she had happened to be among the discards in Salzman's barrel he could never guess, but he knew he must urgently go find her.

Leo rushed downstairs, grabbed up the Bronx telephone book, and searched for Salzman's home address. He was not listed, nor was his office. Neither was he in the Manhattan book. But Leo remembered having written down the address on a slip of paper after he had read Salzman's advertisement in the "personals" column of the *Forward*. He ran up to his room and tore through his papers, without luck. It was exasperating. Just when he needed the matchmaker he was nowhere to be found. Fortunately Leo remembered to look in his wallet. There on a card he found his name written and a Bronx address. No phone number was listed, the reason—Leo now recalled—he had originally communicated with Salzman by letter. He got on his coat, put a hat on over his skull cap and hurried to the subway station. All the way to the far end of the Bronx he sat on the edge of his seat. He was more than once tempted to take out the picture and see if the girl's face was as he remembered it, but he refrained, allowing the snapshot to remain in his inside coat pocket, content to have her so close. When the train pulled into the station he was waiting at the door and bolted out. He quickly located the street Salzman had advertised.

The building he sought was less than a block from the subway, but it was not an office building, nor even a loft, nor a store in which one could rent office space. It was a very old tenement house. Leo found Salzman's name in pencil on a soiled tag under the bell and climbed three dark flights to his apartment. When he knocked, the door was opened by a thin, asthmatic, gray-haired woman, in felt slippers.

"Yes?" she said, expecting nothing. She listened without listening. He could have sworn he had seen her, too, before but knew it was an illusion.

"Salzman—does he live here? Pinye Salzman," he said, "the matchmaker?"

She stared at him a long minute. "Of course."

He felt embarrassed. "Is he in?"

"No." Her mouth, though left open, offered nothing more.

"The matter is urgent. Can you tell me where his office is?"

"In the air." She pointed upward.

"You mean he has no office?" Leo asked.

"In his socks."

He peered into the apartment. It was sunless and dingy, one large room divided by a half-open curtain, beyond which he could see a sagging metal bed. The near side of a room was crowded with rickety chairs, old bureaus, a three-legged table, racks of cooking utensils, and all the apparatus of a kitchen. But there was no sign of Salzman or his magic barrel, probably also a figment of the imagination. An odor of frying fish made Leo weak to the knees.

"Where is he?" he insisted. "I've got to see your husband."

At length she answered, "So who knows where he is? Every time he thinks a new thought he runs to a different place. Go home, he will find you."

"Tell him Leo Finkle."

She gave no sign she had heard.

He walked downstairs, depressed.

But Salzman, breathless, stood waiting at his door.

Leo was astounded and overjoyed. "How did you get here before me?"

"I rushed."

"Come inside."

They entered. Leo fixed tea, and a sardine sandwich for Salzman. As they were drinking he reached behind him for the packet of pictures and handed them to the marriage broker.

Salzman put down his glass and said expectantly, "You found somebody you like?"

"Not among these."

The marriage broker turned away.

"Here is the one I want." Leo held forth the snapshot.

Salzman slipped on his glasses and took the picture into his trembling hand. He turned ghastly and let out a groan.

"What's the matter?" cried Leo.

"Excuse me. Was an accident this picture. She isn't for you."

Salzman frantically shoved the manila packet into his

portfolio. He thrust the snapshot into his pocket and fled down the stairs.

Leo, after momentary paralysis, gave chase and cornered the marriage broker in the vestibule. The landlady made hysterical outcries but neither of them listened.

"Give me back the picture, Salzman."

"No." The pain in his eyes was terrible.

"Tell me who she is then."

"This I can't tell you. Excuse me."

He made to depart, but Leo, forgetting himself, seized the matchmaker by his tight coat and shook him frenziedly.

"Please," sighed Salzman. *"Please."*

Leo ashamedly let him go. "Tell me who she is," he begged. "It's very important for me to know."

"She is not for you. She is a wild one—wild, without shame. This is not a bride for a rabbi."

"What do you mean wild?"

"Like an animal. Like a dog. For her to be poor was a sin. This is why to me she is dead now."

"In God's name, what do you mean?"

"Her I can't introduce to you," Salzman cried.

"Why are you so excited?"

"Why, he asks," Salzman said, bursting into tears. "This is my baby, my Stella, she should burn in hell."

Leo hurried up to bed and hid under the covers. Under the covers he thought his life through. Although he soon fell asleep he could not sleep her out of his mind. He woke, beating his breast. Though he prayed to be rid of her, his prayers went unanswered. Through days of torment he endlessly struggled not to love her; fearing success, he escaped it. He then concluded to convert her to goodness, himself to God. The idea alternately nauseated and exalted him.

He perhaps did not know that he had come to a final decision until he encountered Salzman in a Broadway cafeteria. He was sitting alone at a rear table, sucking the bony remains of a fish. The marriage broker appeared haggard, and transparent to the point of vanishing.

Salzman looked up at first without recognizing him. Leo had grown a pointed beard and his eyes were weighted with wisdom.

"Salzman," he said, "love has at last come to my heart."

"Who can love from a picture?" mocked the marriage broker.

"It is not impossible."

"If you can love her, then you can love anybody. Let me show you some new clients that they just sent me their photographs. One is a little doll."

"Just her I want," Leo murmured.

"Don't be a fool, doctor. Don't bother with her."

"Put me in touch with her, Salzman," Leo said humbly. "Perhaps I can be of service."

Salzman had stopped eating and Leo understood with emotion that it was now arranged.

Leaving the cafeteria, he was, however, afflicted by a tormenting suspicion that Salzman had planned it all to happen this way.

Leo was informed by letter that she would meet him on a certain corner, and she was there one spring night, waiting under a street lamp. He appeared, carrying a small bouquet of violets and rosebuds. Stella stood by the lamp post, smoking. She wore white with red shoes, which fitted his expectations, although in a troubled moment he had imagined the dress red, and only the shoes white. She waited uneasily and shyly. From afar he saw that her eyes—clearly her father's —were filled with desperate innocence. He pictured, in her, his own redemption. Violins and lit candles revolved in the sky. Leo ran forward with flowers outthrust.

Around the corner, Salzman, leaning against a wall, chanted prayers for the dead.

LEO LITWAK

Leo Litwak, a Middlewesterner, has taught philosophy at Washington University in St. Louis and elsewhere. He not only writes well but thinks clearly. He is at present working on a novel.

The Solitary Life of Man

Melford Kuhn had done his duty and with courage. He had received a Silver Star for carrying a wounded buddy a thousand yards while under fire from a pillbox. He mocked the decoration. He cursed brass hats. He disdained all that was rear echelon. He was judged to be the most effective platoon sergeant in the company. This judgment was the buttress of his pride.

There were a few truths that had so affected him that all else seemed irrelevant. A shell fragment has a trajectory defined by its initial velocity and direction and the successive forces impressed upon it. Flesh and bone were not impressive forces. The fragment could act as bullet, knife, cleaver, bludgeon. It could punch, shear, slice, crush, tear. It could be surgical in its precision or make sadistic excess seem unimaginative.

And what happened to brass-hat zeal when the brain was exposed, when guts unfolded, when a flayed stump drooled blood? Didn't the lieutenant turn away from Morgan's shredded stump, mumbling, "I can't. Oh, no!"? Kuhn fixed the tourniquet. Yet they became zealots again when the dying was a few days past and they were in the company of their brother officers and they could begin the falsification of history which proposed heroes and cowards and right action and blunders.

He had learned that the dread of dying is a knife that hacks at all sentiments and kills those which have no validity. He scorned those who approached combat from the perspective of honor, ambition, and the other sentiments of gallantry which flourish when there is no risk of dying.

He felt that ignorance had been pared away from him until only the core of truth was left. The more imminent death became, the narrower was his focus, until now, after two years of combat, he had reached hard fact. Not country, not family, not buddies, but only he himself was relevant. And as his focus narrowed, he became more taciturn, less concerned with the vanities which depended on a wider community.

He loathed Solomon. Solomon was a supply sergeant, assigned to battalion headquarters, who had no reason for being at the front. He should have been two miles back, in a village already secured, nicely housed, nicely fed, profiting from the German obsequiousness which made everything available to acquisitive hands. Solomon was forty-five, a swarthy, big-nosed man, his face creased, tall, gaunt, with a gentle manner. He was dressed like a soldier, yet Kuhn regarded him as a caricature of a soldier. His clothes were glistening new issue, and he used all the tricks of dressing which the combat soldier learns through necessity. He wore a field jacket over his wool sweater, OD trousers tucked into combat boots, a knit wool cap under his helmet liner and steel helmet. Solomon, with his pious talk, his admiration for heroes, his fear of cowardice, his flagrant sympathizing, had become intolerable to Kuhn. Solomon used the sanctimonious language which charmed officers back in battalion headquarters, but he had no flair for the bitter invective which the GI recognized as the language of a friend.

The platoon was assembled, ready to mount the truck. The company jeep arrived with a galvanized can filled with hot coffee. The men lined up and dipped into the coffee with their canteen cups. It was a chill morning, and Solomon stood at the rear of the line, his arms wrapped around his chest, his hands tucked into his armpits.

"Solomon—" Kuhn waved him over to his side and walked him out of earshot of the others. "What are you doing here, Solomon?"

Solomon smiled, misunderstanding Kuhn's intention. "I think I should take my chances with the rest of the boys, Mel. Let them have their coffee first."

"That's damn nice of you. You could be sitting down to breakfast back in battalion."

"It weighs on my conscience, Mel, that I should be safe while the boys up here take all the risks."

"This isn't a club for healthy consciences. I'm not interested in your conscience. There isn't one of us who wouldn't be back in battalion if he had the chance. All you're doing up here, Solomon, is taking someone's coffee."

Solomon shivered. He pulled one arm free and shrugged with it. "You're right. I'll go without coffee."

"Solomon! We're going to take a village this morning. Suppose we have trouble? What do you do, Solomon?"

"What I can do I don't know. But whatever you want I should do, I'll try."

"I've got no job for you." He wanted to snarl, "Stop cringing, Stupid!" Instead he glared his dislike. "Rodansky tells me you bother him with your kraut pitying. How come you're giving Rodansky trouble?"

Solomon rubbed his eyes. He wore OD wool gloves with leather palms. He was more than twenty years older than Kuhn. "Rodansky is bothered by the German boy. I know he's bothered. So he didn't offend me."

"I don't care if you're offended. You're no problem of mine. I care about my platoon. And you're just trouble for me. I don't want you around, Solomon."

Solomon nodded. "I'll ride back with the jeep. I apologize, Mel."

Kuhn walked away from him.

Rodansky had been on guard duty the day before. He had heard a noise in the bushes at the edge of the platoon area. He had challenged, then had fired, and Kuhn had found

him standing beside the dying man. The German lay behind
a bush, his arms extending through it. He wore a greatcoat.
His wool cap had fallen off. His hair was in the midst of the
bush, an abundant, dirty yellow. He wasn't armed, and
Kuhn rolled him over. The German wheezed through his
chest.

"I told him to put up his hands. *'Hands auf,'* I said."

"What a mess. He's a kid."

The boy was already soggy gray. The slug had hit at an
angle, swerved within the compass of the chest, and his
heart was bared. *"Warum hast du—"* Neither Kuhn nor
Rodansky understood German and they did not respond to
the boy's muttering.

Kuhn straightened up as others in the platoon joined
them. "He won't last till the aid station. Leave him here. Is
the medic around? It doesn't make any difference."

Then Solomon came up, gasping with fear, blanching
when he heard the moans. He fell to his knees beside the
boy and touched his face. He listened to the muttering. "He
wants to know why did we shoot." Solomon looked up,
asking the question in his own right. "He says he wanted to
surrender. *'Wir haben nicht gewissen,'* " he explained to the
boy, his voice trembling with compassion. "He wants to
know if he's dying."

"He's dead, Solomon! Tell him he's dead. *Tot,*" Rodansky shouted at the boy. "Kraut *tot!*"

"Nein," Solomon said in turn. He told the boy they
would soon have him in a hospital. *"Wir haben nicht gewissen,"* he concluded in a hopeless apology.

A few weeks before, twelve men from the platoon had
been killed in front of a pillbox. There had been considerable variety in their deaths. They'd been zeroed in by
eighty-eights. The GIs had swallowed these deaths as part
of the nourishment of combat whose grotesqueries provi-
sioned their daily fare.

Rodansky caught Solomon's arm as they left the boy to
the medic.

"What the hell you doing in the army, Solomon—an old
man like you? Why aren't you back with the girls, getting

the dough, saluting the flag? What are you here for, Solomon?"

Solomon was still shocked by the sight of the naked heart beating in a sheath of slime. His face mirrored the open-mouthed pallor of the dying German.

He raised his arms waist high and let them flop. He repeated this gesture several times before answering Rodansky. "He asked is he dying. He came to surrender. Why did we shoot, he wants to know. He's maybe only sixteen. The poor boy!"

"Poor boy!"

"It doesn't matter to me all of a sudden that he's German. His chest was breathing, Harry. Did you hear it? Ah! I wish we didn't shoot. It's a pity, a pity, Rodansky."

Though they had recently come from a reserve area where shower facilities were available, Rodansky hadn't washed or shaved. His helmet was set low on his forehead, and he peered from under it like a man taking a cautious look in the midst of a barrage. He released his grip on Solomon's arm to squeeze his rifle with both hands. He shook the rifle at Solomon, his lips twisting for an adequate expression of his outrage. "I shot, you old bastard, not you! You bastard! We fight your wars and then you come around and preach!"

It was clear that he meant the "you" generically. Solomon revealed his identity with every shrug, with every anecdote, with his intonation, with his liberal use of such notions as Pity and Justice, with his faithful attendance at Saturday services.

Kuhn shared Rodansky's loathing for this old man who presumed to give them lessons in sentiment when he was so little experienced in the passion that proved integrity, the fear of death. The following morning he ordered Solomon back to the rear.

They had come so fast into Germany that they passed through villages still entrucked, leaving the security of the area to the reserve companies that followed. The widely spaced convoy rattled down poor country roads, claiming a new segment of Germany with each turn of the wheels. The

Germans who lined the streets cheered the convoy with the enthusiasm of the liberated. When the soldiers dismounted and formed squads to scour a village, they found the Germans more tractable than any ally. *"Nach kirche!"* the GIs shouted. The Germans took up the cry and without further urging streamed to church where they were instructed by the military government. The town was left in the hands of the GIs. These were irreverent hands, not limited by any law. They stripped watches from the grinning Germans. They ransacked the German houses for guns and cameras and silver and food. The Germans yielded their homes to GI boots which trampled their linens and muddied their beds. The women were cheerful offerings to appease the conqueror. Good food, good servants, good plumbing, good women, they were a magnificent fee to conquer. Kuhn despised them. Good cameras, good watches, good pistols, they were as good to Kuhn as any European. Kuhn had a Luger, a Leica, a fine Swiss watch.

Ahead of them, beyond the reach of GI boots, there was law supported by a seemingly death-defying ardor. There was German law and German pride ahead of them. Ahead of them were boasts that the German spirit would endure death rather than humiliation. Behind them they left a disordered mob prepared to sacrifice everything German and human to preserve themselves. Without urging, the Germans denied all that they had been and betrayed any compatriot whose betrayal benefited them.

Kuhn had so far not failed himself. He had not lost himself in the solvent of dread. He had made trembling legs advance. He had made his panicked hands obey him. He had refused to be overwhelmed by fatigue. Whatever beliefs he possessed he was sure of, since they had endured. Yet his victories had not relieved him from oppression. He was more and more oppressed. Instead of being restored by the intervals between hazards, he spent the time anticipating future catastrophes. He didn't know the extent of his endurance. He feared that moment when his courage would fail him and he would act badly.

As the truck bore them across a German valley, he

scanned the sky for aircraft. He studied the roadside for cover. He planned his escape from the truck. The sky was too clear, the land too hilly, the opportunities for ambuscade unsettling. He didn't rely on the scouting jeeps to discover snipers. He only trusted his own vision. He tried imagining the city of Helo where they were to dismount and assemble for an assault. He wondered whether the Germans would be supported by tanks and artillery, whether they would be yielding or would resist.

The banter of the GIs irritated him. He considered their ability to forget hazards a kind of amnesia, fortunate if one could settle for something other than truth. The men were crammed on benches that ran the length of the truck on both sides. They squatted on the floor. They pressed together, shoulders and hips joined, knees against backs, rifles held between legs, loosened helmet straps clanging against steel with each toss of the truck.

"—outside of Triers, remember?" Reilly summoned his buddies to hear the anecdote. "That pillbox with the railroad tunnel?" He and Rodansky had left their squad to check a farmhouse. It was a place with an inner court and a ripe compost pile and pigs and chickens and Russian laborers. Rodansky found a book filled with sketches. These showed a man and woman going all out for love. Various attitudes were sketched in provocative detail. The farm wife entered. Rodansky looked at her, then at the sketchbook. "This is you?" He held up the book and tapped his finger on the woman depicted. The farm wife nodded. "This is me!" Rodansky shouted, pointing to the man. He threw off his harness, dropped his rifle on the table, and pursued her into the bedroom.

Rodansky admitted his conquest and in response to their urging detailed it. He was filled with a charge that raised him mile high. "She didn't run no further than that bed. All feathers it was, so she sunk out of sight with her legs poking up. We didn't get past page one. It's lucky for me there was a war on."

What perhaps the men most admired was Rodansky's ability to forget the pillbox where a few hours previously they had lost an entire squad. Rodansky was able to lust when only terror seemed appropriate. He made places and people who were strange to the GIs less intimidating by humbling them. He'd had limey women in England, Frog and Belgian girls, fräuleins—and in circumstances which seemed to rule out any passion but fear. Once he'd disappeared into a cellar with a fräulein while they struggled for a village. Machine guns directed tracers at the GIs from the high ground beyond. They could see Tiger tanks maneuvering on the hillside for a counterattack. And afterwards what they remembered of that village was, not the GI and German dead, not their panic when it seemed that the enemy tanks would assault them, but Rodansky taking a recess from war in order to satisfy an appetite they were delighted had survived.

Kuhn saw in this eagerness to return to manageable passions a betrayal of experience which he attributed not only to GIs, but to allies and enemies everywhere, and above all to those who remained in the rear echelons, never risking death. Instead of being readied for disaster by his relaxing intermissions, Rodansky was becoming untrustworthy. He bitched too much, he talked too much. He failed to tend himself when they were in reserve. And Kuhn believed that if fear hadn't predominated, Rodansky could have taken the German boy prisoner.

The convoy ascended a steep hill. From the crest they looked down upon a valley. The day was clear, and they were able to view a dozen villages, each centered around a church, ringed first with plowed fields and then with forest. The wind came from the east and brought a piney smell and a vague sound which seemed composed of church bells, the lowing of cattle, the barking of dogs, but nothing of war. Across the valley, straggling beneath the distant hills was the city of Helo. No tanks were visible, no Germans, there was no sound of artillery, no machine-gun staccato to presage resistance ahead. On the left, some two miles distant, they observed another column, preceding them toward Helo. The information was passed back that B and C Companies of their battalion would take the city, with small resistance expected, and that their company would follow in reserve.

The men were jubilant. This was a fine big city that had been spared air raids, and they were getting it peacefully. What novelties in bedding, what steals in cameras, what city fräuleins were available? They relished the chickens they would gut; hams, sausages, preserves they would loot; wine from cellars; and finally sleep.

They dismounted six miles from Helo with orders to sweep the area before the city. Kuhn's platoon controlled a sector three hundred yards wide, consisting mainly of open field and farmhouses. He broke the platoon into squads, instructing the squad leaders to keep track of their men. "There's a crossroads about three miles from here. We'll assemble there in two hours. Keep moving. Call me if there's any trouble."

The mission was uneventful. Kuhn reached the assembly point with time to spare. The day had warmed sufficiently to make the march uncomfortable. Chester Grove, the platoon messenger, accompanied Kuhn. Grove was a farmer from Oklahoma, a lumpish man who admired Kuhn. He nervously broached topics which he hoped would interest Kuhn.

"If we get it now, Sarge, when it's almost over, what a joke."

"It's a long way from over."

"It's been a couple weeks since we run into artillery. Everyone's relaxed. I tell you, Sarge, you can be trained for a lot of things. Experience makes you better if you want to be an athlete or a farmer or for screwing. You get smarter reading books. There's a lot of things where practice makes perfect. But, Sarge, when I hear a shell I don't have the nerve I first had. I figure that every time I wasn't killed I was in luck and there's only so much luck a man has before the cards change."

The squads arrived, Reilly's squad reporting last. The men sprawled along the roadside, munching at K-rations and food looted in the course of the march.

"Everybody here?"

"Rodansky ain't showed up," Reilly reported. "Give him a few minutes, Sarge. He'll be along."

"Where is he?"

"You know old Rodansky, Sarge. He could find himself a woman and a bed Sunday morning in church."

"Where is he?"

"Back in that farmhouse." Reilly pointed to a farmhouse in a grove of trees, half a mile from the assembly point.

"He's got five more minutes." When the five minutes passed, Kuhn nodded. "Okay, Reilly. Let's get him."

Plodding and sour-faced, there were a few buddy indiscretions Reilly wouldn't forgive. He might regret excess in killing, cowardice, gold-bricking, but so long as it was family that was in error he was tolerant. The broadness of his view did not extend beyond the family of buddies.

"Old Rodansky, when he's on tail, it takes a direct hit from a eighty-eight to get him off."

"I'll get him off."

"Take it easy, Sarge. Harry's okay."

"You think this war is a joke, Reilly?"

They walked directly into the kitchen, Rodansky's rifle was on a counter near a tile oven. His field jacket, hung with grenades, lay in a chair.

Kuhn shouted for Rodansky. He walked to the door beside the oven and kicked it. "Rodansky! Come out of there!"

Reilly caught his arm. "Hold on, Sarge. He'll come."

Kuhn shoved the door open. The room was dark. There was a burst of motion from the high bed. Rodansky scrambled from the bed, gripping his pants. He came toward the light, fumbling with his belt, his shirt undone, blinking, stunned, a sweaty smell accompanying him. The woman crouched on the other side of the bed.

"That's a lousy trick, Kuhn. It's no skin off your nose. What are you getting so goddam GI for?"

Kuhn struggled with a murderous impulse he didn't understand. "I catch you again leaving your rifle around like that and I'll bust the hell out of you."

"Bust me. I'm a PFC."

"I can bust you good, Rodansky. You know what I mean? You want to push harder and find out?"

Kuhn hurried back to the platoon without waiting for Reilly and Rodansky.

C Company had the outskirts of Helo. A tank man pissed from a doorway, his free hand gripping a bottle of wine. Chemical mortars had fired the bordering houses, and no efforts were made to stop the burning. B Company had sequestered an entire block, and the men of B Company had already cashed in on the available bounty.

Instead of approaching the heart of town, the reserve company was directed along its periphery. For a moment, peering down a winding street, they glimpsed a sizable plaza that promised the amenities of city life they had long missed. They were marched through a residential area, then to a dirt road, and soon the city was on their left, open field on their right, and it was evident they were not intended to share the fortunes of the other companies in the battalion.

In an open field, two miles beyond the city, they came to barracks enclosed with barbed wire. There were three buildings that formed a *U*-shape. The buildings were mere boxes, with small windows covered with steel mesh. The ground surrounding the buildings was hard clay.

The prospect was barren, and Kuhn shared the general dismay. The battalion jeep was at the entrance to the compound. A group of officers huddled around the jeep while the company halted. The captain and platoon leaders conferred with the major. Solomon was with them. He waved to Kuhn.

Kuhn's platoon was detached from the company and entered the grounds where they assembled around their officer. The rest of the company returned to the city.

"We're only going to be here a few hours. We have to make Brumberg by morning. We go by truck. There'll be hot chow. Get some rest, boys." Lieutenant Gordon was a ruddy-cheeked man of twenty-five, his natural stoutness trimmed down by rigorous living. "Now, about this place— I'm not going to give you the usual crap about looting and fraternizing. I know what goes on. This is a *Lager*. The middle barracks there has thirty women in it—Hungarians. These girls have had a very rough time. Stay away from them. They think the GI is something different, and I want them thinking that way when we leave. Sergeant!" He summoned Kuhn. "Sergeant, I want you to put out a guard detail for the women's barracks. Any man caught fraternizing I'll court-martial."

There were wooden bunks in the long room. A potbellied stove was in the center of the room, firewood heaped behind it. The men flung down their rifles, helmets, and harness. They sprawled in their bunks on bare springs.

Kuhn waited for them to settle down before assigning details. He felt dizzy and knew the dizziness to precede a blackout. These periods of amnesia had become frequent. Dread settled on him like a fog and, sometimes for several moments, he couldn't distinguish his place, his role, his purpose. He nerved himself to endure these moments. He took off his helmet and swabbed his forehead with his wool cap. Their names tumbled across his tongue, and he scanned the barracks but couldn't find the faces to fit the names. Then slowly their faces merged with the fog. He felt as distant from them as if they had been background to a dream. He couldn't pluck out the sense of their words. He fumbled for his detail book and turned the pages. The headings were senseless, there was no clue in the words recorded. He felt nauseated but was determined not to reveal his panic and continued turning the pages. Rebel, Reilly, Rodansky. Grove, Nelson, Schultz. The words became a rhythm which was compulsively reiterated.

"Mel, Mel." The blackout lasted a few seconds. He was not detected. Solomon gripped his sleeve. "Can I talk to you, Mel? In private? A few seconds? Are you busy?"

The smiling, seamed face was in focus.

"Reilly, your squad takes the first tour of guard duty. Let's make it till eleven. Nelson, from eleven to three. Schultz, from three if we need your squad. One post in front, one in back."

He followed Solomon into the yard. The jeep had left. The yard was empty. The sun was already low over the plowed fields. They could hear the distant motors in the city, the heavy rumble of tanks, a faraway shout.

"They're Jewish girls, Melford. Yesterday, before the Germans left, they cut off their hair and marched them naked through the streets. They're lucky they are alive. They come from a village, Mel, where all the Jews are dead except these girls. The Germans made them whores."

"What do you want from me, Solomon?"

"In two days it's Pesach—Passover—Mel. Tonight, while we're still here, I want that you and I should help these girls to celebrate their luck. I want we should have a meal which we can pretend is a seder."

The sun was covered by the clouds rolling in from the horizon. Long shadows spread from the forest across the furrows of the encompassing fields. The forest hadn't been cleared of enemies. Germans, by-passed by their column, might now be waiting at the edge of the forest. The road to Helo went through the forest, and Kuhn was to be briefed at company headquarters in Helo. There were rumors that Brumberg, their next objective, was a focus of resistance. He had to get to town before dark to secure the password.

"I want you to meet the girls, Kuhn. It will give them a real pleasure."

"What time is it?"

"It's four o'clock. I have permission from the major to hold a seder, Mel. These poor kids. There are some of them babies yet—fifteen, sixteen."

"I got troubles without you around, Solomon. What do you want? A seder?"

Rebel came out to begin the first tour of duty. "Where shall I dig in, Sarge?"

"In back. Near the wire."

Solomon caught his arm, and Kuhn shoved him away. "Don't touch me, you jerk."

But his single-mindedness brooked no offense. "It's not a question do I annoy you or do you like me or are you worried. The question has to do with these girls. I don't ask any big sacrifice from you, like to give up your life. I only ask you to be a little decent to some girls who, because you are a Jew—even if it annoys you—they would feel some pleasure to meet you."

"You're what annoys me, Solomon."

"Do you so much value yourself, Kuhn, that you can't take a little time for these poor girls?"

"Get off my back." He left Solomon abruptly and returned to the barracks. He told Reilly to take over the platoon while he and Grove went to headquarters for the briefing.

Rodansky lay on his bunk, still harnessed, his knees raised, his arms folded across his chest, his eyes closed.

Reilly accompanied Kuhn to the barbed-wire gate. "How about these gals, Sarge?"

"You heard the lieutenant. They're off-limits."

"What he don't know won't hurt him."

"It'll hurt you, Reilly. It's my orders you listen to. Stay away from them. I hold you responsible, Reilly. You're in charge. Don't get smart."

"What the hell. We're moving out in a few hours."

"I'm telling you straight. I'll break you, Reilly. Don't give me any of that buddy business. No screwing around. Get it?"

Reilly winked. "Got it."

Lately, Kuhn had sensed resistance among the men. He felt eyes following him, averted when he turned. They were handling him as they did officers, accepting orders with sardonic geniality, grins becoming smirks.

"I'll make it a point to check, Reilly."

There was no part of army life which was natural to Kuhn. He had no flair for communal living. He had early discovered that his efforts to establish himself as a buddy made him foolish. He could only pretend sympathy and when the pretense wearied him his antipathy showed.

Forests were strange to him. Initially he had not been able to orient himself in forests. He was not familiar with forest sounds, had poor vision in the murkiness of the forest gloom. There were men who could walk confidently in the dark. They could discriminate sounds and know when to be easy and when to be tense. They could relax vigilance. A snapped twig, a sensed motion, danger felt, and without doing violence to their nerves, they were again prepared. But to Kuhn, all sounds were ominous. He had no sense for danger and was always on guard. He feared the infiltration of enemies and he couldn't take advantage of lulls. Yet Kuhn had mastered his natural disadvantages and by never yielding to terror he had established himself as the equal of any soldier in the company.

The pines leaned together across the road. Kuhn and Grove advanced into pockets of gloom, the only sound being the gravel scattered by their boots. Kuhn held his carbine ready, bracing against panic whenever they approached an area of darkness. He felt himself vulnerable to any violence. If a German should leap from the forest, he would turn and run. He would abandon Grove. If captured, he would beg. He clicked off the safety of his carbine and hunched his shoulders.

He was trembling when finally they were past the forest and had entered the town.

"Maybe we'll get a ride back," Grove suggested.

"They don't run a taxi service."

Cobbled streets twisted up the hill toward the church. Half-timbered houses fronted solidly on the narrow streets, their upper stories cantilevered. The gutters were strewn with wires laid by the Signal Corps. The intersections were placarded with directions indicating the various units in the area. MPs supervised traffic at intersections. Convoys of trucks rolled through. The front which had been at Helo a few hours previously was already several miles beyond.

Company headquarters were located in the main square which centered about the church. Market stalls, shuttered and locked, fringed the square. The area was being used as a motor-pool and was crowded with trucks and jeeps. There were no civilians in sight, and the soldiers who were not attending to their vehicles were rummaging for loot.

The captain briefed them on the coming objective. Brumberg was defended by twelve batteries of German artillery.
This was, perhaps, a sizable element of the remaining enemy
resistance. Their company was to participate in a task force
that included tanks, TDs, and air support. They had earned
this privilege by virtue of their great record. The captain
was proud. The lieutenants were proud.

Kuhn loathed himself after a session with the officers. A
gentlemanly jargon was in common use. The noncoms, as
well as the officers, lent themselves to a collegiate view of
war. Even Kuhn while in the company of officers was impressed by their vision of combat. They had seen what shell
fragments could do. They had smelled blood and knew that
it was a fecal smell. They had seen how the perspective of a
dying man narrows until it is confined to himself. And yet
they could still approach combat with collegiate sentiments.
They ate well. They drank the best of Scotch, served from
German tumblers. They were established in the mayor's
residence and handsomely bedded. Kuhn withdrew from the
party spirit that prevailed. He saw them as a spic-and-span
hazing crew with a boy-scout ardor for protocol and a soph-
omoric concern for reputation.

The major, who had joined the briefing, approached
Kuhn. "How's my boy Solomon doing, Sergeant? You keep
an eye on that old man, hear?" The charge was confided
with the easy bonhommie that a master—a decent paternal-
istic master—has for his underlings. He was a ruddy, bulky,
senatorial type, his uniform tailored to fit his bulk, his
polished, stiff bearing a mark of his caste. "I love that big-
hearted sonofagun. He found himself some Jewish girls
who were treated very badly. And Solomon—well he
couldn't have been more concerned if it was him the krauts
tortured. We could do with more like Solomon." He held
Kuhn's elbow and spoke confidentially: "By the way, Sergeant, I've fixed a little surprise for Solomon. Some of the
mail has arrived from Division, and the chaplain has sent up
some Jewish flat bread—matzos—and I sent it on to your
outfit together with the hot chow. The old man will get a

kick out of it. See that he's taken care of, Sergeant. Right?"
He squeezed Kuhn's elbow.

The password was Easter Bunny.

The twilight was well advanced when they started back
toward the platoon. It was chill again, and Kuhn shivered
in his woolens which were still damp from sweating. They
left the town. The moment they were on the country road
the clamor of motors and rummaging GIs diminished. They
entered the forest. Grove walked down the center of the
road, his rifle clanking against his canteen, the sling of his
rifle slapping against the buckles of his harness. Kuhn
listened to him chew the chicken leg he had taken from the
officer's mess. He used both hands to hold the leg, his head
jerking back as he tugged at the meat. He flung the bone
away and wiped his hands on his trousers. He belched, then
reached into the pocket of his field jacket for a chocolate
bar. He stripped the paper, crumpled it into a ball, flung it
into the underbrush beside the road. Kuhn was dizzy with
expectation of a bullet. He felt like a target.

"You pig!"

"What?"

"Quiet!"

"I was just eating, Sarge."

"They can hear you eating in Berlin. Where did you
learn to eat, on your pig farm? You'll bring every kraut in
ten miles."

"There're no krauts around."

"You're not getting me killed, Grove. This is enemy terri-
tory. How do you know this forest is secure? There are
twelve batteries of kraut artillery at Brumberg. Brumberg
is only ten miles from here."

"I won't eat then. If my eating is going to lose the war,
okay, I won't eat."

"Whisper, Stupid! This isn't an officer's club."

"You're making more noise than me, Sarge."

"Shut up and let's move."

They trudged on opposite sides of the road, less concerned now with possible ambushes than with their hatred

of each other. Kuhn listened to Grove's muttering, realized his own childishness, and yet couldn't restrain his loathing for this and all other buddies. He felt himself dying in a stupid war among stupid men whose understanding was confined to what sex and stomach could sense.

"Twelve batteries—they're honored."

Grove steamed with the insult. "You'd think you was General Patton. Who the hell are you to tell me how to eat? I can eat any damn way I please. I was the only friend you had in this platoon. With the friends you got, it ain't kraut shrapnel you have to worry about. Sonofabitch. They better section-eight you before you crack wide open."

They were still far from the barracks when they heard the party. It was night, and the windows hadn't been completely blacked out, and cracks of light sprayed over the plain.

"We move out in three hours and they're screwing up! I warned Reilly!"

The guard was near the door. It was Rebel. He was so intent upon the sounds from the barracks that he didn't observe their approach.

"*Hands awf*, you jerk! Put down that rifle. If I was a kraut you'd be a dead man and so would everyone else in this platoon. This isn't your post, Rebel. I could court-martial you, Stupid. What the hell's going on?"

"Solomon brought them in, Sarge. He said it was okay. He said he'd take responsibility. The major gave him permission."

"Who's running this outfit, me or Solomon!"

"It ain't my fault, Sarge."

"The password is Easter Bunny. Got it? We're moving out in three hours. We're joining Task Force Onaway. We've been volunteered. There's twelve batteries of kraut artillery at Brumberg. You feel like kicking your heels, Rebel?"

"How come us, Sarge? Why don't they give some other company the chance?"

"We're honored, Stupid. What's the password?"

"Easter Bunny."

A long table had been constructed from planks fitted over saw-horses. There were candles on the table. Mess kits had been placed in front of the seated women. Hot chow was presented in huge GI pots. The women were shawled. They wore knee-length smocks, half-sleeved, open-throated. They were pallid and puffy-faced, an unhealthy taint that was as much the color of apathy as the consequence of poor food and imprisonment. Dead men had this color. Bodies moldering in trenches had this smell.

Yet now they could laugh. Now they felt no pain. Now they were ready to forget the several hundred krauts who had mounted them. So newly rescued from terror, could their equilibrium be so quickly restored? Kuhn shrank from the sight of them. How could they laugh? How could they respond to the buddy teasing? How could they live after their complete humiliation? They had given everything away.

The men stood behind them, helping with the preparations for the feast. They beckoned Kuhn to share the fun. "Climb in, Sarge. There's room for everybody."

"Grab a matzo, Sarge. Good old Solomon—"

Solomon beamed. Solomon, with his brood of chicks, thought he was among gentlemen.

"Reilly! What did I tell you!"

"Solomon's got orders from the major. I figured you was outranked, Sarge."

"I saw the lights a mile away. Is this what you call a blackout?"

"It ain't hardly dark."

"Clear out these women. I don't want any more screwing around. We move out in three hours."

"That's three hours. That's not now."

"I said, clear them out, Reilly," he slowly advised.

"What's the pitch? We're nice boys. These are friendly gals. What's eating you, Kuhn?"

"Twelve batteries of kraut artillery. That's what's eating me. Come morning we'll be at Brumberg."

"I'll be there, Kuhn, and so will the boys. Meantime, I don't see any artillery. Maybe I'll get kilt in the morning. Right now I'm not getting kilt."

"Melford!" Solomon shouted. "My friend! I want you to meet someone." He beckoned Kuhn with both hands, speaking excitedly to the woman beside him.

"Melford, I want you to meet Leona." In German he told Leona that Kuhn was the Jewish sergeant he had told her about. All the women turned to watch the introduction.

She was the only one not shawled. Her straight black hair was cropped at the neck. Leaning on her elbows, puffing a cigarette, she had seemed a beauty across the room —a dark, slim woman, great-eyed, fine-featured. But up close the ravage was apparent. The skin was jaundiced, and the face was dry and brittle. The swollen cords of her throat traced her gauntness. Her sprawled legs exhibited the welts of lice bites. There was a sore on her lower lip.

"It is a year now since I see a Jewish man," she told him in a rasping voice. She arose to greet him. She didn't bother to find out whether he would accept the identity she imposed on him. She came to him with the stiff gait of a pregnant woman, her arms half raised, and walked up in reach of the embrace she expected.

He was so strongly repelled by her that it required a physical effort to remain in her presence. She seemed to him fouled by all the abuse she had suffered. Her walk was infirm. The broadness of her hips, the puffy ankles, were an unnatural contrast to the bony shoulders and skinny arms. The musty smell which repelled him seemed to have its source in her scabs and her welts. That she was still a young woman made her seem even more repellant. What hadn't she allowed to happen to her? What hadn't she endured in order to avoid death? Dared she claim him as kin? Face him as her equal?

"Everyone's had it tough." He stood his distance.

"Solomon has much praised you to us."

"Solomon is sometimes foolish. Solomon is a big talker. Pardon me, Leona, but now I have to talk to Solomon. I have to speak privately."

He took Solomon outside and when the door was closed, seized him and slammed him against the barrack wall. Solomon's helmet fell across his forehead. He lost his balance and grabbed Kuhn's arm.

"Mel!"

"I hate the way you smile, Solomon! I hate the way you wiggle on your belly to get laughs. I hate you for all the asses you've kissed. I hate you for being so stupid!"

"Because I'm a Jew maybe?" Solomon hissed, gasping under the hand that pinned him to the wall. "You hate me because I'm a Jew, Kuhn?"

"In three hours we go for a ride. At the end of the ride we get out and walk. And while we walk we get killed. The man ahead, the man behind, they get killed. Their bellies open. Their legs tear off. Their heads explode. That's what I concentrate on, Solomon. That's the important thing. And you, Smiley, you Fat-lips, you Big-heart—you drag your ass up here where it doesn't belong and you clap your head and say, 'Poor little kraut who doesn't have a chest—' You come up here and hunt out Jews and you say, 'Okay! Let's stop everything, boys, let's be nice to the Jew girls. They've had it so bad, take pity. Pity the poor Jews who are whores.' And you know what the boys think of you, Solomon? Who is this old jerk with the clean uniform and good food in his belly who comes up here and says, 'Time out, let's take pity.' Pity? What's that word? They use it back in headquarters? Those gentlemen back there, the ones who tell us we have the honor to get killed? They use words like honor, too, don't they, Solomon?"

He shook Solomon while he spoke. He clutched the lapels of Solomon's field jacket, and the old man gasped and choked, his head wobbling as he submitted to what appeared to him a murderous assault. His lips slackened, white showed in his eyes, his face was gray with shock, he embraced Kuhn's hands with his own.

"You want to kill me?" he hissed.

Kuhn felt the trembling hands on his own and tightened his grip.

"I'm old enough to be your father," Solomon said as if amazed. "Is this the way you treat me?"

"What have you ever learned, you bastard!" But suddenly he couldn't endure the terror in Solomon's eyes. He pushed Solomon against the wall once more and dropped his hands.

"Are you a Hitler or a God you can treat me like this? What gives you the power?"

Kuhn felt drugged in the aftermath of violence. He looked at Solomon as if he could see there the reflection of himself, see his brutishness mirrored there, see reflected in the older man's disillusionment his own deterioration.

"I learned how it is about dying," Kuhn muttered. "I learned what is bullshit. What I learned you have no idea of. Why are you so surprised, Stupid? Don't you know what the world is like?"

Solomon breathed deeply, his seamed face now resolute. "Don't be too proud, Kuhn," he answered hoarsely. "Don't think you only have felt what no one else has felt. There is always someone has had it worse."

"Have your seder, Solomon. But stay away from me. Stay away from me and stay away from this platoon."

He did not respond to the bitter dignity of Solomon's defiance, "It's not only your war, Kuhn."

Toward the east, in the direction of Brumberg, the sky pulsed from dark to lightening white. This was the artillery preparation of Brumberg. The damp chill pinched his toes and shivered his thighs. He raised the collar of his field jacket. It required intense listening to discern the pervasive bass rumble of the distant shelling. The furrows in the field seemed to writhe and twist after steady scanning. Clots of gloom separated from the forest wall and merged with the field. There was laughter in the barracks behind him. They were snug in their lighted room, warmed by the stove, guarded front and rear by entrenched GIs. But what was this one drop of light contrasted with the great puddle of darkness in which they were immersed?

When Solomon left, Kuhn felt the darkness swarm over him. It pressed a bubble of loneliness that rose from his guts to his throat. He despairingly summoned his exhausted pride to suppress this gas of pity.

He was close to tears when Rodansky came around the corner, followed by the girl. She was no more than seventeen. Shawled, her form distorted by the poor-fitting smock, there was still no mistaking her beauty. There was an idiot innocence in her eyes, as though she had preserved herself from further defeat by withdrawing her awareness from all that her body had suffered. She clutched Rodansky's arm when she saw Kuhn. She cowered at the sight of him.

Rodansky was in a fever, tensed from head to toe, his eyes darting in quest of escape. He jerked to a halt and spread out his arms to stop the girl when he saw Kuhn. His fear showed. He stood his ground, nerving himself for punishment. "Okay . . . so what are you going to do about it?"

He was strangely saddened by Rodansky's terror. Was his effort to find release of such pathetic consequence that he could now turn pale at the sight of Kuhn?

"There's kraut artillery waiting for us, Rodansky."

"You can wait for it, Kuhn. I don't ask any favors. At least I got my kicks in."

"Take the girl in, Rodansky. Get some chow. We move out in two hours."

Rodansky guided the girl into the barracks. She followed him docilely, averting her face as she passed Kuhn.

A flare ignited with a hiss, turning the sky greenish-white. It was the first of a series of flares aimed toward Brumberg. Planes flew overhead toward Brumberg. In front of him, the forest appeared in silhouette, the trees as sharply defined as paper cutouts. He remained frozen after the darkness again settled.

He had to clean his carbine, get the ammo distributed, receive the final briefing from the lieutenant. But until his loneliness was relieved, no action was possible.

Solomon was seated at the head of the table. He addressed both the seated girls and the standing GIs. Kuhn went to the opposite end of the table and sat by Leona. He did not reject her hand which gripped his under the table.

Somehow Solomon had made a congregation of his audience. There was pious intensity in their listening.

"—so that is why tonight we talk about the meaning of this day. And to make this meaning clear is why I ask why this night is different from all other nights. It has to do when our people were in Egypt. They were slaves."

ISAAC ROSENFELD

The death of Isaac Rosenfeld in 1956 deprived American literature of a writer of immense stylistic and intellectual gifts. He was perhaps the most brilliant member of his generation, a philosopher and critic as well as novelist. Born in 1918, he grew up on the northwest side of Chicago and attended the University of Chicago where he studied literature and philosophy. From the early forties he lived in New York City. He was for a time a junior editor of the *New Republic,* and literary editor of *The New Leader.* He is the author of *A Passage from Home* and the posthumously published *An Age of Enormity.* The translation of Sholom Aleichem's "On Account of a Hat" in this collection is his work.

King Solomon

1. With His Women

Every year, a certain number of girls. They come to him, lie down beside him, place their hands on his breast and offer to become his slaves.

This goes on all the time. "I will be your slave," say the girls, and no more need be said. But Solomon's men, his counselors, can't bear it—what is this power of his? Some maintain it is no power at all, he is merely the King. Oh yes, admit the rest, his being the King has something to do with it—but there have been other kings, so it can't be that.

Nor is it anything else. Consider how unprepossessing he is, what a poor impression he makes—why, most of the counselors are taller, handsomer, and leaner than he. To be sure, he has an excellent voice. But his voice comes through best on the telephone, and he has an unlisted number which no one would give out. Certainly not, say the men. Still, the girls keep coming, and they lie down beside him with their hands on his breast.

It is not enough to say the counselors are jealous. After all, there is something strange here, the like of it has not been seen. But who shall explain the King?

Solomon himself makes no comment, he does not speak of his personal affairs. He may drop a hint or two, but these hints are contradictory and vague, and he drops them only for his own amusement; perhaps he, too, doesn't know. Every few years he publishes a collection of his sayings, most of which he has never said, but the sayings have little to do with the case, and their melancholy tone is held to be an affectation. The wisest counselors pay no attention to his words. If anything is to be learned, the wise men say, it had better be sought among his girls.

But the girls also say nothing. The rejected go away in tears—in which case one cannot expect them to speak coherently or with regard for truth; or they are determined yet to win his love—and again they will tell lies. As for the women he accepts, they are useless. Almost at once they become so much like Solomon, adopting his mannerisms of gesture and speech and sharing his views of things, that they say only what he would say—and Solomon does not speak his heart.

So it has become the custom in the court to study Solomon's women in their work; perhaps the manner in which they serve him will make it clear. The counselors watch over the harem, each chooses a woman to follow about the palace, over the grounds and through the town. One woman . . . there she goes! . . . sets out early in the morning with a basket, trailed by a counselor. She makes her way to the largest and most crowded kosher market, where she will stand in line for hours, haggling and hefting, crying

highway robbery! And what delicacies does she buy? Surely
pickles and spices, the rarest and the best. . . . Not necessarily, it may even be noodles. So who is the wiser? And as
for the obvious conclusion—that Solomon sets store by
economy—this has long since been drawn. He even lunches
on left-overs.

Others clean his shoes, open and sort the mail, tend the
garden and the vineyards, keep his instruments polished and
in tune. A few go to the well for water—a curious assign-
ment, as the palace has had hot and cold running water for
years. Perhaps he sends them to the well on purpose, to confuse the counselors. But if this occupation serves only to deceive, why not all the rest? This may well be the case. King
Solomon has a staff of regular servants, quite capable of
looking after his needs.

Therefore nothing has been learned. The counselors are
always confronted by the same questions at nightfall, when
their need to know the King is greatest. Much of the time,
he sits quietly with a girl or two, pasting stamps in an album, while they massage his scalp. On festive nights, the
counselors note the revelry and participate, when invited, in
the dancing and carousing. Not that this enchants them;
many counselors complain that the King has no taste in
entertainment, that he relies, for instance, too heavily on
tambourines, which he has his dancing girls flutter in their
hands till the jingling gives one a headache; that much the
same or better amusements can be had in the cabarets about
the town which—so much for Solomon's originality—have
been the source of many a spectacle of the King's court—
and they even have newspaper clippings to prove the point.
Nevertheless, they succumb to the King's merrymaking, and
even if it makes them puke with disdain, still they lose the
essential detachment. And then at the hour when the King
retires to his chamber with his chosen love, all is lost, the
counselors are defeated and go disgruntled to their own
quarters, to lie awake or dream enviously through the night.

All the same, a pertinacious lot. What stratagems, dis-
guising themselves as eunuchs or hiding in vases or behind
the furniture to learn what goes on at night! Here, too,

they have been disappointed. Though Solomon burns soft lights beside his couch, no one has witnessed anything—or at least has ever reported what he saw. At the last moment the hidden counselors have shut their eyes or turned away; no one has dared look at the King's nakedness, dared to witness his love. Still, sounds have been heard floating in deep summer air over the garden and the lily pond, mingling with the voices of frogs—but the intrusion has been its own punishment, maddening those who have overheard the King and driving them wild with lust or despair. Sooner or later, the counselors have been compelled to stopper their ears. Now when these sounds issue from the King's apartments, the counselors take up instruments and play, softly but in concert, to hide his sounds within their own.

None has seen the King's nakedness; yet all have seen him in shirt sleeves or suspenders, paunchy, loose-jowled, in need of a trim. Often in the heat of the day he appears bare-headed, and all have looked upon his baldness; sometimes he comes forth in his bare feet, and the men have observed bunions and corns. When he appears in this fashion with, say, a cigar in his mouth and circles under his eyes; his armpits showing yellowish and hairy over the arm holes of his undershirt; his wrinkles deep and his skin slack; a wallet protruding from one hip pocket and a kerchief from the other—at such moments, whether he be concerned with issues of government or merely the condition of the plumbing, he does show himself in human nakedness after all, he is much like any man, he even resembles a policeman on his day off or a small-time gambler. And sometimes, unexpectedly, he summons the cabinet to a game of pinochle—then all are aware he has again transcended them.

Of late, King Solomon has turned his attention to the young. He has organized bicycle races for children, entertained them with magicians, taken them on picnics and excursions to the zoo. He loves to sit on a shady bench with a youngster on either knee, a boy and a girl, about four or five in age. They pull at his beard, tug at his ears, and finger his spectacles till he can no longer see through the smudges.

Sometimes, the children are his own, more often not. It makes no difference, the King has many sons and daughters. He tells stories, not nearly so amusing as they should be, old stories which the children grew tired of in the nursery, or poor inventions, rather pointless on the whole. And he seldom finishes a story but begins to nod in the telling, his words thicken and stumble; eventually he falls asleep. Solomon is a disappointment to the young, seldom will children come twice to his garden. Yet for them he is truly a king: robed and gowned, golden-sandaled, wearing a crown, his hair trimmed, his beard washed lustrous, combed, and waved, and the hairs plucked out of his nostrils.

And in this splendor, in which he seldom appears, not even for the reception of ambassadors, he loves to bounce a rubber ball and play catch with the children. He is unskilled at these games, they call him butter-fingers. A man turning sixty, an aging king.

But how clear is the expression of his eyes as he plays with the children—if only one knew what it meant! Perhaps he longs to reveal himself but does not know how; or does not know that the people await this revelation; or is unable to see beyond the children, who are bored with him. Perhaps he has nothing to reveal, and all his wisdom lies scattered from his hand: he is merely this, that, and the other, a few buildings raised, roads leveled, a number of words spoken, unthinking, on an idle afternoon. Occasionally, when he recognizes the expectation of the people, he tries to remember an appropriate saying from one of the collections he has published. Most of the time, he is unaware of all this.

The children are fretful in the garden, they wait to be delivered. They have been brought by mothers, nurses, older sisters, who stand outside the gate, looking in through the palings. The mothers and nurses whisper together, their feet and eyes and hands are restless, they look at his shining beard. Later in the afternoon, when the children have been led home, perhaps one of the older girls, one of the sisters, will enter the same garden, approach the spot where the

King lies resting, lie down beside him, fold her hands upon his breast, and offer to become his slave.

2. The Queen of Sheba

From all over they have come, and they keep coming, though the King is now an old man. It may be owing to his age that he has grown lenient, admitting women to concubinage whom, the counselors swear, he would have sent packing in the old days. He has reached the years when anything young looks good to him. This may not be true, there may be other reasons; but the counselors have a point in saying that the standards have fallen, and they tell the story of the Queen of Sheba.

A letter came, it was the first application to be received by mail. From a foreign country, the woman signed herself The Queen. She flattered Solomon's wisdom, word of which had reached her from afar; her own ears longed to hear his discourse, her own eyes, to behold his person. An unorthodox application, written in a powerful, forward-rushing, though feminine hand on strangely scented paper: the King said it reminded him of jungles. He inspected the postmark, clipped off the stamp, and pasted it on a page by itself in his album. His expression was hidden in his beard.

The woman meant it. Boxes began to arrive, plastered with travel stickers. They came on sand-choked, sneezing camels, in long trains, attended by drivers, natives of the Land of Sheba. The next day, more boxes, and again on the third. Gifts of all description, of money and goods, spangles and bangles for the entire court. It made an excellent impression, but Solomon, who distributed the gifts, did not seem pleased. . . . Here the counselors pretend to know the King's mind. First of all, they say, he was annoyed at having to put up so many camels, whole droves of them—his stables were crowded, and there was a shortage of feed for his own animals. Then the camel drivers, rough and barbarous men, were inflamed by the sight of Solomon's women, and the King had to double the guard and pay overtime; this killed him. But their greatest presumption lies in saying that Solomon thought, *"Adonai Elohenu!* Is she coming to stay?"* No one knows what the King thought.

He may well have been glad that the Queen was coming. No queen had ever before asked to be his slave—and she was a queen for sure, and of a rich country, think of the gifts she had sent. Solomon put his economists to work and they submitted a report: the financial structure was sound, and the country led in the production of myrrh, pepper, and oil. Now to be sure, the Queen's letter made no direct application; apart from the flattery, it merely said, *coming for a visit,* as an equal might say. But the interpretation was clear. An equal would not come uninvited, only one who meant to offer herself would do so—unless the Queen was rude; but the gifts she had sent took care of that. Yet as a queen, writing from her own palace, she could not have expressed the intention, it would have been treason to her own people. Nevertheless, she had every intention: otherwise, why would she have gone to the trouble? The fact is, there was rejoicing in the palace, Solomon himself led the dancing, and he declared a holiday when the Queen of Sheba arrived.

She came in a howdah, on a camel, preceded by troops of archers and trumpeters. Solomon helped her down, and washed and anointed her feet in the courtyard. This didn't come off so well. Sheba used coloring matter on her toenails and the soles of her feet, and the coloring ran; Solomon was out of practice, he tickled her feet a few times and made her laugh. The ceremony was supposed to be a solemn one, the people took it very seriously, and they were offended by her toenails—feet were supposed to be presented dusty: as for the giggling, it was unpardonable, and the priests took offense. A poor set of omens.

Besides, Sheba was not quite so young as the autographed picture, which she had sent in advance to Solomon, would have led one to expect. Her skin was nearly black, and her black hair, which she had apparently made some effort to straighten, had gone frizzled and kinky again in the heat of the desert crossing. She wore anklets of delicate chain, gold

bracelets all over her arms, and jewels in both obvious and
unexpected places, so that the eye was never done seeing
them; their light was kept in constant agitation by the mas-
sive rhythm of her breathing, which involved her entire
body. A sense of tremendous power and authenticity emanated from her breasts. Some thought she was beautiful,
others, not.

No one knows what the King thought; but he may well
have felt what everyone else did who came to witness her
arrival—drawn, and at the same time, stunned.

But the King is glad in his heart as he leads Sheba to the
table, where he has put on a great spread for her. He is attended by his court and surrounded by his women—and
how lordly are his movements as he eats meat and rinses his
mouth with wine! At the same time he is uneasy in the
Queen's presence—after all, this is no maiden lurking in
the garden to trip up to him and fold her hands upon his
breast. The meal goes well enough: Sheba asks for seconds,
and seems impressed with the napkins and silverware. But
suddenly, right in the middle of dessert, she turns to him
and demands, in front of everyone and that all may hear,
that he show her his famous wisdom. This comes as something of a shock. The implication is two-fold: that so far
he has spoken commonplaces; and secondly, that he is to
suffer no illusions, it was really for the sake of his wisdom
that she made the difficult trip. The people turn their eyes
on the King, who handles the awkward moment with skill;
he clears his throat on schedule, and raises his hand in the
usual gesture, admonishing silence. But nothing comes.

In the official account of the visit, which Solomon had
written to order, he was supposed to have

> . . . told her all questions: There was not anything . . .
> which he told her not. And when the Queen of Sheba
> had seen all Solomon's wisdom, and the house that he
> had built, and the meat of his table and the sitting of
> his servants . . .

etc.,

*there was no more spirit in her. And she said to the
King, It was a true report that I heard in mine own
land, of thy acts and thy wisdom. Howbeit, I believed
not the words, until I came and mine eyes had seen it;
and behold, the half was not told me: Thy wisdom and
prosperity exceedeth the fame which I heard. Happy
are thy men . . . which stand continually before thee
and that hear thy wisdom.*

After which there was supposed to have been a further exchange of compliments and gifts.

Now this is not only a bit thick, it gets round the question of Solomon's wisdom. What *did* the King say, when put to it by the Queen? That there were so many feet in a mile? That all circles were round? That the number of stars visible on a clear night from a point well out of town was neither more nor less than a certain number? Did he advise her what to take for colds, give her a recipe for salad dressing, or speak of building temples and ships? Just what does a man say under the circumstances?

Certainly, he hadn't the nerve, the gall, to repeat the abominable invention to her face of the two women who disputed motherhood of a child. She would have seen through it right away. And surely he knew this was not the time to quote his sayings; besides, he always had trouble remembering them. Then what did he say?

His economists had worked up a report on the Land of Sheba. He may have sent for a copy; more likely, he knew the essential facts cold, and spoke what came to mind: industry, agriculture, natural resources. Of the financial structure, the public debt, the condition of business. Of the production of pepper, myrrh, and oil, especially oil. Grant him his wisdom.

Certainly, the Queen was impressed, but one need not suppose that the spirit was knocked out of her or that she said, "It was a true report that I heard in mine own land . . ." etc. Chances are, she paid no attention to his words (except to note the drift) but watched him as he spoke, taking in the cut of his beard, the fit of his clothes, and wondering, betimes, what sort of man he was. She saw his initial uncertainty give way and his confidence grow as he reached the meaty part of his delivery. And all along, she observed how he drew on the admiring glances of his girls, soaked up their adoration, as they lay open-mouthed on couches and rugs at his feet, all criticism suspended, incapacitated by love. Love ringed him round, love sustained him, he was the splendid heart of their hearts. She must have forgotten the heat and sand images of the desert crossing, she, too, lapped from all sides and borne gently afloat. . . .

So much, one may imagine. But the Queen spent a number of days or weeks perhaps even a month or two in the King's company, and of what happened during the time of her stay, let alone the subsequent events of the first night, the official chronicles say nothing. A merciful omission, according to the counselors, who report that it went badly from the start. When the King had finished his discourse, they say the Queen felt called upon to answer. But words failed her, or she felt no need of words: she was the Queen. What she did was to lean forward and, in utter disregard of the company, take his head into her hands, gaze at him for a long time with a smile on her thick lips, and at last bestow on him a kiss, which landed somewhere in his beard.

Then she jumped onto the table, commanded music, and danced among the cups and bowls, the dishes and the crumpled napkins. The counselors were shocked, the girls smirked painfully, the servants held their breath. Nor was Sheba so slender as the autographed picture may have led one to believe. When she set her feet down, the table shook, and the carafes of wine and sweetened water swayed and threatened to topple. Solomon himself hastily cleared a way for her, pushing the dishes to one side; his hands were trembling. But she proceeded with the dance, the chain anklets tinkled, her fingers snapped, the many jewels she wore flashed wealthily. Her toes left marks on the tablecloth, as though animals had run there. And run she did, back and forth over the length of the table, bending over the counselors to tweak this one's nose and that one's ear. But always she glanced back to see if she had the King's eye.

She had it, darker than usual. To her, this meant that he was admiring her, gravely, as befits King and Queen, and her feet quickened. How stern he was! Already she felt the King's love, harder than any courtier's and so much more severe. She increased the tempo, the musicians scrambling to keep up with her, and whirled. Round and round she sped, drawing nearer the end of the table where the King sat. It was a dance in the style of her country, unknown in these parts, and she did it with the abandon of a tribes-girl, though one must assume she was conscious, in her abandonment, that it was she, the Queen, none other than Sheba, who abandoned herself to King Solomon. That was the whole point of it, the mastery of the thing. Pride did not leave her face, it entered her ecstasy and raised it in degree. Already cries, guttural, impersonal, were barking in her throat; then with a final whoop she spun round and threw herself, arms outstretched and intertwined, like one bound captive, to fall before him on the table where his meal had been.

It was a terrible mistake. The women and the counselors knew the King so much better than she, and their hearts went out in pity. The Queen had offered herself in the only way she knew—majesty, power, and reign implied—throwing herself prone with a condescending crash for the King to rise and take her. What presumption! He did not move. He sat infinitely removed, almost sorrowing over this great embarrassment. The music had stopped, there was an unbearable silence in the banquet hall. The King rumbled something deep in his beard; perhaps he was merely clearing his throat, preparatory to saying a few words (if only his wisdom did not fail him!). Some of the servants took it to mean more wine, others, more meat, still others, finger-bowls. They ran in all directions. Sheba lowered herself into her seat at the King's side. Her dark face burned. . . . Somehow the time went by, and the evening was over. Solomon led Sheba off to his chamber, as courtesy demanded. Even

as she went with him, it was apparent that she still went in
hope; even at the last moment. The older women wept.

Day by day, the strain mounted. Sheba was sometimes
with the King, they played chess or listened to the radio,
they bent their heads over maps, discussed politics, and
played croquet. But there were no festivities and she did
not dance again. She bore herself with dignity, but she had
grown pale, and her smile, when she forgot herself, was
cringing and meek. Sometimes, when she was alone, she
was seen to run her finger over the table tops and the wood-
work, looking for dust. She could not bear the sight of her
waiting women—lest the revival of her hope, as they did
her toilet, become apparent to them—and would chase them
out of the room; only to call them back, and help her prepare for an audience with the King. Finally, she quarreled
with some of the girls of the harem. And when this happened, Sheba knew that the day had come and she began
to pack.

A pinochle game was in progress when the Queen of
Sheba, unannounced and without knocking, came into the
room to say she wanted a word with the King. He dismissed
his counselors, but one of them swears he managed to hide
behind the draperies, where he witnessed the scene.

The King was in his undershirt, smoking a cigar. He
apologized for his dishevelment and offered to repair it. The
affairs of state, he explained, were so trying lately, he found
he worked better in dishabille. Had he been working? asked
the Queen with a smile. She thought this was some sort of
game, and she fingered the cards with pictures of kings and
queens. Solomon, knowing that women do not play pinochle, told her the cabinet had been in extraordinary session, trying fortunes with the picture cards. The times were
good, but one must look to the future, and he offered to
show her how it was done.

"No, I don't want to keep you," said the Queen of Sheba,
"I beg only a few words."

"Speak," said Solomon.

"Solomon, Solomon," said the Queen, "I am going away. No, don't answer me. You will say something polite and regretful, but my decision can only be a relief to you." She paused, taking on courage. "You must not allow this to be a disappointment to you, you must let me take the whole expense of our emotion upon myself. I did a foolish thing. I am a proud woman, being a Queen, and my pride carried me too far. I thought I would take pride in transcending pride, in offering myself to the King. But still that was pride, you did wisely to refuse me. Yes, you are wise, Solomon, let no one question your wisdom. Yours is the wisdom of love, which is the highest. But your love is love only of yourself; yet you share it with others by letting them love you—and this is next to the highest. Either way you look at it, Solomon is wise enough. Understand me—" She took a step forward, a dance step, as though she were again on the table top, but her eyes spoke a different meaning.

"I am not pleading with you that you love me or allow me to love you. For you are the King, your taking is your giving. But allow me to say, your power rests on despair. Yours is the power of drawing love, the like of which has not been seen. But you despair of loving with your own heart. I have come to tell the King he must not despair. Surely, Solomon who has built temples and made the desert flourish is a powerful king, and he has the power to do what the simplest slave girl or washerwoman of his harem can do—to love with his own heart. And if he does not have this power, it will come to him, he need only accept the love which it is his nature to call forth in everyone, especially in us poor women. This is his glory. Rejoice in it, O King, for you are the King!"

The counselor who hid behind the drapes said he regretted his action, to see how his King stood burdened before the Queen. His own heart filled with loving shame. Solomon looked lost, deprived of his power, as though the years in the palace and the garden had never been. He made an effort to stand dignified in his undershirt, he bore his head as though he were wearing the crown, but it was pitiful to see him.

"The Queen is wise," said he. Then he broke down, and the counselor did not hear his next words. He did hear him say that the Queen was magnificent, that she had the courage of lions and tigers . . . but by now his head was lowered. Suddenly, he clasped the Queen to his breast in an embrace of farewell, and the Queen smiled and stroked his curly beard. They did not immediately take leave of each other, but went on to speak of other matters. Before the Queen of Sheba left the country, King Solomon had leased her oil lands for ninety-nine years.

But on the day of her departure, he stood bareheaded in the crowded courtyard to watch her set out, with her trumpeters and archers mounted on supercilious camels. He extended his hand to help her up, and she, with her free hand, chucked him under the chin. Then she leaned out of the howdah to cry, "Long live the King!" King Solomon stood with bowed head to receive the ovation. Now more than ever they yearned for him.

When Sheba moved off, at the head of the procession, Solomon led the people onto the roof, to watch the camels file across the sand. He stood till evening fell, and the rump of the last plodding animal had twitched out of sight beyond the sand hills. Then he averted his face and wept silently lest the people see their King's tears.

3. With His Fathers

So the counselors have a point when they say the standards have fallen. Once the Queen of Sheba herself was unable to make it; and now, look. But no wonder, her like will not come again, and besides, Solomon is old. He has been running the country forty years, and has begun to speak of retiring; but the people know he will never retire, and so they whisper, it is time for the King to die.

How does this strike him? To look at him—his beard is white, his spotted hands shake, he walks bent, his eyes are rheumy and dim—to look at him one would suppose he dwells on the thought of death. But he is no better known now than he was in his prime. The only certainty is that the King is old.

But what follows from this, how does it reveal him? Or this?—that he had an attack of pleurisy not long ago, and since then his side has been taped. And what does it mean to say that he now has more women than ever cluttering up the palace, one thousand in all, including seven hundred wives? (Is it merely that the standards have fallen?) It was necessary to tear down the harem (while the women, to everyone's displeasure, were quartered in the town) and raise a new building, so large it has taken up ground formerly allotted to the garden. They are a great source of trouble to him, these women, and the counselors complain —that's where all the money is going, to support the harem. Harem? Why, it's a whole population, the country will be ruined! And the priests complain, every week they send fresh ultimatums, objecting to the fact that so many of Solomon's girls are heathen; they have even accused him of idolatry and threatened him with loss of the Kingdom and the wrath of God. And the people grumble, it's a shame, when they find his women loitering in beauty shops or quarreling right out in the open, as they have begun to do, in the very streets. But Solomon ignores the discontent and goes on collecting women as he once collected stamps.

Why? Or what does this mean?—that he seldom takes the trouble to interview applicants, but establishes a policy for several months, during which time the rule is, no vacancies. Then he will change the rule and take on newcomers by the dozen, most of whom he does not even see, the work being done by the counselors. And how complicated the work has become, compared with the old days, when all that was necessary was for a girl to lie down beside the King with her hands upon his breast. Now there are forms to fill out and letters of recommendation to obtain, several interviews and a medical examination to go through, and even then the girls must wait until their references have been checked. The filing cabinets have mounted to the ceiling. What sense does it make?

And above all in view of the following? The counselors

vouch for it, they swear they have seen the proof. That King Solomon now takes to bed, not with a virgin, as his father, David, did in his old age, or even with a dancing girl, but with a hot water bottle. If this report is true, then doesn't something follow? For this is the extreme, between life and death, where all thoughts meet; an extreme, not a mean; and a wrong guess is impossible, everything is true, as at the topmost point, where all direction is down. It follows that he warms his hands on the water bottle, presses it to his cheek, passes it down along his belly.

Now when he thinks of his prime, he of all men must wonder: what was the glory of the King? Who bestowed the power, and what did it consist in? When he had it, he did not consider, and now it is gone. Passing the rubber bottle down to his feet and digging with his toes for warmth, he sees he did everything possible in his life, and left no possibility untouched, of manhood, statesmanship, love. What else can a man do? There is no answer. Except to say, he was in God's grace then? And now no longer? Or is he still in a state of grace, witness the water bottle at his feet? And perhaps he is only being tried, and may look forward to even greater rewards? Such are the advantages of being a believer. If he were one, he would know—at least believe that he knew. But a man who knows only that once love was with him, which now is no more—what does he know, what shall he believe, old, exhausted, shivering alone in bed at night with a hot water bottle, when all's quiet in the palace? And if all's not quiet, that's no longer his concern.

No, if there were any rewards, he'd settle for a good night's sleep. But sleep does not come. He hears strange noises in the apartment, scratching. . . . Mice? He must remember to speak to the caretakers. . . . At last he drowses off, to sleep a while. And if he does not sleep? Or later, when he wakes, and it is still the same night? . . . Does he think of the Queen of Sheba and wonder, whom is she visiting now? Does he remember how she danced upon the table? Or the song he wrote soon after her departure, with her words still fresh in his mind, when he resolved to pour out his love for her, but from the very first line poured out, instead, her love for him? *Let him kiss me with the kisses of his mouth, for thy love is better than wine.* It has been years since he heard from her. . . .

Meanwhile, the bottle has grown cold. Shall he ring for another? He shifts the bottle, kneads it between his knees. *And be thou like a young hart upon the mountains of spices.* Look forward, look back, to darkness, at the light, both ways blind. He raises the bottle to his breast; it does not warm him. He gropes for the cord, and while his hand reaches, he thinks, as he has thought so many times, there is a time and a season for everything, a time to be born and a time to die. Is it time now? They will lay him out, washed, anointed, shrouded. They will fold his arms across his chest, with the palms turned in, completing the figure. Now his own hands will lie pressed to his breast, and he will sleep with his fathers.

PHILIP ROTH

Philip Roth, born in Newark, N. J., in 1933, received his B.A. from Bucknell, and his M.A. from the University of Chicago. *Goodbye, Columbus,* his first volume of stories, brilliant and controversial, appeared in 1959. In 1960 he was honored with the National Book Award. Mr. Roth's first novel, *Letting Go,* appeared in 1962.

Epstein

1

Michael, the weekend guest, was to spend the night in one of the twin beds in Herbie's old room, where the baseball pictures still hung on the wall. Lou Epstein lay with his wife in the room with the bed pushed cater-corner. His daughter Sheila's bedroom was empty; she was at a meeting with her fiancé, the folk singer. In the corner of her room a childhood teddy bear balanced on its bottom, a VOTE SOCIALIST button pinned to its left ear; on her bookshelves, where volumes of Louisa May Alcott once gathered dust, were now collected the works of Howard Fast. The house was quiet. The only light burning was downstairs in the dining room where the *shabus* candles flickered in their tall golden holders and Herbie's *jahrzeit* candle trembled in its glass.

Epstein looked at the dark ceiling of his bedroom and let his head that had been bang-banging all day go blank for a moment. His wife Goldie breathed thickly beside him, as though she suffered from eternal bronchitis. Ten minutes before she had undressed and he had watched as she dropped her white nightdress over her head, over the breasts which had funneled down to her middle, over the behind like a bellows, the thighs and calves veined blue like a road-map. What once could be pinched, what once was small and tight, now could be poked and pulled. Everything hung. He had shut his eyes while she had dressed for sleep and had tried to remember the Goldie of 1927, the Lou Epstein of 1927. Now he rolled his stomach against her backside, re-membering, and reached around to hold her breasts. The nipples were dragged down like a cow's, long as his little finger. He rolled back to his own side.

A key turned in the front door—there was whispering, then the door gently shut. He tensed and waited for the noises—it didn't take those Socialists long. At night the noise from the zipping and the unzipping was enough to keep a man awake. "What are they doing down there?" he had screamed at his wife one Friday night, "trying on clothes?" Now, once again, he waited. It wasn't that he was against their playing. He was no puritan, he believed in young people enjoying themselves. Hadn't he been a young man himself? But in 1927 he and his wife were handsome people. Lou Epstein had never resembled that chinless, lazy smart aleck whose living was earned singing folk songs in a saloon, and who once had asked Epstein if it hadn't been "thrilling" to have lived through "a period of great social upheaval" like the thirties.

And his daughter, why couldn't she have grown up to be like—like the girl across the street whom Michael had the date with, the one whose father had died. Now there was a pretty girl. But not his Sheila. What happened, he wondered, what happened to that little pink-skinned baby? What year, what month did those skinny ankles grow thick as logs, the peaches-and-cream turn to pimples? That lovely child was now a twenty-three-year-old woman with "a social

conscience"! Some conscience, he thought. She hunts all
day for a picket line to march in so that at night she can
come home and eat like a horse ... For her and that guitar
plucker to touch each other's unmentionables seemed worse
than sinful—it was disgusting. When Epstein tossed in bed
and heard their panting and the zipping it sounded in his
ears like thunder.

Zip!

They were at it. He would ignore them, think of his other
problems. The business ... here he was a year away from
the retirement he had planned but with no heir to Epstein
Paper Bag Company. He had built the business from the
ground, suffered and bled during the Depression and Roose-
velt, only, finally, with the war and Eisenhower to see it
succeed. The thought of a stranger taking it over made him
sick. But what could be done? Herbie, who would have
been twenty-eight, had died of polio, age eleven. And
Sheila, his last hope, had chosen as her intended a lazy
man. What could he do? Does a man of fifty-nine all of a
sudden start producing heirs?

Zip! Pant-pant-pant! Ahh!

He shut his ears and mind, tighter. He tried to recollect
things and drown himself in them. For instance, dinner ...

He had been startled when he arrived home from the
shop to find the soldier sitting at his dinner table. Surprised
because the boy, whom he had not seen for ten or twelve
years, had grown up with the Epstein face, as his son would
have, the small bump in the nose, the strong chin, dark
skin, and shock of shiny black hair that, one day, would
turn gray as clouds.

"Look who's here," his wife shouted at him the moment
he entered the door, the day's dirt still under his finger-
nails. "Sol's boy."

The soldier popped up from his chair and extended his
hand. "How do you do, Uncle Louis?"

"A Gregory Peck," Epstein's wife said, "a Monty Clift
your brother has. He's been here only three hours already
he has a date. And a regular gentleman . . ."

Epstein did not answer.

The soldier stood at attention, square, as though he'd learned courtesy long before the Army. "I hope you don't mind my barging in, Uncle Louis. I was shipped to Monmouth last week and Dad said I should stop off to see you people. I've got the weekend off and Aunt Goldie said I should stay—" He waited.

"Look at him," Goldie was saying, "a Prince!"

"Of course," Epstein said at last, "stay. How is your father?" Epstein had not spoken to his brother Sol since 1945 when he had bought Sol's share of the business and his brother had moved to Detroit, with words.

"Dad's fine," Michael said. "He sends his regards."

"Sure, I send mine too. You'll tell him."

Michael sat down, and Epstein knew that the boy must think just as his father did: that Lou Epstein was a coarse man whose heart beat faster only when he was thinking of Epstein Paper Bag.

When Sheila came home they all sat down to eat, four, as in the old days. Goldie Epstein jumped up and down, up and down, slipping each course under their noses the instant they had finished the one before. "Michael," she said historically, "Michael, as a child you were a very poor eater. Your sister Ruthie, God bless her, was a nice eater. Not a good eater, but a nice eater."

For the first time Epstein remembered his little niece Ruthie, a little dark-haired beauty, a Bible Ruth. He looked at his own daughter and heard his wife go on, and on. "No, Ruthie wasn't such a good eater. But she wasn't a picky eater. Our Herbie, he should rest in peace, was a picky eater . . ." Goldie looked towards her husband as though he would remember precisely what category of eater his beloved son had been; he stared into his pot roast.

"But," Goldie Epstein resumed, "You should live and be well, Michael, you turned out to be a good eater . . ."

Ahhh! Ahhh!

The noises snapped Epstein's recollection in two.

Aaahhhh!

Enough was enough. He got out of bed, made certain
that he was tucked into his pajamas, and started down to
the living room. He would give them a piece of his mind.
He would tell them that—that 1927 was not 1957! No,
that was what they would tell him.

But in the living room it was not Sheila and the folk
singer. Epstein felt the cold from the floor rush up the
loose legs of his pajamas and chill his crotch, raising goose
flesh on his thighs. They did not see him. He retreated a
step, back behind the archway to the dining room. His eyes,
however, remained fixed on the living room floor, on Sol's
boy and the girl from across the street.

The girl had been wearing shorts and a sweater. Now
they were thrown over the arm of the sofa. The light from
the candles was enough for Epstein to see that she was
naked. Michael lay beside her, squirming and potent, wearing only his army shoes and khaki socks. The girl's breasts
were like two small white cups. Michael kissed them, and
more. Epstein tingled; he did not dare move, he did not
want to move, until the two, like cars in a railroad yard,
slammed fiercely together, coupled, shook. In their noise
Epstein tiptoed, trembling, up the stairs and back to his
wife's bed.

He could not force himself to sleep for what seemed like
hours, not until the door had opened downstairs and the
two young people had left. When, a minute or so later, he
heard another key turn in the lock he did not know whether
it was Michael returning to go to sleep, or—

Zip!

Now it was Sheila and the folk singer! The whole world,
he thought, the whole young world, the ugly ones and the
pretty ones, the fat and the skinny ones, zipping and unzipping! He grabbed his great shock of gray hair and pulled
it till his scalp hurt. His wife shuffled, mumbled a noise.
"Brrr . . . brrrr . . ." She captured the blankets and pulled
them over her. "Brrr . . ."

Butter! She's dreaming about butter. Recipes she dreams
while the world zips. He closed his eyes and pounded himself down down into an old man's sleep.

How far back must you go to discover the beginning of trouble? Later, when Epstein had more time he would ask himself this question. When did it begin? That night he'd seen those two on the floor? Or the summer night seventeen years before when he had pushed the doctor away from the bed and put his lips to his Herbie's? Or, Epstein wondered, was it that night fifteen years ago when instead of smelling a woman between his sheets he smelled Bab-o? Or the time when his daughter had first called him "capitalist" as though it were a dirty name, as though it were a crime to be successful? Or was it none of these times? Maybe to look for a beginning was only to look for an excuse. Hadn't the trouble, the big trouble, begun simply when it appeared to, the morning he saw Ida Kaufman waiting for the bus?

And about Ida Kaufman, why in God's name was it a stranger, nobody he loved or ever could love, who had finally changed his life?—she, who had lived across the street for less than a year, and who (it was revealed by Mrs. Katz, the neighborhood Winchell) would probably sell her house now that Mr. Kaufman was dead and move all-year-round into their summer cottage at Barnegat? Until that morning Epstein had not more than noticed the woman: dark, good-looking, a big chest. She hardly spoke to the other house-wives, but spent every moment, until a month ago, caring for her cancer-eaten husband. Once or twice Epstein had tipped his hat to her, but even then he had been more ab-sorbed in the fate of Epstein Paper Bag than in the civility he was practicing. Actually then, on that Monday morning it would not have been unlikely for him to have driven right past the bus stop. It was a warm April day, certainly not a bad day to be waiting for a bus. Birds fussed and sang in the elm trees, and the sun glinted in the sky like a young ath-lete's trophy. But the woman at the bus stop wore a thin dress and no coat, and Epstein saw her waiting, and beneath the dress, the stockings, the imagined underthings he saw the body of the girl on his living room rug, for Ida Kaufman was the mother of Linda Kaufman, the girl Michael had befriended. So Epstein pulled slowly to the curb and, stopping for the daughter, picked up the mother.

"Thank you, Mr. Epstein," she said. "This is kind of you."

"It's nothing," Epstein said. "I'm going to Market Street."

"Market Street will be fine."

He pressed down too hard on the accelerator and the big Chrysler leaped away, noisy as a hot-rodder's Ford. Ida Kaufman rolled down her window and let the breeze waft in; she lit a cigarette. After a while she asked, "That was your nephew, wasn't it, that took Linda out Saturday night?"

"Michael? Yes." Epstein flushed, for reasons Ida Kaufman did not know. He felt the red on his neck and coughed to make it appear that some respiratory failure had caused the blood to rush up from his heart.

"He's a very nice boy, extremely polite," she said.

"My brother Sol's," Epstein said, "in Detroit." And he shifted his thoughts to Sol so that the flush might fade: if there had been no words with Sol it would be Michael who would be heir to Epstein Paper Bag. Would he have wanted that? Was it any better than a stranger . . . ?

While Epstein thought, Ida Kaufman smoked, and they drove on without speaking, under the elm trees, the choir of birds, and the new spring sky unfurled like a blue banner.

"He looks like you," she said.

"What? Who?"

"Michael."

"No," Epstein said, "him, he's the image of Sol."

"No, no, don't deny it—" and she exploded with laughter, smoke dragoning out of her mouth; she jerked her head back mightily, "No, no, no, he's got your face!"

Epstein looked at her, wondering: the lips, big and red, over her teeth, grinning. Why? Of course—your little boy looks like the iceman, she'd made that joke. He grinned, mostly at the thought of going to bed with his sister-in-law, whose everything had dropped even lower than his wife's.

Epstein's grin provoked Ida Kaufman into more extravagant mirth. What the hell, he decided, he would try a joke himself.

"Your Linda, who does *she* look like?"

Ida Kaufman's mouth straightened; her lids narrowed, killing the light in her eyes. Had he said the wrong thing? Stepped too far? Defiled the name of a dead man, a man who'd had cancer yet? But no, for suddenly she raised her arms in front of her, and shrugged her shoulders as though to say, "Who knows, Epstein, who knows?"

Epstein roared. It was so long since he had been with a woman who had a sense of humor; his wife took everything he said seriously. Not Ida Kaufman, though—she laughed so hard her breasts swelled over the top of her tan dress. They were not cups but pitchers. The next thing Epstein knew he was telling her another joke, and another, in the middle of which a cop screamed up alongside him and gave him a ticket for a red light which, in his joy, he had not seen. It was the first of three tickets he received that day; he earned a second racing down to Barnegat later that morning, and a third speeding up the Parkway at dusk, trying not to be too late for dinner. The tickets cost him $32 in all, but, as he told Ida, when you're laughing so hard you have tears in your yes, how can you tell the green lights from the red ones, fast from slow?

At seven o'clock that evening he returned Ida to the bus stop on the corner and squeezed a bill into her hands.

"Here," he said, "Here—buy something"; which brought the day's total to fifty-two.

Then he turned up the street, already prepared with a story for his wife: a man interested in buying Epstein Paper Bag had kept him away all day, a good prospect. As he pulled into his driveway he saw his wife's square shape back of the venetian blinds. She ran one hand across a slat, checking for dust while she awaited her husband's homecoming.

Prickly heat?

He clutched his pajama trousers around his knees and looked at himself in the bedroom mirror. Downstairs a key turned in the lock but he was too engaged to hear it. Prickly heat is what Herbie always had—a child's complaint. Was it possible for a grown man to have it? He shuffled closer to the mirror, tripping on his half-hoisted pajamas. Maybe it was a sand rash. Sure, he thought, for during those three warm, sunny weeks, he and Ida Kaufman, when they were through, would rest on the beach in front of the cottage. Sand must have gotten into his trousers and irritated him on the drive up the Parkway. He stepped back now and was squinting at himself in the mirror when Goldie walked into the bedroom. She had just emerged from a hot tub—her bones ached, she had said—and her flesh was boiled red. Her entrance startled Epstein, who had been contemplating his blemish with the intensity of a philosopher. When he turned swiftly from his reflection, his feet caught in his pants leg, he tripped, and the pajamas slipped to the floor. So there they were, naked as Adam and Eve, except that Goldie was red all over, and Epstein had prickly heat, or a sand rash, or—and it came to him as a first principle comes to a metaphysician. Of course! His hands shot down to cover his crotch.

Goldie looked at him, mystified, while Epstein searched for words appropriate to his posture.

At last: "You had a nice bath?"

"Nice, shmice, it was a bath," his wife mumbled.

"You'll catch a cold," Epstein said. "Put something on."

"I'll catch a cold? *You'll* catch a cold!" She looked at the hands laced across his crotch. "Something hurts?"

"It's a little chilly," he said.

"Where?" She motioned towards his protection. "There?"

"All over."

"Then cover all over."

He leaned over to pick up his pajama trousers; the instant

he dropped the fig leaf of his hands Goldie let out a short airless gasp. "What is *that?*"

"What?"

"That!"

He could not look into the eyes of her face, so concentrated instead on the purple eyes of her droopy breasts. "A sand rash, I think."

"*Vus far* sand!"

"A rash then," he said.

She stepped up closer and reached out her hand, not to touch but to point. She drew a little circle of the area with her index finger. "A rash, there?"

"Why not there?" Epstein said, "It's like a rash on the hand or the chest. A rash is a rash."

"But how come all of a sudden?" his wife said.

"Look, I'm not a doctor," Epstein said. "It's there today, maybe tomorrow it'll be gone. How do I know! I probably got it from the toilet seat at the shop. The *shvartzes* are pigs—"

Goldie made a clicking sound with her tongue.

"You're calling me a liar?"

She looked up. "Who said liar?" And she gave her own form a swift looking-over, checked limbs, stomach, breasts, to see if she had perhaps caught the rash from him. She looked back at her husband, then at her own body again, and suddenly her eyes widened. "You!" she screamed.

"Shah," Epstein said, "you'll wake Michael."

"You pig! Who, who was it!"

"I told you, the *shvartzes*—"

"Liar! Pig!" Wheeling her way back to the bed, she flopped onto it so hard the springs squeaked. "Liar!" And then she was off the bed pulling the sheets from it. "I'll burn them, I'll burn every one!"

Epstein stepped out of the pajamas that roped his ankles and raced to the bed. "What are you doing—it's not catching. Only on the toilet seat. You'll buy a little ammonia—"

"Ammonia!" she yelled, "you should *drink* ammonia!"

"No," Epstein shouted, "no," and he grabbed the sheets

from her and threw them back over the bed, tucking them in madly. "Leave it be—" He ran to the back of the bed but as he tucked there Goldie raced around and ripped up what he had tucked in the front; so he raced back to the front while Goldie raced around to the back. "Don't touch me," she screamed, "don't come near me, you filthy pig! Go touch some filthy whore!" Then she yanked the sheets off again in one swoop, held them in a ball before her and spat. Epstein grabbed them back and the tug-of-war began, back and ·forth, back and forth, until they had torn them to shreds. Then for the first time Goldie cried. With white strips looped over her arms she began to sob. "My sheets, my nice clean sheets—" and she threw herself on the bed.

Two faces appeared in the doorway of the bedroom. Sheila Epstein groaned, "Holy Christ!"; the folk singer peeped in, once, twice, and then bobbed out, his feet scuttling down the stairs. Epstein whipped some white strands about him to cover his privates. He did not say a word as his daughter entered.

"Mamma, what's the matter?"

"Your father," the voice groaned from the bed, "he has— a rash!" And so violently did she begin to sob that the flesh on her white buttocks rippled and jumped.

"That's right," Epstein said, "a rash. That's a crime? Get out of here! Let your mother and father get some sleep."

"Why is she crying?" Sheila demanded. "I want an answer!"

"How do I know! I'm a mind reader? This whole family is crazy, who knows what they think!"

"Don't call my mother crazy!"

"Don't you raise your voice to me! Respect your father!" He pulled the white strips tighter around him. "Now get out of here!"

"No!"

"Then I'll throw you out." He started for the door; his daughter did not move, and he could not bring himself to reach out and push her. Instead he threw back his head and addressed the ceiling. "She's picketing my bedroom! Get out, you lummox!" He took a step towards her and growled, as though to scare away a stray cat or dog. With all her one hundred and sixty pounds she pushed her father back; in his surprise and hurt he dropped the sheet. And the daughter looked on the father. Under her lipstick she turned white.

Epstein looked up at her. He pleaded, "I got it from the toilet seat. The *shvartzes*—"

Before he could finish, a new head had popped into the doorway, hair messed and lips swollen and red; it was Michael, home from Linda Kaufman, his regular weekend date. "I heard the noise, is any—" and he saw his aunt naked on the bed. When he turned his eyes away, there was Uncle Lou.

"All of you," Epstein shouted. "Get out!"

But no one obeyed. Sheila blocked the door, politically committed; Michael's legs were rooted, one with shame, the other curiosity.

"Get out!"

Feet now came pounding up the stairs. "Sheila, should I call somebody—" And then the guitar plucker appeared in the doorway, eager, big-nosed. He surveyed the scene and his gaze, at last, landed on Epstein's crotch; the beak opened.

"What's he got? The syph?"

The words hung for a moment, bringing peace. Goldie Epstein stopped crying and raised herself off the bed. The young men in the doorway lowered their eyes. Goldie arched her back, flopped out her breasts, and began to move her lips. "I want . . ." she said. "I want . . ."

"What, Mamma?" Sheila demanded. "What is it?"

"I want . . . a divorce!" She looked amazed when she said it, though not as amazed as her husband; he smacked his palm to his head.

"Divorce! Are you crazy?" Epstein looked around; to Michael he said, "She's crazy!"

"I want one," she said, and then her eyes rolled up into her head and she passed out across the sheetless mattress.

After the smelling salts Epstein was ordered to bed in Herbie's room. He tossed and turned in the narrow bed which he was unused to; in the twin bed beside him he heard Michael breathing. Monday, he thought, Monday he would seek help. A lawyer. No, first a doctor. Surely in a minute a doctor could take a look and tell him what he already knew—that Ida Kaufman was a clean woman. Epstein would swear by it—he had smelled her flesh! The doctor would reassure him: his blemish resulted simply from their rubbing together. It was a temporary thing, produced by two, not transmitted by one. He was innocent! Unless what made him guilty had nothing to do with some dirty bug. But either way the doctor would prescribe for him. And then the lawyer would prescribe. And by then everyone would know, including, he suddenly realized, his brother Sol who would take special pleasure in thinking the worst. Epstein rolled over and looked to Michael's bed. Pinpoints of light gleamed in the boy's head; he was awake, and wearing the Epstein nose, chin, and brow.

"Michael?"

"Yes."

"You're awake?"

"Yes."

"Me too," Epstein said, and then apologetically, "all the excitement . . ."

He looked back to the ceiling. "Michael?"

"Yes?"

"Nothing . . ." But he was curious as well as concerned. "Michael, you haven't got a rash, have you?"

Michael sat up in bed; firmly he said, "No."

"I just thought," Epstein said quickly. "You know, I have this rash . . ." He dwindled off and looked away from the boy, who, it occurred to him again, might have been heir to the business if that stupid Sol hadn't . . . But what difference did the business make now. The business had never been for him, but for them. And there was no more them.

He put his hands over his eyes. "The change, the change," he said. "I don't even know when it began. Me, Lou Epstein, with a rash. I don't even feel any more like Lou Epstein. All of a sudden, pffft! and things are changed." He looked at Michael again, speaking slowly now, stressing every word, as though the boy were more than a nephew, more, in fact, than a single person. "All my life I tried. I swear it, I should drop dead on the spot, if all my life I didn't try to do right, to give my family what I didn't have . . ."

He stopped; it was not exactly what he wanted to say. He flipped on the bedside light and started again, a new way. "I was seven years old, Michael. I came here I was a boy seven years old, and that day, I can remember it like it was yesterday. Your grandparents and me—your father wasn't born yet, this stuff believe me he doesn't know. With your grandparents I stood on the dock, waiting for Charlie Goldstein to pick us up. He was your grandfather's partner in the old country, the thief. Anyway, we waited, and finally he came to pick us up, to take us where we would live. And when he came he had a big can in his hand. And you know what was in it? Kerosene. We stood there and Charlie Goldstein poured it on all our heads. He rubbed it in, to delouse us. It tasted awful. For a little boy it was awful . . ."

Michael shrugged his shoulder.

"Eh! How can you understand?" Epstein grumbled. "What do you know? Twenty years old . . ."

Michael shrugged again. "Twenty-two," he said softly.

There were more stories Epstein could tell, but he wondered if any of them would bring him closer to what it was he had on his mind but could not find the words for. He got out of bed and walked to the bedroom door. He opened it and stood there listening. On the downstairs sofa he could hear the folk singer snoring. Some night for guests! He shut the door and came back into the room, scratching his thigh. "Believe me, *she's* not losing any sleep . . . She doesn't deserve me. What, she cooks? That's a big deal? She cleans? That deserves a medal? One day I should come home and the house should be a *mess*. I should be able to write my initials in the dust, somewhere, in the basement at least. Michael, after all these years that would be a pleasure!" He grabbed at his gray hair. "How did this happen? My Goldie, that such a woman should become a cleaning machine. Im-

possible." He walked to the far wall and stared into Herbie's
baseball pictures, the long jaw-muscled faces, faded techni-
color now, with signatures at the bottom: Charlie Keller,
Lou Gehrig, Red Ruffing . . . A long time. How Herbie had
loved his Yankees.

"One night," Epstein started again, "it was before the
Depression even . . . you know what we did, Goldie and
me?" He was staring at Red Ruffing now, through him.
"You didn't know my Goldie, what a beautiful beautiful
woman she was. And that night we took pictures, photos. I
set up the camera—it was in the old house—and we took
pictures, in the bedroom." He stopped, remembered. "I
wanted a picture of my wife naked, to carry with me. I admit it. The next morning I woke up and there was Goldie
tearing up the negatives. She said God forbid I should get
in an accident one day and the police would take out my
wallet for identification, and then oy-oy-oy!" He smiled.
"You know, a woman, she worries . . . But at least we took
the pictures, even if we didn't develop them. How many
people even do that?" He wondered, and then turned away
from Red Ruffing to Michael, who was, faintly, at the corners of his mouth, smiling.

"What, the photos?"

Michael started to giggle.

"Huh?" Epstein smiled. "What, you never had that kind
of idea? I admit it. Maybe to someone else it would seem
wrong, a sin or something, but who's to say—"

Michael stiffened, at last his father's son. "Somebody's got
to say. Some things just aren't right."

Epstein was willing to admit a youthful lapse. "Maybe,"
he said, "maybe she was even right to tear—"

Michael shook his head vehemently. "No! Some things
aren't right. They're just not!"

And Epstein saw the finger pointing not at Uncle Lou the
Photographer, but at Uncle Lou the Adulterer. Suddenly he
was shouting. "Right, wrong! From you and your father
that's all I ever hear. Who are you, what are you, King
Solomon!" He gripped the bedposts. "Should I tell you

what else happened the night we took pictures? That my
Herbie was started that night, I'm sure of it. Over a year
we tried and tried till I was *oysgamitched*, and that was the
night. After the pictures, because of the pictures. Who
knows!"

"But—"

"But what! But *this?*" He was pointing at his crotch.
"You're a boy, you don't understand. When they start taking things away from you, you reach out, you *grab*—maybe
like a pig even, but you grab. And right, wrong, who
knows! With tears in your eyes, who can even see the difference!" His voice dropped now, but in a minor key the
scolding grew more fierce. "Don't call *me* names. I didn't
see you with Ida's girl, there's not a name for that? For *you*
it's right?"

Michael was kneeling in his bed now. *"You—saw?"*

"I saw!"

"But it's different—"

"Different?" Epstein shouted.

"To be married is different!"

"What's different you don't know about. To have a wife,
to be a father, twice a father—and then they start taking
things away—" and he fell weak-kneed across Michael's bed.
Michael leaned back and looked at his uncle, but he did not
know what to do or how to chastise, for he had never seen
anybody over fifteen years old cry before.

4

Usually Sunday morning went like this: at nine-thirty
Goldie started the coffee and Epstein walked to the corner
for the lox and the Sunday *News*. When the lox was on the
table, the bagels in the oven, the rotogravure section of the
News two inches from Goldie's nose, then Sheila would de-
scend the stairs, yawning, in her toe-length housecoat. They
would sit down to eat, Sheila cursing her father for buying
the *News* and "putting money in a Fascist's pocket." Out-

side, the Gentiles would be walking to church. It had always
been the same, except, of course, that over the years the
News had come closer to Goldie's nose and further from
Sheila's heart; she had the *Post* delivered.

This Sunday, when he awoke, Epstein smelled coffee bubbling in the kitchen. When he sneaked down the stairs, past
the kitchen—he had been ordered to use the basement bath-
room until he'd seen a doctor—he could smell lox. And, at
last, when he entered the kitchen, shaved and dressed, he
heard newspapers rattling. It was as if another Epstein, his
ghost, had risen an hour earlier and performed his Sunday
duties. Beneath the clock, around the table, sat Sheila, the
folk singer, and Goldie. Bagels toasted in the oven, while
the folk singer, sitting backwards in a chair, strummed his
guitar and sang—

> I've been down so long
> It look like up to me . . .

Epstein clapped his hands and rubbed them together, preparatory to eating. "Sheila, you went out for this?" He gestured towards the paper and the lox. "Thank you."

The folk singer looked up, and in the same tune, impro-
vised—

> I went out for the lox . . .

and grinned, a regular clown.

"Shut up!" Sheila told him.

He echoed her words, plunk! plunk!

"Thank *you*, then, young man," Epstein said.

"His name is Marvin," Sheila said, "for your information."

"Thank you, Martin."

"Mar*vin*," the young man said.

"I don't hear so good."

Goldie Epstein looked up from the paper. "Syphilis softens the brain."

"What!"

"Syphilis softens the brain . . ."

Epstein stood up, raging. "Did you tell her that?" he shouted at his daughter. "Who told her that?"

The folk singer stopped plucking his guitar. Nobody answered; a conspiracy. He grabbed his daughter by the shoulders. "You respect your father, you understand!"

She jerked her shoulder away. "You're not *my* father!"

And the words hurled him back—to the joke Ida Kaufman had made in the car, to her tan dress, the spring sky . . . He leaned across the table to his wife. "Goldie, Goldie, look at me! Look at *me*, Lou!"

She stared back into the newspaper, though she held it far enough from her nose for Epstein to know she could not see the print; with everything else, the optometrist said the muscles in her eyes had loosened. "Goldie," he said, "Goldie, I did the worst thing in the world? Look me in the eyes, Goldie. Tell me, since when do Jewish people get a divorce? Since when?"

She looked up at him, and then at Sheila. "Syphilis makes soft brains. I can't live with a pig!"

"We'll work it out. We'll go to the rabbi—"

"He wouldn't recognize you—"

"But the children, what about the children?"

"What children?"

Herbie was dead and Sheila a stranger; she was right.

"A grown-up child can take care of herself," Goldie said. "If she wants, she can come to Florida with me. I'm thinking I'll move to Miami Beach."

"Goldie!"

"Stop shouting," Sheila said, anxious to enter the brawl. "You'll wake Michael."

Painfully polite, Goldie addressed her daughter. "Michael left early this morning. He took his Linda to the beach for the day, to their place in Belmar."

"Barnegat," Epstein grumbled, retreating from the table.

"What did you say?" Sheila demanded.

"Barnegat." And he decided to leave the house before any further questions were asked.

At the corner luncheonette he bought his own paper and sat alone, drinking coffee and looking out the window beyond which the people walked to church. A pretty young *shiksa* walked by, holding her white round hat in her hand; she bent over to remove her shoe and shake a pebble from it. Epstein watched her bend, and he spilled some coffee on his shirt front. The girl's small behind was round as an apple beneath the close-fitting dress. He looked, and then as though he were praying, he struck himself on the chest with his fist, again and again. "What have I done! Oh, God!"

When he finished his coffee, he took his paper and started up the street. To home? What home? Across the street in her backyard he saw Ida Kaufman, who was wearing shorts and a halter, and was hanging her daughter's underwear on the clothesline. Epstein looked around and saw only the Gentiles walking to church. Ida saw him and smiled. Growing angry, he stepped off the curb and, passionately, began to jaywalk.

At noon in the Epstein house those present heard a siren go off. Sheila looked up from the *Post* and listened; she looked at her watch. "Noon? I'm fifteen minutes slow. This lousy watch, my father's present."

Goldie Epstein was leafing through the ads in the travel section of the *New York Times,* which Marvin had gone out to buy for her. She looked at her watch. "I'm fourteen minutes slow. Also," she said to her daughter, "a watch from him . . ."

The wail grew louder. "God," Sheila said, "it sounds like the end of the world."

And Marvin, who had been polishing his guitar with his red handkerchief, immediately broke into song, a high-pitched, shut-eyed Negro tune about the end of the world.

"Quiet!" Sheila said. She cocked her ear. "But it's Sunday. The sirens are Saturday—"

Goldie shot off the couch. "It's a real air raid? Oy, that's all we need!"

"It's the police," Sheila said, and fiery-eyed she raced to the front door, for she was politically opposed to police. "It's coming up the street—an ambulance!"

She raced out the door, followed by Marvin, whose guitar still hung around his neck. Goldie trailed behind, her feet slapping against her slippers. On the street she suddenly turned back to the house to make sure the door was shut against daytime burglars, bugs, and dust. When she turned again she had not far to run. The ambulance had pulled up across the street in Kaufman's driveway.

Already a crowd had gathered, neighbors in bathrobes, housecoats, carrying the comic sections with them; and too, churchgoers, *shiksas* in white hats. Goldie could not make her way to the front where her daughter and Marvin stood, but even from the rear of the crowd she could see a young doctor leap from the ambulance and race up to the porch, his stethoscope wiggling in his back pocket as he took two steps at a time.

Mrs. Katz arrived. A squat red-faced woman whose stomach seemed to start at her knees, she tugged at Goldie's arm. "Goldie, more trouble here?"

"I don't know, Pearl. All that racket. It sounded like an atomic bomb."

"When it's that, you'll know," Pearl Katz said. She surveyed the crowd, then looked at the house. "Poor woman," she said, remembering that only three months before, on a windy March morning an ambulance had arrived to take Mrs. Kaufman's husband to the nursing home, from which he never returned.

"Troubles, troubles . . ." Mrs. Katz was shaking her head, a pot of sympathy. "Everybody has their little bundle, believe me. I'll bet she had a nervous breakdown. That's not a good thing. Gallstones, you have them out and they're out. But a nervous breakdown, it's very bad . . . You think maybe it's the daughter who's sick?"

"The daughter isn't home," Goldie said. "She's away with my nephew, Michael."

Mrs. Katz saw that no one had emerged from the house yet; she had time to gather a little information. "He's who, Goldie? The son of the brother-in-law that Lou doesn't talk to? That's his father?"

"Yes, Sol in Detroit—"

But she broke off, for the front door had opened, though still no one could be seen. A voice at the front of the crowd was commanding. "A little room here. Please! A little room, damn it!" It was Sheila. "A little room! Marvin, help me!"

"I can't put down my guitar—I can't find a place—"

"Get them back!" Sheila said.

"But my instrument—"

The doctor and his helper were now wiggling and tilting the stretcher through the front door. Behind them stood Mrs. Kaufman, a man's white shirt tucked into her shorts. Her eyes peered out of two red holes; she wore no make-up, Mrs. Katz noted.

"It must be the girl," said Pearl Katz, up on her toes. "Goldie, can you see, who is it—it's the girl?"

"The girl's *away*—"

"Stay back!" Sheila commanded. "Marvin, for crying out loud, help!"

The young doctor and his attendant held the stretcher steady as they walked sideways down the front steps.

Mrs. Katz jumped up and down. "Who *is* it?"

"I can't see," Goldie said. "I can't—" She pushed up on her toes, out of her slippers. "I—oh God! My God!" And she was racing forward, screaming, "Lou! Lou!"

"Mamma, stay back." Sheila found herself fighting off her mother. The stretcher was sliding into the ambulance now.

"Sheila, let me go, it's your father!" She pointed to the ambulance, whose red eye spun slowly on top. For a moment Goldie looked back to the steps. Ida Kaufman stood there yet, her fingers fidgeting at the buttons of the shirt.

Then Goldie broke for the ambulance, her daughter beside her, propelling her by her elbows.

"Who are you?" the doctor said. He took a step towards them to stop their forward motion, for it seemed as if they intended to dive right into the ambulance on top of his patient.

"The wife—" Sheila shouted.

The doctor pointed to the porch. "Look, lady—"

"I'm the *wife*," Goldie cried. "Me!"

The doctor looked at her. "Get in."

Goldie wheezed as Sheila and the doctor helped her into the ambulance, and she let out a gigantic gasp when she saw the white face sticking up from the gray blanket; his eyes were closed, his skin grayer than his hair. The doctor pushed Sheila aside, climbed in, and then the ambulance was moving, the siren screaming. Sheila ran after the ambulance a moment, hammering on the door, but then she turned the other way and was headed back through the crowd and up the stairs to Ida Kaufman's house.

Goldie turned to the doctor. "He's dead?"

"No, he had a heart attack."

She smacked her face.

"He'll be all right," the doctor said.

"But a heart attack. Never in his life."

"A man sixty, sixty-five, it happens." The doctor snapped the answers back while he held Epstein's wrist.

"He's only fifty-nine."

"Some only," the doctor said.

The ambulance zoomed through a red light and made a sharp right turn that threw Goldie to the floor. She sat there and spoke. "But how does a healthy man—"

"Lady, don't ask questions. A grown man can't act like a boy."

She put her hands over her eyes as Epstein opened his.

"He's awake now," the doctor said. "Maybe he wants to hold your hand or something."

Goldie crawled to his side and looked at him. "Lou, you're all right? Does anything hurt?"

He did not answer. "He knows it's me?"

The doctor shrugged his shoulders. "Tell him."

"It's me, Lou."

"It's your wife, Lou," the doctor said. Epstein blinked his eyes. "He knows," the doctor said. "He'll be all right. All he's got to do is live a normal life, normal for sixty."

"You hear the doctor, Lou. All you got to do is live a normal life."

Epstein opened his mouth. His tongue hung over his teeth like a dead snake.

"Don't you talk," his wife said. "Don't you worry about anything. Not even the business. That'll work out. Our Sheila will marry Marvin and that'll be that. You won't have to sell, Lou, it'll be in the family. You can retire, rest, and Marvin can take over. He's a smart boy, Marvin, a *mensch*."

Lou rolled his eyes in his head.

"Don't try to talk. I'll take care. You'll be better soon and we can go someplace. We can go to Saratoga, to the mineral baths, if you want. We'll just go, you and me—" Suddenly she gripped his hand. "Lou, you'll live normal, won't you? *Won't you?*" She was crying. " 'Cause what'll happen, Lou, is you'll kill yourself! You'll keep this up and that'll be the end—"

"All right," the young doctor said, "you take it easy now. We don't want two patients on our hands."

The ambulance was pulling down and around into the side entrance of the hospital and the doctor knelt at the back door.

"I don't know why I'm crying." Goldie wiped her eyes. "He'll be all right? You say so, I believe you, you're a doctor." And as the young man swung open the door with the big red cross painted on the back, she asked, softly, "Doctor, you have something that will cure what else he's got—this rash?" She pointed.

The doctor looked at her. Then he lifted for a moment the blanket that covered Epstein's nakedness.

"Doctor, it's bad?"

Goldie's eyes and nose were running.

"An irritation," the doctor said.

She grabbed his wrist. "You can clean it up?"

"So it'll never come back," the doctor said, and hopped out of the ambulance.

GRACE PALEY

Grace Paley is one of the liveliest writers of her generation. Born in the Bronx in 1922, she attended Hunter
College and New York University. Her first stories appeared in *Accent* and other little magazines. Her collection of stories, *The Little Disturbances of Man*, was
widely and handsomely reviewed. She is married and
lives in Manhattan with her husband and two children.

Goodbye and Good Luck

I was popular in certain circles, says Aunt Rose. I wasn't no
thinner then, only more stationary in the flesh. In time to
come, Lillie, don't be surprised—change is a fact of God.
From this no one is excused. Only a person like your
mama stands on one foot, she don't notice how big her behind is getting and sings in the canary's ear for thirty years.
Who's listening? Papa's in the shop. You and Seymour,
thinking about yourself. So she waits in a spotless kitchen
for a kind word and thinks—poor Rosie. . . .

Poor Rosie! If there was more life in my little sister, she
would know my heart is a regular college of feelings and
there is such information between my corset and me that
her whole married life is a kindergarten.

Nowadays you could find me any time in a hotel, uptown
or downtown. Who needs an apartment to live like a maid
with a dustrag in the hand, sneezing? I'm in very good with

the bus boys, it's more interesting than home, all kinds of
people, everybody with a reason. . . .

And my reason, Lillie, is a long time ago I said to the
forelady, "Missus, if I can't sit by the window, I can't sit."
"If you can't sit, girlie," she says politely, "go stand on the
street corner." And that's how I got unemployed in novelty
wear.

For my next job I answered an ad which said: "Refined
young lady, medium salary, cultural organization." I went
by trolley to the address, the Russian Art Theater of Second
Avenue where they played only the best Yiddish plays. They
needed a ticket seller, someone like me, who likes the public
but is very sharp on crooks. The man who interviewed me
was the manager, a certain type.

Immediately he said: "Rosie Lieber, you surely got a
build on you!"

"It takes all kinds, Mr. Krimberg."

"Don't misunderstand me, little girl," he said. "I appreciate, I appreciate. A young lady lacking fore and aft, her
blood is so busy warming the toes and the finger tips, it
don't have time to circulate where it's most required."

Everybody likes kindness. I said to him: "Only don't be
fresh, Mr. Krimberg, and we'll make a good bargain."

We did: Nine dollars a week, a glass of tea every night, a
free ticket once a week for Mama, and I could go watch rehearsals any time I want.

My first nine dollars was in the grocer's hands ready to
move on already, when Krimberg said to me, "Rosie, here's
a great gentleman, a member of this remarkable theater,
wants to meet you, impressed no doubt by your big brown
eyes."

And who was it, Lillie? Listen to me, before my very eyes
was Volodya Vlashkin, called by the people of those days
the Valentino of Second Avenue. I took one look, and I
said to myself: Where did a Jewish boy grow up so big?
"Just outside Kiev," he told me.

How? "My mama nursed me till I was six. I was the only
boy in the village to have such health."

"My goodness, Vlashkin, six years old! She must have had shredded wheat there, not breasts, poor woman."

"My mother was beautiful," he said. "She had eyes like stars."

He had such a way of expressing himself, it brought tears.

To Krimberg, Vlashkin said after this introduction: "Who is responsible for hiding this wonderful young person in a cage?"

"That is where the ticket seller sells."

"So, David, go in there and sell tickets for a half hour. I have something in mind in regards to the future of this girl and this company. Go, David, be a good boy. And you, Miss Lieber, please, I suggest Feinberg's for a glass of tea. The rehearsals are long. I enjoy a quiet interlude with a friendly person."

So he took me there, Feinberg's, then around the corner, a place so full of Hungarians, it was deafening. In the back room was a table of honor for him. On the tablecloth embroidered by the lady of the house was "Here Vlashkin Eats." We finished one glass of tea in quietness, out of thirst, when I finally made up my mind what to say.

"Mr. Vlashkin, I saw you a couple weeks ago, even before I started working here, in *The Sea Gull*. Believe me, if I was that girl, I wouldn't look even for a minute on the young bourgeois fellow. He could fall out of the play altogether. How Chekhov could put him in the same play as you, I can't understand."

"You liked me?" he asked, taking my hand and kindly patting it. "Well, well, young people still like me . . . so, and you like the theater too? Good. And you, Rose, you know you have such a nice hand, so warm to the touch, such a fine skin, tell me, why do you wear a scarf around your neck? You only hide your young, young throat. These are not olden times, my child, to live in shame."

"Who's ashamed?" I said, taking off the kerchief, but my hand right away went to the kerchief's place, because the truth is, it really was olden times, and I was still of a nature to melt with shame.

"Have some more tea, my dear."

"No, thank you, I am a samovar already."

"Dorfmann!" he hollered like a king. "Bring this child a seltzer with fresh ice!"

In weeks to follow I had the privilege to know him better and better as a person—also the opportunity to see him in his profession. The time was autumn; the theater full of coming and going. Rehearsing without end. After *The Sea Gull* flopped *The Salesman from Istanbul* played, a great success.

Here the ladies went crazy. On the opening night, in the middle of the first scene, one missus—a widow or her husband worked too long hours—began to clap and sing out, "Oi, oi, Vlashkin." Soon there was such a tumult, the actors had to stop acting. Vlashkin stepped forward. Only not Vlashkin to the eyes . . . a younger man with pitch-black hair, lively on restless feet, his mouth clever. A half a century later at the end of the play he came out again, a gray philosopher, a student of life from only reading books, his hands as smooth as silk. . . . I cried to think who I was— nothing—and such a man could look at me with interest.

Then I got a small raise, due to he kindly put in a good word for me, and also for fifty cents a night I was given the pleasure together with cousins, in-laws, and plain stage-struck kids to be part of a crowd scene and to see like he saw every single night the hundreds of pale faces waiting for his feelings to make them laugh or bend down their heads in sorrow.

The sad day came, I kissed my mama goodbye. Vlashkin helped me to get a reasonable room near the theater to be more free. Also my outstanding friend would have a place to recline away from the noise of the dressing rooms. She cried and she cried. "This is a different way of living, Mama," I said. "Besides, I am driven by love."

"You! You, a nothing, a rotten hole in a piece of cheese, are you telling me what is life?" she screamed.

Very insulted, I went away from her. But I am good-natured—you know fat people are like that—kind, and I thought to myself, poor Mama . . . it is true she got more of an idea of life than me. She married who she didn't like, a sick man, his spirit already swallowed up by God. He never washed. He had an unhappy smell. His teeth fell out, his hair disappeared, he got smaller, shriveled up little by little, till goodbye and good luck he was gone and only came to Mama's mind when she went to the mailbox under the stairs to get the electric bill. In memory of him and out of respect for mankind, I decided to live for love.

Don't laugh, you ignorant girl.

Do you think it was easy for me? I had to give Mama a little something. Ruthie was saving up together with your papa for linens, a couple knives and forks. In the morning I had to do piecework if I wanted to keep by myself. So I made flowers. Before lunch time every day a whole garden grew on my table.

This was my independence, Lillie dear, blooming, but it didn't have no roots and its face was paper.

Meanwhile Krimberg went after me too. No doubt observing the success of Vlashkin, he thought, "Aha, open sesame . . ." Others in the company similar. After me in those years were the following: Krimberg I mentioned. Carl Zimmer, played innocent young fellows with a wig. Charlie Peel, a Christian who fell in the soup by accident, a creator of beautiful sets. "Color is his middle name," says Vlashkin, always to the point.

I put this in to show you your fat old aunt was not crazy out of loneliness. In those noisy years I had friends among interesting people who admired me for reasons of youth and that I was a first-class listener.

The actresses—Raisele, Marya, Esther Leopold—were only interested in tomorrow. After them was the rich men, producers, the whole garment center; their past is a pincushion, future the eye of a needle.

Finally the day came, I no longer could keep my tact in my mouth. I said: "Vlashkin, I hear by carrier pigeon you have a wife, children, the whole combination."

"True, I don't tell stories. I make no pretense."

"That isn't the question. What is this lady like? It hurts me to ask, but tell me, Vlashkin . . . a man's life is something I don't clearly see."

"Little girl, I have told you a hundred times, this small room is the convent of my troubled spirit. Here I come to your innocent shelter to refresh myself in the midst of an agonized life."

"Ach, Vlashkin, serious, serious, who is this lady?"

"Rosie, she is a fine woman of the middle classes, a good mother to my children, three in number, girls all, a good cook, in her youth handsome, now no longer young. You see, could I be more frank? I entrust you, dear, with my soul."

It was some few months later at the New Year's ball of the Russian Artists Club, I met Mrs. Vlashkin, a woman with black hair in a low bun, straight and too proud. She sat at a small table speaking in a deep voice to whoever stopped a moment to converse. Her Yiddish was perfect, each word cut like a special jewel. I looked at her. She noticed me like she noticed everybody, cold like Christmas morning. Then she got tired. Vlashkin called a taxi and I never saw her again. Poor woman, she did not know I was on the same stage with her. The poison I was to her role, she did not know.

Later on that night in front of my door I said to Vlashkin, "No more. This isn't for me. I am sick from it all. I am no home breaker."

"Girlie," he said, "don't be foolish."

"No, no, goodbye, good luck," I said. "I am sincere."

So I went and stayed with Mama for a week's vacation and cleaned up all the closets and scrubbed the walls till the paint came off. She was very grateful, all the same her hard life made her say, "Now we see the end. If you live like a bum, you are finally a lunatic."

After this few days I came back to my life. When we met, me and Vlashkin, we said only hello and goodbye, and then for a few sad years, with the head we nodded as if to say, "Yes, yes, I know who you are."

Meanwhile in the field was a whole new strategy. Your

mama and your grandmama brought around—boys. Your
own father had a brother, you never even seen him. Ruben.
A serious fellow, his idealism was his hat and his coat.
"Rosie, I offer you a big new free happy unusual life." How?
"With me, we will raise up the sands of Palestine to make a
nation. That is the land of tomorrow for us Jews." "Ha-ha,
Ruben, I'll go tomorrow then." "Rosie!" says Ruben. "We
need strong women like you, mothers and farmers." "You
don't fool me, Ruben, what you need is dray horses. But for
that you need more money." "I don't like your attitude,
Rose." "In that case, go and multiply. Goodbye."

Another fellow: Yonkel Gurstein, a regular sport, dressed
to kill, with such an excitable nature. In those days—it
looks to me like yesterday—the youngest girls wore under-
garments like Battle Creek, Michigan. To him it was a matter of seconds. Where did he practice, a Jewish boy? Nowadays I suppose it is easier, Lillie? My goodness, I ain't asking you nothing—touchy, touchy. . . .

Well, by now you must know yourself, honey, whatever
you do, life don't stop. It only sits a minute and dreams a
dream.

While I was saying to all these silly youngsters "no, no,
no," Vlashkin went to Europe and toured a few seasons . . .
Moscow, Prague, London, even Berlin—already a pessi-
mistic place. When he came back he wrote a book, you
could get from the library even today, *The Jewish Actor
Abroad*. If someday you're interested enough in my lonesome years, you could read it. You could absorb a flavor of
the man from the book. No, no, I am not mentioned. After
all, who am I?

When the book came out I stopped him in the street to
say congratulations. But I am not a liar, so I pointed out,
too, the egotism of many parts—even the critics said something along such lines.

"Talk is cheap," Vlashkin answered me. "But who are
the critics? Tell me, do they create? Not to mention," he
continues, "there is a line in Shakespeare in one of the
plays from the great history of England. It says, 'Self-loving
is not so vile a sin, my liege, as self-neglecting.' This idea

also appears in modern times in the moralistic followers of Freud. . . . Rosie, are you listening? You asked a question. By the way, you look very well. How come no wedding ring?"

I walked away from this conversation in tears. But this talking in the street opened the happy road up for more discussions. In regard to many things. . . . For instance, the management—very narrow-minded—wouldn't give him any more certain young men's parts. Fools. What youngest man knew enough about life to be as young as him?

"Rosie, Rosie," he said to me one day, "I see by the clock on your rosy, rosy face you must be thirty."

"The hands are slow, Vlashkin. On a week before Thursday I was thirty-four."

"Is that so? Rosie, I worry about you. It has been on my mind to talk to you. You are losing your time. Do you understand it? A woman should not lose her time."

"Oi, Vlashkin, if you are my friend, what is time?"

For this he had no answer, only looked at me surprised. We went instead, full of interest but not with our former speed, up to my new place on Ninety-fourth Street. The same pictures on the wall, all of Vlashkin, only now everything painted red and black, which was stylish, and new upholstery.

A few years ago there was a book by another member of that fine company, an actress, the one that learned English very good and went uptown—Marya Kavkaz, in which she says certain things regarding Vlashkin. Such as, he was her lover for eleven years, she's not ashamed to write this down. Without respect for him, his wife and children, or even others who also may have feelings in the matter.

Now, Lillie, don't be surprised. This is called a fact of life. An actor's soul must be like a diamond. The more faces it got the more shining is his name. Honey, you will no doubt love and marry one man and have a couple kids and be happy forever till you die tired. More than that, a person like us don't have to know. But a great artist like Volodya Vlashkin . . . in order to make a job on the stage, he's got to practice. I understand it now, to him life is like a rehearsal.

Myself, when I saw him in *The Father-in-law*—an older man in love with a darling young girl, his son's wife, played by Raisele Maisel—I cried. What he said to this girl, how he whispered such sweetness, how all his hot feelings were on his face . . . Lillie, all this experience he had with me. The very words were the same. You can imagine how proud I was.

So the story creeps to an end.

I noticed it first on my mother's face, the rotten handwriting of time, scribbled up and down her cheeks, across her forehead back and forth—a child could read—it said, old, old, old. But it troubled my heart most to see these realities scratched on Vlashkin's wonderful expression.

First the company fell apart. The theater ended. Esther Leopold died from being very aged. Krimberg had a heart attack. Marya went to Broadway. Also Raisele changed her name to Roslyn and was a big comical hit in the movies. Vlashkin himself, no place to go, retired. It said in the paper, "an actor without peer, he will write his memoirs and spend his last years in the bosom of his family among his thriving grandchildren, the apple of his wife's doting eye."

This is journalism.

We made for him a great dinner of honor. At this dinner I said to him, for the last time, I thought, "Goodbye, dear friend, topic of my life, now we part." And to myself I said further: Finished. This is your lonesome bed. A lady what they call fat and fifty. You made it personally. From this lonesome bed you will finally fall to a bed not so lonesome, only crowded with a million bones.

And now comes? Lillie, guess.

Last week, washing my underwear in the basin, I get a buzz on the phone. "Excuse me, is this the Rose Lieber formerly connected with the Russian Art Theater?"

"It is."

"Well, well, how do you do, Rose? This is Vlashkin."

"Vlashkin! Volodya Vlashkin?"

"In fact. How are you, Rose?"

"Living, Vlashkin, thank you."

"You are all right? Really, Rose? Your health is good? You are working?"

"My health, considering the weight it must carry, is first-class. I am back for some years now where I started, in novelty wear."

"Very interesting."

"Listen, Vlashkin, tell me the truth, what's on your mind?"

"My mind? Rosie, I am looking up an old friend, an old warmhearted companion of more joyful days. My circumstances, by the way, are changed. I am retired, as you know. Also I am a free man."

"What? What do you mean?"

"Mrs. Vlashkin is divorcing me."

"What come over her? Did you start drinking or something from melancholy?"

"She is divorcing me for adultery."

"But, Vlashkin, you should excuse me, don't be insulted, but you got maybe seventeen, eighteen years on me, and even me, all this nonsense—this daydreams and nightmares—is mostly for the pleasure of conversation alone."

"I pointed all this out to her. My dear, I said, my time is past, my blood is as dry as my bones. The truth is, Rose, she isn't accustomed to have a man around all day, reading out loud from the papers the interesting events of our time, waiting for breakfast, waiting for lunch. So all day she gets madder and madder. By nighttime a furious old lady gives me my supper. She has information from the last fifty years to pepper my soup. Surely there was a Judas in that theater, saying every day, 'Vlashkin, Vlashkin, Vlashkin . . .' and while my heart was circulating with his smiles he was on the wire passing the dope to my wife."

"Such a foolish end, Volodya, to such a lively story. What is your plans?"

"First, could I ask you for dinner and the theater—up-town, of course? After this . . . we are old friends. I have money to burn. What your heart desires. Others are like grass, the north wind of time has cut out their heart. Of you, Rosie, I re-create only kindness. What a woman should be to a man, you were to me. Do you think, Rosie, a couple of old pals like us could have a few good times among the material things of this world?"

My answer, Lillie, in a minute was altogether. "Yes, yes, come up," I said. "Ask the room by the switchboard, let us talk."

So he came that night and every night in the week, we talked of his long life. Even at the end of time, a fascinating man. And like men are, too, till time's end, trying to get away in one piece.

"Listen, Rosie," he explains the other day. "I was married to my wife, do you realize, nearly half a century. What good was it? Look at the bitterness. The more I think of it, the more I think we would be fools to marry."

"Volodya Vlashkin," I told him straight, "when I was young I warmed your cold back many a night, no questions asked. You admit it, I didn't make no demands. I was softhearted. I didn't want to be called Rosie Lieber, a breaker up of homes. But now, Vlashkin, you are a free man. How could you ask me to go with you on trains to stay in strange hotels, among Americans, not your wife? Be ashamed."

So now, darling Lillie, tell this story to your mama from your young mouth. She don't listen to a word from me. She only screams, "I'll faint, I'll faint." Tell her after all I'll have a husband, which, as everybody knows, a woman should have at least one before the end of the story.

My goodness, I am already late. Give me a kiss. After all, I watched you grow from a plain seed. So give me a couple wishes on my wedding day. A long and happy life. Many years of love. Hug Mama, tell her from Aunt Rose, goodbye and good luck.

ISAIAH SPIEGEL

Isaiah Spiegel, a Polish Jew, born in 1906, who remained
in Poland during the war, is one of the survivors of the
Warsaw Ghetto and of the Nazi concentration camps. He
now lives in Israel where he devotes himself almost exclu-
sively to a single theme, the destruction of the Polish
Jews.

A Ghetto Dog

Anna Nikolaievna, widow of Jacob Simon Temkin, the fur
dealer, had only time enough to snatch up a small framed
photograph of her husband, for the German was already
standing in the open doorway shouting, *"R-raus-s!"*

There were no more Jews in the house by now, and if she
had failed to hear the noise they made as they fled it was
because with age she had grown hard of hearing and because that very morning, before the light had seeped
through the heavy portieres, a desire had come over her to
open her piano—a grand piano, black—and let her old
parchment-like fingers glide over its yellowed keys. One
could scarcely call what she was playing music, since her
fingers, which were as gnarled as old fallen bark, had been
tremulous with age for years. The echoes of several tunes
had been sounding in her deaf ears the whole morning, so
that she had failed to hear the German when he appeared
shouting on the threshold.

Translated by Bernard Guilbert Guerney. From *A Treasury of Yiddish
Stories,* edited by Irving Howe and Eliezer Greenberg. Copyright 1954
by The Viking Press, Inc., and reprinted by their permission.

All the while Nicky, the widow's dog, had been lying near
one of the heavy portieres, dozing and dreaming an old
dog's dream, his pointed muzzle resting on his outstretched
paws. He was well along in years; his coat was shedding and
light patches showed in its sandy hue. His legs were weak,
but his big eyes—brownish with a blue glint—reminded
one that he too had once been a puppy.

The widow and her dog led a lonely life. Nicky wandered through the rooms on his weak stumpy legs, his head
drooping, and swayed mournfully, his whining quieted by
weary thoughts. The Temkins had got him from a farm a
long time ago. After his master's death the widow used to
listen all day to Nicky moving through the stillness of the
house. Whenever she sat by the table and Nicky was in the
bedroom opposite (he had refused for several days to leave
the bed where his master had died), it seemed to her as
though her late husband were again walking through the
bedroom in his house slippers. She used to listen to the least
noise from the bedroom, pricking up her deaf ears, and as a
sudden pallor spread over her wrinkled forehead she seemed
actually to hear Jacob Simon's soft slow tread. Any moment now he would appear on the threshold of the bedroom, seat himself in the plush *fauteuil,* reach out for a
plaid rug, and throw it over his knees, which had been rheu-
matic for so many years.

Between the widow and her dog there had formed a mesh
of other-worldly thoughts and dreams. She saw in his drooping old head, in his worn-out fur and his pupils with their
blue glints, a shadow of her husband. Perhaps this was because Nicky had been close to his master for so many years
and had been ready to lay down his life for him, or perhaps
because with time he had taken on his master's soft tread
over the rugs, his master's lax mouth and watery eyes—
whichever it was, the widow had never clasped the dog's
head without feeling some inner disquiet. Between them
there was that bond which sometimes springs up between
two lonely creatures, one human and the other brute.

While the German was still in the open doorway, and before the widow had time to snatch up the photograph,

Nicky had already taken his stand at the threshold. He raised his old head against the German, opened his mouth wide to reveal his few remaining teeth, let out three wild howls, and was set to leap straight for the German's throat. One could see Nicky's hackles rise and hear his old paws scrape as he dashed about, ready to leap at the stranger in the outlandish green uniform. Suddenly the dog had shed his years; his legs straightened and hot saliva drooled from his muzzle as if he would say, "I know you're our enemy, I know! But you just wait—wait!"

The German at the door became confused for a moment. Taken aback by the fire glinting in the old dog's eyes, he clutched at his pistol holster.

"Have pity!" the old woman quavered. "It's only a poor animal—"

With her old body she shielded Nicky from the German and at the same time began patting the dog. In a moment he lay quiet and trembling in the old woman's arms. At last the widow tugged at his leash, and the two of them made their way through the dark hallway and into the street. As she hurried through the hallway she seized a small black cane with a silver knob; without this cane, a memento of her husband, she could hardly take a step.

She found herself in the street, leaning on the black cane with the silver knob, the rescued photograph safe in her bosom, and tugging the dog on his leash. Her eyes could scarcely be said to perceive what was going on around her. The day was frosty, blue; a blue silvery web of mist, spun by the early Polish winter, was spreading over the houses, the street, the sidewalks. The faces of the fleeing Jews were yellow, pallid. Nicky was still restless and was drawing back all the time; he did not know where his mistress was leading him. From time to time he fixed his eyes on the widow's face, while she, as she trudged along, felt a sudden icy fear grip her heart. From the dog's eyes raised to hers there peered the watery, lifeless gaze of her late husband. And here were the two of them, linked together in the web of frosty mist that was swirling under a lowering dark sky. The two of them were now plodding close to each other,

their heads downcast. Cold, angry thoughts kindled in her
drowsy old mind. She actually felt a chill breath swishing
about her ears and she caught words—far-off words, cold
and dead.

The widow who had for so long lived a life apart from
Jews and Jewishness had suddenly come to herself, as if
awaking from a state of unconsciousness. She had been
driven out of her house, of course, as a Jew like any other,
although for many years her house had been like any Christian's. Her only son had become an apostate, had married a
Christian girl and gone off to Galicia, long before the war,
where he was living on his father-in-law's estate. During the
Christian holidays various gifts would arrive from him. She
knew beforehand what he would send: a big, well-fattened
turkey and half a dozen dyed Easter eggs. The turkey she
could use, but when it came to the colored eggs the old
woman had a strange oppressive feeling. They would lie
around for months, gathering dust on their shells, until some
evening she peeled them in the bright light of the girandole
and then left them on the window sill for the hungry sparrows.

She herself had been estranged from Jewishness since her
very childhood. For years on end no Jewish face appeared
at her threshold. The war, which had come so suddenly to
the town, had during the first few days failed to reach her
comfortable home. The catastrophe that had befallen the
Jews had not touched her, and the angry prophecy of the
storm that was raging in the streets had not beaten upon
her door.

When the German had opened it that morning, he had
aroused the little old woman from her torpor and had reminded her that she was a Jew and that heavy days had
come for her and all other Jews. And though the old woman
had during so many years been cut off from Jewishness and
Jews, she had accepted the sudden misfortune with courage
and resignation, as if an invisible thread had connected her
to her people all through the years.

Now she was trudging through the streets with so many
others whose faces were strange and distracted. She recog-

nized these faces from her remote youth, faces framed in black unkempt Jewish beards and surmounted by small round skullcaps, which Jacob Simon used to ridicule so in his lifetime. Jews in gaberdines, Jewish women wearing headkerchiefs and marriage wigs, were dragging their children by the hand. Anna's heart was filled with a friendly feeling as, leaning on her black, silver-knobbed cane, she led Nicky with her left hand. The fleeing Jews cast surly sidelong looks at her and the dog. Nicky plodded on without once lifting up his head; the light had gone out of his eyes. A small spotted dog suddenly emerged from the crowd, ran up to Nicky, and placed a paw on the old dog's neck as if seeking consolation; thereafter both dogs walked side by side.

Nicky sensed the strange atmosphere as they turned into the next street. It was poorly paved, with gaping pits; the press was greater here. He could barely make his way among the thousands of unfriendly feet. They kept stepping on his paws, and once his mistress almost fell. Anna held her head higher and was pulled along by the crowd of Jews. She drew the leash closer to her, every so often saving Nicky from being trampled. By now he kept closer to her, mournful, and with his head still lower.

Fine, wet snowflakes swirled in the air, unwilling to fall to the ground, and settled on Nicky's grizzled, closely curled coat.

The widow found herself in a narrow squalid street in the Balut district of Lodz, where all the hack-drivers, porters, and emaciated Jewish streetwalkers lived. She had come here with a host of strangers who quickly made themselves at home in a huge empty barn. The Jewish streetwalkers brought them all sorts of good things baked of white flour. The widow sat in the barn, her gray disheveled head propped on the silver knob of her cane, while Nicky sprawled at her feet and took in the angry din made by the strange people.

It was late at night before everyone in the barn was assigned quarters in the district. The widow found herself in the room of a tart known as Big Rose—a very much disgruntled tart, who did not want a dog in the house.

"It's enough that I have to take in a female apostate!"
she kept yelling. "What do I need a sick old hound for?"

Anna stood on the threshold before the tart, the dog close
to her on his unsteady legs; his body emanated a forlorn-
ness that was both animal and human.

"Quiet, quiet!" The widow's hand fell shakily on Nicky's
drooping head and patted it.

The room where Big Rose lived lay under a gabled roof.
It held a small shabby sofa, strewn with yellow and red
cushions. A low ceiling made the place dreary and depress-
ing. Outside the window was the hostile night, spattered
with the silver of the first frost. This night-silver interlaced
with the reflections of light from the room and fell on the
windowpanes like dancing stars.

The nook that sheltered the widow and her dog was very
dark; the warmth lingered there as if in a closed warm
cellar. Throughout the room there hovered a sour odor of
sin and lust. The old woman did not realize where she had
come to; nothing mattered any longer. She and her dog
huddled in their nook and for a long while squatted there
like two huge rigid shadows. From time to time Nicky put
his head in her lap, and a soft, long-drawn-out whine issued
from the dark nook, like the moan of a hopelessly sick man.

Later that night, when the old woman and the dog had
stretched out in their nook on some rags, Big Rose closed
the red hangings which screened the shabby sofa from the
rest of the room. The little red flame of the small night-
lamp hanging on the wall wavered slowly and angrily, licking at the musty darkness around it.

Only now, when everything had become utterly quiet,
did certain huge shadows appear in the darkness of the
threshold. The shadows entered one by one; each hovered
for a moment on the threshold, looked about, then disappeared within the hangings. In the dark little hallway on
the other side of the door other shadows gathered and
waited for the door to open. They did not have to wait long:
each shadow, after darting out from behind the hangings,

rushed through the door and disappeared down the dark stairs.

The widow was dozing by now. From time to time she awoke and put her arms around Nicky's warm neck. The dog continued snoring with a low, canine snore. Each time the door opened and a shadow darted within the hangings, from which there immediately issued Big Rose's witchlike snicker, Nicky would emit a low growl.

This suddenly angered Big Rose. She sprang up naked by the drawn-back hangings and, brandishing her arms, shouted at the widow in the nook, "My grand madam! May a curse light on you! Maybe madam would like to step out for a little while on the balcony with the hound? He's driving everybody away, may the devil overtake him! I'll poison that hound!"

The widow, startled from her sleep, was frightened by Big Rose's stark nakedness and its pungent reek.

"Sh, sh, sh!" she at last managed to whisper to the dog.

She stood up in her nook, took Nicky's head, and started for the door. Through the small dark hallway the two of them, the widow and the dog, reached the deserted balcony. Below them lay a tangle of dark Balut streets. The wind drove nearer and scattered the grayish, tenuous whiteness of the still swirling night snow. From the south side of the city the dusty glow of electric lights was borne through the night. The widow watched these lights blinking on and off, like inflamed eyes.

"See there, Nicky? Over there—there. That's our house, our street—"

The dog lifted his head, stood up on his hind legs, and peered into the darkness. For a while he stood thus, with the widow's arms around him, then suddenly let out a howl. It rent the sky like lightning, beat against the clouds, and then died away in the cold darkness of the earth.

In the morning, when the chilled widow awoke in her nook, the dog was no longer by her side. Nobody had any idea where he had vanished to. Big Rose kept saying that this was no dog but a werewolf and that she hadn't even heard the dog leaving the house.

He was gone the whole day, and only toward evening did they hear him scraping at the door. He fell into the nook in great excitement, with foam on his hanging tongue, and threw himself on the frightened widow's lap.

Nicky lay on her knees, quivering with an ardent, old-dog sob. The widow took his shivering head and for some time gazed into his watery pupils, as if into the small openings of two wells. She could not understand what had happened to the dog. He barked in a subdued way, as if some words were struggling to escape him, as if he were straining to tell everything to the old woman bending over him. His whole body quivered, and his narrow face seemed to wear the twisted grimace of a dog in lament. Yet this was not whining; rather a noisy outburst of joy and consolation. He kept lifting his paws and putting them on the old woman's knees. The widow took the paws and brought them to her aged, withered lips, bent over, and for a long, long time, with her eyes closed, rested her head upon them.

For a long time the widow sat in the darkness embracing the dog, while the night-lamp, which had been turned low and had been burning all day near the red hangings, now cast a mysterious reddish reflection on the wall. The sharp silhouette of the dog's pointed head and the widow's arms swayed on the ceiling in a network of dancing shadows.

The next morning Nicky again disappeared and did not come back until nightfall. This was repeated day after day.

These disappearances coincided with the time the Germans built a wall around the ghetto, barbed wires dividing the Balut from the rest of the city. Nobody was allowed to leave or enter the Jewish district. But just the same Nicky used to disappear every day and come back only at night.

Once, when Nicky returned as excited as always, the old woman put her hands on his head and drew them back: they were sticky with blood. His fur was split and torn with open wounds. He was holding his paws on her knees, as always, but this time his pupils were reddish, glowing, and little green fires kept dancing across his watery eyes.

The widow applied rag after rag soaked in cold water to the dog's open wounds. Only now did she realize that Nicky had been crawling through the barbed wire, that each morning he had run off to the city and each evening he had come running home. The widow kept on washing the warm blood and applying the cold wet rags, while Big Rose ran to fetch basins of water. The bitterness she had felt in her heart for the dog had quickly vanished. She took a white blouse from her closet and tore it into narrow bandages; she also procured from somewhere a salve that was good even for human wounds. She smeared torn strips with the salve and then, kneeling by the door, started to bind the dog's wounds.

A sudden fright came over Big Rose; an other-worldly expression appeared on her face, as if she felt a cold breath upon her. She could have sworn by all that was holy that, as she had been binding the dog's wounds, he had given her a mournful human look.

From the day Big Rose had bound the open wounds the dog had got by crawling through the barbed wire strung around the ghetto—from that day her attitude toward the widow had undergone a complete change. She took down the red hangings that had divided the room in two and asked the old woman to leave her dark nook and share the room with her. All three of them, the two women and the dog, now used the sofa. Nicky lay propped up by the colored cushions, lost in an old dog's dream.

This happened just about the time when the Germans issued an order that all animals—horses, cows, goats, and dogs—must be turned over to them. Only two broken-down horses were allowed to remain in the whole ghetto. For generations the old Jewish residents of the Balut had made their meager living as animal-breeders. The hack-drivers and cabbies, the milk dealers, small middlemen, organ-grinders, and innkeepers had to give up the horses and cows they had tended in the crowded dark stables and stalls. They unharnessed their horses for the last time and embraced the warm necks of their cows; they led out the mournful Jewish

cows and the frightened Jewish goats. The draymen led
their beautiful, glossy chestnut draft horses through the
streets, the whole family marching in step with them, wring-
ing their hands as if they were following the dead to a yawning grave. The women dragged the cows and goats along—
the animals became stubborn and refused to budge. At the
tail end of the procession, on ropes and leashes, other Jews
were leading watchdogs, Dalmatians, poodles with mournful
eyes, and common household pets with bobbed tails. The
Jews hoped that their dumb creatures would be better fed
than they had been in the ghetto. The horses and cows were
taken into the city, but the dogs were immediately shot in a
field close to the market place.

At daybreak Big Rose had thrown a torn black shawl
with long fringes over her, and the widow, without uttering
a word, had taken Nicky on his leash with one hand and
her small silver-knobbed cane in the other. Both women
were going to take the dog to the market place. Big Rose
kept mauling her cheeks and softly weeping. The widow's
disheveled hair, gray and lifeless, hung over her ashen face.

The compulsory surrender of her dog had come as such
a shock to the widow that at first, when Big Rose had
shouted the news into her face, she had clutched her head
with her withered fingers and had remained still for several
minutes. Big Rose thought the old woman had died, standing with her fingers in her hair, and her eyes not even blinking. She just stood there, stunned and stone-cold.

The dog let them do with him whatever they liked. He
dropped at their feet and held his pointed head up to them,
then yawned and let his muzzle sink to the cold floor.

The two women started out through the small courtyard,
Nicky on his long leash between them. The snow was coming down in flakes as slender and chill as needles and
stabbed their hands, their faces, and the dog's fur. It was
bitter cold. Although dawn had broken a comparatively
short while ago, the ghetto seemed already to be in twilight
—night can fall abruptly in that region.

Big Rose bit her lips as she walked along. She peered out
from the black shawl in which she was wrapped and could

see nothing but the widow's half-dead face. Nicky still had his back bound in rags.

As they neared the market place they saw Jewish children emerging from the surrounding little streets, leading gaunt, emaciated dogs on ropes and leashes. There was a pound in the market place where the Germans collected the dogs. The horses and cows had already been transferred to German civilians to bring into the city proper. The dogs within the pound were looking out on the ghetto through barbed wire, their eyes watering. A shadowy terror was frozen upon their frightened, pointed muzzles.

A German stationed near the wicket leading into the pound relieved each owner of his or her dog, pushed the wicket open, kicked the dog with the point of his boot— and the animal found itself in the pound. Rarely or ever did any dog snarl at the German. Sudden shock paralyzed the dogs, depriving them of their strength and numbing their rage. Perhaps this was due to the reek that now came to them from the field where the dogs were being killed.

By the time the widow and Big Rose approached the pound with Nicky it was full of Jewish dogs. They were jammed together, huddled in twos and threes, their heads resting on one another's shoulders. Perhaps they did this because of the cold, which beat down upon them from the sky. A few of them were close to the barbed wire, prodding it with their paws in an attempt to get free. But they had to fall back with a childlike whimper when they felt their paws become sticky with blood. The barbs of the wire were sharp and rusty and stuck out like little knife points.

The widow and Big Rose halted before the German. He was waiting for the old woman to let go of the leash. But, instead of letting go, she wound the leash still tighter about her wrist and even her forearm. She did this with her eyes closed, the way a Jew winds the straps of a phylactery on his forearm. The German snatched at the leash. The widow staggered on her old legs, since Nicky was by now pulling her into the pound. She let herself be dragged along. In the meantime the German kicked the wicket shut. His loud, tinny laughter ran along the barbed wire.

Big Rose saw the widow standing inside the enclosure ringed by a pack of dogs and still holding Nicky on the leash. In her left hand she had the small cane with the silver knob and was keeping it high over the heads of the dogs. She stood there with her cane raised, her hair disheveled, the dogs circling at her feet. Some of the dogs lifted up their mournful heads and looked into the old woman's face. Nicky alone remained unperturbed. His back was still bound up in the white rags torn from Big Rose's blouse. From time to time he lifted his head toward the wicket where Big Rose was standing, petrified.

Exhausted, the widow sank to her knees in the snow. By now one could barely make out her body. The snow was falling more heavily, in bright shimmering stars. The widow's head stood out in the whiteness like a dazzling aureole.

Big Rose saw another wicket fly open on the other side and someone begin driving the dogs out into an open field. The widow stood up, leaned on her small silver-knobbed cane, and, with Nicky leading, started toward the field. . . .

Big Rose wrapped the small black shawl more tightly about her head. She did not want to hear the dull, tinny sounds that came from the sharp-edged shovels scooping up the frozen ground of the Balut. It was only the wind, playing upon the shovels that delved the narrow black pits —only the wind, chanting its chill night song.